NOAH'S ARK

By
Steve Pizzolato

DEDICATION

This book is dedicated to my wife, Nancy Pizzolato, who puts up with me disappearing, when in plain sight, for hours on end while I write. Special thanks also goes to Ted Wright my good friend, fishing buddy and illustrator extraordinaire who designed this book cover plus, Diane Swain, who took care of all the proofing and editing. Also thanks to my 6th grade teacher and my oldest brother, Greg, who provides insight and support along the way. I also want to thank my daughters, Julie, Lauren, and Andrea, for their support and critique, good or bad. Also love and kisses to my grandchildren Wesley, Wyatt, and Walker, all born naturally and our IVF miracle Alessi. Hope you all enjoy the read.

Original inspiration for Noah's Ark cover from Wesley, age 9

Author's Notes

The idea for this book came from a conversation I had with my daughter who was going through IVF treatments. She had successfully created ten viable embryos and was soon pregnant. When the Supreme Court overturned Roe v. Wade with the Dobbs v. Jackson decision there was some quiet talk in conservative state legislative bodies that perhaps the disposition of unused IVF embryos would be treated the same way as an abortion. Criminal prosecution of the mother, the doctor or the clinic. She asked me, concerned, "Do you think I could be charged with murder if I chose to donate my unused embryos for medical research?"

An interesting and scary question for all women, partners, and fathers. Noah's Ark hopes to educate you and let your mind think about the possibilities of that happening.

DISCLAIMER

SYNOPSIS

STLPD Detective Rhonda Simon has been suspended from the police force while a past shooting is being investigated however the day before she is reinstated, Dr. Layla Brazini, a woman from her past, calls her desperately looking for her help in solving a crime committed at her IVF Clinic.

While the crime seems open and shut, Detective Simon and her personal private investigator, and lover, Richard Leary uncover many more secrets and suspects including a loner, Noah Sharpe who can only relate to the apes that he feeds at the St. Louis Zoo; a mysterious online influencer who goes by Harvest and seeks upheaval in American society; a far right aspiring politician Missouri Representative Billy O'Dell who will say anything to stay in power, and a far left domestic terrorist, Marianne Hylany who takes everything personally, and who believes violence is the only ends to the means in this battle between left and right. Simon and Leary need to determine how these people intersect to stave off a local crime from becoming a national crisis creating social chaos and violence among ordinary citizens on both sides of the pro-life vs. pro-choice debate.

Noah's Ark is the second book in the Perfect Match Series, where readers are first introduced to Detective Rhonda Simon and her ability to solve crimes that challenge societies norms about choice and upheaval of the status quo for financial gain and political power.

Table of Contents

Chapter 1

NOAH

"**N**oah, get off your ass and clean up the damn ape cages, then feed them!" yelled Noah's supervisor at the St. Louis Zoo.

"Jesus, Lou, get off my back. I'll do it in a minute," Noah angrily replied.

He wanted to finish reading and comment on an article on his phone. Noah's online followers demanded to hear his opinion, and no matter what an asshole Lou was, Noah had to take the time to provide a thoughtful response to his fans. They expected it from him. Once done with his response, he got up, grabbed a shovel and a broom, and headed toward the primates. As he walked to the cages, he thought how much more he liked the primates than his co-workers and humans, especially Lou, his overbearing boss of the last five years.

While he did not have any close relationships with people he had met in person or interacted with, he did have a special bond with the primates he kept fed and whose cages he kept clean. He understood animals, especially apes, chimpanzees, and gorillas. Eat, Sleep, Shit, Procreate. That was their life. In a way, he was jealous of the simplicity in their lives.

He believed that humans, also considered primates, evolved from apes. Still, from Noah's perspective, the animals he cared for were the more intelligent creatures, even now, thousands and thousands of years after evolution occurred. They even looked forward to seeing people, especially Noah, as his arrival for first cleaning the cage, followed by a feeding, was a daily ritual both man and beast looked forward to. He had worked at the zoo for nearly twenty years since graduating from community college with an associate degree in exotic animal training and management. His original plan was to be a veterinarian because he loved animals. He thought of being a biologist as he spent many summer days observing the formation of life in the ponds around his family's land in southeast Missouri. But as he got older, he thought a zoologist would be the best path for him as it could combine all his interests, so he planned to get a zoology degree at the University of Missouri. But shit happened, and Noah's life turned dark and desperate. As a precursor to Noah's future, whatever grand plans he had fizzled out, as most of his plans did, and he ended up at community college. Some labeled Noah a genius with a reported IQ of one hundred and fifty, but he was a genius who barely finished community college and could scarcely hold a job. At forty-one, Noah, genius or not, had reached the pinnacle of his career – if cleaning ape shit could be called a career. But he never cared about his career trajectory as he set the bar low. When he was teenager, his life turned to shit, and he had no desire to raise or exceed the bar. His personal life was no better than his career. He had no one in his life. There was no wife, girlfriend, or family because of his stupid actions. He had come to grips with this life being his destiny. It was lonely, except for the life he lived online.

But that was fine for Noah, as in his mind, had an entire online family. He believed he was a significant influencer in people's everyday lives as he spent most of his time posting comments primarily on sports stories, but occasionally, he would comment on local or world events. The commentary handle he used with his online posts was *NoahItAll*. He thought his handle was a clever play on his full name, Noah Sharpe, and his belief that he did know it all. Noah sensed his fellow commenters thought he was smart, as many gave positive reviews to his comments, which he thought made him quite an important online influencer. Noah believed he had true friends, not just fans. Online, people seemed to listen to what he had to say about sports and life in general. He primarily commented on the pitching and hitting woes of the Cardinals, the goal-scoring woes of the Blues, or the lack of offense or defense for the area's college teams. In his mind, he should be on a sports radio station or TV as a sportscaster, but he knew those jobs went to ex-athletes, women, or mandatory minority hires. Noah thought he was better than all of them and whenever he went to sports memorabilia shows where athletes or the media would gather, he would always attempt to engage them in conversations, trying to impress them with his vast knowledge of sports. However, they usually pulled away from the conversation sooner than Noah liked. "*Pompous assholes,*" he thought as they walked away from him. Everyone, it seemed, in Noah's life scurried away or ghosted him. He silently accepted it and his fate, but in his mind, he hoped for something more. And he would soon find it, significantly changing his life and what people thought about him.

Chapter 2

LAYLA

Dr. Layla Brazini was always the first to work at the New Beginnings
Fertility Clinic, an In Vitro Fertilization (IVF) business on South
Grand Avenue near Tower Grove Park in St. Louis. Being first to work
meant being at work at 5:00 a.m. as she wanted to get in her workout at
the facility's private fitness center she installed when she started the clinic
ten years ago. As soon as she arrived, she noticed something amiss. The
door to her private entrance to the clinic had been tampered with, and
she could see what looked like crowbar marks embedded between the
doorframe, and the now open door.

"Dammit," she thought, "had I not set the alarm before I left last night?"
She held her breath as she walked through the door, unsure if the
intruders were waiting for her in her office or the clinic. She turned on
the lights, but only after she released the safety on her gun that she always
kept in her purse. While Dr. Brazini's life's work helped create life for
those who could not conceive, she was not naïve and was aware that the
dangers of her job, now increasingly politicized, and the neighborhood,
now deteriorating, made owning a gun the easiest way to protect her

life. Years ago, a doctor's life, much like a policeman, teacher, or social worker, was sacrosanct and usually untouchable by crime. Not anymore, unfortunately.

As she walked into her office, she immediately saw what few files she had left on her desk the night before strewn on the floor. She kept no patient information in hard copy files, so she ignored the mess and looked down at her desk, noticing that the few drawers her desk contained were wide open. She never kept anything significant in the drawers; there may have been some theater tickets and some petty cash, but the thieves would have been disappointed if this were a robbery for drug money. Feeling a little relieved, she clicked the safety back on the gun, left her office, and entered the clinic's medical areas. What she saw made her blood run cold. The thieves had been both sophisticated and focused on specific items in the clinic: her most valuable ones, her patients' cryogenically frozen embryos that were being staged for the next cycle of implantation. These embryos were normally stored off site, as all her thousands of embryos were now, due to insurance costs, potential system failures, and physical space, and she had only just received about one hundred of them a day ago from the off-site storage center in Texas. In three days, they would have been implanted into excited and nervous women, and now their hopes for a family was gone.

While someone had smashed the freezer doors open, there was no damage to the embryo containers. The thieves had removed the embryos from the holding tank without leaving a shard of glass. They had removed the vials as cleanly as one of her lab technicians would do.

"But why?" she wondered.

She knew clinics like hers, from time to time, were targets of religious zealots and protesters who thought conception between a man and a woman should not be done scientifically. Some people were still against the use of IVF, despite it being a salvation for nearly fifty years for women who could not conceive naturally. Her business did not have as many protesters as those who commonly marched and argued around Planned Parenthood clinics, historically the center of the ongoing abortion battle.

Most of the time, any protesters who visited her center did so because they did not know what an IVF center did, thinking it performed abortions. When they learned otherwise, just for the hell of it, they stayed there to yell some pre-programmed chants and left after a few hours. But she also knew that with the 2022 Dobbs v. Jackson Supreme Court ruling essentially giving states the right to eliminate abortion established by Roe v. Wade, the topic was as heated as it had ever been, although the focus had shifted a bit. While abortion was being challenged nationally and overturned or entirely protected in some states, attention was beginning to focus on reproductive medicine, including IVF clinics and the embryos created by the process. More specifically, there began to be quiet whispering in state legislative chambers and by pro-life advocates regarding the discarding of unused embryos. She received communications from ASRM, The Association of Reproductive Medicine, that IVF clinics might be targeted by both protesters and by future regulations. Perhaps this break-in was just an isolated event, or perhaps someone wanted it to become part of the growing debate.

Layla was uneasy, but mostly she was angry that her business had been violated. Regardless of the thieves' motivation, a crime had occurred at her clinic. She needed to report it to the police immediately, but she did not want them storming in and treating it as a normal robbery. She wanted to consult with someone she trusted who would look beyond the obvious. She picked up her phone and dialed the one person she could trust professionally but the one who hurt her so many times personally. Detective Rhonda Simon.

Chapter 3
RHONDA

Her three-month suspension was ending tomorrow as the investigators had determined that St. Louis Detective Rhonda Simon had acted properly in her handling of the attempted murder of Marvin Applebaum by Vinnie Calabrese. Simon felt the police board should not have suspended her at all. The board was serving her up as an example of how the police and the government officials would have a zero-tolerance policy for cops involved in questionable shootings. Never mind that Simon probably saved Applebaum's life; the protesters and the media demanded an investigation and the immediate suspension of Simon, a thirty-year veteran on the force.

Simon, though, was burnt out, and the timing of the suspension was a godsend. 2022 was brutal in St. Louis with murders and crime, although the final numbers were slightly below past years. She also wanted to forget 2022, as the big case she had in her grasp eluded her, partly because of her suspension but mostly because the suspect, Dr. Alex Finnegan, had disappeared.

The Finnegan case featured multiple murders to cover up past crimes and newer murders to aid in an organ donation scheme. It was now the responsibility of the FBI and the SEC to find him because Dr. Finnegan had also absconded with millions of dollars of investor money intended to finance his vision of the Arch City Transplant Center.

Simon was hours away from putting the cuffs on Finnegan for a crime that had made national and international news. It was a crime that had become yet another topic in the culture wars regarding the rights of humans to choose their own destinies without government intervention. A crime so big that Simon might have ridden its notoriety to become police commissioner or even mayor of St. Louis if she wanted that. But Finnegan was gone, leaving Simon as only a footnote and foot soldier to a bigger story.

However, Rhonda Simon did not wallow in self-pity during the three months she was suspended, spending most of that time in the powerful arms and soft bed of Richard Leary, the former private investigator whose research had helped Simon solve the Finnegan case. Most cops who are suspended and under investigation hit the bottle, but Simon, in her past, had done plenty of drinking, so that did not interest her as a stress reliever. Sex, lots of it, did the trick for Simon.

Richard Leary fit the bill for now, but Rhonda Simon had no interest in anything more than a few laughs and many sweaty nights. Maybe Leary thought more of their relationship, but they had not reached the point of having that uncomfortable conversation discussing where the relationship was headed. Regardless of her personal life, Simon was excited to restart her professional life tomorrow and hit the streets of St. Louis, where abundant crime would provide her another kind of stimulation.

But this morning, hitting the sheets with Richard again became more enticing than hitting the streets and catching bad guys. However, as Richard reached for her, Rhonda's phone buzzed. She knew from the name listed only as "**L**," identifying the caller that was the only person who could get her out of bed and out of Richard Leary's arms. She paused for a moment, thinking perhaps about all the times "**L**" had passed in and out of Rhonda's life, and with both trepidation and a bit of nostalgic tingling inside, answered, "Layla. It's been too long."

Chapter 4
BECCA

At forty, Becca Stevens felt she was running out of time. But Becca Stevens always would have of options. She was determined to achieve her goals, and no door would ever be closed. Becca was going through a messy divorce, which had soured her on ever remarrying. As she would tell her friends, while she was not interested in women, at this point in her life because of what her husband had done to her, she certainly hated him and all men. Becca especially hated men who felt entitled to tell her what she could or could not do with her mind or her body. Now, as part of her divorce battle, men were deciding what she could do with her possible future children. Everything with her ex-husband was a tooth-and-nail battle over who owned what. He was always jealous of her success, and their marriage was doomed to fail from the beginning, but like many couples battling to save a marriage, they felt having a baby would be the cure. But even that was not easy as they found out that they could not conceive naturally, and who was at fault and thus blame became another chapter in their epic battles.

However, this failure to conceive naturally initially turned into a blessing because Becca and her husband decided to use IVF to start their family. Doing their research about the processes, philosophy, success rates, and costs of IVF around the United States, they chose the New Beginnings Fertility Clinic in her hometown, St. Louis. New Beginnings was expensive. In fact, with an upfront fee of $40,000, it was on the upper end of costs for comparable options. Money was not a concern to them as Becca was a successful entrepreneur who had started a women's swimwear line several years ago, now generating $15 million dollars annually in revenue. She had also turned down several purchase offers for three times that amount because she still loved the business, but Becca thought that if her IVF treatments were successful, having a baby would change her priorities on how she wanted to spend her time, including saving her marriage.

After going through the grueling IVF process of testing, preparatory hormones and other shots correcting reproductive deficiencies, and answering invasive and embarrassing questions, Becca and her husband were able to produce sixteen viable eggs. One of them would become, after fertilization, the embryo to be implanted in Becca, which would be become a baby that hopefully would start their family and repair their marriage. But as they waited each month for the optimum timing cycle for the embryo to be implanted, Becca and her husband delayed the decision because of anger at each other and self-doubt about themselves as a couple. They swung from stony silences to screaming fights. Their volatile marriage and the stress of a future family crept into every conversation. Becca realized that not a baby, not anything could save their marriage, so she and her husband filed for divorce, but even that process was fraught with bitterness as one of the major issues to resolve was the ownership or disposition of the embryos stored at the New Beginnings Fertility Clinic. While normally a couple when entering into IVF treatments is required to sign extensive documentation on the disposition of unused embryos, because Layla and Becca were friends, and more importantly Layla knew what was in Becca's heart and on her mind with regard to the viability of her marriage, she, probably unethically, did not make Becca and her husband sign the documentation. It would not be the first, or last time,

Layla betrayed her medical oath to protect Becca, her embryos, and her possible future children.

Now that Becca and her husband were committed to the divorce, they had to decide whether to destroy the embryos, save them in the hopes that they would reconcile, split them up so each of them owned eight, or use them for medical research. There was no answer they could agree on, and to make matters worse, while Becca and her husband always thought they were morally aligned along the issues of pro-life and pro-choice, when it came down to making those decisions for their future offspring, they were at greater opposites than they thought possible. While they were generally both pro-choice, his choice since they were divorcing, was to destroy all the embryos or give them up for science with no chance any of their mutual offspring would reach conception. It was all-or-nothing for him. Whatever decision they eventually would come to would affect all sixteen embryos. Becca was pro-choice as well, saying to him, *"It's my damn choice what I do with my embryos."* While this issue put their divorce at an impasse and created a divorce lawyer's dream of excessive unlimited billings, the ordeal was spilling over to downright hatred and threats to each other over the embryos.

Despite the trauma surrounding Becca's failed marriage and the battle over their embryos, her decision to use New Beginnings brought Becca closer to the owner, Layla Brazini. While she never told her husband this, after doing all her research on IVF centers, the deciding factors for Becca choosing New Beginnings were not only their success rates and ability to select the gender of her baby, but the vision and philosophies of the dynamic owner of New Beginnings, Layla Brazini, who Becca had met at a Women in Leadership conference six months previously. While in different businesses, Becca, who did her research much more than her husband, heard Layla speak on the efforts she and the clinic made to ensure reproductive medicine would always be available to women of any income level, race, or sexual orientation. Layla and Becca were close to the same age and clicked at once upon meeting. It seemed they had the same drive about business and the emerging role of women as business leaders.

They also were aligned culturally and politically, as they both believed in women having more control in their own lives, including income equality, if not superiority if they outworked men, which they both did regularly. They also had little use for men, although for different reasons. Layla was completely open regarding her sexual preferences. Becca was at the point where her marriage had failed, and men she generally believed, did not reach the intelligence, maturity, and open-mindedness Becca was looking for in a partner. Becca and Layla grew exceedingly close because Layla was an ear that was willing to listen to Becca as she agonized about the decision to proceed or not with IVF. Becca confided in Layla about the state of her marriage and discussed with her the pros and cons of proceeding with IVF while her marriage was on the rocks. They also discussed decisions Becca might have to make about the ownership of the embryos. By the time Becca had filed her divorce, the relationship between the two women was beyond one of a doctor and her patient. In each other, they both had an equal and someone who would listen and accept, without judgement, the decisions each of them made in their lives.

Becca had made big career decisions her entire life. If she were a man, she would be described as having balls because when she made a decision, she committed to it. Becca knew she was making a life-changing decision going through IVF, especially since her marriage was shaky. She also knew she was making a life-changing decision regarding what to do with her embryos and how to settle this issue with her husband. She knew the only person she could trust to guide her through the process was Dr. Brazini, whose New Beginnings Clinic now possessed Becca's most precious gift, her embryos now contested in a divorce proceeding. As her doctor, Layla could only talk to her about medical options, whether that be live birth, donation, or medical research. She could not advise her on ownership or how to settle with her husband because, technically, he, as the other owner of the embryos, was Layla's client too. However, no matter how much Layla's hands were tied legally, her friendship with Becca flourished, and she would do anything for Becca regardless of Layla's moral code and Hippocratic oath all doctors followed.

Chapter 5

RHONDA AND LAYLA

It was 6:30 a.m. by the time Rhonda pulled herself away from Richard and showered away the sweaty scent from last night's marathon love-making sessions and this morning's quicker but no less satisfying encounter.

At 7:00 a.m., she was at the New Beginnings Fertility Clinic and about to knock on Dr. Layla Brazini's private office door. It had been two years since she had last seen Layla. She did not know how this reunion would go as their relationship seemed to teeter between great love or anger and resentment. Would it be police-like and professional? *"Tell me the facts, nothing but the facts,"* or would it be warmer, each woman accepting their shared past and looking towards a brighter future.

Rhonda sensed, mostly in Layla's tone on the phone call, that it would be a warm embrace, not a cold professional encounter. They had overcome too much bad history, and while they often fell into bad habits and stupid arguments, Rhonda hoped their future was much brighter than their past had been. Plus, Layla, by nature, was warm and forgiving, and while Rhonda was not, Layla was and would always be, an important person in Rhonda's life.

Rhonda entered Layla's office and saw Layla rattled. Rhonda had never seen Layla not composed. Rising from her office chair behind her ransacked desk, Layla approached Rhonda, professionalism aside, hugging her and whispering, "Thank God you are here, Rhonda." After the embrace, which seemed to Rhonda to be fueled by more relief than longing, Layla stepped back, and Rhonda could immediately see the fire that burned in Layla's eyes. Layla was not a weak woman; whatever happened today in her clinic did not weaken her but rather put more steel in her resolve.

Layla's voice, now steady and strong, looked Rhonda in the eye and said, "Those bastards aren't going to destroy my life and those of my patients."

Before Rhonda could ask her to explain, Layla grabbed Rhonda's hand and led her into the clinic. Once in the clinic, Rhonda could see tables overturned, drawers rifled through, and computer screens pulled out from their fixtures. The office looked ransacked as if vandals had come in looking for something to steal but found nothing of value they could hock on the street, so they just trashed the place.

"Looks like you were vandalized. Is anything important missing?" Rhonda asked.

"Just my patient's lives, hopes, and dreams," Layla said, as she opened the door to the clinic's laboratory.

Once inside, Rhonda immediately cast her eyes toward the area containing the liquid nitrogen embryo storage tanks, which, while not destroyed, were tampered with as numerous test tubes containing the embryos were missing. These vials had contained the incredible possibility of Layla's patients becoming parents, and perhaps, Rhonda thought, the future generation that may be saving the world from the mistakes of the current generation. But Rhonda did not have time to think about philosophical what-ifs. Layla was important to Rhonda, and Layla was shaken. But putting those emotions aside, Rhonda was a cop, and a crime was committed, so she immediately went into cop mode.

"Layla, any idea who might have done this?"

"I don't know who might have done this, but once I figure out why, I think I can tell you who is behind this," Layla answered.

"Ok. Why do you think someone broke in?" Rhonda asked.

"Well, it could be because people are just evil, or they are greedy and after money, or to make a political statement for or against science, religion, or women's rights," Layla answered.

Rhonda said nothing, so Layla continued, knowing Rhonda well enough to see she was thinking it through one step ahead of where Layla was taking her.

"It is hard to say the specific reason or reasons as it could have been done by someone with multiple agendas. I know this was not a robbery by the local neighborhood thieves looking to turn what was stolen into a quick buck. This was a professional robbery because the thieves knew what they wanted, the embryos, and took care extracting them from the chambers," Layla said.

Rhonda interrupted, "Sorry for my ignorance with this question, but how long would an embryo survive without the proper storage you have here?"

"Not long at all, which may answer the important question of why. If the thieves who took them did not have proper storage, the embryos would not last two hours. It would also be questionable if their genetic integrity would remain intact if they were placed in the proper storage two hours from now," Layla answered.

"So, how long would they last if they were correctly stored immediately? "Rhonda followed up.

"Years," Layla answered. "Embryos as old as ten years can remain viable and produce babies."

"Ok, Layla, let's follow the line of thinking that the embryos were stolen, not to destroy them but rather to protect them. Who does that tell you might have stolen them?"

Layla answered, "If they were stolen with the intent to protect the embryos, the thieves would have to be medically intelligent to know what they were handling and backed by a lot of money as these storage units and the liquid nitrogen are very expensive."

"So," Rhonda said, "in that scenario, protection of the embryos, for whatever reason, was the goal. Correct?"

"Yes. I would assume so," Layla answered pensively.

"Ok, Layla, let's take scenario two. The embryos were taken, but they were taken to be destroyed. Give me your thoughts on that."

Layla answered, "If that was the case and the goal was to destroy the embryos, why not just take them out of the chambers and smash them on the floor? Why carefully remove them?"

"Yeah, that is what I was thinking as well," Rhonda confirmed and added, "Of course if this is a sophisticated crime, it seems to me, they could just have taken them as a redirect, to take us and you away from the real motive and the people behind the crime."

"Layla, are there any people or groups that have been causing you or the clinic trouble in any way and did this to make a statement?" Rhonda asked.

"Well, there are always the usual nut jobs who, after all these years, still think IVF is the devil's work, but that has quieted down. However, with the Supreme Court decision and continued pressure on reproductive rights, especially in states like Missouri, I have noticed more and more people protesting outside my doors or occasionally sending me a nasty email or letter. Sometimes, we have a couple who are angry we did not have success with their ability to conceive, but they are mostly angry because they are heartbroken. And most, if not all, our clients have the means to spend $40,000 plus on the procedure, so their standing in life would not seem to lead them to a criminal act," Layla said. Then thinking about Becca and her husband, added, "and then we have couples going through divorce who are fighting over the ownership and disposition of their embryos."

Ignoring Layla's last comment about divorcing couples, Rhonda pressed on. "I have found the boundaries of criminal intent are not necessarily restricted based on a person's net worth or standing in the community. You said yourself, Layla, if someone were to take the embryos to protect them, they would have to be smart and have money. I will also need to see any letters or emails you may have received recently from anyone upset with what you are doing here, whether it was a personal issue or not."

"I can't give you any information for anyone who is a current or past patient due to HIPPA laws, but there are plenty of other crazy people out there, with lots of motivation and anger, who have sent me emails and such," Layla answered.

"General crazy anger covers about eighty percent of the population, so I am hoping we can whittle that down to people who are specifically irate over the IVF concept," said Rhonda, now thinking about her next steps and thinking about Richard Leary's special skills.

Changing gears because Rhonda knew this was a very intricate case that would require additional resources, plus she had personal reasons, she said to Layla, "It's a bit problematic that you called me first and not 911, especially since I am a homicide detective, and I am still technically suspended until tomorrow, so I will have to tell my superiors why you called me."

"Why did you call me, Layla?"

"I called you because I wanted to talk to someone first before some beat cop and forensics came down and stomped all over my clinic. And because I trust you and only you to handle this for me. I am sorry about your suspension. I read about the case you handled chasing down Dr. Finnegan and his transplant center. It seemed to me you did everything right and still got suspended," Layla said.

Rhonda, nodding, said, "That case proves my point that crime knows no status level. Finnegan is a scumbag that frankly thought he was untouchable because he was intelligent, wealthy, and had connections that he thought would protect him," adding, "Did you know Dr. Finnegan?"

"I did not know him personally but knew of the work he was doing at the center and frankly thought it was fascinating how he pushed social and perhaps moral boundaries. In a way, that is what IVF did in the early years. When I heard you were involved, I knew he was toast. I wish I contacted you then to congratulate and support you during your suspension. I am sorry I didn't."

"Thanks, Layla. It would have been nice to hear from you," she said softly, then turning back into a cop, "Do you know his business partner, Dr. Calabrese?"

"I do know her. In fact, I am on one of her advisory boards."

Rhonda was quiet for a minute, still thinking Calabrese was also more involved with Finnegan's crimes than she let on and wishing she had another crack at her. She also did not like that Layla was close to Calabrese, but Rhonda could see why the two women would know each other as they were both in the medical field and perhaps Layla saw Dr. Calabrese as an older mentor, a role that Rhonda had failed to provide.

Rhonda pushed those thoughts to the back of her mind and now holding Layla's hand, said, "I am here now, Layla, and while I obviously will need to get additional STLPD resources on this, I am glad you called me first. And don't worry that we lost touch. Much of that is on me, but let's get your life and business back on its feet and catch the bastards that made a mess of things here."

Chapter 6
MOLONEY AND LAYLA

It had now been a very long and stressful morning for Dr. Layla Brazini. This was a day that she never in her life thought would happen to her and her profession. Layla knew that Rhonda could not officially work on the case, but she would do some off-the-grid investigating using a friend of hers. That was all she said. Layla knew Rhonda tended to work off the grid quite a bit, which was partly the reason she had so much success in solving cases as well as so much condemnation from her superiors regarding her tactics. Rhonda got things done, and she promised Layla that there was no one more important in her life than Layla and that she would do everything possible to help her. Layla had heard those words before, and she hoped Rhonda would not let her down as she had done before.

Layla stood in the middle of the office, trying to decide what to do next when there was a knock at the door. A young woman in uniform stood in the doorway. "I'm Officer Ally Moloney, STLPD, ma'am, and I've been assigned to investigate the robbery. I'd like to ask you some questions to get up to speed on the case."

Layla sighed and thought, "*This is all I need; she's just a kid.*"

Moloney began by asking some standard robbery questions: Was the alarm turned on? Any video devices? No was her answer on the alarm, as Layla forgot to set it the previous evening, and no was her answer on video devices, as Layla thought that was an invasion of patient privacy. Moloney asked about disgruntled employees or patients. Layla gave Moloney the same answers she gave Rhonda.

There were no disgruntled employees, and while some patients were disappointed IVF did not work, none, Layla thought, would be audacious or desperate enough to steal embryos. And even though couples could get crazy when they found out their ability to have a child with their DNA was coming to an end, they would have enough sense, Layla hoped, to realize it was the woman's body telling them it was over. Stealing someone else's embryos to get pregnant would make no medical or moral sense. But Layla knew that crazy now seemed to be the most popular trait shared by Americans, so she could not rule anything out. However, when Moloney asked to see the records of patients whose embryos were taken, Layla answered "no" as she had to consider patient privacy. Layla told Moloney that she would have to discuss this with her lawyer to determine the legality of releasing patient records. Thinking about her patients gave Layla a sick feeling as the most precious things in their lives right now were gone. Then Moloney asked about the value of what was stolen or damaged. Layla rattled off the estimated value of destroyed furniture or computers.

Moloney then asked about the value of the embryos, a question that burst the false calmness Layla had tried to exude throughout the morning.

"Value? What is the value of the embryos? Is that what you want to know, Officer Moloney?"

Using false bravado and knowing she had just asked the question that had upset Layla, Moloney followed up as professionally as she could and said, "Yes, Dr. Brazini, the value. What is the value of the embryos?"

Responding factually rather than emotionally, Layla answered, "I guess you could value them based on the cost each patient pays to go through IVF. That is between $40,000 to $60,000 spent in my clinic." Then she added, "But most of these patients have spent double that on other techniques tried and failed."

Sensing the way Layla had answered, Moloney knew a more caustic answer was coming, so she stayed quiet. She was not as green as Layla assumed she was.

"Or, Officer, you can value each embryo as a life. How much is life worth to my patients who have no children, and this was the only chance to start a family? Or how much will a failed marriage be worth when my patients realize their dreams, and now their marriage is broken? How do you put a financial number on their value, Officer? You tell me," Layla said more defiantly than she meant.

"You are right, Doctor. I can't put a value on life. No one can," Moloney said.

Then Moloney asked a question Layla did not expect. "Doctor, and I apologize for being so direct, but at this stage, is an embryo considered a life?"

Layla thought about the answer, then sighed and took a breath. She also eyed Moloney, thinking this question was less about being a cop and more about being a woman or perhaps a woman planning to have children. Because of that, Layla softened her tone a bit with Moloney. "That is a complex question, Officer, and one I think we will hear a lot about after the Roe decision. Medically speaking, until the embryo is implanted into a woman's uterus, it doesn't have life. We freeze them close to absolute zero to ensure no biological activity of cells can occur. This activity only happens after they are implanted. Even then, because of many factors, including the woman's health, age, and embryo viability, maybe forty to fifty percent of the embryos become viable and form a life. So, you tell me, which embryo, of the ones stored here, becomes a life if the IVF success rate is only forty to fifty percent?"

"Doctor, do you think the recent overturning of Roe-Wade will impact the IVF business and the embryos?" Moloney asked, thoughtfully.

"Are you asking related to the investigation of this break-in or asking for your general education," Officer Moloney?"

"Well, general education and curiosity, but depending upon your answer, maybe for investigating the break-in," Moloney said.

Now, eyeing her differently than when she first met her, Layla answered, "That is an interesting question and one that Detective Simon and I discussed earlier. Are you getting counsel or advice from her on this case?"

"Let's just say I have followed Detective Simon's career since I have been on the force, and I try to think as she thinks."

"Good, I have faith in Detective Simon looking beyond the obvious, and maybe my trust in you has risen a few notches. Now, to answer your question, I think IVF and embryos are going to be the next battleground for the true crazy zealots and legislators of pro-life. I think they are coming after the embryos and are going to claim that if a woman or a clinic destroys them, they should be convicted of murder based on the abortion laws where the clinic or the woman resides."

"That seems crazy, Doctor. Do they expect the embryos to be forced into a woman to have as many kids as the embryos can produce?"

Layla, now more animated than before, said, "As bat shit crazy as that appears, I think some of them believe so. I also think that the other option is for the embryos to be given out to those who can't have children, so in essence, a man or woman would be forced to give up their embryos and have many of their biological children roaming unknown to them on the earth."

Layla was now getting a pounding headache, and all she could think about was that she needed to contact her lawyer again to prepare for all the lawsuits she knew were coming and call her insurance company to understand what type of liability coverage she had, as she knew the losses could be astronomical.

After a quiet moment, Moloney finally said, "Dr. Brazini. I am not yet sure what happened at your clinic and why, but what you just described about how embryos may be treated in the future sounds like someone, or some group would have the motive to steal the embryos for possible financial gain or to make a social statement."

"Officer Moloney, you are more like Detective Simon than you think. After the break-in, she came to the same conclusion, but we both had three unanswered questions. Who, why, and most importantly, how?"

Moloney nodded, saying, "Whoever took them, took them to protect or destroy them." She added, "Doctor, based on my report, which can only state facts, not opinions or conspiracies, this case will be handled like a break-in and robbery. We will do some cursory examination of the evidence, look out for similar crimes in the area, and keep our eyes on social media to see if anybody talks about this crime. Normally a case like this gets shoved to the back burner along with the other hundred or so burglaries that happen each month in the city."

Layla answered, "I figured that is how this will go. But it will be tough to explain to my patients how their futures will be so easily discarded because of police and prosecution backlog."

"Well, Doctor, Let's hope this case does not get backlogged, and I have an idea how we can avoid that and perhaps how Detective Simon can be assigned to it. She may be the only one who can solve it and muscle her way past the political and social hurdles she will surely face."

"Officer Moloney, I like the way you think. Tell me what you think my next step should be."

Chapter 7

Layla Calls Her Patients

After Officer Moloney left, Layla dreaded the calls she needed to make to her patients, but she knew she only had a few hours before they read or heard about it on the news. Although her lawyer had advised her not to do or say anything to the media, citing patient confidentiality, Layla felt she owed it to her patients, many of whom Layla was emotionally connected to as she had known them for months and sometimes years through the roller coaster of IVF.

Her lawyer wanted Layla to keep the discussion with her patients very vague. Do not offer guilt or take blame. Do not make promises of what might happen next. Just stick to the facts of what she knew and do not speculate on why and what she thought might have happened. Her instructions were to convey that New Beginnings was broken into and vandalized. *"Our equipment and some of the embryos were destroyed or missing. The police are investigating."*

As Layla began looking at the list of her patients whose embryos were missing and possibly destroyed, she thought it might be easier if she started with the most recent patients. They were early on the journey and could restart the process. Her heart told her she should try to re-start their treatments at the lowest cost possible. Perhaps insurance money could cover that.

The most difficult conversations would be those who had spent well over the initial $40,000 fee and had spent multiple years in IVF trying to get pregnant. She knew these would be the ones who saw New Beginnings as their last possible hope, either because they were out of money or were aging out of the viability window to even carry a baby. These were the people whose hopes had been dashed so many times, and this news would cripple them emotionally.

The first call she did make, though, was with one of her newest patients, who now was one of her dearest friends, Becca Stevens. Layla and Becca were two peas in a pod. They were both women not only breaking into a man's world but trying to dominate it. Layla through medicine, and Becca through entrepreneurship. They talked now nearly every day, and there were no secrets between them, so Layla thought this call would be a good trial run for the calls she would have to make to all her patients.

Becca immediately sensed something wrong in her friend's usual cheerful demeanor. "Is everything ok, Layla? You seem preoccupied and a bit subdued."

Layla hesitated before answering, thinking about her lawyer's instructions. However, at this point in her life, Becca was the person she could trust the most, so she decided to be honest and ignore her lawyer's advice.

"Before you hear it on the news or from someone else, I want to tell you what happened at the clinic this morning, or maybe it happened last night."

"What news? Is everything all right?" Becca asked, now with worry in her voice.

"This morning, I discovered that the clinic was broken into."

"Oh no. Are you ok? Was anything stolen?" Becca immediately showed genuine concern as a friend, not as a patient.

"I am a little shaken up, but I am fine now. We did have some damage, and some valuable things were stolen," Layla answered.

"What valuable things?" Becca asked, but Layla sensed she already knew the answer.

"Umm. Layla stalled. "They stole our embryos."

"What?" was all Becca could say as she seemed too stunned to say anything more.

Now, anger was coming back and coursing through Layla, as she said with anger and then tears that she had held back all day, "Those bastards stole some of my patients' embryos and trashed the clinic."

In her heart, Becca knew it was best to comfort Layla, but her heart also knew that her future was also stored at the clinic, so she asked a question she did not want to know the answer to. "Layla, did they take mine?"

After a few tense seconds, Layla softly said, "Yes, I am so sorry, Becca."

Just silence from Becca. Then she finally spoke, and her response was what Layla expected from her friend. This friend was going through a horrible divorce, a friend whose embryos were in the middle of the divorce litigation. This friend had a fantastic career future but looked at the embryos as life changing. But rather than lay guilt, Becca did what she always did, she comforted her friend, not complaining about how this news affected Becca's own life. "Layla, I am there for you and will do whatever I can to help you."

Layla, now crying, said, "Becca, I am not sure what I can or should do. I feel so helpless and violated, which pisses me off frankly. I let my patients down. I let you down, and I know how much your embryos mean to you and how hard you are trying to keep ownership of them. I feel especially bad for you, Becca; you have gone through so much hell during your divorce trying to protect them."

Becca then said something that surprised Layla, "You know, Layla, while I hope my embryos can be recovered, in retrospect, my creating embryos was a last-ditch attempt to save a marriage gone bad. I should never have done it, and if they are gone for good, maybe next time I will just harvest eggs and get them fertilized by an anonymous donor if I don't find anyone I love enough to have a baby with."

Becca's statement sent a jolt to Layla's brain, not because Becca so casually thought about the creation of embryos as a mistake to save a lost marriage, but the comment about just harvesting her eggs instead of having them fertilized in Layla's lab.

"Her eggs," she thought. Then, visualizing the damage to the clinic and the test tubes storing the embryos, she remembered something very important. The thieves had only taken embryos, eggs fertilized with a man's sperm, but many of Layla's patients had not gone through the fertilization process yet. The eggs were from patients who had gone through egg extraction but had not fertilized them for various reasons. Sometimes it was because a spouse or an anonymous sperm donor for a single or gay woman had to arrange to come into the IVF Clinic to fertilize a woman's eggs before she proceeded with IVF. Layla kept the eggs on site for many of the women who were in the process of contracting with Cryobanks or a sperm donor to fertilize their eggs. It made more sense and cost less to keep the unfertilized eggs in her clinic temporarily and then, after fertilization, ship them off site to one of the large embryo Cryo-storage units now part of the IVF business and store them for a later date in their lives when they were better prepared to raise a family.

"Becca, as I think about it, they didn't take the eggs." Then, she said it again but now with excitement in her voice. "They didn't take the eggs. I just realized that they left the unfertilized eggs alone. They only took the embryos." Then, talking to herself, forgetting Becca was on the line, Layla asked herself, *"Why? Why did they take the embryos and not the eggs?"* That question haunted Layla, but she now knew that the break-in was not a random act of violence but rather a well-planned theft, and the thieves knew the embryos were what they wanted to steal.

Now, with a sense of urgency, Layla said, "Becca, I hate to cut you off, but I need to call my other patients before this news comes out. I think the fact that they only stole embryos and not the eggs means something significant as to who the thieves are and what they wanted."

"Do what you need to do, Layla, and take care of your other patients as their situation is much more dire than mine. But let's talk again soon when you are able. Love you, Layla." Becca hung up and sat in silence, thinking about their conversation. While Becca felt helpless to Layla, she also felt anger rising inside her. If someone had taken the embryos, they had done it for a purpose. In Becca's mind, the only people capable of doing something like this were the people who made her blood boil every day, the damn pro-lifers who seemed to feel emboldened to take away all women's rights, first abortion and now perhaps the rights of ownership and disposition of a woman's embryos. While the battle she was fighting with her husband was personal, she saw that maybe this battle was more existential, and it was a battle she was ready to engage in. The next opportunity to do that would be tomorrow at a planned Pro-life rally in Tower Grove Park, across the street from Layla's clinic. Becca knew where she and her friends, Layla's friends, would be tomorrow and precisely what they hoped to accomplish.

Chapter 8
RHONDA AND LT. TARALLO

Rhonda certainly did not ease into her first day back on the job after her suspension.

Yesterday morning's surprise call from Layla and the subsequent visit to her clinic, while immediately getting her juices flowing, also got her in hot water with Lieutenant Andrea Tarallo, who was pissed off that Rhonda took the call from Layla without going through the proper police protocols. While many people would call a cop they knew to help them out before making it an official request, a cop like Detective Simon, who just got off suspension, should have handled it by the book.

Tarallo dressed down Detective Simon in her office. "Shit Simon, your first day back from suspension, and you take a call yesterday without notifying the precinct. Hell, it was just a break-in. Not something I would have even assigned to you."

"You are right, Lieutenant. I took the call because Dr. Brazini is someone I am close to, and based on what she told me on the phone, I felt she needed someone she could trust before we called in the troops."

"What is your relationship with Dr. Brazini?" Tarallo asked.

Tersely Rhonda replied, "My relationship with Dr. Brazini could best be described as none of your fucking business, Lieutenant." Rhonda had always had a bad relationship with Tarallo, and her suspension had not improved it because Rhonda felt instead of having her back, Tarallo stabbed her in it and threw her to the wolves.

"Ok, Simon. I see your suspension has not had any effect on your bullshit attitude. Still, unless something warrants it in the future, you are off any investigation of the clinic break-in. I gave it to Officer Moloney and her partner to see what they could turn up. It was a simple smash and grab anyway done by some of the locals looking for drugs or money."

After talking to Layla, Rhonda knew it was more than just a simple smash and grab. She sensed that it was something more significant, but she knew Officer Moloney from the Finnegan case. If needed, Rhonda knew Moloney would give her back door information as the case progressed. And Tarallo was right. The robbery was a junior-level offense in a city that had a Ph.D. in murder. She was a homicide detective. One of the best in St. Louis, and she would have to accept Tarallo's decision. She would explain to Layla that she would have to *"officially distance"* herself from the case and Layla. Unfortunately, distancing herself from Layla had been Rhonda's history with Layla in their complicated past.

As Detective Simon was about to leave Tarallo's office, Tarallo looked down at her cell phone and, with a look of surprise after reading her official police notifications, said, "Well, today is your lucky day, Simon. It seems your first day back will have you in the swamp immediately. Looks like all hell is breaking loose in Tower Grove Park with a shooting between protest groups."

"Shit Tarallo. It's my first day back. Let me catch up with what the guys on my team have been up to and see what has been going on in the big picture in this city before I deal with this run-of-the-mill protest bullshit."

Now, with a slight grin, Tarallo said, "Oh, you will want in on this one. While the protest started at the park, it seems the shooting was across the street from the New Beginnings Fertility Clinic, which I believe is owned by your mystery woman, Dr. Brazini. No, this one is all yours, Simon, but try not to shoot anyone like you did with your last case."

Tempted to tell Tarallo to go fuck herself, Rhonda knew bringing up the Finnegan case, which got her suspended, was Tarallo's way of baiting her. Tarallo rose through the ranks because she was not only politically shrewd within the department but also a very thorough and analytical investigator on the cases handled in her department. Rhonda was like her in that way, but Rhonda was a bit more of a bull in the china shop, literally and metaphorically crashing and destroying any obstacles that got in her way. She preferred a simple level of crime solving, including shooting the criminal when possible. Hell, why did she carry a gun if she did not use it? Rather than take the bait and continue the ongoing feud between her and Tarallo, she sensed that perhaps Layla was in danger. Perhaps the break-in and this protest and shooting were all part of the same crime. Thinking big picture and not wanting to be dragged down in the mud with Tarallo, Rhonda gave her a fake salute because she could not give her the one-finger salute she wanted to, just said, "Got it, Lieutenant," and left Tarallo's office.

Chapter 9

A Protest and a Murder

The protest and shooting at Tower Grove Park, near New Beginnings Fertility Cinic, took place, not over a drug deal or gang fight, but it involved a bunch of primarily white, predominately middle-aged, normally law-abiding residents within the St. Louis metro area. The locale was Tower Grove Park on the city's southwest side, usually a genteel area as the park abutted the tranquil Missouri Botanical Gardens at its northwest border. During the day, people came to the park and the Botanical Garden to relax, take a walk, have a picnic, or practice yoga in nice weather. The park, which also included the land on which the Botanical Gardens now sits, is considered one of the largest and best-preserved 19th-century Gardenesque-style city parks in the United States.

Detective Simon always marveled at the abundance of beautiful parks the St. Louis area was blessed to have for its people to enjoy. She visited Tower Grove Park many times as she enjoyed a peaceful walk or some people-watching during lunch at a picnic table or park bench. In the past, she often had lunch with Layla, whose clinic was nearby on Grand, bordering the park's east side. At night, unfortunately, as in many city parks, Rhonda did some watching of a different caliber of people with other intentions than a friendly lunch.

During most days, the park was fortunately a wonderful oasis of greenery and tranquility. Tower Grove Park also featured the largest multi-cultural event in the city, The International Institute, Festival of Nations, where food, music, and dance representing over forty countries were enjoyed by immigrants just arriving in St. Louis and perhaps the country as well as immigrants who called St. Louis home for years and generations.

But the festival attendance was not limited to immigrants, recent or long-time settled, as any St. Louis resident looking to expand their viewpoint of the world, its people, and perhaps its exotic food would come to enjoy the festival. Simon herself always made a visit, primarily as a purveyor of new experiences, scents, and tastes, and this past year, she brought Richard Leary, who had never been to the festival despite living in St. Louis for most of his life. He, like many first-time visitors to the festival, was shocked at the ethnic diversity in the city. St. Louis has the largest Bosnian population in the United States. In the past few years, the city and area were getting an influx of Afghans fleeing their country after the Taliban violently filled the void when the Americans finally and haphazardly pulled out. Rhonda assumed now the city would see an influx of Ukrainians and maybe Palestinians fleeing their war-torn countries.

Rhonda was not surprised by the influx of immigrants in St. Louis as it was an affordable and relatively safe place, but she encountered them more frequently than she had wanted in her line of work. In most cases, it was because some immigrants, because of skin color, inability to speak English, or religious preferences, were being attacked. The attacks and violence were not done by those whose brutality they were escaping back in their homeland but often by members of the St. Louis immigrant community who were all struggling to assimilate. Many were current St. Louis residents, perhaps recent immigrants, who felt the new arrivals were taking a higher spot on the lowest rung of the societal ladder.

Rhonda also got to know many of the immigrants who came together after an attack to aid the victims or clean up the broken windows and racist messages painted on shop owners' storefronts or restaurants. In observing and aiding in these interactions, Rhonda knew immigrants were not afraid of hard work, would not be intimidated by others, and would leave sooner than later the lowest rung on the ladder of success. Rhonda knew in talking to the immigrants that anything the streets or violent criminals of St. Louis would throw at them was nothing compared to the oppression, poverty, and violence they experienced daily in their original homelands. Pursuing the American dream and the violence and vitriol they experienced was nothing compared to the land they left. America may seem broken to some, but to newly arriving immigrants, it is still a beacon of hope that drives many immigrants from all over the world to settle in the U.S. and in St. Louis specifically.

This morning at the park, though, it wasn't a battle between those fighting over the ladder's bottom rung. It was a battle of ideology between two groups of people, both wanting to save America, not from foreign enemies, but from each other, based on political beliefs. Today, unfortunately, the heated rhetoric originating from and passed along by cable news and extremist websites grew beyond angry shouts from the protest lines and turned into a murder scene.

Pulling up to the primary area where the violence unfolded, Rhonda sought out the city cops and park rangers who had gotten there first to get their take on what had happened. The city had issued a permit for a lecture/demonstration of the pro-life advocates and supporters of Dr. Joseph Merkel, a prominent pro-life supporter and speaker from Boca Raton, Florida. The recent Supreme Court decision might potentially eliminate abortion nationwide, but for now, it was still a state-by-state decision. Merkel and his supporters, feeling the wind at their back due to the Supreme Court, did not want any progress made from women and liberals in large cities such as St. Louis and its surrounding suburbs, which were actively trying to pass protections, access, and funding to ensure women still had a choice, even those living in conservative states like Missouri. Dr. Merkel was invited to speak in St. Louis by an up-and-coming vocal right-wing firebrand in the Missouri state senate, Billy O'Dell, who was trying to suppress the ability for Missouri citizens to put the right to abortion on the ballot, rather than dictated by his peers, in the Missouri state senate.

O'Dell knew that messages and messengers like he and Merkel were critical at rallies like this one, especially in St. Louis, since the liberal-leaning city and its media could not only try to influence statewide politics in Missouri but, due to its proximity to Illinois, could influence the messaging there which was ramping up its access to abortion clinics.

O'Dell, Merkel, and their advocates came armed with loud voices and the usual messaging on signs, denigrating everybody with an opposite opinion. The crowd was small, with less than one hundred people, and ignored by other parkgoers as it seemed most people just wanted to enjoy a nice day in the park with their families, and a protest march, regardless of the focus, was not of any interest to them.

According to the cops on the scene, the relative peace of the protest changed when the pro-life attendees noticed a smaller group of people walking in front of The New Beginnings Fertility Clinic, Layla's business, vocalizing support for her and her clinic after news of yesterday's break-in and robbery hit the media. This group was made up of primarily women, young and old, white and black, who came with their own slogans and signs. Many might have been the clinic's patients or friends of the owner, Dr. Brazini. If anything, the Supreme Court decision seemed to re-energize the pro-choice crowd who had been complacent over the years. They never thought Roe v. Wade would be overturned, but now that it had been, they saw the energized right move swiftly and aggressively in state legislatures to expand their positions and reach on the issue. The pro-choice crowd feared how far the conservative bent of the Supreme Court and the conservative states would go. Beyond pro-choice vs. pro-life on abortion, the signs and the chants of the group in front of Layla's clinic shouted that every human right was now on the table. Positions for and against same-sex marriages, interracial marriages, contraceptive devices, the use of science to conceive, and the ownership of embryos and eggs created and stored in IVF labs and Cryobanks now seemed to be a fair and threatened target that needed protection.

While the decision on the disposition of unused IVF embryos had been broached in some state legislatures, no real movement on the issue had progressed, probably because state-by-state abortion access was still being contested and protected even in conservative states such as Kansas and Ohio. While normally the two groups might have protested separately, each, frankly, was looking for a fight, and today would be the day for that fight. The group outside the IVF clinic seemed content to show their support for New Beginnings and did not want to engage in a larger, all-encompassing right vs. left battle. They were mostly friends of Layla and were there to support her and her business. But all that changed when a large group of the pro-life gathering wandered from the park over to the sidewalk in front of the IVF clinic and decided to throw what could only be described as clear plastic balls with red paint in them, depicting blood, and contained inside the balls were plastic replicas of what an eight-week-old fetus, the size of a strawberry, would look like. This group was looking for a battle today and they found one.

This action whipped up the frenzy and anger, and the police and park rangers could contain neither group as both groups broke through the human and wooden barricades and rushed toward each other with vulgarities and fists flying. The pro-life crowd was a little bit older, whiter, and generally years from being in fighting shape. The pro-choice group was more diverse and younger, and their youthful exuberance overwhelmed the pro-life crowd quickly. The small contingent of police waded into the fight carefully as they were outnumbered as well, and the police knew through breaking up these types of events, the fight would extinguish itself very soon; most of the combatants would throw a few punches and then tire from exhaustion. After a year of dealing with these groups, week after week of never-ending philosophical or political differences, the police, like most people, were pretty much fed up and did little to intervene. But then, they and all the protesters heard several gunshots, and all hell broke loose.

First, there were the shots, then screams, then most of each group running or seeking cover, with the cops, guns drawn, looking for the shooter or the direction of the shot. Everyone was running, except for six people standing, peering at the woman who was shot and now lying on the ground screaming in anguish. "Call 911. Theresa has been shot," someone yelled. Those surrounding Theresa were a mixture of both groups and were all visibly shaken and, in an odd way, consoling each other without blame for the time being. Three cops rushed in, moving the onlookers to the side, performing an assessment of the wounded woman's injuries and radioing in to get emergency medical personnel on the scene quickly. But today, quickly was moot because the woman would be dead within two minutes of the emergency call. The cops knew it. The protesters knew it, and Noah Sharpe, who had silently observed the scene unfolding from two hundred yards away, knew it.

While he was not involved in the protest, Noah witnessed the whole scene from beginning to end. Mayhem had ensued, and everyone was either running away or tending to the injured woman. Noah quietly moved closer and sat at a nearby bus stop, shaking his head and laughing over the chaos caused by the mindless protesters, sheep as he called them, who were in shock that name calling and taunting had turned into actual violence and actual death. Now that a death was involved, the stakes got significantly higher, and Noah knew these weekend warriors did not have the stomach or calling to do what he had been called to do, and that was to make a real, permanent change in a world spiraling out of control; it was a world that seemed to ignore Noah, but soon it would have to reckon with him.

The cops at once sequestered six protesters who seemed to be the primary agitators, to hold them for questioning from Detective Simon, who was just pulling up in her car. As she did, she also looked around the perimeter of the demonstration area to see if any bystanders not involved in the protests but being in the vicinity would have seen anything. Rhonda's experience told her that many shooters in these types of events hovered close enough near the crime, in part due to ego and in part to make sure their target was hit.

She scanned the crowd and saw pain, anxiety, anger, and sorrow. These were normal emotions from people who had seen actions gone too far or perhaps ones who had never seen violence up close. Detective

Simon had seen more than her share of up-close violence, and today, her first full day back from suspension, she was back in the hateful, violent, murderous stew, which simmered constantly on the streets of St. Louis. She was about to turn away from the onlookers and back to the cops on the scene who were surrounding the body and giving the paramedics room to work, but soon their work would be done, and the coroner would be arriving to start his grim task. Before she turned her attention to the dying woman, she glimpsed a man, white, perhaps late thirties or early forties, sitting quietly at the bus stop with an expression, not of fear or interest, but almost complacency as if the scene unfolding before him were commonplace, and, in some areas of town, it was. But there was something else that struck her about him. He seemed almost relaxed as if he was waiting for his daily bus to take him to work, which perhaps he was, but his lack of interest in the madness occurring just two hundred yards in front of him seemed odd. He seemed odd, but for now, Detective Simon could not identify why. Perhaps her suspension had dulled her usual sharp instincts, but she would have to put the guy out of her mind because she had what would be, in about sixty more seconds, a murder to solve. However, if the guy were still around after she dealt with the matter at hand, that being a dead woman, she would make sure to go over and talk to him.

Chapter 10

WITNESS TO A MURDER

Detective Simon turned to talk to the cops on the scene and learn whatever she could from their initial assessment. The victim of the shooting, now identified as Theresa Cahill, had already died and was covered with a tarp. Simon did a cursory review of the body, looking at where the bullet entered the woman, through her back, then exiting her chest, and along the way shredding her vital organs that probably thirty minutes ago were pumping blood through a woman who was excited to be part of a protest for a cause she believed in. Now, her lifeless eyes stared back at Simon, who always used this moment to humanize the victim, which, in a way, motivated Simon to solve this case quickly before it became yesterday's news and the only ones who cared about Theresa Cahill were the family she left behind.

Simon spoke with the cops who had just concluded interviews with any possible witnesses. While close to one hundred people were on the scene, some protesters and some curious onlookers, the cops narrowed the primary witnesses to a handful that had stayed behind so Simon could ask them additional questions. After the shock of the shooting, the brief moment of shared compassion and humane actions over a tragic event ended, and finger-pointing and arguments began again as to who started the fight between the pro-choice and pro-life groups. There was no doubt that the victim was part of the pro-choice crowd as her blood-stained t-shirt read, "My body, My choice." The identity of the shooter, however, was still a mystery as no one with any degree of certainty could or would identify who it was, though some felt the shot rang out from a distance and pointed in the direction of a park statue. Others thought the shot came from above, in any one of the high-rise apartments on Grand. Despite no one seeing the shooter, everyone had assumptions as to who it was. Naturally, depending on who you asked, their assumptions were biased. Some people said they saw a white male running from the scene, and others said it was a black male. Some thought they had seen a shady-looking stranger lurking near the protest who was wearing a t-shirt that said, "Jesus Saves You and Your Fetus." Still, others were sure the t-shirt said, "Keep your hands off my Uterus." Thirty minutes after Simon's arrival, the crowd was still larger than Simon wanted to deal with. They began taunting each other and the cops again until Simon could stand it no more.

"Shut the fuck up," she yelled at the remaining people. "Go home. Do something productive today because right now, you are wearing out my patience, and all of us are sick of dealing with your crap." She was probably referring to the police, but the entire crowd at the park that was not part of the protesting group yelled in agreement. Most citizens wanted to live life peacefully and quietly. Still, the lunatic fringe, on the extreme right or left of most arguments, was slowly sucking the hope and civility out of our society.

Simon turned to Sargent Jacoby, saying, "If these assholes don't disperse in the next five minutes, arrest them all."

"Will do, Detective," and then nodding to a small group of people to his left, said, "I have pulled a few of these folks aside as I think you should hear what they have to say. I interviewed them separately, but their stories are nearly identical, which I found interesting since they were on opposite sides of the protests."

With that, Simon made her way through the larger groups, now becoming more obedient as the threat of arrest seemed to take steam out of their zeal. But Simon had already dismissed them as loudmouth assholes wasting her time as they had nothing to offer. But she wanted to talk to the man and woman Jacoby had pulled aside and now sat on a picnic bench.

"Ma'am, sir, I am Detective Rhonda Simon. I understand you had some interesting things to say to Officer Jacoby about what you saw here." The man, about sixty, balding, looking like a preacher or an insurance agent, spoke first.

"Detective, I am Craig Kane. It's not what I saw. It is about what I heard before the protest started. I heard that there would be a shooting, but I did not know who would do the shooting nor who would be the victim. Just that there would be a shooting."

Interrupting before Rhonda could ask a follow-up question, the woman, about forty but with pre-mature graying hair, spoke up. "I heard the same thing, Detective."

"And you are?" Rhonda asked.

"Oh, sorry. I am so nervous. I am Diane Carmody."

"Okay, Ms. Carmody, what did you hear?"

"I did not hear but rather read the same thing. There would be a shooting. More specifically, there needed to be a shooting."

Turning to both, Rhonda asked, "Where did both of you hear or read about the protest and the possibility of a shooting?"

Simultaneously, they said, "Online."

"Can you get more specific?" Rhonda asked.

They both looked at each other and then back to Simon and said simultaneously, "No, we can't."

"Why can't you tell me where you heard or read about this shooting?"

Now Kane answered. "Because those of us here fighting for the cause keep our sources of information private as we don't need or want the government snooping in our lives. We still have the right to privacy in America. Don't we, Detective?"

Simon did not like Kane's tone, so she said to scare him a bit, "Sure, you have all the right to privacy you want until I subpoena you and call you in as a material witness to a murder."

Turning to Diane Carmody, Simon asked, "Ms. Carmody, are your lips sealed as well?"

"Well, despite the fact I can't stand him," she said, pointing to Kane, "and the hate he believes in, yes, I also believe in privacy. We are trying to be of some help, but we don't want our private lives exposed as part of an investigation that has nothing to do with us and this murder."

Exasperated that in today's culture, every contact a cop had with a citizen seemed to be captured on an iPhone and turned into a lecture on civil rights or worse, Rhonda turned up the heat a bit more but was cautious.

"Well, you both knew of a possible murder happening at a rally that you were planning to attend, and neither of you bothered to alert the police."

Carmody answered first, "She said not to."

"Who said not to?"

"Harvest."

"Who the hell is Harvest?" Simon asked.

This time, Kane answered, "If you don't know who Harvest is, then you don't know the grand plan, Detective. Maybe you should pull your head out of your ass and learn the truth about the real battle happening in America."

The disrespect that people gave the police was appalling to Simon, and it was getting worse daily. Police now seemed to be the enemy, but one thing that Simon improved upon during her suspension was patience. So, for now, she let that comment slide, only asking both, "Is Harvest a local St. Louis person?"

Kane spoke, "I don't know where she is from, but that does not matter. She is the voice I and others listen to."

Surprisingly, Carmody also nodded her head in affirmation, which confused Simon as Carmody and Kane were on opposite sides of the pro-life vs. pro-choice protest issues.

"She is the voice of your cause as well as Ms. Carmody? Aren't you two on opposite sides of the fence politically and culturally?"

Carmody answered this question: "We are on opposite sides of single issues, such as pro-choice or pro-life and perhaps others, but Harvest speaks to all who want a permanent solution to society's collapse and re-birth and only talks to those who realize there is no right or wrong, only a center or agreement that will be reached when a new society is formed. We probably interpret her message differently to suit our own goals."

Now more confused and perhaps thinking Carmody and Kane were a bit nuts, Simon took another tack asking, "Do you think Harvest was at the protest today?"

"We could only pray and hope she was. Her appearance would give strength to our movement," Kane said.

"Our movement," Carmody quickly countered.

"I don't care whose movement you believe she supports. Can either of you describe her?"

They both shook their heads no.

Then Carmody said to Simon, "Detective, no one can tell you what Harvest looks like. It does not matter, just her message matters. You are thinking about her in the physical sense, and that is a mistake."

"Jesus,", Simon thought to herself, *"What a crazy first day back on the job."*

Sensing this conversation was going nowhere and feeling a major headache coming on, Simon gave her card to both Carmody and Kane, who she sensed would pitch it immediately after they left. Simon looked down at her notes, wondering what the hell she had learned from these two nut jobs plus others who randomly gave out their opinion on the shooting that, frankly, were all dead ends. There were no actual witnesses who saw anything conclusive. She was about to get back in her car when she looked around again and then back at the bus stop where the guy who had caught her attention previously was still sitting. It had been nearly an hour since Simon arrived, and this guy was still there. This time, he stared directly at Simon as if waiting for her. Simon made a beeline to him. His wait would be no more.

Chapter 11

RHONDA AND NOAH

Detective Simon approached the man, who instead of looking pan-icked because he had just witnessed a shooting, sat on the bus stop bench very calmly, looking directly at Simon as if he was expecting her. Most people panic and flee at the sound of gunfire. This man seemed perfectly calm, almost enjoying watching the scene unfold and patiently waiting for Detective Simon. She saw him looking at her, and she assumed he was also thinking about her and the conversation they were about to have, but unbeknownst to Detective Simon, this strange fellow was thinking about another woman. A woman who changed his life. Who had already been encouraging him to do things he never would have contemplated before. He had been sitting on the bus stop bench for nearly an hour, hoping today was the day he would meet his lover. His eyes were closed as Simon approached. Simon thought perhaps he was asleep or maybe passed out from an early morning drunken buzz. But his eyes were closed because he was thinking of her and waiting for her to come to him, embracing him, kissing him. In his mind, she was dazzling and mysterious. She had long, tousled blonde hair that fell to her waist. She was always dressed in a long, flowing, leopard-patterned duster, fitting loosely over tight blue jeans and lizard-skin boots. Her face was alabaster in color, offset by ruby-red lips. Wrapped around her face was a white feathered boa. Her appearance alone would have drawn the attention of almost everyone there if there had not just been a shooting, but she was only there to see one person: him.

His eyes still closed, he watched her come towards him, and he felt himself slowly rising to embrace her, to kiss her, but when he opened his eyes, she was not there. He only saw the detective who was eyeing him, now only a few feet in front of him. He seemed confused as he tried to look past where Detective Simon was now standing. Simon focused on the man, and then she also turned in the direction in which his gaze was focused. Simon could not decide what he was looking at, but to her, he was transfixed, almost catatonic, as he just stared and smiled.

Shaking his shoulders to snap him out of his gaze and thinking he might have seen something, Simon asked, "What are you looking at, bub?"

He said nothing, so she tapped his shoulder and more forcefully said, "Sir, I am not sure what you are looking at, but look at me now."

He turned to Simon, looked up with a slight smile and said, "Oh, I am sorry. I was thinking about my girlfriend. We were supposed to meet here in the park before the protest and shooting happened, and I thought I saw her, but I guess not. She probably left when she heard the shooting."

"Okay. Let's talk about what you might have seen. I am Detective Rhonda Simon. What is your name, sir?"

"I am Noah Sharpe."

"And what were you doing here at the park this morning?"

"Like I told you, I was here to meet my girlfriend, " Noah answered.

"Okay. Is this your day off, Mr. Sharpe? What do you do for a living?"

"I work with monkeys and apes at the zoo. I like them."

"That sounds like an interesting job," Simon answered but not with much conviction.

"Monkeys are better than humans. They are smarter and nicer to each other," Noah offered as if it was an important distinction to make.

Picking up oddness in Noah, especially in how his answers, tone, and eyes seemed distant, even when talking to her, Rhonda just shook her head, saying to herself, *"Another psych patient off his meds."*

"That's nice, Mr. Sharpe. Would you mind if I asked you a few questions about what you may have seen here this morning?"

"Sure. What do you want to know, Detective?"

"Did you see who did the shooting, Mr. Sharpe?"

"No."

"Do you think your girlfriend saw who did the shooting?"

"Well, I don't know if she did because I am not sure she was even here, but she did not need to see the shooter; she knew it was going to happen."

Now perking up, Simon edged closer to Noah's face.

"How did she know it would happen, Mr. Sharpe?"

"Everyone knew it was going to happen," said Noah.

"Who is everyone, Mr. Sharpe?"

"Everyone who showed up here today. They knew because she told them it was going to happen. She wanted it to happen. She is the reason all these people were here today."

"She, meaning your girlfriend?" asked Simon.

"Yes. She has been helping us understand that we have ruined this society and must form a new one. Everyone here and those in other conflicts around the country and world want to form a new society. Our anger should not be at each other because while we all have different opinions, we all want the same thing. We just believe in different paths to get there."

"And what is it that we all want? Mr. Sharpe.

"While we all want to feel we will win in the end, the only way for all of us to triumph is for our current society to crumble and self-destruct. That will not happen by going at each other's throats but by realizing that a complete and total rebirth of our species is what needs to happen. Our species is doomed, Detective, and a new species will rise that will come out of the ashes of our current society. We have reached the end of humankind, and we will soon be extinct. While these little skirmishes that we saw today and the much larger ones happening worldwide might portend humankind's end, they are only distractions, an opening act of what is to come, so we must prepare for that."

"Pretty deep thoughts for a guy who works with monkeys and has a mystery girlfriend," Rhonda said sarcastically and with reduced patience.

"You are rude, Detective. I have an I.Q. of over one hundred and fifty. I know I am smarter than you. Some people say I am a genius. You also insulted my monkeys, who have a higher intellect than you," Noah responded, this time, not from an absent gaze in his eyes, but from somewhere deeper and more sinister in his soul.

Slightly unnerved, perhaps because she was out of practice dealing with the psychos roaming the streets of St. Louis, Simon pushed on with a little more tact and perhaps more empathy. "Okay, Mr. Sharpe, I apologize if I insulted you and your girlfriend. I am just trying to solve the murder of a young woman, who right now is being grieved by her family and friends. And while I will agree with you that the world is fucked, I am trying to make it less fucked, one captured criminal at a time, and any help you or your girlfriend can give me would be great. Can you tell me your girlfriend's name?"

Pausing for a minute to determine if Simon was sincere or feeding him a bunch of bullshit, Noah sat for a moment and finally said, "Her name is Harvest."

"*Harvest.*" Simon thought, "*The same name those two witnesses had mentioned.*"

"This is the second time I have heard this person's name. Two witnesses I interviewed earlier also mentioned her name."

Looking unfazed by this news, Noah answered, "That does not surprise me, Detective. Anyone who wants to be enlightened and shown the way knows Harvest."

Detective Simon continued, "They would not tell me how to find Harvest. Since you seem to know her better than they do, could you tell me where to find her or how I can reach her? Do you have any contact information on her? Phone number, email perhaps? Where does she live?"

Noah answered, "You can't find her unless you are open to her message. If not, you will never find her."

"So, how does she contact you?"

"We talk online among like-minded visionaries, but she and I have a much deeper relationship. She sometimes goes to the zoo and watches me work. She is evaluating me to ensure I am worthy of her and can carry out her mission."

"But you have never seen her in person?" asked Simon.

"No. I see her online through chat and videos, but we have never been with each other physically, but that will happen as soon as I prove my worth to her. She told me I was her chosen one, and I believe her."

Now, Simon was shaking her head as she was sure Noah Sharpe was missing a few tools in the shed, and she was possibly wasting her time with him, at least in this case. Still, she thought, while he was very odd and maybe even mentally unstable, she did sense he was extremely bright, and highly intelligent people make extremely cunning criminals. The crazier they are the more it is a cat-and-mouse game.

She asked, "Mr. Sharpe. Are you on any medication? Under the care of a psychiatrist by any chance?"

Noah answered with a crisper sharpness than in his earlier tone, "If I were, which I am not, I would not need to tell you as that is privileged information. Are you on any medication, Detective Simon? After all, you were involved in a shooting last year in Forest Park. I believe you got suspended for it, didn't you?"

She was shocked that Noah Sharpe would know any information about her. The shooting in the Finnegan case was often in the news several months ago, but for Noah Sharpe to recall that and bring it up now sent some shivers down her spine. Was he stalking her? Was this killing at the park somehow connected to him and his desire to flush her out? Was it a coincidence the shooting took place on her first day back from suspension?

As spooked as Simon was by his comment, she also knew not to let Noah Sharpe change the focus of the conversation from him to her, so she ignored him for now. She was not going to get anywhere with Noah

Sharpe today or maybe any day if he was just a random psycho trying to bait her. She did not want him to know that he rattled her more than she thought possible. Simon needed to think about all this, so she handed Noah her card. "Okay, Mr. Sharpe. Please call me if you can remember anything else about today's events. Also, while I will try to track your girlfriend down, if she is willing or interested in talking to me, please give her my information."

With her sea legs back underneath her, Simon knew she had one more thing to say to him before she left Noah Sharpe. Getting right in his face, she said, "Mr. Sharpe, since it seems you know a little about me, let me give you some more to think about. I have seen it all, from cold-blooded murderers who would kill their mothers for ten bucks to psychopaths who believe voices told them to gun down children in a school. I have seen evil in humans, and nothing you do or say scares me or will stop me. If you are involved in anything that happened today or any other day in my city, believe me, Mr. Sharpe, I will be down at the zoo wiping your smug face in monkey shit right before I bust your ass. Are we clear, Mr. Sharpe?"

Looking her back in the eyes, he quietly said, "Very clear, Detective, but I will decide when that time to meet again comes about, perhaps like we did today. But I hope our next meeting comes soon before all time runs out on us because it will be too late once that happens. Harvest, I, and other believers will be well on our way to leading the new society we will have built. And Detective, it will be a society that your kind will not be needed or wanted."

Detective Simon turned and walked away, but her walking was un-steady, and her thirty years of mental toughness had taken a hit, courtesy of Noah Sharpe. Perhaps just a harmless loner living in a fantasy world or someone much, much worse—a killer whose intelligence and psychosis would pose a risk more significant than any criminal Simon had ever encountered.

Chapter 12

Pro-Life Plan for Revenge

While Detective Simon was ending her conversation with Noah Sharpe, other discussions were taking place at two bars, not more than two miles from Tower Grove Park and The New Beginnings Fertility Clinic, where the killing of Theresa Cahill had just taken place.

These conversations dealt with a more traditional form of violence for Simon and the STLPD. Revenge. The post-protest meet-up place for the pro-life crowd was O'Connell's Pub, an old, dark, burger and beer place just north of Tower Grove Park and with easy access to Interstate 44 in case the group ran into trouble, which it certainly had during this morning's demonstration.

Only twenty members of the much larger original protest group showed up at O'Connell's. Typically, a larger group would participate in post-protesting comradery, resulting in a rehashing of the day's event, claiming victory, owning the higher moral ground, and debasing counter-protesters who showed up. Then, as a few drinks became many drinks, drunken revelry would take over, and outlandish boasting would occur about what should have happened or what could have happened if only the police had not arrived. But the shooting at today's protest, rather than scaring the crowd, gave them a new sense of purpose, a new enemy, a new focus, and goal.

In most protest marches or demonstrations, regardless of the subject, the drunks and the loudmouths were the least committed to the cause yet caused the most trouble. Their passion was to stir up anger rather than solve the problems they were protesting. Many of the protesters just wanted to feel they were part of something. However, to the core pro-life believers, those who strategized rather than reacted, despite winning the fifty-year battle to repeal Roe v. Wade knew the war was not over and opened new fronts to be fought on the issue. They wanted to make the pro-choice supporters pay for their fifty years of killing babies. Still, abortion rights battles had moved from the Supreme Court to state legislative bodies and in a growing movement, actual state elections where the issue was voted upon by the citizens of the state and which, so far, the pro-life crowd had come up on the losing end in every state election, even surprisingly in conservative states. The restriction of abortion rights was once again impacting national politics, and wise politicians began to walk back some of the more stringent restrictions that they fought to put in place. The extreme hard right said no abortions for anyone or 6-week limits regardless of the circumstances even if the mother's life was in danger, or if the pregnancy was caused by rape or incest. But slowly because of actual state elections, stances changed from no abortions, period, to legal abortions up to six weeks, then maybe twelve, then perhaps when life is viable outside the womb at twenty-two weeks or about five months. Election after election in each state clearly showed that when put to a vote, stricter abortion limits would fail, and politicians, as they always do when they sniff which way the wind was blowing, would change, or soften their positions. But this group assembled in O'Connell's were not politicians; in fact, most of them hated politicians. They wanted to be domestic terrorists whose goal was to create unrest in society, and they knew the best way to do so was to find a new cause, a new enemy. They found it this morning while fighting with New Beginnings Fertility Clinic supporters. In this clinic, embryos that they believed formed life could be discarded like garbage if they were no longer needed by the couple that produced them. They had just won the battle to restrict abortion wherever possible, and to the most radical of this group, many in this room, like hell would they let embryos be destroyed. They wanted a world to go back in time when large families were the norm. When a woman's priority was to stay home and raise their kids. Marriage was only between a man and a woman, and conception was God's will, not the outcome of medical advancements such as IVF. That is why things got out of hand when they confronted a group marching to support the New Beginnings Fertility Clinic. They found a new enemy, a new focus: the ownership and protection of embryos coming out of IVF procedures.

The core members of this group sat silently in a corner booth, watching the revelry and the boasting until the last of the group began to finish up and head home. They knew that after today, their focus would change. They may not be able to win abortion restriction measures if all states let citizens vote on the issues, but they could win a more significant battle, one that would yield perhaps one hundred-fold the number of babies they would save through the elimination of abortion. These men and women in the bar thought they were revolutionaries. While all revolutions started with one shot, they could feel in their bones that this new revolution, this new battleground, started today with the one shot that killed a supporter of the IVF clinic. They had no idea who had fired the shot, but they felt it was one of their supporters, a true patriot and soldier in the battle like they were. They also knew that after today, they needed a new leader, someone who would take up a new struggle with a new strategy and a potentially growing national presence. Someone who today encouraged the attack of the IVF supporters because he knew the game had changed already. And while he was a politician they usually did not trust, he was one of theirs, a local up-and-comer from southwest Missouri, State Senator Billy O'Dell. He would take them to the promised land. But what this group at O'Connell's did not know was just a mile away, there was a force who would match them in anger, ferocity, money, and, most importantly, strategy to win this battle, if not in the courts, then on the streets, city by city, across the country.

Chapter 13
Pro-Choice Plan for Revenge

Not more than a mile from where the pro-life group was meeting, the counter-protesters who were out that day supporting the New Beginnings Fertility Clinic, which had recently been robbed, met at Sasha's Wine Bar, north of Tower Grove Park just bordering the Botanical Garden. Usually, their post-protest meet-up was low-key, softened by glasses of wine and philosophical discussions about what was wrong with the world and what they needed to do to fix it. They would always talk about how to have honest conversations with those who disagreed with them, hoping they could see eye to eye on many points, but today was different. Today, most people in this room were just out on the street showing solidarity with New Beginnings IVF Clinic and its owner, Layla Brazini, many of whom were her patients. They were shocked when their peaceful rally turned deadly.

Had they known their enemies, the presumed killers of Theresa Cahill, were meeting at O'Connell's, just a short walk away, they might have gathered up the enthusiasm to face off with them once more, but they were somber, with anger only occasionally rising to the surface of their conversations. But their anger was starting to affect their planning. Like the pro-life crowd, this group had a mixture of personalities who all had different reasons to protest. Many supported government intervention and overreach regarding public health, such as in the Covid lockdowns. Still, none of them believed the government had the right to tell women what they should do with their bodies, whether it be abortion, contraceptives, or reproductive choices such as IVF. The group also had its core believers and casual followers, those who were just along for the ride and wanted to be part of something. While they were all in shock over the killing that they assumed had been done by a pro-life supporter, they were at a loss of what to do because, for the most part, they shunned violence. But the leaders of this group knew violence was called for. They felt that for years, pro-life supporters were more aggressive, more violent, and more vocal. The just-concluded rally and shooting proved that they could either be lions attacking their prey or lambs being attacked. They were tired of being lambs.

The leaders of this group were like their counterparts, regular people, and in many instances stood for the same values the pro-lifers wanted. They wanted safety for their families, good schools, bright futures, and a fair shake in life. It was not necessarily a group comprised only of elitist liberals as the media and the other side might want to portray them, but a group consisting of a melting pot of Americans, young, old, male, female, white, and those of color. They were both blue-collar, white-collar, wealthy, or saddled with debt. Many were college-educated, and many were not. That was what was so confounding about the conflicts between these causes. The group's arguing and, in some cases, fighting each other over pro-choice or pro-life would, in many other instances, be aligned on issues. Mostly, on any other day, they would be friends, neighbors, and co-workers.

Much like their counterparts sitting at O'Connell's, the leaders of this group sat apart from the larger group. They strategized quietly among themselves about what happened and why. They were the leaders of this group, as much for their longevity in attending every rally as it was for their calm demeanor and strategy when dealing with a crisis, and this was a crisis. Was attacking them and their support of the IVF clinic a new battleground? They were all aware of the chatter out there that IVF-created embryos may be a new battleground of pro-life vs. pro-choice. Still, until today, they had never seen an attack on people supporting IVF. While the wind temporarily went out of their sails when the Supreme Court abortion decision came down, they had gotten the momentum back by winning state-by-state elections on these issues of abortion rights. That was a battle worth fighting for, but perhaps so too was IVF, and because IVF attracted perhaps a different socioeconomic group of people, more educated, wealthier, and whiter than abortion rights did, so perhaps they would have different types of supporters. One member of their group who was one hundred percent pro-choice was even more behind the right of choice regarding IVF embryos. Trying to understand how big of an issue this was, Becca Stevens, a top female entrepreneur in St. Louis and someone everyone respected, stood up to speak to the group.

"We are in a fight for not only our rights but our lives. Today, they want to halt all abortions, but they won't stop there as they feel encouraged to take away all our rights. Tomorrow, it will be marriage equality, perhaps access to contraceptives. I hear that embryos created in IVF clinics are now being targeted. What will we do to fight back, and how far are you willing to go to protect these rights?"

Becca did not mention to the group that she and her soon-to-be-divorced husband had used an IVF procedure to produce embryos. She also did not mention that the ownership and disposition of the embryos were part of a legal battle between her and her husband and that she would do anything possible to protect her rights to the embryos. Becca knew the conversation or debate around embryos was based on the definition of when life begins, but she also knew, regardless of the outcome of that debate, in her mind, it was one hundred percent her choice of what to do with her embryos, and come hell or high water, no one would take that choice from her. Not her ex-husband, not the government, and not religious leaders' calls to action.

Sitting in the back of the bar, taking all this in, was Marianne Hylany. She was unknown to most of the group except one attendee who had invited her. She had not been at the protest but knew to be at the bar when the protest was over as she had been invited by a silent financial supporter to speak to the group. She thought her speech would be about motivation, organization, focus, and fundraising, but the shooting changed what Hylany would say, much to her delight as she sought conflict and violence. After Becca Stevens spoke, Hylany got up to speak. She turned to Becca Stevens and the group, saying, "You don't know me, but I am not here to talk about embryos or conception, or marriage equality or many of the other ideas progressives pursue. I am here to talk about revenge. Revenge for Theresa Cahill and others who will die in this struggle." The room was now dead silent, turning all their attention on Marianne Hylany, who continued, "If those assholes want to use the blood of babies to prove their point, then we need to use their blood to prove ours."

"How many of you here own a gun?" Out of the twenty people there, seven raised their hands. Hylany then asked, "How many of you gun holders could use it to protect your rights in the next protest?" After what seemed like minutes of silence, feet shuffling, glances held downward, one of the seven raised their hand. It was Becca Stevens.

An uncomfortable silence overtook the room, as no one else wanted to acknowledge that they would use a gun to protect their rights. Hylany knew some would approach her afterward expressing solidarity, but most wanted anonymity. She was glad Becca Stevens came forward as Hylany knew that Becca was a leader, and all this group needed was a few leaders, and the rest would follow.

Marianne Hylany waved her over to her table. "Thank you for speaking up," she said. "I was not sure anyone would." Becca Stevens nodded, then huddled quietly with Marianne Hylany. Becca's future was once stored in test tubes at Layla Brazini's New Beginnings Clinic. Becca knew that the robbery of embryos at the clinic might be the first act of a new battleground over the unborn. Still, to Becca, it would be a personal assault on her future and change her involvement in the battle from a follower to a leader.

Chapter 14
NOAH'S NIGHTMARES

If the meeting between Noah and Detective Simon spooked Simon, it had the opposite effect on Noah. After the events of the day, including the protest, the shooting, and the interrogation by Simon, most people would be on edge and paranoid. But not Noah; he was calm and even keeled, thanks to Harvest and his relationship with her. Generally, after every day that Noah was an adult on earth, he would sit home alone, eating whatever he could microwave quickly. Then, he would turn to his online community to share his opinions with his followers. He thought of them as his friends but never met them in person. That was okay with Noah. He assumed if he met them in person, they would disappoint him as he could not imagine any of them being able to convey thoughts in such a deep and intelligent manner as Noah. *They were a bunch of losers in real life,* he thought.

Usually, Noah went to bed early and tried to find sleep and peace, but that was when the real demons in his life began to surface. He would try to push them out of his mind, and while they might go away temporarily, they never went away completely. Every night, regardless of when he went to bed, Noah always woke, if he ever did sleep, at 2:00 a.m. At the same time, every night. Noah awoke with the same terror haunting him and following him for most of his adult life. While he thought he recalled vividly and accurately what happened so many years ago, each time the nightmare reappeared, it seemed changed, maybe blurred around the edges. The result was always the same. Noah could never escape the nightmare or the feeling that he was responsible for it happening. His mind would race, his head would hurt, and his stomach would burn with indigestion. Then the night sweats came. Then, the anticipation of vomiting that he would assume would come but never did. It had been over twenty-five years since that fateful night and the following day that Noah last vomited. Noah wondered about the significance of that. After fifteen minutes of painful memories and lucid recall, he got up to take a piss. He did not bother to flush the toilet because he would be pissing again and again until the morning because sleep, or whatever you call what he did at night, would never come again. Noah would wander into the kitchen in the dark, taking two Tylenol with a glass of orange juice and go back to bed, not to sleep, but to think about his past, present, and future. For over twenty-five years, his mind had convinced him his future was dark and bleak. Devoid of life, love, and laughter. He had no genuine human companionship. But all that changed once he met Harvest, and she outlined a future for him and, more importantly, with her. It was a future that he felt he was owed. A future where he would no longer be alone or a loner. A future that would not be shaped by his 2:00 a.m. night terrors that replayed how his life had unraveled and fallen apart. But now, rather than sitting up in bed staring into the darkness and waiting for dawn to come, Noah thought about Harvest and his future with her. But he knew that he would have to earn Harvest's love. Noah would have to prove to her he was worthy of being chosen by her, so every night, starting at 2:00 a.m., he planned what his next steps would be. Today, though, while at the protest shooting, he felt he took a big step in proving to Harvest that he could be the partner she sought. His actions at the protest, hopefully seen by her, would demonstrate his commitment to her.

If Noah were rational, he would think she was crazy, and her plan was bizarre. But whether crazy or rational, he thought he loved her. But he was unsure as he had never loved anyone before, so he did not know what love felt like. It was 2:37 a.m., and Noah was still awake, so he grabbed his phone, the bright LED display illuminating his darkened bedroom. Noah was careful in searching for her online as everyone was watching him, and he had to cover his tracks so the government would not discover the plans she had asked him to execute.

As an active and engaged online commentator, Noah felt he knew how to cover his tracks digitally. He did not log into any specific information sites under his online persona of *NoahItAll,* which he used as an online commentator. He first visited the movie streaming services of Amazon, Netflix, Hulu, and AppleTV to see if they had documentaries on the subjects Harvest told him to study. He searched documentaries on the end of times, biblical stories, race segmentation or uprisings, government intervention and spying, Artificial Intelligence, survivalism, cloning, and reproductive medicine. Noah noted them, with the plan to watch them later. He also knew that once he watched one of the documentaries, the streaming services would set up a preferences algorithm and feed him related shows on similar subjects. They were doing his work for him. Next, he went to the major news sites to see if they had any stories on recent topics in the news, such as pro-life vs. pro-choice, protests and violence, legislative movements nationally or at the state level, and subjects he was interested in. He scanned Facebook, CNN, Fox News, the Wall Street Journal, the Post-Dispatch, the New York Times, and One America News. Every outlet had covered the subject in some detail, primarily from a religious, political, legislative, and, importantly, financial angle. Who would profit, and how would they do that? While the subject matter was all the same, the slant or angle in which it was reported was completely different depending upon the liberal or conservative bias each news outlet represented. And depending on how far from the mainstream the "news" outlet was, the more outlandish their predictions and plans were for the future.

It was 3:30 a.m., and Noah had skimmed over most of what was easily researched. He knew if he was to do what Harvest asked, he would have to prove he was committed to her and her plan by showing her the proof of what he was capable of. And he had the proof. He just needed to be able to show it to her in person. He knew if Harvest saw what he could do, his life would be forever changed. But as he lie in bed waiting for his mind to turn off, he thought about his current life, or lack thereof, versus the life she promised. She promised him a life where people took him seriously, not just those he tried to influence online with his commentaries. A life where he was with her forever. Knowing what he had done already for her, Noah was peaceful. Although sleep came, it came haltingly as Noah's agony, which never stopped raging in his brain, would wake him repeatedly before the morning light reached the horizon.

Soon dawn came, and the darkness that always brought Noah loneliness and despair was replaced with light. It was in the light that Noah felt he had the energy to right all the wrongs he suffered at the hands of others in his life. Noah could function again in the daylight because he could interact with his precious primates. Noah was especially excited about this day because he hoped he would finally see Harvest in person. She had told him that if he performed one great act to prove his loyalty, she would perhaps visit him in person. He felt his actions at the protest, in addition to how he handled that pushy bitch Detective Simon, would finally warrant a visit from Harvest. Hell, if Harvest asked, he would kill the detective if it meant he and Harvest would be together sooner than later. But she had not asked him to do that yet.

Noah was unhappy that Harvest was so mysterious, but he accepted her conditions. However, he would always watch for someone who might be Harvest. Someone who would be as kind to his primates as Noah was. Someone who could even communicate with them, like Noah believed he could. He always looked for any woman who could be Harvest, stopping at the monkey cages and talking to his monkeys as if she knew them. If the monkeys were excited versus agitated by a female visitor, Noah would hope the visitor was Harvest. He would then run over to meet her, and they would embrace. But every time he saw a woman he thought could be Harvest, she would look up from the monkey cages and look right through him or, in most cases, grab her children's hands and shrink back in fear. But today might be different, Noah thought. But he had that hope every day, and it had not yet materialized.

After Noah finished his morning chores at the zoo, he took a break to peruse his phone with heightened interest as St. Louis, because of the protest and shooting, was once again in the national news and once again for a story that would create reactions well beyond the local St. Louis metro. But this time, Noah hoped he would be mentioned in the stories, which could catch Harvest's attention.

The headlines, functioning as click-bait vs. unbiased journalism, were both direct and misleading depending on your point of view.

CNN: Pro-life mob suspected in killing pro-choice peaceful marcher.

Fox: After the shooting, a peaceful pro-life group defends itself against a pro-choice mob in St. Louis.

St. Louis Post-Dispatch: Here we go again. Mobs clash, peaceful protester dies outside IVF clinic.

NY Times: St. Louis once again at the center of cultural violence.

Wall Street Journal: Are IVF centers the new battleground for abortion rights?

Noah read each story because he knew what had happened better than anyone. He wanted to see if his name was mentioned and if he would get some well-deserved notoriety. But he was not mentioned in any of the stories. Even that pushy cop who interviewed him, Detective Simon, was quoted, which pissed Noah off because Simon was a known killer who got off because she was a cop. "*Where was that story?*" he wondered. Noah put his phone away and then closed his eyes as a warmer-than-normal winter afternoon, combined with his lack of sleep the night before, began to make him drowsy. He began to think about Harvest. He saw her walking towards him. As she walked towards him, she seemed to be casually chatting with the monkeys that followed her movements just like Noah thought they would. He wanted to say something clever to her, but the words were stuck in his throat. At the last moment, he blurted out, "I think they can understand you."

At first, he thought she did not hear him as she remained focused on the monkeys. Slowly, she turned back to him, walked towards him, and sat down next to him on the bench; she smiled and said, "Of course, they can understand me. They are God's creatures, as am I. We are connected."

Noah sat quietly, again at a loss for words, but before he could reply, he felt her left hand on his knee, and she took her right hand and guided Noah's face and his gaze directly into her eyes.

"God has connected me to you, as well, Noah," she said to him with a smile.

Noah had a feeling of warmth overcoming him. She sensed his anxiety and, lightly stroking his face, said, "Noah, relax. Take some deep breaths. Let's sit here and talk about all you have done and will continue doing to save the world." And then she kissed him.

Noah felt a feeling of lightness, both from being aroused and having clarity in his mind that he was doing what Harvest needed him to. If he continued, they would live together forever in the utopian world they created.

As she pulled back from her kiss, Noah knew his life had changed. No more was he a lonely loser. He would be remembered along with Harvest as the person who saved the world. Visualizing his place in the world, the newfound respect he received from those who mocked or, more often, ignored him, he was peaceful. He was blissful; then, he was awakened by a shake on his shoulders.

"Wake up, you dumb ass and get back to work." It was the sound not of sweetness coming from Harvest, but gruffness coming from his asshole boss Lou. Noah shook the sleep from his eyes and his body, which had become almost limp, as he tried to get back on his feet. He did not say a word to Lou because Noah knew that people like Lou would not be part of the world he and Harvest had planned. Lou and others like him, assholes, not worthy of having a place in society or procreating future offspring, would not be part of Noah's world in the future, and if Noah had anything to do about it, might not have many more days upright and above ground in this world.

Chapter 15
RHONDA AND RICHARD

Rhonda Simon was glad that Richard Leary had entered her life. The companionship made the end of her hard days easy. While the sex they had filled a physical need, but, surprising Rhonda, it also filled an emotional need she hadn't known she had missed. She realized how incredible sex was with a man she liked, for his body and his mind, and who knows, maybe it was even the beginning of love. But as great as it was to fill those voids in her life, what she liked most was that Richard Leary got what she did as a cop. While he always offered her a listening ear and a sense of empathy after she unwound from her day, he, more importantly, helped her look at her cases with an analytical and detached perspective with no emotional bias. She used to be completely detached, completely unbiased. She only looked at a murder analytically: clues, motive, pieces fitting into a puzzle. But over time, her job had begun to wear on her. It was hard to have the desire to help a victim when the victim's family, in many cases, hated you. It was hard to feel you had aided society by taking a dangerous criminal off the streets when, in many cases, the criminal found guilty of a crime was back on the streets in a few years or sometimes only a month, committing another crime. She was also beginning to lose faith in mankind and the criminal justice system. Not just the justice or lack of it for street thugs who terrorized law-abiding citizens, but for the rich, intelligent, and gifted, like Dr. Alex Finnegan and others like him who had enough, but it was never enough. It seemed to Rhonda the best way to avoid being responsible for your crimes was to be either very bright and rich with a lawyer who could get you out of anything or be guilty as sin but be very protected by the overly liberal justice system permeating the large cities and the courts of the country.

But now, resting in Richard's arms, sipping a glass of bourbon over ice, her day's troubles began to melt away. Richard knew it was best not to let the bourbon dull Rhonda's senses too much as he knew it was cathartic for her to talk about her day, even if she did not want to. It was something he and she worked on during her suspension, talking. Richard always saw her bounce back, with a gleam in her eye, as their conversation sometimes sparked an idea or thought on the fringe of Rhonda's mind but had not crystallized yet. Despite all the sophisticated and possible illegal digital and analytical tools Richard used to find information to help solve crimes, he knew that Rhonda's thirty years of experience kept more data points in her head than any computer Richard could access.

"So, babe. Tell me about your day. What will keep you up tonight that maybe we work through now?"

Rhonda replied, "I am so beat; nothing will keep me up tonight. One more glass of Blanton's," holding up her now empty glass, "and I may be out like a light in about thirty minutes."

Richard laughed, knowing that Rhonda never slept through the night. She tossed and turned and got up frequently, sometimes writing a note on the pad beside her bed, and sometimes, when she was hot on an idea, she got up to do some research online.

Richard decided to ask more directly, "What new case has your attention currently?"

Sighing and sitting up, knowing Richard would not stop asking questions until Rhonda began talking, she said, "Well, throw a couple of steaks on the grill, refill my glass, and then I will start talking."

That was one of the reasons he loved Rhonda. A gal who liked bourbon, red meat, and catching criminals was all the woman Richard Leary needed. "I am ahead of you, babe," as he poured two fingers of bourbon into her glass. "The steaks are marinating, the grill is simmering, so let's get talking."

"My day, like many, involved another day in the human race shitshow. A protest group of pro-lifers and pro-choice tangled up today at Tower Grove Park. One of the protesters, I believe siding with the pro-choice group, was shot and killed, presumably by a member of the pro-life group," Rhonda started in, then adding, "but frankly, I am not sure who did the shooting and why." For some reason, Rhonda did not mention that the pro-choice group was marching in support of the New Beginnings Fertility Clinic. Rhonda didn't because she was not ready to tell Richard about the past relationship between her and Dr. Brazini, the owner of New Beginnings.

"Well, Roe v. Wade was...still is a big issue, and I think the Supreme Court probably inflamed it more or perhaps gave a little more fuel to it for the pro-choice crowd who probably never thought it would be overturned. But protesting is part of the fabric of America. In our day, it was stopping wars, building of nuclear power plants, political assassinations," Richard said solemnly.

Trying not to drag Richard down to Rhonda's level of despair, she lightened the conversation by adding, "Yeah, but we had kick-ass songs to go along with the protests. Now it seems we have a bunch of out-of-work or retired loudmouths with nothing better to do than yell at each other over the government telling them what to do when every fucking day they do what the government tells them to do. And none of these people would know a good protest song if it hit them in the head. But I need to correct you on one thing, Richard. We have gone beyond protesting. Unfortunately, violence and murder are now part of the fabric of America."

Going on, Rhonda added, "You know, Richard, every murder I would investigate, while I could never get over how casually people took another's life, I always understood the motivation because it was so primal, maybe even biblical—an eye for an eye kind of stuff. You have what I want! You took what was mine! You are the reason I am in this dark place! Greed, anger, jealousy, revenge. All reasons that made murder so easy to do and solve in the cases I investigated, but now it's different."

Nodding and knowing Rhonda was deadly accurate in her assessment of the world and its violence, Richard wanted her to focus on today's events as he knew that was cathartic for her in winding down and then solving the case. He knew these types of protests were common in St. Louis and around the country and usually overblown or overhyped by an individual's TikTok, Facebook, or Twitter post; Richard asked, "So how did this one turn into a murder?"

"I am not sure. It may have been an accident. It did not seem to me premeditated. Just tempers boiling, and when half the people in the crowd are carrying a gun, something like this is bound to happen," Rhonda replied.

Richard, looking quizzically at Rhonda, knowing she still had more to say about the day, added, "Okay, the normal basic price we pay for freedom...a daily shit show...now tell me the interesting part of today's events," and as he got up to put the steaks on the grill added, "or I am going to burn your steak."

Ignoring Richard's comments, Rhonda continued, "The interesting part was these witnesses I interviewed. No one saw anything specifically, but several of the witnesses mentioned that they knew a killing would take place because a woman named Harvest told them so."

"Well, that seems like a good lead, "Richard said.

"Maybe, but they could not or would not provide more information about her, except to say they connect with her online. And believe me, the more witnesses I talked to, the weirder they got."

Knowing that a sarcastic comment was just on the tip of his tongue and that if said, it might stop Rhonda from opening up, Richard nodded in affirmation, and Rhonda continued.

"Another witness I talked to told me it was his girlfriend who told him a murder was to happen today at the park."

"Is his girlfriend the same woman, Harvest?" Richard asked.

Laughing, Rhonda said, "Well, if you had met this guy, you would not even believe he has a girlfriend. Total loner, loser, psych job. Beyond knowing his girlfriend's name, he did not seem to know anything about her except to say they talk online or, get this, through the monkeys at the zoo."

Richard concurred, saying, "Well, you know Rhonda, at these protests, every nut job shows up to be part of the action or to watch the train wreck. It seems like your monkey guy might have been off his meds and was just at the park talking to the squirrels since he can talk to monkeys."

"Yeah, that is what I thought, but here is the weird thing. The first two witnesses, who seemed normal, seemed to communicate with Harvest online, but they would not tell me anything more. Privileged information, they claim. But the weird thing is they described Harvest's insight into what would happen at the protest and her vision about the future end of civilization in the same way as the monkey guy did."

Richard nodded, then added, "So, I will ask you again, do you think the monkey guy, as weird as he was, is the boyfriend of the mysterious Harvest?"

"Doubtful. Harvest, whoever she is, seems to be an online influencer with some believability and perhaps intelligence. She would seem to be a leader of people or ideas, and that would make her way out of monkey guy's league in my opinion, but that is where you can help fill in the blanks though your little snooping machine there," Rhonda said, pointing to Richard's laptop. "I want you to search the dark corners of the web and find out if we are dealing with normal, local crazy or if we are dealing with something or someone else. I know you tell me the information and opinions you read in the deep and dark web would scare the shit out of me, but I think I am ready to see how depraved society might be."

Rhonda's last comment stopped Richard from saying anything because he knew Rhonda was one of the mentally toughest, most practical, and analytical cops he had ever known. He knew Rhonda could handle anything he found. Still, he was concerned knowing what he knew or would find would give Rhonda an overwhelming sense of powerlessness to be able to make a difference. Rhonda held on to the belief, naïve as it was, that if she and her fellow STLPD officers took care of daily crime on the streets of St. Louis, they could try and create some semblance of normalcy for decent folks who wanted to feel safe. But once Rhonda saw the deep, dark web, she would realize, as Richard already had, that normalcy and decency in society were gone, never to come back, and the talk of an unraveling society was not fantasy; it was reality. Richard and Rhonda's relationship survived by feeling like they lived in a cocoon, and while they talked about the bad stuff, they kept it at bay. Once Richard let Rhonda see deep, deep into Richard's world, and once she understood how Richard accessed this information, he was concerned it would darken her outlook on humans, and perhaps also on him. Rhonda might have to think like a criminal sometimes to catch a criminal. In many cases, to find the danger lurking in the deep, dark web, Richard had to become a criminal and use tools that he knew were illegal. But he would do anything for Rhonda and allowing her to get deeper into his world was a chance he was willing to take.

But entry into Richard's world could wait, and finally, after what seemed a long silence, both deep in their thoughts, Richard grabbed Rhonda's hand and led her to the dining room table. Once seated, with wine poured and a filet and baked potato on each plate, Richard offered what he hoped was a plan to get Rhonda to focus on her functions as a local detective. Work the streets, follow leads and clues. He did not want her to venture too deeply into the online world. Not until Richard had entered that door first and determined its danger.

"Rhonda, let's team up on this. You have your hands full just getting back into the swing of things returning to work after the suspension. The protest shooting is going to spawn, my guess, larger and potentially more violent protests, so I think investigating that shooting at the local level should be your priority number one. Also, you are still on thin ice with Lieutenant Tarallo based on how the Finnegan case came down. So, you should ease into your work and keep it locally focused." Richard knew that comment would irritate Rhonda, so he continued before she could say anything.

"Let me do some online snooping on this Harvest person, or whatever her name is, and see if she is connected to any larger online groups spouting the same nonsense, locally or nationally. There are a lot of crack-pots out there on the fringes among us, just looking for a way to cause trouble or make a name for themselves."

Surprisingly, Rhonda was quiet and not about to burst into anger over Richard's comments about getting back into her job, probably because she knew he was right but also because she was already planning to ignore him. As socially advanced and sophisticated as Richard was, he was still a man and a throwback to an era when men felt they had to protect their women. Maybe years ago, she would have discarded a guy like Richard after a few good lays, but now, although he was still a bit of a chauvinist, she found his concern for her somewhat endearing. She had not had a man in her life who genuinely cared for her well-being for a long time. They made a good team, whether it be for companionship, sex, or a shared interest in solving crimes and putting the bad guys away. She was also quiet because her head was spinning thinking about the protest shooting and the break-in at Layla's clinic; she now wondered if the two were connected. She wanted to tell Richard about it and ask for his help, but she also wanted to keep some secrets from him, like her relationship with Layla. She knew Richard was excellent at his job, and the more he investigated online connections, perhaps the more likely he would dis-cover Rhonda's past with Layla. But at this point in Richard and Rhonda's relationship, she felt he could handle the truth, and if he found out, he might even like it.

Rhonda was still quiet and had not answered Richard's question about how to proceed with the investigation. Still, she offered, "All this evil scheming may have my head spinning, but it's probably because of hunger. Let's eat and lay out a game plan to understand where your head is on this." Now more hungry than energetic, Rhonda finally looked down at the steak sitting on her plate for ten minutes and said, "Richard, this steak looks awesome. Cooked perfectly, though it's a little cold," she said, laughing as she knew she had delayed the meal. Instead of talking, she ate ravenously as if the last ten minutes of their conversation never happened.

Chapter 16
MOLONEY AND RHONDA COMPARE NOTES

While the break-in at New Beginnings made the news and quickly faded, the shooting outside the clinic during the pro-life rally ensured any short-term peace and tranquility in St. Louis was about to end. Detective Rhonda Simon, as always, would be in the middle of it.

Officer Moloney stopped by Simon's desk after she returned from interviewing Dr. Brazini at the clinic and asked Rhonda to meet her when she got off her shift later that afternoon. They planned to meet for drinks at Tucker's Place, a popular restaurant and bar in the French-influenced Soulard district, one of the oldest areas in St. Louis, nestled off Broadway between the Arch and the Anheuser-Busch In-Bev headquarters and brewery.

Rhonda went into the restaurant and headed to the back where no one could see or hear them. She slid into a booth that Moloney was already occupying. Moloney, knowing Rhonda's reputation for using alcohol to blow off steam regardless of the time of day, had two cold Budweiser's already on the table. Rhonda did not refuse hers, and with a clink of the bottle to Moloney, she said, "Thanks for the beer, Moloney. Your request for a clandestine meeting has piqued my interest, so what gives?"

"Two things, Detective Simon, that I believe will be of interest to you," Moloney jumped in.

"So, tell me what is on your mind, Moloney," Rhonda said, with some impatience in her voice. She wasn't ready to be chummy with Moloney just yet. Rookies are like deer in headlights; they can be unpredictable and freeze on you. Rhonda wanted to make sure Moloney was solid before she would let her guard down. Expecting this rookie hazing from Simon, Moloney was unfazed, so she waded into the conversation.

"I wanted to talk to you out of the office to update you on my conversation with Dr. Brazini and my investigation of the break-in at her clinic. I asked Dr. Brazini her opinion about the motive for the break-in, which is why I thought we should have this meeting off-premises."

Rhonda just sipped her beer and said nothing, so Moloney continued.

"Well, I interviewed Dr. Brazini, asking her not only about possible motives, but about the value of what was stolen, and the names of disgruntled employees or patients. I got the answers and outcomes you probably did when you first met with her. Dr. Brazini is also protecting the confidentiality of her patients for now. We then talked about possible motives, she shared some of the same hypotheses she shared with you about the embryos being stolen as part of some whacked-out new battleground of the Roe v. Wade legal fight."

"So, what do you think of that hypothesis, Moloney? Tell me your gut reaction."

"My gut is never underestimating the stupidity or savagery of humans, as well as the vitriol taking place within our society, so yes, I think this could be that," Moloney paused, " or it could be just a break-in, and when the thieves found nothing of value, they took the embryos because they didn't know what else to take." Then she added, "but the protest shooting might have added a new wrinkle to this."

"How has Lieutenant Tarallo instructed you to proceed on the case?" Rhonda asked.

"As you would expect. Do some calling around. See if any copycat break-ins have been reported. Look at the local suspects, maybe drug dealers, look online for any social media chatter, and then, as most cases like this seem to end nowadays in St. Louis...put it on the back burner and then forget about it."

Thinking the meeting was over and draining her beer, Rhonda said. "That's about what I thought would happen. I'm not sure we needed this conversation outside the office, but thanks for the beer and update." Rhonda started to get up to leave. Before she could, Moloney grabbed her arm and, with a look more than a command, gave Rhonda the signal to sit back down.

Waving her arm at the server for two more beers, Moloney said, "I told you I had two things to discuss with you. One was what Tarallo told me to do with the case, and the second one is what I think *we*," pointing her bottle of Bud at Rhonda, "should do about this. So, you might want to have another beer."

Laughing slightly, Rhonda said, "I am beginning to like you, Moloney." Before she could continue, Moloney jumped in and said, "That is just what Dr. Brazini said when she told me I think like you."

Smiling now, Rhonda just swigged her beer, leaned back, and gestured to Moloney as to say, *"I am all ears, so let's have it."*

Moloney continued. "The other interesting part of my conversation with Dr. Brazini was establishing the value of the embryos. She said value could be determined by the cost of a medical procedure that creates just biological cells, or value could be applied if one of those cells becomes a human life. She told me that they are just cells medically. However, in the court of public and perhaps legal opinion, they could be considered humans. Thus, the value is inestimable because how do you place a value on a life, even ones that are perhaps never born."

"That is a good train of thought, Moloney. Tell me why it is important to establish the value of the embryos," Rhonda said.

Sensing she was being lectured or tested, Moloney went on with more confidence. "Why? In a court of law, a jury is asked to place value on an accident victim who dies, or a person murdered and award a settlement to the survivor based on the value of the deceased. The value may also help or hurt with the lawsuits Dr. Brazini expects to come from the aggrieved men and women who produced the embryos and had their dreams shattered," Moloney said.

"Well, if that shit ever came to trial, it could be the trial of the century. Supreme Court kind of shit, right Moloney?" asked Rhonda.

"Well before it hits the Supreme Court docket, it could come to trial with as much sensationalism as the Scopes Monkey Trial back in 1925.

Did you ever read about that trial, Detective Simon?"

Simon laughed out loud, and shook her head, "No Moloney, I am just a country girl turned cop. I think I missed school the day they covered that trial. But my question Moloney, is how do you know about it and what the hell are you talking about?"

Smiling back at Simon and knowing Simon, like all cops enjoyed razzing other cops who tried to sound pretentious or know-it-alls, Moloney said, "I know about the trial because I was pre-law before I decided to become a cop and I took a course that covered groundbreaking trials, and this was one of them. Plus, I am a bit of a book nerd Detective Simon."

"Ok, Ok, Moloney. I'll bite. Explain what you are getting at."

"What I am getting at is in that trial, they debated teaching evolution vs. creationism, you know sort of 'where life comes from argument.' Maybe an early 1900's debate of conservatives versus liberals, or religious versus a secular beliefs. Do you see any parallels here Detective?"

Simon nodded saying, "And today the same factions are arguing over when life begins. I see the parallels Moloney, but I still don't see your point."

"My point Detective is after talking to Dr. Brazini, I, feel this case was bigger than a break-in and could be something related to the unanswered question of when does life begin. If I am right, it would be as big as the trial you would have had if Dr. Finnegan had been caught and his case had come to trial over the right to die and to choose who gets an organ. That would have been a trial of the century with one detective, Rhonda Simon, the star. Right Detective?"

Rhonda bore her eyes deep into Moloney's with curiosity and slight anger as she felt perhaps Moloney was goading her over the Finnegan case. In fact, Moloney was goading Rhonda as she wanted to illicit the emotion she was now getting from her. She wanted Detective Rhonda Simon to get angry that not only did Alex Finnegan get away, but now maybe a more significant case right under her nose and impacting someone close to her might also elude her grasp.

Rhonda, now visibly angry, bit on Moloney's taunts. "So, what are you getting at Moloney? What wild conspiracy are you chasing?"

"Not ones I am chasing. Ones *we* are chasing," pointing her finger at Rhonda and then back to herself.

"We?" Rhonda said, swatting Moloney's finger with faux aggression but also with curiosity.

"Yes, we are chasing them, along with Dr. Brazini. She expects something great from you as I sense you have a past to make up for."

Now Rhonda was pissed that Layla's name and perhaps their shared history was being brought up by Moloney for some sort of leverage, saying, "Moloney, any past issues between Layla," then hesitating, "I mean Dr. Brazini, and I are personal, so stay the hell out of them."

"Detective, I could not care less about whatever relationship, issues, or conflicts you have had with Dr. Brazini. I care about solving a case that may be way above my pay grade, and Dr. Brazini and I need and want your help.

Rhonda answered, "I told you I can only be a sounding board on the case, and besides, it sounds like it will be backlogged as a breaking and entering case that will be shoved in a drawer by Tarallo soon."

"Well, it might be and still could, if not for yesterday's shooting. I know it is too early for you to determine if the shooting was also connected to the break-in, which could all be connected to a new battleground regarding women's rights over their bodies and now embryos, which, by the way, is what Dr. Brazini believes. If this is all connected, we convince Tarallo that it is the crime of the century with all the publicity that comes with it. It is a crime that Tarallo's best detective, hell, the best detective in St. Louis, needs to be on. This is not a standard B and E case, Detective

Simon. This may be a crime involving mass murder, child kidnapping and endangerment, and perhaps an eruption of violence on the rights of women."

Shaking her head, Rhonda said, "Mass murder, kidnapping. What the hell are you talking about, Moloney? One person was killed at a protest rally who may have no connection. No one was kidnapped. You are getting way over your skis here, Moloney."

Moloney, calm as a twenty-year veteran, proceeded undaunted by Simon's doubt. "If you believe life begins at conception and conception occurs when a cell is created, which many people do, then whoever stole those embryos, if their intent was to destroy them, is possibly the murderer of hundreds of embryos that could become fully developed humans. If, however, those who took the embryos did it to protect them from those who would destroy them, then you have a mass kidnapping or child endangerment crime. We don't have to prove motive as that is the prosecutor's job. We just need to find out who did it and why, and to do that, we just need to get you on the case now, so this does not get shoved in a drawer by Tarallo."

"So how do we convince Tarallo to agree to this, might I say crazy, slightly unhinged, conspiracy-laden idea, Moloney?"

"Before the Scopes Monkey Trial became a serious debate on one of the greatest unsolved questions mankind wrestles with, it was the largest media event ever in the history of the United States. The media made it a spectacle that everyone wanted to be associated with and our media today will create a feeding frenzy where everyday people, like cops and lawyers become stars and…

Rhonda stopped her to finish the sentence. "And Tarallo will not want this case to be buried so she will have to keep the case open and put me on it."

"Exactly," Moloney said. "Now, if you are interested, let's discuss how to set this up."

After a twenty-minute outline of her plan, Moloney sat back, somewhat smugly waiting for Rhonda to respond.

"Moloney, in another life, you might have been a criminal; this plan is so good. But we need something more solid for Tarallo to move on this. We need to also make this a political win for her. Give me a week to have a friend of mine dig up some information you and I won't have access to. When he does, we will wrap it in a nice package and deliver it to Tarallo. When we do, she will be chomping at the bit to keep this case open and, much to her chagrin, put me on it."

As they left Tucker's and Rhonda got in her car, she dialed Richard Leary's number.

"Ready for a wild ride, Richard? Stay sober; I am coming home."

Chapter 17
RICHARD DISCOVERS HARVEST

Richard was sober when Rhonda got home and anxiously awaited the wild ride that Rhonda had promised. But it was not the ride, at least for now, he expected.

"Grab your laptop," she said to Richard. She then looked around and saw Richard had turned the lights low, lit some candles, and had mood music on.

Laughing, she said, "Easy hoss. This is not that kind of wild ride. Or at least not yet."

Grabbing his laptop, Richard played along a little more, asking Rhonda if they would at least check out an obviously fictional website he called "Bad Cops Get Naked."

"Get your mind out of the gutter, Richard, because I have something juicier for you to sink your teeth into. Something I know that will get you excited." Now Richard was laughing, especially in the fake sultry voice in which Rhonda delivered the news.

"You will be turned on, my dear Richard, by digging deep into the background of some unsavory characters in our beautiful metropolis.

And if you are a very good boy, I will let you investigate my new conspiracy theories."

Laughing loudly, he said, "Well damn, Rhonda, conspiracy theories. You know how much they turn me on, you tease. Now, just tell me what you want me to do."

"I will tell you all about my conspiracy theories after you tell me what you learned about Harvest." Rhonda was unsure how she wanted to approach Richard about her and Moloney's conversation about the larger crime that perhaps occurred at the New Beginnings Fertility Clinic. Richard could read Rhonda's mind well and was not shy about telling her when to plow forward or back off from the direction she was taking a case. Richard was detail-oriented and methodical in assembling all his data and coming to his conclusions. Rhonda was a break-the-door-down-first-then-knock-on-it kind of person. Rhonda knew she needed Richard's help to prove that Moloney and Layla's theories had some merit, but she needed to first ensure she was doing all she could to solve the protester murder as a standalone because no matter how explosive the theories could be that she, and Moloney concocted, Tarallo would still have to be sold. Rhonda was paid to solve real murders of real people, not theories about embryos being stolen or destroyed. She would wait till Richard told her everything he had on Harvest before she would take him down another path.

"Okay, Richard, before I get into my newest conspiracy, I want you to tell me everything you have learned about the woman I asked you to investigate, Harvest."

Richard started, "Okay, here goes. I started looking into women with some variation on the name Harvest. First name, last name, married name, stage name, etc. As you would expect, there are thousands of them nationwide, which is normally the case when I first start doing my investigations. Still, based on what you told me people said about her and her beliefs, I built an algorithm that integrated the name Harvest with certain keywords your witnesses used. Words like new society, the rebirth of civilization, cultural wars, conspiracies, government overreach, protest marches, pro-choice, and pro-life. Now, normally, those words by themselves would have the opposite effect of drilling down on someone or something because they are so prevalent in the online world of TikTok, Twitter, Facebook, and other more off-the-grid types of digital sites, but what became apparent quickly was that while millions of unconnected people use these words in their online postings, I wanted to find people who had huge number of followers and frequently speak on the subject, some with far right views, like Alex Jones, Lin Wood, Nick Fuentes, Dr. Merkel, or some with huge followings on both side of the argument, like Joe Rogan, as well as some of our more social media savvy and incendiary politicians like Marjorie Taylor Green or AOC, the ones who put out every passing thought in a tweet or post. This was easy to do as most influencers get paid a lot by having the most followers and supporters willing to pay for memorabilia or weekly newsletters. This group of people are very PR savvy and, as such, want to be found, and they are not hidden."

Rhonda interrupted, "So, is this how you found Harvest?"

"Well, not directly, because these people really have gone mainstream. Slick websites, newsletters, blogs, speaking gigs, merchandise with catchy slogans. It seems revolution has become big business nowadays." He added, "If Adolf Hitler were around in today's digital world, he would make millions selling Nazi gear, I am sure."

"Scary thought," Rhonda chimed in.

"Scary but not too far-fetched, to be honest with you, as you can market any kind of hate digitally. But that is not the world where Harvest lives, at least for now. She is content to be the influencer of the influencers," said Richard.

"What do you mean by that?"

"Harvest is connected with links to many influencers regardless of their political or cultural position. Her positions are cited and, in fact, linked to in many cases by both conservative and liberal influencers. Ones on the extreme or ones that are relatively moderate. Whatever Harvest espouses, she does so in a way that all people think she is representing or talking to them. It's quite incredible how omnipresent she is."

Richard continued, "What is also quite incredible is that while she has a very active digital footprint exposing her viewpoints, I have found almost no trace of her physical existence or personal history. Basic stuff like date of birth, birthplace, education and employment history, social security number, tax records, and real estate records. All the information or history we accumulate over time that shows how life is lived is missing from Harvest."

"Do you know what she looks like?" asked Rhonda. "The witnesses at the park were so vague or secretive in trying to describe her."

"There are many photos and, in fact, videos of her espousing her views, and in all the photos and videos of her, she is beautiful. But here is the weird thing: she is too beautiful," Richard said.

"What do you mean, too beautiful?"

"Flawless. Perfect. Never aging," Richard said.

"Never aging?" asked Rhonda. What does that mean?"

"It means that the explosive use of photography and videos in the digital realm, including social media sites such as YouTube and Facebook, began in the late nineties and early two-thousands, and as such, digital imagery of a person could be circulating for the last twenty years let's say. Based on the imagery I see of Harvest, I would put her in her age at late thirties or early forties. If that is the case, there would be some historical images of her over the last twenty years. Photos of her in college or as part of a professional association like a speaker's bureau or panel. Since she also happens to be an online influencer, even if she only became very active in the last three to four years, there would have to be some older images of her that would show her normal progress of aging. But the lack of information about her physical presence and the lack of imagery showing anything but a stylized perfect image would eventually show up online, especially with me searching for it."

"I am not sure what you are getting at Richard."

"Well, have you ever taken a bad photo, Rhonda? Ever with your hair out of place, or in a less than flattering outfit, or maybe when you were ten pounds heavier or lighter? Have you ever been in a group photo that someone posted about you, and the image showed you in a setting that was out of your control, maybe with a drink in your hand at a restaurant, a bar, or a sporting event?"

"Sure, I have. Everyone has."

"Not everyone. Not Harvest. Every image of her is just her, never in a group, and she always looks perfect. I can't find one photo of her at a different age or when her weight has fluctuated; a wrinkle or two appeared that wasn't there the last time. Also, every video of her is in the same setting, like a hotel room, with the same angle and lighting. Almost as if they are done at a studio or some fixed location. Every outfit is generally the same. Not much variety in what she wears and the patterns of her clothes."

"Here, look at these photos and video clips of her," Richard said, "and tell me what you see."

Rhonda began swiping the photos and clicking on the videos, one after another, still confused about what point Richard was making.

"So what? Harvest is a woman who manages her look and online persona perfectly and professionally, as it is how she makes a living in many cases. Lots of celebrities do that, and many professional women generally wear the same type of outfit and simple color schemes, so they can mix and match easily," Rhonda said.

Richard added, "Ok, maybe I will buy that she is an incredibly organized dresser with a tailored and matching wardrobe. But think about, let's say, the Kardashians. They probably manage their personas better than most online celebrities. But I know you have seen bad photos of them, right?"

"Of course, I have," said Rhonda. "Coming out of a gym or shopping. You can't be perfect every second of the day. So, Richard, you are telling me Harvest is perfect?"

"I can't say whether she is perfect, but she seems to have crafted a perfect online persona that reveals nothing about her but what she wants to communicate. Lots of information comes from her, but very little about who she is. Everyone talks about her as if they know her. Still, I wonder if anyone has really seen her in person. I can't find any photos of her with another person in them, which is very weird. Someone, somewhere, would have poised for a quick iPhone photo with her or snapped a shot of her leaving her home, a restaurant, or a gym. She has too much of an online following, in the hundreds of thousands, to be completely invisible in the physical world."

"It's funny you say that because two of the witnesses who could not or would not describe her said who she is or what she looks like is not important; it's her message that is important," added Rhonda.

Richard went on, "She seems like a person from folklore whose existence and stories are passed down from one person to another. Her name is both vague and meaningful. Harvest comes from an old Norse foundation that means to gather and pluck. Harvest is also associated with pleasant thoughts like fall festivals or the Harvest Moon. It's a soothing name, almost one that could be the name of a Native American princess, long since gone, but perhaps whose philosophies, theories, or manifestos she emulates. It's a trusting name, which is why, perhaps, many of her followers, those who have never seen her in person but seem to follow her blindly, believe everything she says is some sort of manifesto or message that needs to be acted upon."

"So, what are her messages and theories?" asked Rhonda.

"She espouses a theory that humanity needs to be replaced and reborn. How people interpret that is based on their own personal beliefs. Some on the right may think she is talking about a pure, white, Christian race with the ultra-conservative values that we have lost over time. However, those on the left may think she is talking about a new society where the color of your skin, your sexual preferences, or religious beliefs don't matter. All people are equal and created under the eyes of God."

"Harvest or her writings and messages appeal to both sides based on how they interpret what she says. It's almost as if the left and right co-opt what Harvest says or thinks and apply it to their vision of how that new world might look."

"So why or how does society get replaced and reborn?"

"Think about what the origin of her name means," Richard said. "To gather and pluck. Is it her intent to gather her followers and pluck the strongest or the most like-minded from those followers to create a new civilization? Or does it mean gathering those with the most like-minded views, perhaps based on political, religious, or even environmental and climate change opinions, or does it mean causing a social or civil war among these camps, and she gathers the survivors, the strongest, to form this new society? I am not sure she cares who wins; I think she wants to create chaos and upheaval now and finally turn civilized vitriol to open warfare against each other."

Rhonda added, "Well she must be proud of us because this is already happening every day. People espouse opposite views, and from those disagreements, violence occurs. It happened the other day in the park. It happens every day in America."

Richard somberly said, "Yeah, but that violence is normally one-on-one, or maybe a mentally ill person with an AR-15 who wants to wipe out a school or a church to make a name for himself or correct some perceived wrongs. I am talking about widespread violence conducted by and against all spectrums of society. I am talking about hundreds, if not thousands, of people engaging in violence against those with different views. I think this is perhaps what Harvest is after. In a way, what she espouses is tribalism."

"Okay, so she is not a white supremacist, religious warrior, some woke ideologist, or a BLM supporter. So, what is she, a cult leader? A David Koresh or Jim Jones type of person?" asked Rhonda.

"Well, if she was a cult leader, the closest similarity I can find would be to a woman named Clementine Barnabet and her Church of the Sacrifice way back in the early twentieth century. "And although thousands of people follow her, she did not have a physical enclave or colony located somewhere. She seems to have led a movement, but she seems not to have a physical footprint, or at least I can't find one yet, but I will."

"Is she charismatic, incredibly intelligent, or just insane?" asked Rhonda.

"While her rantings may seem insane, she seems extremely intelligent. Her speech, diction, and vocabulary are perfect. Her messages are very persuasive and hit every hot-button current at the time, almost to the day the topic is trending online. She created a movement of followers based on a message that appeals to the lunatic fringe who will follow anyone if that person amplifies or parrots their beliefs. Different from the past, today's digital world has allowed millions of people to follow someone or something without ever having physical proof of who is providing the message or whether the message is true or based on any facts," Richard explained. "And while it seems strange that so many people have faith without proof, is it different from the followers of Jesus, Mohammed, or any other great religious leader? Very few people ever physically saw Jesus, yet his word traveled from village to village, and everyone believed his word because they wanted to. Harvest and the thousands of others like her don't have to be seen. They just have to be believed."

Rhonda thought about that for a minute and then added, "Technology and social media have really fucked up our country and our minds, Richard. I hope you don't have anything else because you are scaring the shit out of me. Confronted with a street punk with a handgun, I know what to do, but some online influencers or messiah giving marching orders to the radical fringe is way beyond my pay grade," said Rhonda, pouring herself another glass of wine.

Richard saw that Rhonda poured herself a glass of wine to the brim and held out his own glass, signaling her to fill it up, while saying to Rhonda, "You may need another stiff drink for this, but Harvest believes that after this great battle, after the cleansing of humanity, to survive this cataclysmic event, we need to go Biblical."

"Biblical. What do you mean?" asked Rhonda.

"Biblical like after the great war, she will lead new followers and those not yet born to create a like-minded, purified society. All who are not her followers or all that are born to non-purified parents will be cast aside and left to die."

With that comment, Rhonda spit out her wine, laughing hysterically, partly because of the booze and partly because of Richard's absurdity.

Richard just shrugged, saying, "I told you this was going to be a crazy tale."

"Okay, Richard, please don't tell me Ms. Harvest or her followers plan on bringing animals two by two onto an ark to prepare for a biblical flood. Please tell me that is not what you have found out."

"Well, so far I have not read anything like that, but you never know how some people might interpret her message of what this new society will look like or how it will flourish and grow."

Rhonda's skin crawled upon hearing what Richard said, and a chill came over her. Then, there was silence between them as they sat digesting the conversation. Finally, Richard broke the silence.

"Rhonda, I know you think this is all fucking crazy, and I know you deal with sick and demented people all day, but you don't see what I see deep online in the darkest rooms of the web. If you did, you would realize that what you deal with is child's play. The web is the reason these sick fucks, primarily young white males, decide it is their destiny to shoot up a school or a church. There are a bunch of aimless losers out there who live in a digital fantasy echo chamber. They are sheep waiting to be led somewhere. Maybe to slaughter or to be the slaughterer. While you may not believe Harvest and that her viewpoints can be taken seriously, I am telling you they can and probably are already. Crazy is America's top export, and it is being fueled by the advancements in technology and unchecked and rampant growth of social media."

"Richard, I have looked into the vacant eyes of an eighteen-year-old as his finger twitched on the trigger of a gun. I have seen gruesome murder scenes where wives and children were gunned down by a 'loved one.' I have seen torture that I could not imagine a human could inflict on another human. None of that scares me as much as what you just told me. Nothing."

"It scares the shit out of me as well," Richard replied.

They then sat silently, lost in their thoughts, until the late evening darkness enveloped the living room.

Finally, Richard said, "I think I am going to bed. I can't think any more about this."

After formulating her thoughts, she turned to Richard and said, "What you told me about Harvest is way beyond what I can comprehend. I am not even sure I believe it. To maintain my sanity, I need to focus on my day job and solve the protest shooting, but I need your help on something else. Something that if I investigated openly would really put me in hot water with Tarallo, who already told me to back off."

Richard laughed, "First week on the job, and you already pissed Tarallo off. How did you do that?"

Rhonda answered, "I'm not sure you remember the call I got the other morning, but it was from a friend, Dr. Layla Brazini. Her clinic was broken into a few days ago, in fact, the day before the protest shooting, which, by the way, was in front of her clinic." With everything that had already happened on Rhonda's first week back from suspension, she thought, *"Has this all happened this week?"*

Smiling mischievously to Rhonda, Richard said, "Well, I remember you got a call, but perhaps you don't remember we were a little busy before and after that call."

Rhonda said nothing initially as she was focused on what she was about to say and how she would say it to Richard without raising any alarms. "Richard, I think it is good you investigated and tracked the on-line history and whereabouts of Harvest, and as bizarre as your findings are, I need you to dig deeper into her, but I need you to do me a favor and look into something else."

"And what would that favor be, Rhonda?"

"It's personal and something I need you to do quietly, so I stay out of hot water with Tarallo. After I got the call from Layla," Rhonda began and then stopped herself to keep it more professional, "I mean Dr. Brazini, I went down to her clinic to see what had happened. She is usually very calm, but I knew something terrible had happened in talking to her. When I got there, my first inclination was that it was a run-of-the-mill robbery of a medical facility, probably done by someone looking for drugs, cash, or both. But, after talking to Dr. Brazini and looking around, I think it could be something more significant, possibly done by locals or possibly by someone or something with much more sophisticated and perhaps darker motives."

"Okay. Your intuition is always right, but why do you think you will get in hot water with Tarallo by investigating the case?" Richard asked.

"The case on the surface may be just a break-in by someone looking for drugs. That is not what I do. I investigate homicides. I was reminded of that because Tarallo had already slapped my hand for going down to investigate the clinic on my own and not involving some local officers. In the simplest of terms, Tarallo told me to lay off and focus my time on solving the protest killing and other run-of-the-mill killings that will soon follow."

"Well, without knowing what else is on your mind, I agree with Tarallo. I get that Dr. Brazini is your friend," but the way he said it was more of a question than a statement, "and I know you went down there to help, but why do you want to dig a little deeper? What do you expect me to find that will either help you solve the case or get in the good graces of Tarallo?"

"I think the case is more significant than a smash-and-grab. More sophisticated like what we uncovered with Finnegan and his operation, and if it is, I want to be damn sure I get put on the case. I need you to see if any threads exist to something bigger, and I need you to find out before Tarallo calls it simple robbery and shuts the investigation down due to the backlog in the department. I need you, my handsome and sexy snoop, to find me something no one else can, something like murder, so I can convince Tarallo to get me back on the case."

"Well, compliments will get you everywhere, my dear. But I am confused. Are you talking about the murder of the protester outside her clinic? You are already on that case. What am I missing, Rhonda?"

Rhonda just looked at Richard with a sly smile, and Richard just sat back and laughed out loud, then said, "Oh my God, Rhonda. What will your fertile imagination have me looking into now? Please explain while I still have some lucidity tonight."

"Not a fertile imagination. Just following my instincts on something, and as you know, my instincts are rarely wrong."

Richard just nodded his head and gestured to Rhonda to continue.

"Okay, Richard, just sit back without interrupting or judging me. The cop working on the break-in, Officer Moloney, and I have a possible theory that the New Beginnings break-in may be part of a larger and more complicated crime."

"Okay, that is easily investigated, but I am still waiting for your explanation connecting the break-in to a murder."

"Murders, Richard, potentially mass murders," Rhonda said very seriously.

Richard sat up. More attentive than he had been, he realized that Rhonda was deadly serious, and he knew never to doubt her instincts or the intensity with which she pursued them. "Mass murders, Rhonda? You are going to have to explain that theory to me. Sounds far-fetched."

Rhonda continued. "On the surface, it will sound farfetched, even perhaps like what you just told me about Harvest, but let me explain this in a way that challenges you to expand your thought process of what reality is today versus what reality could be, so please be open-minded."

Richard said nothing, so Rhonda continued.

"Richard, as a man, and one not necessarily driven by religious principles, you probably do not follow the extended potential downstream effects of the Roe v. Wade decision. And frankly, it is not something that directly impacts me at my stage in life anymore. Still, in talking to Dr. Brazini and Officer Moloney and reading on the subject, my eyes have been opened to the possibilities that greater forces are at work regarding the IVF break-in and possible motives."

"How so, and what greater forces?" Richard asked.

"Potentially, and I emphasize potentially, there is a possibility that the break-in and the stealing of the embryos were done by fringe groups who want to take a stand or make a statement one way or another on the IVF industry and the outcomes it produces."

"The outcome that fertilized eggs form embryos and they eventually form humans. Then they are part of the 'when does life begin battle.' Those outcomes, Rhonda?"

Looking at Richard and realizing his comments indicated he had a grasp on the issues, and he should since he was brilliant, curious, and constantly researching social trends, she continued without patronizing him.

"What if, Richard, those embryos were stolen for a specific reason? And that reason, depending on which side of the bread you want to butter, was either to protect the embryos from being destroyed by the clinic or the owners of the embryos or destroy the embryos before someone else decided for the owners what their future use would be."

Rhonda waited a moment to let Richard answer.

"Rhonda, that is certainly an interesting theory, and as you said, a theory that current reality, legal or political, does not necessarily support, but knowing what I see and read every day, I am not closed-minded to it, and frankly, I could see it happening. And while we and others could debate forever on when life begins, at a minimum, the taking of the embryos for whatever reason is a crime that could be debated as potentially amounting to kidnapping or child endangerment."

Rhonda nodded, knowing that while perhaps Richard did not necessarily believe her, he was at least open to the possibility that her theories might carry water. His openness would motivate him to dig as deep as needed into the deep dark web.

Richard continued with exasperation in his voice, "So you want me to see if any outside players, either locally or nationally, have any involvement in the break-in at New Beginnings, then you want me to see if this local crime is connected to any similar crimes around the country, and lastly you want me to see if any of these crimes are somehow being done by pro-life or pro-choice forces and if the crime or crimes is also a building block in the newest battle over abortion. And whatever I find out, hopefully, it supports your case to go to Tarallo and have you assigned to the case. Is that about right, Rhonda? Did I miss anything?"

Rhonda laughed a bit, saying. "No, I think it keeps you busy enough, but don't take your eye off the ball on the continued investigation of Harvest and her potential involvement in the protest killing. You know I must keep my day job, which means I must solve that crime."

Richard laughed as well. "Oh, I forgot about Harvest. Up to an hour ago, I thought she was the craziest thing we would discuss, but now I think she may be taking a back seat to this new assignment."

Then Richard was silent, thinking momentarily, so Rhonda said nothing. She knew Richard was in that mind space where he was oblivious to everything, including her, as he worked something out in his brain.

Eventually speaking, he asked Rhonda something that surprised her.

"Do you think Harvest is at all connected to the protester murder, the break-in at New Beginnings, and the larger nationwide conspiracy you are asking me to investigate?"

"I don't know. Do you?" Rhonda answered.

"Well, I have found in my line of work that crazy tends to seek out crazy, and while I am not sure there is any connection, the fact that a protest and killing occurred between pro-life and pro-choice demonstrators the day after the fertility clinic break-in would give me enough reason to at least think of the possibility that there is a connection. Plus, Harvest is still too mysterious and an unknown, and for her to surface now and in St. Louis seems too coincidental. Still, there is too much I don't know to give you anything solid. Let me ask you something, Rhonda. Do you want there to be a connection? Does that help you with your presentation to Tarallo?"

"Just dig, Richard, and dig deep and fast. I will do the rest once I know what I am working with. And if my hunches are correct, I think I might be able to convince Tarallo that perhaps a murder or murders did occur at the clinic and perhaps elsewhere. If I do, Tarallo will let me run with both cases."

"And if Tarallo does not believe you and thinks this is too far-fetched, or worse case, she believes you and gets the feds involved because these crimes are connected and occurring in multiple states, then what happens?"

Rhonda knew Richard had a point. "Tarallo has rank on me, but I know what drives her, and it is ego and glory. If she sees a larger crime, she will do whatever possible to avoid getting the feds involved. Tarallo missed out on the Finnegan case, and it still burns her. She won't want to lose local control of this case."

Richard, now exhausted, said, "Okay, this is a lot to digest, and I am tired. Let me start digging into all this New Beginnings stuff tomorrow since I need to figure out where to start. Let's go to bed."

Rhonda began to unwind from the couch and let out a sigh. *"New Beginnings."* If only Layla and her patients knew how ironic that name is. They want a new beginning, to start a family, to start a rich and full life. But if they knew what world they may be bringing their child up in, they would not consider it a new beginning, more like the end."

With that, she grabbed a valium from her purse. She broke one in half, swallowed one, and handed one to Richard, who did the same. They both hoped a deep sleep would come, but they knew it wouldn't.

Chapter 18
LAYLA SHARES A THEORY

Both Rhonda and Richard woke up groggily as neither had slept very well, partly because of the large amount of booze that they had both drunk but more so because of the discussion they had about Harvest, the break-in at Layla's clinic, the protest shooting, Noah Sharpe, and Tarallo. Rhonda knew she better have her facts solid if she was going to weave this all together and present it to Tarallo. Otherwise, she might be put on permanent leave for being delusional. But Richard's investigations, critical to putting together many of the missing pieces, would take time, and right now, Rhonda had an actual murder to solve. As exciting as it could be that there was a more significant national conspiracy at play, at the end of the day, Rhonda had to go back to being a street cop and doing the basics of investigation, interviewing witnesses. However, her gut told her there was something bigger brewing, and beyond her professional interest in the case, she had a personal and emotional interest. Solving the protest murder was her job. Layla was her life.

Rhonda, unable or unwilling to finally get out of bed and out of Richard's arms, said, half joking, "Please tell me that I just was dreaming about a psychopath named Harvest on the loose."

"Sorry, my dear. That was real or as real as things can be online. I hope to have more information on Harvest, but as you commanded, I will start digging deeper into the IVF clinic break-in to see if that has any connections beyond St. Louis. But you, my dear, must get up, and as much as I wish you wouldn't, shower and get some food in you as you need to get back to being a cop and start interviewing witnesses to the protest shooting."

Rhonda reluctantly slid out of bed and jumped in the shower, hoping Richard would join her. After a few minutes, she realized she was showering solo. She dried off, got dressed, and sat down to a huge breakfast that Richard had prepared. They were each surprisingly quiet during breakfast, each inside their own heads about what their day had in store. Breaking up the silence was a text ping from her phone, and looking down, she saw it was from Layla. "Rhonda. Urgent we meet today. Can you meet asap? My house. LMK."

Looking at her watch, knowing all hell would break loose as her day unfolded, she texted back. "9:30 am. Your place."

Rhonda, now with curiosity mixed with adrenaline, jumped from her chair, strapped on her gun, kissed Richard goodbye, and headed out to meet Layla. As she drove over to Layla's house, she wondered why Layla chose to meet at her home instead of the clinic. Rhonda assumed Layla had something sensitive to talk about, and the less Rhonda was seen at the clinic, the fewer questions would be asked. It took twenty minutes for Rhonda to drive to Layla's home, located in the DeMun area west of Forest Park but near the Clayton business district and Washington University. It was a very fashionable and livable community that many professors, doctors, and young urban professionals called home. Layla lived in a one-hundred-year-old, four-bedroom condo on Rosebury within a short walk to the DeMun area parks and restaurants. Layla had beautiful taste, and her condo showcased the architecture of its grand past, featuring modern and chic interior design and impeccable furnishings to reflect Layla's love of art, music, and literature. It was bigger than what Layla, single and with no children needed, but it was perfectly suited to her lifestyle and joy of entertaining. Rhonda had not been to Layla's home in several years, so she was apprehensive when she pulled up. Until the call from Layla a few days ago when her clinic was broken into, Rhonda had been absent from Layla's life, an absence that wore on Rhonda more than she wanted to admit. Because the street was typically crowded with parked cars that had yet to leave for work, Rhonda did not notice an STLPD police cruiser parked one hundred yards west of Layla's condo, not that an STLPD cruiser would be the cause of any concern for Rhonda.

What caused Rhonda some concern was who she saw after Layla greeted Rhonda and ushered her into her home. Sitting in the living room, surprising Rhonda a bit as she assumed this was to be a private conversation, was Officer Ally Moloney.

Before Layla could make any introductions or explain why Moloney was there, Rhonda opened that door by saying, perhaps more gruffly than she intended, wondering if Moloney and Layla had started to form a bond, "Moloney, what are you doing here?"

Taken aback a bit because of Rhonda's tone and surprising reaction to her presence, Officer Moloney, holding her ground and demanding some modicum of professional respect, shot back in an official tone of voice, "Detective Simon, I am here at the behest of Dr. Brazini and the case I am working on at her clinic." And perhaps because she wanted to establish some turf ownership from Simon, she added, "You do remember that Tarallo assigned me this case, don't you, Detective?"

Eyeing Moloney a bit differently with a hint of respect for the toughness she just showed, Rhonda softened a bit and, as a way of defusing an uncomfortable scene, said to both Layla and Officer Moloney, "I am glad you are on the case Moloney. I tried to reach you on the way over," pointing to Moloney's phone, "as I wanted to tell you I was coming over here."

Moloney knew that was obviously a lie, but to get down to business and stop the pissing match, she just said, "We are all here, I guess, to compare notes and determine a strategy, so let's get down to business."

Rhonda nodded in affirmation, but Layla was taking charge as usual and asserting her position as the queen bee in this pack of three, jumping in to explain why she called this meeting.

"Detective Simon, I called Officer Moloney and you over today because I have some additional information as to why my clinic was robbed, what the thieves may have been after, and more importantly, what they weren't interested in stealing or maybe destroying. I also know how this information can help you get on this case and do what you do best, Detective."

Rhonda nodded as if to say *"continue,"* knowing that what she had Richard Leary investigating would also be additional information to make a stronger case to present to Lieutenant Tarallo. And, while she was intrigued with what Layla was about to divulge, she turned to Officer Moloney as both a sign of respect and an olive branch. "Whatever new information you have, Dr. Brazini, until this case is officially assigned to me, it is Moloney's case, and I will take her lead. If it never gets assigned to me, I will gladly help you behind the scenes in whatever way I can."

Moloney nodded to Rhonda with an affirmation of the gesture. Seeing the air was cleared, Layla dived into what new information she had.

"Yesterday, I was in the process of informing my clients that their embryos may have been stolen for unknown reasons, and their whereabouts or even viability was unknown. These were tough conversations as not only were these people clients, but they were also friends, and the IVF process they were going through might have been their last chance to ever have a baby."

Both Detective Simon and Officer Moloney nodded in understanding.

Layla continued, "My first call was to a patient, who is more than a patient, really a very dear friend, whose embryos were stolen."

That comment got Rhonda sitting up a little more erect in her chair, her eyes questioning who this person was and what her relationship was with Layla. Rhonda knew she was still overly possessive of Layla, who noticed Rhonda's sudden shift in demeanor but ignored it and continued.

"Anyway, my friend, who because she is also protected by HIPPA laws and will remain nameless, said something that got me thinking about the break-in and what the thieves took and, more importantly, did not take."

Looking puzzled, Rhonda was about to ask what the thieves took, but before she did, Moloney, twenty-five years younger than Rhonda and in prime childbearing years, piped in with a burst of enthusiasm as if she had the correct answer in class. "Dr. Brazini, if I might. Unfertilized eggs were not stolen, correct?"

"That's right, Officer Moloney," Layla answered. "I am impressed you would know that."

"I bet you keep the unfertilized egg storage separate from the embryos, and none of the eggs you might have had at the clinic were stolen. Correct Dr. Brazini?"

"Absolutely. I checked, and none of the eggs were stolen," Layla said, smiling at Ally Moloney as if they had already formed a bond, perhaps beyond this case. Rhonda looked at the two of them and wondered.

Moloney then turned to Rhonda. "Detective Simon, remember when we last talked, I shared with you the idea that perhaps this case would be treated not as a break-in but more as a possible murder or even a kidnapping scene."

"I remember, which is why I have asked Richard Leary to investigate the case more. I hope to have some information that may be related but go on."

Moloney then looked at Layla as if to ask, "Do *you want me to continue, or do you want to finish up this story?*" Layla just nodded with her eyes, indicating Officer Moloney should continue.

Continuing and reaching a conclusion, as a trial lawyer might do in closing arguments, Officer Moloney turned to Detective Simon and said, "The thieves did not take the eggs because they weren't as valuable to them as the embryos were."

"Why weren't they?" Rhonda asked.

"They weren't fertilized. They weren't fetuses. They weren't potential human beings. They were incapable of forming life in their current state. They were just eggs, and while it may be a crime to steal eggs, as far as I know, it is not a murder, but..."

"But," Rhonda completed Moloney's sentence, "stealing only the embryos clearly indicates the thieves specifically wanted those because they believe those are humans and..."

This time, Layla jumped in. "And...over one hundred embryos were stolen for safekeeping or to be destroyed, so either you have a mass kidnapping case on your hands or a mass murder case. Either way, this is a case you need to get on Detective, and I think we have the proof for your lieutenant. I think she will be very interested in it because this case is much more visceral and personal than the Dr. Finnegan organ donor case. After all, childbirth is a full life experienced and cherished by more people than organ donations.

Rhonda thought about that last statement. This case was more visceral. In the Finnegan, Arch City Transplant case, the crime was committed by and against the underprivileged and poor. And if you looked beyond the greed of Dr. Finnegan and perhaps his partner Dr. Calabrese, the result of the crime was to find more organ donors so others could live. *"Righteous in a sick way,"* Rhonda thought. But if what Moloney and Layla were laying out was accurate, this crime was unfathomable. Stealing or destroying embryos before life could begin, and at the same time, destroying the dreams of all those people whose lives were hurt by not being able to have children. In addition, unlike organ transplants, which might affect hundreds of thousands of people, the entire adult population of the United States was in a daily argument about when life begins. The national debate would intensify this case, the investigation, the media frenzy, and trial.

Rhonda did not want to get ahead of herself as she was a cop who based every decision on evidence, not emotion, visions of grandeur, or publicity of the case. Putting her cop hat back on, she turned to Layla and Moloney.

"Okay. We have the beginning of some possible theories we can present to Tarallo, which are more significant than the break-in at the clinic."

"How so, Detective?" Moloney asked.

With that, for the next thirty minutes, Detective Simon laid out the entire conversation she and Richard had shared over the last twenty-four hours regarding the protest, the protest organizers, and the mysterious Harvest. She then explained what she had Richard investigating regarding the possible cause and connections of the IVF break-in and its possible links to other IVF centers beyond St. Louis. The women were intelligent and nodded in agreement with Rhonda as they followed her theories to a logical but preposterous and frightening conclusion.

While excited and believing in her gut that they were on to something, Layla was cautioned by Rhonda to slow down and let her, and Officer Moloney methodically investigate the cases they each had before them. Rhonda, the old pro, knew they might have a significant case to present to Tarallo that could be one of the most vile and heinous crimes the city or the country had ever encountered. She also knew that it could be politically and culturally supercharged, and they needed to focus on being cops and doing their jobs, or else Tarallo would have their badges. For Simon, doing her job meant, for the time being, continuing to investigate and interview anyone who might have seen or heard something at the protests. Period. That was her assignment. She told Moloney the same thing. Keep your head down and do your job. Keep quiet about your theories and tell no one anything you are thinking until the three of them can compare their notes and the ones Richard was compiling.

Chapter 19
O'CONNELL'S PUB

While the meeting with Layla and Detective Moloney had Rhonda's head spinning with the scope of the possible crime committed at the New Beginnings Fertility Clinic, she still had the shooting at the protest in Tower Grove Park to investigate. Perhaps information based on Richard's research would add some credence to the theories she, Layla, and Moloney discussed, but that would have to wait. She needed to take her own advice and concentrate on the Tower Grove Park shooting. The best place to do that would be to visit the two meeting places that the protest groups went to after the shooting in the park. As a detective, she found bartenders or servers were some of the best sources of information, either overheard or witnessed.

She thought she would start at O'Connell's for a fundamental reason. She was hungry, and they had food, which appealed to her more today than Sasha's Wine Bar. O'Connell's was a century old burger and beer bar that had lost pretentiousness, if it ever had any, years ago. It was a place where almost everyone ordered a beer and burger or some other dead animal and onion rings or fries. Or, in case you wanted to pretend you were watching your weight and cholesterol, a side salad instead. She had been there many times and never ordered a side salad. While she was not at O'Connell's often enough to be called a regular, the badge on her belt buckle and the gun clearly visible in her shoulder harness let everyone know she was a cop, so they treated her like a regular. O'Connell's was a place that respected cops and always appreciated their presence.

Sitting at the bar, she caught the eye of the bartender, who walked over to her and, without placing a menu in front of her, just asked, "How do you want your burger cooked, Detective?" "Medium rare, with a side of rings and, unfortunately for me, iced tea, though I am dying for a beer," Rhonda answered.

"So, this is a work visit, Detective? No drinking on the job? I can't say that is a hard and fast rule followed by most of your co-workers," replied the bartender.

Rhonda just laughed. "I get in enough trouble just being a general shit disturber, so drinking on the job is probably the only thing I don't do." Then, before the bartender left, Rhonda asked, "What's your name?"

Holding her hand to his, he shook it and said, "Nick."

"Good to meet you, Nick. I am Detective Simon on this side of the bar. I know you may get busy soon, so can I ask you a few questions before the lunch crowd starts piling in?"

Rhonda could tell he got a bit of a worried look on his face like most people do when they talk to cops, but she assured him, saying. "My questions are not about you but about a group of folks who might have been here after the protest and shooting outside Tower Grove Park the other day."

Relaxing a little, Nick said, "Let me put your order in, and you will have my undivided attention when I get back."

As Nick placed her order in the kitchen, Rhonda looked around the bar and restaurant to see if any of her co-workers were knocking off some cold ones. However, there was no one in the place she recognized, but it was still thirty minutes before the big lunch crowd would swarm the place. As she turned back around to face the bar, Nick, on the other side, pulled up a stool, saying, "I am all yours, Detective, and your food should be out here in about ten minutes, but here are some wings on the house in case you can't wait."

"Thanks, Nick. I am famished, so if you don't mind talking while I eat, let's get at it."

"Last Saturday, I understand that a group of people came in here after the protest and shooting at Tower Grove Park. Is that accurate?" Rhonda asked.

"Yep, it is. This group comes in a lot when they are involved with protests in this part of the city, which now seems to be a weekly occurrence, so I did not think anything of it. Then, when they started talking about a shooting, I thought back to all the sirens I had heard an hour earlier. I put two and two together and figured they were at the scene."

"Anything more than being at the scene? Like anyone confessing anything or maybe boasting about what they had done?" Rhonda asked.

"No, nothing specific or tied to any one person, but when I figured out they were near the shooting, I did try and eavesdrop a little more than I usually do. They were initially more subdued, but then, after getting some liquid courage in them, they started boasting, not about the shooting but about their supposed "ass-kicking" of the other group. I think the folks that come in here are more conservative, right-wing oriented as I have seen them after anti-government protests, anti-masks protests, and now after pro-life vs. pro-choice protests. Frankly, I don't listen to much of anything they say as they eventually turn into just another bunch of drunks and bad tippers, no different than any other group of people who can't hold their liquor."

"Do you have any names of the people that were here?" asked Rhonda.

"Just first names when they might yell across the room. When they talk about someone or something a little more private, they huddle up in small groups, and their voices go down to a whisper," said Nick.

"When they whisper, do they ever mention the name of a woman who goes by Harvest? Does that name ring a bell, Nick?"

"No. I have never heard that name mentioned, but I hear another one mentioned occasionally and, I might say, with some degree of reverence or respect," Nick answered.

Rhonda silently thought about Harvest and was disappointed that Nick had not heard her name mentioned. Based on some interviews at the shooting scene, it seemed Harvest liked to stay in the shadows. Snapping out of her brief pause, she asked, "So, who was the name of this other person?"

"Well, I heard them talking about a guy named Billy O'Dell."

"O'Dell. Hmm. Was he here that afternoon or any afternoon after a protest?" Rhonda asked.

"Not that I can recall. But I definitely would know what he looked like because his photo is on the flyer," said Nick.

"Flyer?" Rhonda asked, and as she did, Nick went to the back side of the bar and, after shuffling around some papers, handed Rhonda the flyer.

As Rhonda looked the sheet of paper over, Nick confirmed what she was reading by commenting, "This guy seems to be the organizer or headliner of the event. They seem to talk about him with reverence. He seems like one of the group's leaders or at least the most charismatic in a slimy sort of way. I think he is some sort of state senator from down near the Branson area of the state."

Rhonda thought for a minute, then said, more to herself than to Nick, "O'Dell. I knew that name sounded familiar, but I did not make the connection. It makes sense that he is part of this group as he seems to be one of the biggest rabble-rousers down in southwest Missouri; he seems to weigh in on every right vs. left issue, even if it has nothing to do with his district or the state he is supposed to represent."

Nick added, "Typical politician, always running for another office without working in the job he was originally elected to hold."

"Nick, this information is beneficial. I will track O'Dell down to see how deep his fingerprints are on this protest and shooting. But before I go down another path, I want to ask you whether anyone here spoke specifically about the shooting, the shooter, or the victim."

"No, I did not hear them talk about anything specific to the shooting, and I did not pick up any other names mentioned, but I can tell you these folks seemed out for blood and maybe gleeful that someone had died. The weird thing was they were just common folk. Looked like my parents' friends or neighbors. The guys could have been here after a golf match, and the women could have been here after attending their kid's soccer practice. They weren't all tatted up. They looked and spoke as if they were relatively affluent and educated, which made their anger so scary."

"How so, Nick? What was scary about their anger?"

"Detective, I have been a bartender for many years. I can spot a bad seed or troublemaker ten seconds after they walk into the bar. I expect him or her to be trouble as soon as they have a few belts, or someone looks at them the wrong way. But these people were normal. They probably never raised their voice in anger to their neighbors, friends, or colleagues. But their anger towards the other protesters and their views had so much venom, it scared me that if supposedly normal people could act and think like this, what hope do the rest of us have?"

Rhonda shook her head in the affirmative as she felt the same way and answered Nick by saying, "The power of the mob, Nick. Individually, most of us are decent and docile humans. We stay to ourselves and respect others. But when the mob forms, all sensibility and decorum go out the door. It's ugly, Nick, and it will get uglier. Something needs to break this cycle of hate, but we are not there yet. I think more people will be killed, more hatred will be stoked, and assholes like Billy O'Dell, who has a political pulpit from which to espouse his views, are the most dangerous. The snake does not lie in the grass, Nick. His venom comes at us from behind a microphone, whether that microphone is at a rally or on stage, or even online." The last words were sentiments Richard shared with her daily.

Sensing the lunch crowd was beginning to build, Rhonda asked Nick one more question. "Nick, one last question, and I will let you go as you are getting busy. Beyond talking about the protest they had just come from, did any of them mention the New Beginnings Fertility Clinic?"

"No, I did not hear that name mentioned. What is that?"

'It's an IVF center, in vitro fertilization, and the shooting took place across from Tower Grove Park, on Grand, right in front of this clinic."

"Detective, I did not hear that specific medical term, but I did hear a couple of the guys talking about the next battleground being "taking control of these test tube babies." I am not sure that helps, and I am sorry I don't have any more to tell you, but I need to get back to work."

As the lunch crowd began taking Nick's attention off Rhonda and onto the thirsty souls needing a burger and a beer, Rhonda grabbed $20 and her business card and slid both to him.

Nick took the card but not the money. "Your money is no good here as long as I am bartending, Detective, but I will call you next time this group comes in. I am sure it won't be long."

Chapter 20

SASHA'S WINE BAR

It was 12:30, and Rhonda wanted to visit Sasha's Wine Bar, about a mile away. It wasn't too far to walk, and although it was a relatively nice winter day, Rhonda drove the mile and waited in the car, thinking she would have better luck once Sasha's lunch crowd thinned out. Besides, she could use the time to call Richard Leary to see if he had discovered anything new to add to the plan she would present to Tarallo tomorrow. Richard did not answer Rhonda's call, but thirty seconds after she hung up, her text chimed, indicating inbound from Richard: *"Can't talk. Heads down on something interesting. Cover it tonight when you get home. Love ya."*

Rhonda was intrigued by Richard's message and wondered what else he had found, but the last two words threw her. "Love ya." Rhonda knew those words were throw-away words with many people as she heard so many of her male peers saying it to their wives after every phone call, which Rhonda thought hypocritical as she knew most of them had some strange ass on the side.

But Rhonda, whose life was riddled with infidelity, booze, violence, and nightmares from the job, had not been in love with a man for years.

She had not heard those words spoken to her in a long time. Not even from Layla, who disappointed her by never saying it to Rhonda despite Rhonda breaking down one night and telling Layla that she loved her. Rhonda thought about Richard and wondered if she had finally found someone she could live a fairy tale with at this later stage of her life. Could Rhonda, after three failed marriages, let someone break through her armor? Rhonda thought that if anyone could, it would be Richard, as she felt something for him beyond sexual. She was in love with his brain. After thinking for thirty minutes, Rhonda realized the lunch crowd had thinned out. Sasha's was not as crowded as O'Connell's, so she turned off the car, checked her remaining messages, and entered the restaurant.

While in the same neighborhood as O'Connell's, Sasha's had a different vibe. Where O'Connell's could be described as gritty and dark, a working man's drinking and burger spot, Sasha's was leafy, bright, and airy. The lunch crowd was more women than men, and the menu had more salads than beef. O'Connell's was where beer was the drink of choice, and sports blasted from the TVs. Sasha's was a wine bar featuring a lighter fare, and the sounds of acoustic singers piped over the Pandora station they subscribed to. Rhonda, though, could feel at home in both places, and she had been to Sasha's several times with Layla, which now seemed years ago. Rhonda wondered if she and Layla would become close again. Ironically, the break-in at Layla's clinic might bring them back together again.

Instead of walking to the bar as she did at O'Connell's, Layla went to the host stand and asked to see the manager. The host, after sizing Rhonda up for a few seconds, wondering if she was a food supplier, salesperson, or disgruntled customer, just shrugged indifferently and pointed to a booth in the back where a young woman worked on her laptop.

Approaching the table, Rhonda waited a few seconds for the manager to look up, as she seemed deep into a task on her computer. Finally, with a sigh indicating the task had been completed, she looked up warmly to Rhonda, saying, "Oh, hi. Sorry, I was so focused I did not see you standing there. How can I help you?"

Rhonda, simultaneously flashing her badge and sliding into the bench across from the manager, said, "Do you have a few minutes to answer some questions I have?"

Reacting just as Nick did, with a mixture of worry and dread on her face, Rhonda quickly assured the manager. "Relax. What is your name?"

"Lauren. My name is Lauren Stevens."

"Okay, Lauren, please relax. You are not in trouble, and I am not here to deliver bad news about someone you may know. I need to ask a few questions about some people who were in your restaurant a few days ago."

The stiffening in Lauren's body eased a bit, and she asked Rhonda if she could get her a drink, some coffee, or iced tea, but Rhonda politely declined.

Rhonda was a bit preoccupied thinking about Richard's message and what he found, so she wanted to get this interview over and get back home to talk to Richard. She was less casual than she was with Nick and started in on her questions for Lauren.

"Lauren, were you working here last Saturday?"

"Yes, I was. I opened the place for the lunch crowd and was here around 9:00 or so, finishing the prep work. I worked the lunch crowd, then took off when the night manager showed up around 4:00."

"Do you usually have a big lunch crowd? I noticed today seemed a little light."

"Today was typical for a Tuesday. Saturdays are usually bigger, as people enjoy a leisurely lunch on the weekend, mainly if a special event occurs at the Botanical Gardens or Tower Grove Park. We usually get good traffic from those events."

"How was last Saturday's crowd?" Rhonda asked.

Thinking for a moment to remember a day in a string of days that ran together, Lauren said, "Last Saturday was busier than usual. It was also a little crazier as a big crowd came over from the protest march at Tower Grove, and once I heard about the shooting, I understood why they were in the mood they were in."

"What was the mood?" Rhonda asked.

"First, very, very somber. Quiet. Lots of tears and hugs. Then, after they settled in, ate, and drank a little, there was lots of anger. Lots of anger. More than I have ever seen with this group, as they usually are pretty mellow, thoughtful, and introspective about many topics."

"So, this is a group of people you have seen before?"

"Yeah. Mostly the same fifteen to twenty people, a few new ones now and then, but I guess they all participate in political protests because they always come in with some of their signs or, in some cases, they have the messages written on their bodies."

"Did anybody stand out to you as a leader of the group? Someone who was more vocal than the others?"

"Well, they all seemed more vocal, raising their voices more than in the past. As I said, usually they are mellow when they come in. Engrossed in conversation. Drinking wine. Chilling out. Almost decompressing after every event."

"But they were different this time. A little more animated?"

"Yeah, Good word to describe them. Animated," Lauren said.

"About what?" asked Rhonda.

Now not looking at Rhonda, Lauren said, "About the shooting, I think a lot of them knew the woman who was shot and killed, Theresa somebody. I did not hear the last name from them."

"Theresa Cahill was her name. The woman that was shot," Rhonda clarified.

"Just another day in the Lou," Lauren said to Detective Simon, referring to yet another murder in a city full of them.

Rhonda eyed Lauren with more suspicion that perhaps she knew more than she was letting on. Her demeanor wasn't guarded but cautious, as if she was weighing how much information to give Rhonda. A cop's intuition kicking in, Rhonda said, "Lauren, I will be out of your hair in a few minutes because I know you are busy. Outside the regulars whom perhaps you know or at least know their first names, did you hear anyone in the group talking about a woman named Harvest?"

"No. Does not ring a bell, Detective. But you know I am watching the entire operation, in and out of the front of the house, the bar, the kitchen. Maybe one of the servers heard something," Lauren said as she looked around at her wait staff.

Sensing this, Rhonda asked, "Are any of the servers who worked Saturday here now?"

"No. I was checking to see, but no one here today was here on Saturday. It is tough getting labor, as you know, so it's kind of a crap shoot who shows up to work."

"Okay. Well, if you remember anything else, or if one of the Saturday servers wants to give me a call, here is my card. I appreciate your time and help."

"Sure thing, Detective. I will look at the schedule to see who was here last Saturday."

Changing tactics, Rhonda pulled out the flyer from Nick that featured O'Dell's name. "How about this guy? Did anyone mention his name or talk about him?"

Lauren just laughed and said, "O'Dell. That scumbag politician is on everyone's most hated list, and his name is usually brought up every time the group meets. Frankly, I am surprised he was not the person shot based on how extreme he is." Rhonda knew O'Dell was an extreme right-wing conservative, very pro-life and anti-LGBQT. She assumed the group that met here was opposite to what Billy O'Dell stood for. Still, Billy O'Dell was not her focus yet, so Rhonda did not press the issue. She handed Lauren her card and asked her to call her if she or the Saturday servers remembered something about the group.

Leaving with the feeling that she was not getting all the information Lauren Stevens had and wondering, while being tight-lipped throughout the conversation, why she suddenly became very animated when the discussion turned to Billy O'Dell. Rhonda sensed she had hit a nerve with Lauren Stevens.

Rhonda headed back to her car and decided she would head home early after making a few more calls to see what Richard had found out. She had a meeting with Tarallo in the morning, and she was hoping Richard would find something that would give Rhonda some ammunition to tie in the protest, the killing, and the break-in to the IVF clinic. Without

Richard's information, Rhonda's assumptions were nothing more than assumptions, and they were hard to believe. Rhonda knew this was not enough to get her re-assigned to the clinic case.

Lauren, as soon as she saw Detective Simon pull away, pulled out her phone and whispered, "Hey, a Detective was asking about last Saturday and what we were talking about after the protest." After listening for a few more minutes, Lauren hung up the phone and sat in the booth instead of returning to work, thinking about where all this was headed for her and her friends.

Chapter 21
RICHARD SEES THE BIG PICTURE

Somewhat deflated that her interviews at both O'Connell's and Sasha's did not result in any bombshell or breakthrough information, especially no knowledge of anyone named Harvest, Rhonda wondered if her theories were just that, theories and, in fact, she was trying so hard to help Layla that she was grasping for straws to make connections that were not there. Rhonda also wondered if her adrenaline and notoriety from breaking the Finnegan and Arch City Transplant case was clouding her typically pragmatic approach to things. Did she want to help Layla for personal reasons, or did she want a big splash case for her professional advancement, and yes, ego? Regardless, she headed to Richard's house with great anticipation about what Richard had found.

While Richard and Rhonda spent most of their evening hours together at her house, as it was larger and *"less manned up and more livable,"* as Rhonda used to say, during the day, Richard did his investigative work at his house. While it reflected Richard's masculinity and testosterone-driven interest in sports, hunting, fishing, and all things military, it was also, as Rhonda liked to say, *"'geeked up' like a teenage nerd's room."* Richard's office looked more like a high-tech data center or a scene from a spy movie, darkened with only the ambient light from the five large monitors all displaying different websites, analytical sites, and social media sites. While some were mainstream, many sites were found only in the deep, dark metaverse and only secretly accessible by someone as intelligent as Richard. As Richard would like to say, anybody looking for evil could find the sites. The skill was keeping your identity secret while you perused the sites.

Richard orchestrated all this technology in the darkness, but not in silence, as he loved listening to eighties rock and roll, which was louder than his neighbors and Rhonda were comfortable with. His neighbors knew Richard and all he represented, so they rarely confronted him about the noise because they felt Richard Leary was better to befriend than to have as an enemy in these turbulent and violent times. Besides what Rhonda was getting to know and as his long-time neighbors knew, Richard was a good guy and would always be there for you if you needed him.

Richard had given Rhonda the code to his front door as he knew she was trustworthy. He was always unresponsive about answering a knock on his door because of his intense focus and lack of hearing from years of listening to loud music and louder weaponry in his original military work. Rhonda let herself in, and entering his office, hoping Richard saw her image reflected on his computer screen, kissed him on the back of his neck, indicating it was her arriving, not an assassin hired to kill him. They liked to joke about that, but Richard said he knew Rhonda would not make a good secret assassin because her familiar and alluring scent gave her away.

Turning down the music and minimizing a few of the screens on the monitors, he got up and embraced Rhonda with a warm hug and a dazzling smile. Rhonda sensed and perhaps felt he was aroused a bit.

"It seems, Richard, you are happy to see me, or is that the information turning you on?"

Laughing loudly, Richard said, "Damn, you figured me out. Information stimulates my brain, not my body, and you control 100% of that."

Rhonda pulled away a bit because she needed to ensure some work was done before the fun started. She did not trust herself to keep that from happening, so she said, "Richard, for the next few hours, I need to be stimulated by your brain. So, tell me what has got you so mentally excited."

"Okay. Well, sit down, and I will amaze and impress you with what I have found and what you can present to Tarallo tomorrow."

Sitting comfortably on a couch in Richard's office, he told Rhonda to pay attention to the largest center screen and, for the next thirty minutes, dazzled her with independent pieces of information and then integrated it all to tell a story.

"Let's start where we left off about Harvest. We know she has an on-line following by both the radical left and the fringe right, and they all believe in her theories that the world needs to be reborn. We know she has spouted off some crazy ideas about biblical end-of-time scenarios."

"When you say that out loud in the sober light of day, it does sound more like a dream or nightmare," Rhonda said, but growing impatient because Richard had covered most of this, she added, "Okay, we discussed all that previously. What do you think the connection is, if any, to the clinic?"

"The connection I have, as of now, is somewhat disjointed, but follow me for a minute. I will try to connect some dots, but the connection so far is not a straight line. At your protest march, a protest that perhaps was inspired by Ms. Harvest's online rantings, several individuals were involved, if not at the protest, who, unbeknownst to you, are followers of Ms. Harvest, and you may find their beliefs interesting."

"Who were the followers? I want to make sure I interview them," Rhonda asked.

"Well, you interviewed one of her followers, Noah Sharpe. The monkey man who believes he and Harvest are in some lover's relationship, right?" Richard asked.

"He is a lunatic, in my opinion, and while delusional, possibly only a harmless loner," answered Rhonda.

"Possibly harmless, but you know what makes lunatics dangerous, Rhonda? Lunatics, even the delusional ones, become more dangerous when two things happen. First, they find people who share their views and, in fact, make their views seem rational. The other dangerous thing is when they are encouraged by their new group of peers to act on their views. In Noah Sharpe's case, both those things are happening."

"He has followers?" asked Rhonda.

"Sharpe probably believes he has followers, especially since he also believes he has been chosen in some regard by Harvest, and as such, this gives him street cred or maybe online credibility. But all these people just float in and out of each other's online presences, trying to find out who would swallow what level of bullshit to push an agenda. Sometimes, it is to make some big bucks, stroke their ego, and tout how many followers they have. Remember when Facebook first came out, and you felt you were judged based on how many online friends you accumulated. A few young people, unfortunately, would go as far as committing suicide if they did not have enough online friends."

Richard continued, "In Harvest's case, a whole lot of people believe her bullshit and her agenda, and the key is finding those who are the most ardent believers because, invariably, those core believers seem to gravitate to each other for confrontation or confirmation. Everyone is trying to become the most influential influencer. They find the more radical their agenda, the more followers they will get. And by the way, followers may not be just those who believe in what you say. Followers may also be people who passionately hate what you stand for because hatred of a person's views and affinity towards them achieves the same purpose. Online notoriety is created from connections or conflict. Based on what I have found, we have some key people who, I believe, are connected. This may be the link you are seeking to tie-in the protest killing with possibly the IVF clinic break-in here in St. Louis and perhaps others that are taking place around the U.S."

Rhonda sat silently, looking at the flashing computer screens and all the information on them. She was temporarily dazed by the potential magnitude of what she may have stumbled into, but she knew Richard would break it all down for her.

"Okay," Richard said, as he typed in some information, "let me try and outline as simply as possible what I have found and the connections I have made. There is a lot here, so be patient. I needed to build a case around the known activities or people versus the unknown activities and people and see if there is a connection."

"I first plugged into my algorithm all the facts I knew about or could learn about the St. Louis protest and, of course, the shooting. The pre-protest activity primarily created only local chatter, and many of those who shared common threads were local participants. Things like time and place of the protest and where to meet up afterward. Nothing jumped out to me in terms of violence or collusion with something greater, like a connection to the IVF break-in. But post-protest, the chatter became more interesting, violent, and widespread. I will cover that in a minute."

"Secondly, I did the same search on the break-in at Layla's IVF clinic, and as I expected, most of the chatter was local, germinating from the local news coverage about the break-in, which is limited since there were probably thirty crimes committed that day in St. Louis, some much more violent. I looked to see if any of the protest participants' online voices also wandered into the online discussions about the break-in, and there were a few random comments. So, the break-in and the protest were the two primary fixed events that I knew happened. Still, not much to get me or you excited."

Confirming Richard's comment, Rhonda just said, "Well, I agree with you on that."

Patting her on the knee with a mischievous grin, Richard said, "Don't lose faith Rhonda. You are about to get very excited."

"So, knowing what was said online about both events, which were, in fact, independent events, I then plugged in two known entities who may be somehow connected to the protest. The mysterious Harvest and the nut case Noah Sharpe. You had given me the names of some others you interviewed, and aside from some harmless pre-protest event comments, nothing jumped out at me. But, when I then cross-referenced those people with Harvest and the postings she had made, it started to get interesting as those you interviewed, including Sharpe, indicated Harvest's involvement with or encouragement to others to attend the protest. She does this with pro-life versus pro-choice protests around the U.S. She seems to voice her opinions and influence those who plan to attend. What she posted after the event and who clicked on and shared her comments made this interesting."

"What did she say after?" Rhonda asked impatiently.

Instead of telling her what Harvest said, Richard pulled up the post, and Rhonda read it.

Dear believers, the battle to purge our current society from its sicknesses and sins to form a new society is being fought in towns and cities across America. If lives are lost, they are lost for a greater cause, ensuring a like-minded species survive and prosper in peaceful harmony. Today in St. Louis, in addition to the battles fought between citizens in our town squares and city streets, a new battlefront has opened to protect the unborn, not only in utero, but where science and nature clash at IVF centers around this country. These perfect humans have not yet formed but will be born and will be raised mentally and philosophically to become the future leaders in our new society. I encourage all my followers to understand what opportunity IVF centers offer us to create this new society. A society that can be pre-determined before birth and re- programmed after birth to serve our needs. Understand that many of you will survive this battle, and many of you won't. Only the strongest and most determined will, but once we come out of this epic struggle, we must replenish our population and do it rapidly and permanently. Over the next weeks, I will share with those willing to become my soldiers in this fight the blueprint of how to achieve this new society with the living and the unborn."

After she finished reading it, Richard said, "Rhonda, in the old days when police did investigations without online research, this could be considered a smoking gun, or at a minimum, accessory to a crime. Is she asking people to commit violence on her behalf, and if so, did they?"

Rhonda sighed, then commented, "As much as I want this to be the answer, it might be a big leap, Richard, because, for one thing, we do not even know where Harvest is. Secondly, we do not know specifically who may be acting upon her requests except Noah Sharpe. Is he one of her soldiers she mentions? I think I need more than this to go to Tarallo."

"And more you shall get, my dear," Richard said. "Knowing what Harvest posted after the event, I looked at two things. Who reacted, commented, shared, or retweeted the post most frequently and with possible incendiary comments, and were any of those re-shared comments related to the protest and people who attended? What I found interesting was that three people surfaced as reacting the most to Harvest's posting. While many reposted, three prominent ones that rose to the top based on the number of posts and linkages to other violent sites were, of course, Noah Sharpe, who enthusiastically agreed with Harvest, also posting, "I am doing my part." The two other prominent commentators were a Missouri right-wing, incendiary downstate politician named Billy O'Dell and a woman named Marianne Hylany.

Rhonda interrupted, "O'Dell was featured on a flyer circulating at the protest march, but the woman does not ring a bell."

If Richard was annoyed by Rhonda's interruption, he did not show it. He knew he had a convincing story to tell, and he would let it unfold as quickly or slowly as Rhonda could digest the information.

"Bingo, Rhonda. You know of two connected to the protest, and I believe the third, Hylany, was also connected, and I will tell you why in a minute."

He continued. "We know a little about Noah Sharpe, but I encourage you to dig deeper as I think he could be key to this. Billy O'Dell, who, in addition to being a general shit disturber, is a Missouri state rep from a deep red district in the southwest part of the state down by Branson. While he plays the part of the aw-shucks rube fighting for rural America, he is very calculating, politically, as he has his eyes on a much bigger prize. He is the primary organizer of many protests in the Midwest. But before you assume that O'Dell's views and Sharpe's outright craziness directly connect them to both the protest and the IVF break-in as part of some far-right agenda, let me introduce you to someone who may be scarier. A woman named Marianne Hylany, while not necessarily an organizer or participant in the St. Louis protest, is a throwback to the sixties flag-burning, anti-war liberal but modernized to fight today's left-leaning battles. She is five feet and four inches of hell on wheels, a professional agitator and a first-class one as she goes from protest to protest, firing up the crowd and beyond, demanding justice and violence. I would equate her to the radical philosophy of the Irish Republican Army. Violence as a means to an end."

Thinking about this information silently and then laughing, Rhonda said, "If they were all at the protest, I am sure sparks would fly. Were they all at the protest at the same time?"

"We know Sharpe was there, probably at the behest of Harvest, but Sharpe is a tool. He's a small-time player, more like a foot soldier, but he wants to be much more. We know O'Dell was there as he was a featured speaker promoted on websites and Facebook pages and on the flyer you mentioned. Based on O'Dell's Twitter posts, it seems he was already at another political fundraising event in the suburbs shortly after the protest, so I do not think he was there to see the skirmish and shooting."

"He just comes in to stir the pot and leave, right?" asked Rhonda.

"Seems so," said Richard.

"What about Hylany? Was she actively involved in the protest?"

"No, and thank God she wasn't, as she has particular hatred towards O'Dell. If they were both there at the same time, you might have had two additional murders on your hands. To me, it seems the hatred stems beyond their political differences. There is something deeper there, but I am unsure of their history together. She clearly was in route from Chicago when the protest started based on her online postings, even commenting that she would be late for the main event but would be meeting "true believers" at the after-party at Sasha's Wine Bar. Based on your interviews, it seems many of the pro-choice crowd met afterward at Sasha's, and many of the pro-life crowd met at O'Connell's."

Rhonda nodded, saying. "Yeah, I talked to people at both places, but interestingly enough, the restaurant manager at Sasha's, Lauren Stevens, made no mention of Hylany, and if this woman is as dynamic as you paint her to me, you would think that Lauren Stevens would have mentioned her. However, she did get quite animated when I mentioned O'Dell's name. Perhaps she and Hylany have the same shared history with O'Dell?"

"I may need to add Lauren Stevens to my list to investigate because she is local, and I need to tie in local activity to help you make your case with Tarallo, but the list is getting longer and longer, so we need to focus on the primary players," Richard said.

Rhonda nodded, not in agreement but more so that she was already formulating her thoughts on presenting this information to Tarallo. Knowing she was deep in thought, Richard waited for Rhonda to focus on him to begin formulating a plan of action.

"Richard, this has all been excellent information, and I appreciate your special, off-the-grid investigative skills, but I think you are holding onto your last card, and I need that card to somehow link any or all these people to the protest and most importantly, the break-in to Layla's clinic. That is the connection I need to make to Tarallo: Perhaps the protest was just a smokescreen hiding the real reason for the break-in.

"Well, dear, a less skilled investigator may have stopped with what I just gave you but knowing how much I like being rewarded by you for my good work, I dug deeper into the online historical postings, content sharing, Twitter feeds of all the players, and cross-referenced them to the historical postings of the ever-mysterious Harvest plus anyone else sharing her views. Plus, I expanded my search beyond U.S.-based sites. I looked into Russian, Chinese, and Arab sites that few Americans can access or know exist. I also built an algorithm to look for phrases such as IVF, embryos, Rowe vs. Wade, and that algorithm will feed us in real-time any online activity that may be connected. And if the results are what I expect them to be, meaning a connection between people and events, I may hold several hole cards. One of them is an ace that might make your case for Tarallo." Richard sat back with a smug smile on his face.

"Being a bit irritated with Richard and impatient, Rhonda said, "So, what is the ace you are holding, Richard? I know you did not tell me the whole story."

"Ever since Roe v. Wade was overturned in the Dobbs v. Jackson ruling, the chatter has become stronger and, in my opinion, much more volatile. The left and the right are gearing up for a new fight and that fight may be the IVF industry, per the posting by Harvest, which I shared. I think Layla and her clinic might be a trial run for something bigger, something national, maybe international," Richard said.

"Jesus, that seems so fucked up. These poor women who can't have children and rely on IVF may now be torn apart emotionally by being in the middle of another culture war," an exasperated Rhonda said. "You need to help me make the connection between the protest killing and break-in at the clinic. It could not have been a coincidence that it happened outside Layla's clinic the day after the break-in."

Richard concurred, "I have always said there are no coincidences because, in any crime, you follow the money as the money leads you to the truth, and the truth is social causes are not grassroots; they are created and fueled for financial gain, and based on what you told me Layla said about the sophistication of her break-in and the careful removal of the embryos, this crime was not done or funded by amateurs. This crime, whether it was a canary in a coal mine to test society's reaction or the harbinger of more audacious, more frequent crimes of the exact same nature, was done by someone with the financial wherewithal to, not only fund it, but to profit from it. Together, we will see if this all adds up, but you have enough to present to Tarallo, and if she does not salivate about this case and put you on it, then she is a fool."

Richard had taken seemingly unrelated data points from various sources and wove them into a tightly connected story that left Rhonda not only in awe of Richard's expertise but also afraid of what he had found out. She was not afraid for herself. She was afraid for the future of mankind or the disintegration of it that may have begun in the protests, the break-in at Layla's clinic, and the people possibly involved in both. But this was beyond St. Louis. This was a powder keg about to explode all over the country. Before any shots are fired, the most potent weapon is the disinformation being distributed, shared, and repeated among people all over the U.S. and the world.

Sensing perhaps what Rhonda was thinking, Richard quietly said, while patting her on the knee, "I have lived a life where bullets and bombs killed people and made our cities unlivable. I also know more than I should about the possibility of nuclear annihilation, but what I just showed you might be more powerful than any weapon I have seen. Information or disinformation may be the weapon that destroys us all because eight billion people on earth all have access to it, and all can manipulate and distribute it without any checks or controls."

"Well, I must get assigned the case first, and I think I can convince Tarallo to let me do that. Not just because of what you found out, but I will appeal to her political savvy and career aspirations to become chief of police. She won't want to miss out on a big case like she did with the Finnegan and Arch City Transplant Center case. Tomorrow, come hell or high water, I am on this case, and Tarallo, damn whatever she decides, is not going to stop me," Rhonda said defiantly.

Chapter 22
NOAH'S PAST REVEALED

Noah knew what Harvest had wanted him to do, and because of the past trauma in his life, he knew exactly where he would start his work for Harvest. He knew that despite his crappy, dead-end job at the zoo, he was super intelligent, and only his lack of ambition and motivation kept him from achieving more. Harvest and his love for her and her love for him gave him the motivation to be more than he was now. Noah would figure it out on his own as he felt if he went to her for guidance, she would see weakness in him, and for the first time in his life, he wanted to exude strength. But to get that strength, he needed to go where he was once very strong and then became very lost.

His answer of where to build the future Harvest laid out for them was easy. It was the only place in his life, albeit years ago, that Noah felt he belonged. His long-owned family property ninety miles south of St. Louis, near Caledonia, Missouri, whose rolling foothills were the start of the ancient Ozark Mountain range. Noah and his parents were there as much as possible through Noah's childhood. It was an outdoor wonderland with rugged and hilly terrain, hiking paths, deep woods, and beautiful, clear

Ozark Mountain streams crisscrossing their land. As a youth, Noah had a carefree life hiking, riding bikes, swimming, and fishing in the deep, clear waters of the streams and nearby lakes. Noah learned how to live off the grid, taught to him by his father, who made this wonderland completely solar and hidden from the outside world. He loved it there, and if he could have made a living down there, he would have gladly stayed forever, but that all changed the day his parents died, based in part on Noah's stupidity.

When Noah was sixteen, he was brave and strong and thought he could conquer anything, including the outdoors because of the training his father had taught him. Deciding one early winter day to go hiking, without telling his folks the direction he was headed, Noah hiked for hours, planning to turn around to make it home before the early winter darkness came at 5:00 p.m. Unfortunately, Noah hiked outbound longer than planned, as the day was glorious. Clear blue sky, the leaves on the trees gone, so you could see forever and hear the slightest movements in the forest. At 4:30, with only about thirty minutes left of daylight, Noah realized he would not make it home before dark. The clear day began to turn cloudy, hiding the paths from the moonlight, which usually would have given him enough light to guide him back home. The winds also began howling, indicating a potential storm was coming. Concerned about shelter, Noah found one of the many caves formed in the rocky hills by the streams that traversed this land. Caves or what might possibly be in them, snakes, bats, maybe even a rare mountain lion or bear, did not scare Noah because, at this time in his life, animals were beginning to become his passion that he would continue as he became an adult. Little did he know that animals would, from this day forward, serve as the only species he could genuinely trust. Settling in the cave as the storm grew more intense, Noah knew he was safe and dry, albeit cold. Once a new day's dawn broke, in only twelve hours, he could continue home. While he thought he would probably catch hell from his parents when he got home, Noah did not even think of the panic going through their minds when he had not returned home by 5:00 p.m.

But Noah's parents had been panicking for hours as they knew from listening to the radio that a lot of bad weather and torrential rain was coming their way. They knew Noah was off hiking but needed to figure out which direction he was going. Noah's father felt he had spent enough time with Noah, teaching him about the woods and the land, and that Noah was more prepared to survive a night in the woods than most sixteen-year-olds. But with the storm approaching and the threat of flash floods impacting many of the streams in the area in which they lived, they took off to try and locate Noah by sight or sound. By 6:00 p.m., the sky turned dark and stormy. By 7:00 p.m., lightning lit up the sky, and with each crack of thunder, the rain seemed to intensify in microbursts. The worry and dread in Noah's parents began to rise as quickly as the streams were rising. By 8:00 p.m., they had a choice to continue looking for him or turn back, hoping Noah would use his survival skills to find a place to shelter and ride out the storm. They decided to turn back before they were in peril as their path crossed several streams that would rise rapidly with this amount of rain. Visitors to their property were always shocked when they saw dry creek beds swiftly become raging torrents, the definition of flash flooding. His parents passed by one swiftly rising stream after another until they went down a final hillside and reached the gravel bar that bordered the last stream they had to cross to get home.

His parents knew from living on this land for thirty years that the water was much higher than when they crossed it hours ago. Still, they were unaware of exactly how deep the water was, how swift the current was, and where the safest place to cross was. While they had hiked across these streams many times when the water was a meandering flow, and they knew the giant boulders to hopscotch across, tonight, their bearings were off. The large boulders seemed to be swallowed up by the water. They would typically offer a good-sized plateau to jump onto, but now, the dry portions of the rocks were measured in inches, not feet. They had to cross here and now, as turning back was not an option as the streams they had already traversed would be unpassable, and staying put was not an option. The dry creek bed they were presently on would be underwater because they were at a low point in the valley that during flash floods became a lake as all the streams merged into the valley, washing away everything in their path. They only needed to cross over about thirty feet of stream. Hence, with no other choice, they began wading in, grabbing hold of the remaining slivers of each boulder to guide them across. In their younger days, they would jump across these boulders with no fear, but now that they were a bit older, less fearless, and less nimble, the task was much more challenging. They fought against the swift current that pushed their legs from beneath them, almost lifting them parallel to the water. As the current pried their grips off the boulders, they were violently pushed downstream, crashing into one boulder after another. Noah's father, who hoped the current would push them across the stream instead of downstream, soon realized his mistake. The current took them faster and deeper into the water. There would be no escaping the watery grave he had just created for himself and his wife, who soon slipped from both her grasp of his hand and her grasp on the boulder. She went underwater, and Noah's father quickly went under as well, maybe to try and rescue her, but more likely be with her in their final minutes together as he knew well enough that they were not going to survive.

Noah, for his part, had waited in the cave for the storm to end. When morning came, cold and hungry but alive and happy, he started out, blissfully unaware of what had happened to his parents until he reached his family's home. Immediately upon seeing the Reynolds County sheriff and Coroner in his driveway, he knew something was wrong that would change his life. Something for which he would blame himself forever had turned Noah's bright light and future to darkness.

Noah, now an adult, was still haunted about that day and night when he lost his parents due to his stupidity. He thought about his idyllic family home near Ottery Creek, normally quiet but, when raging, could cause death. He thought about his childhood, which was once so promising and full of joy and wonderment, turning into a life of loneliness and despair.

He thought about all of that now as he pulled into his property and began walking around to inspect what he had started to build. He thought about it because of Harvest and the opportunity she had given him to make amends for his life, his sins. Now, twenty-five years after that terrible night, at that terrible place where he lost not only his parents' lives but also his own, he would redeem himself by bringing new life back to this wretched place. For twenty-five years, the area around Ottery Creek symbolized only death to Noah. Now, it would symbolize life and salvation, and the same rains that had killed his parents would hopefully support the vessel he needed to build to create a life he and Harvest would share.

Chapter 23
TARALLO HEARS THE STORY

Rhonda was ready to meet Tarallo and convince her that the break-in at Layla's clinic and the protest where a woman was murdered were possibly connected. Additionally, beyond a local connection, they were perhaps part of a more significant, more sinister, coordinated movement, which could be happening nationwide. And if that was not enough to convince Tarallo, the name Dr. Alex Finnegan would undoubtedly be. Simon and Tarallo missed out on the publicity and probable promotions they would have received had Finnegan been apprehended in St. Louis instead of losing the case to the feds when he fled to the Middle East. However, Richard had cautioned Rhonda not to make the crime beyond what Tarallo held jurisdiction over. He warned her that if Tarallo sensed this was national in scope, she might include the feds and let the FBI run with it. Rhonda appreciated his insight, thanking him before she left. She knew in her heart how to handle Tarallo and what buttons she needed to push to get back on the case without Tarallo getting the FBI involved.

While she did not need Officer Moloney to attend the meeting, Rhonda genuinely was beginning to take a liking to this rookie cop. She felt that if Tarallo saw her as a team player, she would be more inclined to allow Rhonda back on the case. Also, while unconventional, Rhonda asked Dr. Layla Brazini to attend the meeting. She knew Tarallo would push back on a civilian getting involved in a police matter, especially one in which the civilian was also a victim. But in this case, because of the medical aspects that needed to be discussed, Dr. Brazini would serve as an expert in the field to help Tarallo understand, if need be, the science behind IVF.

Rhonda, Moloney, and Dr. Brazini waited in the precinct conference room for Tarallo, who strolled in shortly after the 10:00 a.m. start time. Immediately upon entering, Tarallo took note that Officer Moloney was in the room, and sitting next to Moloney was a woman Tarallo did not know. With some irritation, Tarallo asked Rhonda, "Simon, would you like to introduce me to your guest, who seems to plan on sitting through an internal police meeting?"

Wanting Tarallo to understand Rhonda was prepared and would be in control of anything Tarallo would throw at her, Rhonda calmly set the stage and the agenda for the meeting by saying, "Lieutenant, because I know you are very busy, I have invited Office Moloney to join us, and sitting next to her is Dr. Layla Brazini, owner of New Beginnings Fertility Clinic," adding, "the clinic that you recall was robbed last week. Moloney has been following up with that case. As you know, I have been on the murder at the protest event that happened the day after the clinic robbery. We plan to connect the two events, if possible."

Tarallo, playing an expected cop game of divide and conquer to ferret out the weakest link, turned to Moloney, saying, "So Moloney, you needed help on a routine case, and you thought teaming up with Detective Simon was a smart move to grow my confidence in you?"

Moloney did not flinch under the Tarallo glare, a trait most rookies who worked for Tarallo did not possess yet. "Lieutenant, based on my initial investigation of the break-in and interviews with Dr. Brazini, along with some additional information I uncovered, I felt it was my duty to solicit advice from Detective Simon."

"Maybe I should have been the first person you solicited advice from Moloney, as I am the head of the department," Tarallo snapped back.

Again, with no wavering in her voice, Moloney answered firmly, "We are soliciting your advice now, Lieutenant, which is why we are here. As Detective Simon will lay out, we believe we have several intertwined cases, like the complicated Alex Finnegan and Arch City Transplant case, which Detective Simon solved." Moloney was proud of herself for bringing up a subject she knew would piss off Tarallo.

Knowing she hit a nerve with Tarallo, Moloney nervously looked at Simon to bail her out before she was reassigned to parking meter patrol for the rest of her career. However, the person bailing her out was not Detective Simon but Dr. Layla Brazini, who spoke up rather forcefully.

"Officers, I know I am a visitor here, and probably I should only speak when spoken to, but can we get past the dick measuring bullshit that most men need to get out of their system before any meeting can progress, adding, "I hear enough of that crap when dealing with the ego-maniac doctors in my profession. They equate wearing a skirt to being less intelligent than them, and of course," now looking around the room, "we all know those men out there are just afraid of us and how damn smart and dangerous we really are."

Initially, the room was a bit silent, with some nervous shifting in seats, then a few subtle smiles crossed everyone's face. Internally, Rhonda suppressed a sense of pride in Moloney holding her own and Layla taking charge. It was what she loved about Layla. She did not take shit from anyone.

Sensing it was time to proceed, Rhonda started in.

"Lieutenant, I appreciate you taking the time to listen to us, and now that Dr. Brazini very directly introduced herself and maybe got us to put away our proverbial swords, we believe we have information that you will find very interesting about the clinic break-in, as well as the protest murder. May I begin, Lieutenant?" Rhonda said with some deference to Tarallo's position.

With the earlier heat and tensions dissipated, Tarallo nodded to proceed.

When presenting evidence to anyone, Rhonda liked to start with the final hypothesis and then work her way back to supporting that hypothesis with systematic facts combined with some opinions and assumptions. This usually led her audience to "solve the puzzle on their own," if you will, before Rhonda was finished.

"Lieutenant, we believe that the break-in at the clinic and the murder at the protest, while not necessarily done by the same person, was done by people who shared a common agenda. Using the facts we know about the break-in and the protest and looking at information online may connect the two incidents."

"And what was the common agenda that these perpetrators might have had?" Tarallo asked.

"Well, let's start with the protest murder because this is more straightforward. The protest was a common weekend variety protest happening almost every weekend in our metro area and cities nationwide. Side A is against what Side B believes and vice versa. Most of these protests end peacefully after a few hours of marching, preening for news cameras, and maybe yelling, if not at each other, over each other. But unfortunately, things got more heated, and a shot was fired, killing a member of Side B. In this case, those who were supporting the right to life possibly shot a protester supporting pro-choice, though to be honest with you, we do not have a clear motive or I.D. of the shooter. We also do not know, but we could surmise the shooting, since it was done outside Dr. Brazini's clinic, could be related to the crime at the clinic. Again, we do not know that for sure."

"So far, you have a lot of what-ifs about connections. Where are you at identifying the shooter, Detective Simon?"

"I have interviewed witnesses at the protest and servers and bartenders who interacted with members of both groups when they met up at two local restaurants, O'Connell's and Sasha's Wine Bar. Let me bring that information back into the discussion when we lay out other elements of this investigation," then, turning to Moloney, said, "Officer Moloney, can you outline your findings at the clinic?"

A bit flustered because she thought Simon would handle the entire presentation, Moloney steadied herself and outlined her information to Tarallo in the same confident way she had done confronting Tarallo earlier.

"Lieutenant, while on the surface the break-in at the clinic seems like a smash and grab, maybe by some of the locals looking for cash or drugs, we think it was really a more sophisticated robbery, not done by our run-of-the-mill punks but by someone or some organization way more intelligent, and if I do say, perhaps more organized and professional than a smash and grab would indicate."

"Why do you say that Moloney?" Tarallo asked.

"These guys knew exactly what they wanted and took it, but perhaps as importantly, what they left behind was as telling." Moloney looked towards Dr. Brazini to fill in the blanks, but Layla just nodded to Moloney to proceed, giving her the green light to run with this. If she needed backup, Layla would join in.

"What they took, Lieutenant, were IVF vials containing viable human embryos. Are you familiar with the term IVF, Lieutenant?" Moloney added.

"Yes, I am. "IVF stands for in vitro fertilization, a medical and scientific procedure to help women, or in some cases same-sex couples, who can't conceive naturally, conceive in a lab using a woman's harvested eggs, combined with the sperm of a donor, or husband, or partner."

A brief silence enveloped the room as everyone had the same thought that Tarallo seemed to know about the procedure in a very familiar and personal way, and sensing what everyone was thinking, Tarallo added, "I am personally very familiar with the IVF process, so continue Moloney. You mentioned what the thieves did not take may be more important than what they took. Explain, please."

"During my investigation and in talking with Dr. Brazini, it came to light that not only were the vials and embryos not destroyed, nor the machinery ransacked, but the vials were carefully removed from each cryogenic chamber to not disturb the embryonic cells. But more importantly and surprisingly, as Dr. Brazini pointed out to me, not only were the thieves very careful about handling the embryos, but they left behind vials with eggs that were harvested but not yet fertilized with sperm. And the thieves knew the difference between egg vials and embryo vials."

Now, with piqued interest as it seemed to become personal to Tarallo, she turned to Dr. Brazini, saying, "Doctor, I assume you are here to shed some medical expertise on what happened at your clinic, as well as how and why, so please speak up. You have my attention."

Layla turned to the group and, knowing to use layman's terms, explained what she believed happened and, more importantly, why.

"Thank you, Lieutenant, for allowing me to attend this meeting and give you my insight. I know this is not standard operating procedure, but you will find this valuable. As Officer Moloney gathered evidence at my clinic, I pointed out that while my office was broken into, very little was destroyed or broken in my lab. While the lab and freezer doors had been pried open, generally, all the equipment was left intact, with the exception that the embryo vials which were carefully removed, not ransacked as a thief or vandal in a hurry would be likely to do, especially if he or she did not find any drugs or money on the premise."

Tarallo nodded, saying, "Yes, I would expect that if someone broke in looking for drugs or money and found none, they would have taken their anger out by destroying the lab."

"But the lab, for the most part, was intact, and that is when I noticed something odd. The thieves only took the embryos, not the vials containing the unfertilized eggs. It was very strange that they would leave those in place. Stranger still, they would know how to differentiate between them.

"Hmm. I do find that odd as well, Doctor. Why do you think they did that? Were the embryos stolen for profit for a black-market sale?" Tarallo asked.

"Normally, that would be my first conclusion, and that still may be the reason, but if the thieves wanted to profit, why not take the vials with eggs, as those could also be sold. They were specifically looking for embryos because embryos, while having financial value, may also become the new battleground on the right to life and the right to choose. The other odd thing was since I only have embryos shipped to me from our off-site storage facility for my patient's implantation cycles, the thieves were either very lucky or knew the only times each month when my clinic would be full of embryos."

"That is an interesting assumption, Dr. Brazini, but it seems to be a bit of a stretch that IVF centers have already become a battleground between pro-choice and pro-lifers, but the timing would tell me it was someone who had an intimate knowledge of how your business operates. If true, do you have a theory as to which group and their backers would have committed the crime?"

Turning to Detective Simon, Layla said, "Once we find a connection to who might have done it, we may find the why, but I will let Detective Simon cover what she has found with the online chatter, which may give us more insight in both areas."

Standing up to face the room, Simon said, "I know this is hard to believe, Lieutenant, but, in our job, you know we are never surprised about the human race's depravity or, in some cases, ingenuity. I mentioned when we started, we were going to cover the protest, the break-in, and some online information we have found to hopefully show you how all this ties together and how we have potentially one of the most complicated, politically explosive, and important cases to have fall into your department. The media, local, national and international, will jump all over it."

Rhonda especially wanted to both sensationalize this to Tarallo but also localize it to her area of responsibility, so Tarallo could see the spotlight that might shine on her and her department in this case, as big as it seemed to be, if it was solved by her team. Tarallo's body language and head nodding seemed to Rhonda to indicate that Tarallo knew how big the case could be for her and the department.

Rhonda had to thread the needle very carefully with this last piece of the puzzle as she had to carefully explain that the information she and Richard had found online was not some disinformation, A.I. false flags, or crackpot conspiracy chatter but, in fact, was a movement taking place, online and unfortunately in St. Louis and possibly other communities. She also wanted to avoid spooking Tarallo that the case was outside her local jurisdiction, which would cause Tarallo to bring in the feds. But Rhonda had her plan laid out, and she understood Tarallo's motivation. Tarallo did not get to take the credit for her department's most recent big case, the Alex Finnigan case, and Rhonda knew that Tarallo, like all humans, had a big ego to feed, and when Rhonda was done, Tarallo's ego would be well fed. She laid out the final piece of her case.

Chapter 24

Tarallo Makes Her Decision

"Before I share the next pieces of information," Rhonda began, "let me point out that the information I am presenting now was discovered by one of the most sophisticated private digital snoops in the U.S. I prefer this person to remain nameless for now as doing so allows us freer rein to go into the digital world in areas and ways that perhaps our police resources do not have the means to. I don't want this investigation to take a step backward by being forced to work with local resources that do not have the technical capabilities or smarts that my source possesses. Are you good with this, Lieutenant?"

"I am, as long as what you are learning is being legally obtained and you are not working outside my jurisdiction, like with the feds, for example. For that, Simon, I would cut you off at your knees. I will make that call if we need to bring the feds in. You got that, Simon?"

Simon nodded and was pleased that Tarallo was in line with the plan to keep this close to the vest, a plan that would benefit all of them personally if the case was solved. If the case got too big, too national in scope, Simon knew Tarallo would have no choice but to enlist the feds. Still, it was a private party for now, and only the women in this room were invited. However, Tarallo, if she still needed to, would find the digital snoop Rhonda was using. While Rhonda and Tarallo clashed because of their respective styles, Rhonda knew Tarallo was damn smart and, most importantly, a career climber who knew when to latch onto a big case for personal gain.

"Okay, my contact has dug up the following, and I will topline it for you. We can double back with any questions. First, while the protest in Tower Grove Park and outside Dr. Brazini's clinic was, on the surface, a local event, it had two out-of-town players influencing some of the actions that day. These out-of-town people of interest are Billy O'Dell and Marianne Hylany."

"Do any of these names ring a bell, Lieutenant?" Rhonda asked.

"O'Dell sounds vaguely familiar. Where could I have heard of him?"

"He is a far-right, southwest Missouri state representative who seems to have his sights set on bigger things than he can accomplish from his district near Branson. He has espoused some of the most severe views regarding women's reproductive rights and the outlawing of abortion in all circumstances and timeframes. He is a master on how to use online media and forums to stir up passions among his followers and hatred among his detractors."

"Ok, I get his M.O. What about the woman, Hylany? What is her role in this?"

"Contrary to what you might think, not all these troublemakers are right-wing oriented," Rhonda explained. "Let me introduce you to Marianne Hylany, who may not be a political climber like O'Dell but whose views from the left side of the cheering section are perhaps more dangerous and extreme because they are more violent."

"I am looking forward to meeting her. So far, your cast of lunatics is quite impressive," Tarallo said with a slight smile.

"Hylany," Rhonda stated, is five feet, four inches of pure terror and violence. She has an anger inside of her toward conservatives, primarily men, and frankly, it is hard to understand why since she came from a middle-class, stable background and did not seem to want for much in life. She is from a big family and was raised in Chicago. She went to school at Mizzou and majored in journalism and then went to Georgetown Law, where she graduated top of her class. She is a prolific writer and speaker with a tremendous online presence and following. Her most common theme is the overthrow of our current political and cultural system, fueled mainly by pushing equal rights and pay for all, especially women. She views the next century as the century of women and believes that women, and only women, should run the country and the world. Though, while probably painted as a radical liberal, to achieve her goals, she is surprisingly pro-gun and encourages women to arm themselves for the impending war."

"Wow. Let's hope these two don't end up in the same room together. I'm not sure who would survive, but I will put my money on Hylany as she is fueled by hate, not necessarily by political ambition and riches as O'Dell might be," Tarallo commented.

Simon added, "But here is the rub: in a way, they are already in the same room if you consider the room's digital forums, chat rooms, and dark web meet-up places. They share the same digital space, and while we don't know if they have met in person, they certainly have met online. But before you think about that shitstorm, let me introduce you to perhaps the true ringleader of them all. The woman who stirs the drink, fuels anger, incendiary passion, and, most importantly, calls to action. A woman who is only known by one name, Harvest."

Upon hearing the name, Tarallo laughed, "Seriously, the ringleader is a woman named Harvest. Is this a joke, Detective Simon?"

"Not a joke," Simon said with a solemn face. "If you read her manifestos, regardless of her name, she has tapped into the psyche of some of the most whacked-out people in the U.S. She has done it in such a way to stir intense anger between left and right, encouraging them to do battle to help her achieve her goals."

"And what goals would those be Detective Simon?"

"Now, you may laugh, but I am deadly serious and so are her followers. Her goals are to destroy this society and build a new one. She believes that her followers can cause the end of the world, and they then can help create a utopia that they all live in with like-minded harmony."

Tarallo asked, "I am almost afraid to know the answer, but how will she create a new society?"

"Well, to create a new society, you must destroy the existing one, so that is why she is advocating violence. The violence at the protest was just a small sample, maybe even a trial run. To create the new society, she believes that those who embrace her definition of goodness, or as she calls it, those who are purified from misguided values and principles, will be allowed to be part of her society."

"Ok, well, Harvest, or whatever her real name is, is not the first person to advocate violence or create a like-minded group of people who will be the future when the world is destroyed. We have had cults forever, Simon. I still am not hearing how this is all wrapped up together with the protest killing and the IVF robbery at Dr. Brazini's clinic. I am not sure any of this gets us closer to the triggerman or woman at the shooting, which is my biggest concern. I need to get a killer off the streets," adding, "This all seems a bit crazy, Simon. Are you sure you have had enough time off?"

That last comment stung Rhonda, but if it bothered her, she did not let on. Turning to Tarallo, Rhonda opened her laptop. She showed Tarallo the Harvest manifesto that Richard had dug up regarding targeting IVF Centers as the next battleground and the beginning of her new society. Tarallo read the posting slowly and said nothing, so Rhonda continued.

"I know, Lieutenant, reading what she wrote probably makes her sound even crazier and maybe makes me sound crazy to think it could happen, but remember how crazy Alex Finnegan was? Until the case was solved, could you believe that one person could play God like Finnegan tried to?"

Tarallo thought about what Simon had said and realized she was right. No one would have believed that Alex Finnegan was doing what he was doing had the case not been solved.

But before Tarallo could say anything, Dr Brazini spoke up. "Lieutenant, I know what Detective Simon said sounds insane, and what Harvest has posted sounds even more insane, but from a medical perspective, it's not insane if it's possible, and it is possible to harvest eggs or store embryos for later use. I see more and more women do this daily; they are not ready to be parents yet; still, they do this to have a family when the time is right. In theory, what Harvest is promoting now and encouraging her followers to do is to create future living beings through the storage of embryos, not necessarily by going through the IVF process themselves, but to use current embryos held in IVF centers around the U.S. that are fair game to achieve her utopia."

"Well, Doctor, as far-fetched as her scheme sounds, don't embryos have a shelf life or expiration date that would not make them viable?" Tarallo asked.

"Under the Human Fertilization and Embryology Act of 1990, IVF centers can store embryos for ten years, and now twelve because of Covid. In fact, if a woman at thirty creates embryos and waits to go through with implantation at age forty, the embryos she created are not ten years old. Biologically, they are still embryos made from the eggs of a thirty-year-old woman, and those embryos have a better chance of going to term than embryos used from eggs from a forty-year-old woman." Catching her breath, Layla added, "Embryos have emotional value to the parents who own them, they have financial value if they were stolen and sold to other desperate parents, and they may have some sort of social or societal value in the culture wars as ammunition for the next pro-choice vs. pro-life battle. Because of the problem of more women not being able to conceive naturally or choosing to delay when they want a live birth, the IVF industry around the world is exploding with hundreds of thousands of potential future humans available to anyone for any reason. The future of IVF could prosper or end depending on who wins the culture and legal wars over the embryos."

"If the pro-lifers got legislation to declare that all unused embryos are the beginning of life and, therefore, cannot be destroyed, couples creating these embryos would have to agree not to destroy the unused ones and donate them to other families or worse, perhaps, a government institution. If pro-choice legislation prevailed, a couple who created the embryos would have the sole decision on the disposition of unused embryos. And if they choose to destroy them, possibly hundreds of thousands of these embryos, which have financial and social value, would be off the market, so to speak. For someone who wants to change the course of history or become incredibly wealthy and powerful, protecting these embryos by creating legislation that takes away the rights of the actual owners is critical."

Tarallo took a deep breath before turning to the room. "Ok, while I still think this seems very farfetched, what you are telling me conceivably could happen. Not necessarily the end of the world per se or the start of a new civilization by Harvest, but the stealing of embryos for some other purpose, which more than likely might be for money and power. Simon, in your gut, do you feel that Harvest is behind all this?"

Thinking momentarily, Rhonda said, "Lieutenant, I think just as Harvest is trying to solicit foot soldiers in her supposed battle against current society, I think Harvest herself is only a foot soldier of some entity or someone who is much more well-financed and powerful. Some of the witness I interviewed said not to focus on Harvest herself; focus on her message and who might be behind that message."

Tarallo then turned to Layla. "Dr. Brazini, here is one thing I don't understand. You told me that in your break-in, they stole the embryos and not the unfertilized eggs, and for some reason, that might be significant in determining the 'why' and maybe the 'who' of the crime. Aren't a woman's unfertilized eggs of value as much as embryos?"

Layla answered, "Egg stealing, believe it or not, has happened since IVF was first used as a medical procedure, and unfortunately, most of the crimes were done by IVF doctors reselling eggs for profit or using stolen eggs in women who unknowingly could not produce viable eggs. Many IVF doctors and clinics get paid for how many embryos they insert into a woman. A patient will be charged per attempt. There are more unfertilized eggs than embryos, and embryos have more value to the couple who created them than to someone who wants their own baby. This is why eggs are stolen, and up until now, embryos are not. If vials of unfertilized eggs were stolen, then I would say this was a crime of profit. However, because only embryos were stolen, I would say this was a crime of passion, cultural righteousness or purification, and probably profit."

"Of whose passion, Doctor?" Tarallo asked.

"Based on Detective Simon's overview, it may be the passion of the followers of Harvest, thinking she is instructing them to create a new society by stealing embryos, or maybe something not even that outlandish. It may be the passions of those on either side of the right to life and choice debate trying to create chaos with the public on how to deal with unused embryos. You know, shine a light on a subject few people today are focused on. Since Roe v. Wade was overturned by the Supreme Court, there has been speculation that the next battleground will be embryos. Perhaps the theft of embryos was only for publicity to stir up passions or shine the spotlight on the issue, for now. Based on what I have read in the medical publications supporting the IVF industry, we and our patients must be prepared."

"Prepared in what way, Doctor?" Tarallo asked, now transfixed on the discussion.

"Prepared to either protect embryos from being destroyed or prepared to destroy the embryos from being used by others to create life from embryos they don't own. Those who believe life begins at conception, even in a test tube done via IVF, and want abortion outlawed at any stage of conception would want to protect the embryos from being destroyed by a couple or woman who perhaps no longer needs or wants to have any more children. Those who believe in the right to choose believe it is their decision or choice to destroy embryos rather than being forced to carry multiple pregnancies until their uterus wears out, or worse, forced to give up their embryos to strangers or the government, and have their offspring running around in the world," Brazini answered.

"And all of you believe this can happen?" Tarallo posed the question to the group.

Dr. Brazini spoke up first. "Yes, I believe it can happen so much that we are starting to not freeze the embryos but rather freeze the eggs and sperm separately and then fertilize each egg right before transplanting into the woman's uterus. It is more expensive, time-consuming, and possibly less successful for the couple. While the original reason was to put off pregnancy, now I hear from patients, especially younger ones, who want to avoid potential legal challenges to the ownership and disposal of their embryos. More of my patients than ever are doing just this. I had a young woman ask me recently if she destroyed her unused and unneeded embryos would she be liable for murder?"

Moloney who had been mostly quiet but was suddenly animated about the conversation said, "There is no way I would want my embryos to be used by others if I could not have any more children. My choice starts with my embryos, and if they are not embryos but just unfertilized eggs, then I avoid that conflict. Also, I am young and single, so I am not ready to have a family, but I certainly want the option in the future when I am ready to do so. I would just harvest my eggs for storage, and wait for the right partner or husband or go to a sperm bank."

"How about you, Simon? Where do you stand on all of this?" Tarallo asked.

"For me, it's simple, Lieutenant, money and power. God complex, and you and I have experience dealing with someone who had that. Plus, we may be the only people in the room who experience this firsthand and way too often. Whenever you think the world cannot be crazier, we are shown by what we see daily that it can and is becoming crazier. Whenever you think human depravity can't sink any lower, it does. We see this every day in our jobs. Crimes are more meaningless and random, where someone is killed for nothing. Plus, there is a huge rise in online hate speech, where seemingly normal people just follow a charismatic leader because they are lost in their lives, and if you consider how passionate this pro-life versus pro-choice debate has become, what we have discussed here can very well happen. While we initially look at unrelated crimes as singular events, when you start putting pieces together, you cannot assume that our protest murder and the break-in at the IVF Center are not connected in some way, maybe not physically as done by the same person, but philosophically, perhaps done by people with shared interests, Harvest followers, for example, or perhaps someone else."

Tarallo nodded in affirmation, then quietly asked, "Where do we go from here? How do we connect the dots on these two crimes, assuming they were connected?"

Simon answered, "I think the answer may start by learning all we can about the one person who I have not mentioned, Noah Sharpe, who is actually a local suspect because he was at the protest and because he seems to know Harvest intimately and says they are a couple."

"So, have you interviewed him? Can he connect Harvest to any of this?" Tarallo asked.

"I interviewed him briefly right after the protest shooting, and his mentioning Harvest got her on my radar screen. But I did not try to determine if he knew anything about the break-in at the clinic because until I got my online information, I did not make that connection," said Simon, adding, "And I think he is off his meds, and maybe delusional."

Tarallo, a bit exasperated, said, "Great. So far, our line-up is a local guy who may be delusional, some online end-of-times conspiracist, a right-wing political rabble-rouser and leftist out-of-town shit disturber looking to grow her influence." Then, knowing the answer before she asked her next question, Tarallo asked, "So now that we have a combination of physical suspects and online chatter tying perhaps several of these people together, what's stopping you from moving forward?"

Without a hint of smugness, Simon, with some humility, just said, "Lieutenant, rightfully, after I came back from suspension, you told me to focus my efforts on the protest shooting. I am a homicide cop, and that is what I do best, solve homicides. But if you think like I do, that perhaps we have something much bigger going on, I need to combine both investigations, the protest shooting and the clinic break-in case."

Tarallo sat silently, so Rhonda continued with what she knew Tarallo wanted to hear. "And Lieutenant, if you would allow it, I would like to team up with Moloney on tying all this information together. We work well together, and I think we can cover more ground and keep you in the loop more frequently. Plus while you want to keep this case close to the vest and local in your jurisdiction, I think this case could explode beyond St. Louis as soon as the media gets wind of it so speed is the essence so we can be in front of the case locally rather than behind it nationally," Rhonda said quietly, waiting to hear what she knew Tarallo would say.

Tarallo nodded. "Ok, Detective, you convinced me. You and Moloney team up. And Moloney, you will learn a lot from Simon, but make sure what you learn are the work aspects of the job, not her after-work habits. Good luck to both of you, and I want a weekly verbal report, or if something big comes up, daily. This is a big case for all of us. And if you find what you think you are looking for, let's figure out how we use the media to our advantage this time. Let's get after it."

With that, Tarallo got up from her chair, shook hands with Dr. Brazini while whispering something into her ear and then left the room. Simon, Moloney, and Dr. Brazini looked at each other silently, knowing they got what they wanted. Still, they had much work to do to stop several crazy people and perhaps thousands of their followers.

Chapter 25

INVESTIGATIVE ASSIGNMENTS GIVEN

After the Tarallo meeting, Rhonda invited Layla and Officer Moloney back to her house to huddle about the next steps and enlist Richard Leary's expertise more prominently in the investigation. They all felt that the large amount of online information he would uncover with some simple keystrokes would more quickly show a connection between the clinic break-in, the protest, and perhaps more significant incidents taking place soon, all under the direction of the mysterious Harvest or others.

Introducing Moloney first to Richard, he held his hand to her and told her he had heard good things about her from Rhonda. Richard's motto was flattery will get you everywhere, and he was a natural charmer. Then, noticeably more clumsily than she had planned, Rhonda introduced Richard to Layla, "Richard, this is Layla," pausing, "I mean Dr. Brazini, owner of the clinic that was robbed." Richard, sensing something had made Rhonda pause, simply said. "Nice to meet you, Doctor. May I call you Layla? I have heard so much about you from Rhonda. I already know you in a sense." He did not have to turn to Rhonda to sense her eyes were boring a hole in the back of his head. Whatever suspicions

Richard was trying to clarify, he knew Rhonda would call him out when they were alone together after everyone left.

After the introductions, Rhonda took the next ten minutes to get Richard up to speed on the meeting with Tarallo. After her summary, she outlined the game plan.

"Ok, we must attack this thing in teams because speed is of the essence. First, Moloney and I will do all the on-the-ground investigative work we can. We must press hard on the protest attendees, including the ones who went to the two bars afterward. Plus, we must re-interview and press harder all the bar staff to see if anybody else heard anything. Moloney, you take the lead on this."

"Next is Harvest and her relationship with Noah Sharpe. It seems he is our only local suspect and the only one who has talked to Harvest or seems to have a personal relationship with her. He is a direct link to Harvest, while everyone else I have talked to seems to just follow her online without really knowing her. I will lead that effort as I have talked to Sharpe already, and I think I can get into his head to tell me more."

"Dr. Brazini, while we can't have you actively involved in asking questions of our suspects, I would like you to tap into your professional network of IVF doctors, clinics, associations, etc., to hear if any other break-ins have been happening in other parts of the country." While Rhonda was speaking, Richard silently wondered why Rhonda suddenly referred to Layla's professional name instead of the more collegial first name she used during her introduction to him and again in front of the group. For some reason, he thought Rhonda was hiding some personal history with Layla Brazini. He knew his online snooping might have to dig a little bit into Rhonda's and Dr. Brazini's past to see where their paths crossed, but it was a web he would weave without arousing any suspicions from Rhonda.

As he thought about Dr. Brazini and Rhonda, he did not hear Rhonda call out his name to give him his assignments, "Richard, we will feed everything we find through me to you, so you can continue monitoring online chatter. I specifically want you to follow the comings and goings of Harvest, Noah Sharpe, Billy O'Dell, Marianne Hylany, and any others who join the party in a significant way and follow their online connections to each other and any other people of interest."

"Got it," Richard said, but in the back of his mind, he was already thinking perhaps that there would be other connections, ones between Rhonda and Layla Brazini, that would also occupy his time.

The meeting concluded with each of them knowing their assignments. However, just as Richard Leary had his suspicions about Layla Brazini, she was wary and untrusting of him. If he was as good as Rhonda said, he might uncover things in her past that would be best left unknown. She knew she must protect all her contacts, including her patients, friends, and IVF network. She did not need her life turned upside down again. Rhonda Simon had done that once and, with the help of Richard Leary, might do it again.

Chapter 26
MARIANNE HYLANY

Sasha's Wine Bar was one of Layla's favorite restaurants as it was her usual hang-out to meet up with many of her friends and colleagues. However, meeting in a private locale would be the more prudent move for what she had to discuss with two of her friends tonight. She pulled into the underground parking lot of The Plaza in Clayton Residences on Carondelet across from the Ritz-Carlton, one of the most prestigious and expensive residential buildings in the St. Louis area. Parking in a guest space, she pressed the elevator to the tenth floor, thinking how much she enjoyed her visits here, especially with all the great restaurants just a few steps away. Many a night, she got a little too tipsy to drive and spent the night at unit 1020. It had been several weeks since she was last here, and she was looking forward to catching up with the women she was closest to and decompressing over what happened to her clinic.

Pressing the doorbell, though she had her own key in case of emergencies or late-night frolicking, the door soon opened. Becca Stevens, radiant as ever, who had bought the condo to escape her husband during the divorce, greeted Layla with a warm embrace. Knowing all Layla had gone through, Becca let the hug continue as long as Layla needed it. After embracing for at least thirty seconds, Layla looked over Becca's shoulder. She saw another friend who made her smile, Becca's sister Lauren, the manager at Sasha's. After hugs between Layla and Lauren, all three settled into their chairs, enjoying a chilled bottle of wine Becca had opened. Before they could take a deep breath and catch up on their lives, careers, and loves, which they usually did when they got together, the doorbell rang again, and Becca got up to answer.

Entering the condo was someone Layla did not know. Becca and Lauren seemed to, but less socially and intimately than they did Layla. Becca did the introductions.

"Layla, this is someone Lauren and I thought you should meet. Marianne Hylany, meet Dr. Layla Brazini."

Despite her shock at coming face to face with Marianne Hylany, Layla was a little subdued when getting up to meet her. She approached her with trepidation because just earlier today, Hylany's name was talked about in earnest about a possible connection to the robbery at her clinic and the protests. Layla just extended her hand and shook Marianne Hylany's hand, hoping she was not telegraphing her uneasiness.

For her part, Marianne Hylany was nothing like the woman Rhonda described in her briefing with Tarallo. Rhonda practically described her as a domestic terrorist, perhaps one of the most dangerous women in the U.S., and here she was, about to spend the evening sipping wine with two of Layla's closest friends. Hylany also did not fit the image of what a domestic terrorist might look like. She was petite, barely over five feet tall. Instead of dressed in military camo, the outfit Layla conjured up in her mind, she was dressed like everyone else in the room, in a pair of black leggings, a stylish blouse, and fashionable boots. Also, Layla thought her language would be much cruder, but she complimented Becca about the décor in her condo, even pointing out correctly some of the artists that hung on the wall. Her use of language was precise and confident, much like the cadence of a college professor teaching a class.

Layla was unsure what to do, as she was unsure why Marianne Hylany was now sitting in the living room with Becca and Lauren. *"How the hell do Becca and Lauren even know Hylany?"* Layla thought, *"and what the hell am I supposed to do? Leave, call Rhonda?"*

While Layla was mulling in her head what options she had, Becca walked Hylany around the condo, pointing out some of the views from the windows and some of the additional art and sculptures Becca had displayed. After a few minutes, all four women sat down, and quickly, Becca broke the ice because she could sense some confusion on Layla's face. However, what Becca did not know was how familiar Layla was already with Hylany, primarily through the descriptions and background Detective Simon had shared. Layla would keep that information to herself until the evening unfolded a bit more.

"Ladies, we have some more wine ready to be opened, and I have some appetizers I will bring out, but I wanted to explain why we are here and why I invited Marianne to join us."

"First, Layla, as background, Marianne and I, and of course, Lauren, all went to Mizzou together about twenty years ago, though it seems longer. After Mizzou, I went to Wharton at the University of Pennsylvania for my MBA, and Marianne went to Georgetown Law School. While we kept in touch sporadically over those last twenty years since Mizzou, we reconnected with more urgency and purpose over the few months. I asked Marianne to come to meet with us, especially you, Layla, since the break-in at the clinic."

Layla thought about Becca describing her reunion with Hylany with the word's urgency and purpose. *"What did that mean?"* she wondered.

"Marianne, Layla, is one of my closest friends in St. Louis. She is a professional peer, as she and I have gotten so close because we share many of the same values and experiences in life. Values and experiences that you also share, Marianne, and I thought it would be great to have you two meet, especially since Layla's clinic was robbed."

Now, Layla was perplexed and almost wanted to bolt from the room. *"Shared values with Marianne Hylany, a supposed domestic terrorist? What was Becca talking about?"*

But Layla suppressed any response indicating her growing concerns. She casually said, "Well, a friend of Becca's is, of course, a friend of mine."

Hoping to manage the conversation more, she asked Marianne, "Are you from St. Louis, Marianne?"

"No, I am actually from Chicago, or at least grew up there, and I keep it as my home base, but I roam a lot for my job, so I'm not sure where I would call home nowadays."

"What do you do?" Layla asked.

Laughing, Hylany answered, "Well, some people who don't like me would call me a domestic terrorist or political agitator, but my friends who know me just call me a social disruptor for just causes."

Upon hearing that, Layla spit out the wine she sipped, laughing to cover up her embarrassment.

Becca said, "Well, that is the normal response when people first meet you, isn't it, Marianne?" That comment caused Becca, Marianne, and Lauren to all double up laughing. Perhaps the laughter lightened Layla's dread, and she was suddenly more comfortable with the situation and the conversation. It might have also been the wine that was taking effect.

"Let me explain a little more, Layla, but please take a sip of wine and swallow it this time since you sprayed me just now." This time, there was laughter from all four women.

As she did, Becca got up to prepare appetizers for the group and grabbed another bottle of wine. Layla then asked Hylany, "I am not sure I have drunk enough wine to hear about your domestic terrorist job, so let's stick with the social disruptor. What is that?"

"I work to change the status quo. I do this through political, social, cultural, educational, and business activities. Much like you, Becca, and Lauren do. In fact, all women must be social disrupters to keep all our advancements and earn more of them."

"Ok, well, maybe domestic terrorists would have been easier to understand. How are all of us social disrupters?" Layla asked with a degree of seriousness.

"Well, you started an IVF clinic to help women or couples who can't conceive naturally to start a family. Many people in this country applaud and need you, while many hate what you are doing, calling it the devil's work. Mixing science with nature. Doing only what God should be allowed to do. Am I right, Layla?"

Layla answered introspectively, "Yes. You are right. I think I am doing something noble, but some think I should be locked up. Not so much now, but when IVF was such a new concept, the early pioneers were either praised or scorned."

"Hold that thought, Layla, because what was past becomes current. What goes around comes around. History repeats itself. All these idioms apply to what you do. To continue doing what you do, you are labeled a disrupter or agitator by those who don't agree with IVF. Becca is the same way. She is a successful entrepreneur who has fought against the glass ceiling to get what she deserves. Some people don't like that. Isn't that right, Becca?" Hylany said, calling into the kitchen.

Yelling back, Becca said, "That's right, Marianne. In years past, I used to be just called a bitch. But I think 'agitator' fits me better. I know I piss off banks, my business partners, lawyers, etc., demanding they treat me like they would treat a man in my position. I fight political, social, and legal battles every day. Sometimes I fight against men, but sometimes it is against women who think I am too uppity. I fight harder than a man in the old boys' club would have to fight. I even fight to get allowed to join certain clubs. Hell yes, I am an agitator and proud of it!"

Lauren then laughed out, "Sis, you are still a bitch to me."

The wine seemed to be getting to everyone's head a bit, but Layla noticed, not to Marianne Hylany's. Although she was drinking wine, she seemed stone cold, sober and focused. It unnerved Layla a bit but also impressed her. She wanted to tell Marianne Hylany that she was on the radar in a police investigation but stayed quiet. She felt she would learn more by staying quiet, and secondly, she had a sense Hylany knew and frankly could care less if she was on anyone's radar. Layla was very successful and was around confident women daily, but Marianne Hylany exuded something else. Power. Strength. Someone to be feared. Layla wanted to learn more, so she asked an innocuous question.

"So, Marianne, what brings you to St. Louis? Disruption, agitation, or terrorism?" Layla asked in a way that she wanted to seem like a lighthearted joke, but the minute the words left her mouth, she could see from the reactions of Lauren and Becca that Hylany did not take it as such. Nothing was lighthearted with Hylany.

"Interesting question, Layla, but before I answer you directly," looking at a nodding Becca and Lauren for confirmation that she could trust Layla, she said, "let me ask you something. What are you the angriest about with the break-in and robbery of your clinic?"

"I am angry at being violated but more so that my patients' lives were violated by someone who has no regard for the pain and suffering they just put my patients and their families through. I will recover, monetarily and from a business standpoint, but my patients may never recover. Whoever did this took away my patient's futures. That is what I am most angry about."

"You know, Layla, you sound just like the talking points of someone who is pro-life and believes aborting a fetus is taking away the future of that fetus, but my guess is someone in your line of work is actually pro-choice. Believing a woman has the right to do what she chooses with her own body."

"That is interesting that you heard it that way, and I guess that makes sense, but I am very strongly pro-choice," said Layla.

"Whether you or your fellow IVF peers and your IVF patients are pro-choice or pro-life, what you need to do is start taking a side and, based on that side, become a social disrupter and political agitator. Whether you like it or not, you and your colleagues in that line of work will be the new battleground of future Roe v. Wade battles, and if you want to protect your patients, you must protect their rights to do what they choose with their embryos. But the irony of that is some of your patients will want to destroy unused embryos, which is their right, and some will want to protect them or put them up for adoption, which is also their right. But more importantly, outsiders will try to make that decision for them. Lawyers and courts will be telling you and your patients what you can and cannot do with those embryos. But before that happens, other social disrupters, other political agitators, and other domestic terrorists will be trying to make these decisions for you and your patients. That is what happened at your clinic last week. You are not the first clinic in the U.S. to be robbed. There are others who, whether they know it now or not, are already in the middle of this cultural battle. They will experience the destruction or saving of embryos for political and social purposes."

Hylany stopped talking for a minute to sip on a glass of water Becca had silently put in front of her. The air was tense, anticipating where this conversation would take, not only Layla, but all of the women in this room, three of them whose friendships and possibly future interests would be intertwined for better or worse.

Finally, Layla spoke. "That was a very interesting take on things," made more interesting, Layla thought, as it was just what Layla and Rhonda had discussed with Lieutenant Tarallo a few hours ago. "But you did not answer my original question. What are you doing in St. Louis, and why were you invited to Becca's place to have this conversation with me?"

Chapter 27
SOCIAL DISRUPTION

"So, what was she doing in St. Louis?" Marianne thought about Layla's question, wondering how to answer it without scaring off an important ally she hoped Layla would become. She decided to wade into the conversation carefully.

"I came in town hoping to run into an old friend of mine, Billy O'Dell."

"Billy O'Dell." Did she just say she came into town hoping to meet yet another person under suspicion in Rhonda's investigation? This was getting too heavy, too real, but Layla was too intrigued to stop. If Rhonda knew that Layla was with Marianne Hylany and was close to linking Hylany and Billy O'Dell together, she would shit herself. Layla decided the best course of action was to continue asking questions because she was still trying to figure out where this was headed. When she last left Rhonda, it was clear that O'Dell and Hylany were on opposite sides of the issues.

"Well, were you able to connect with him?" Layla asked.

"No, I just missed him. We were supposed to be here for the same event, but I got in late, and he probably left early. I will cross paths with him again as we are in the same line of work."

With that statement, it was almost as if Hylany was goading Layla to ask the elephant-in-the room question, so she did.

"So, is he a social disrupter or political agitator as well?" Layla asked.

"First, he is a class "A" asshole, but, yes, he is a social disrupter and political agitator. A very good one. A very powerful one. And a very dangerous one."

Layla asked carefully, knowing the answer to her next question, and hoping Hylany was not onto her ruse. "So, what event were you supposed to be at?" As she did, she looked at Becca and Lauren because she knew they were at the protest. She was looking for hints from them to drop the subject. Still, they were silent as they sensed Layla and Hylany were subtly probing each other, like lionesses, to understand where they each stood.

"We were supposed to attend the Tower Grove Park protest last Saturday. Billy stirred up the crowd with his favorite pro-life catch phases but then left the scene before the shooting. He has always been a pussy as long as I have known him."

"And how long have you known him?"

"About 20 years. We went to Mizzou together. Becca might have known him as well." She looked at Becca to see if she would acknowledge that fact, which she did with a nod. But Becca and Lauren were satisfied to sit back and watch Layla and Marianne play this little chess game.

"So, I take it Billy O'Dell is a long-lost acquaintance but not necessarily a long-lost friend?" Layla asked, knowing the answer, of course.

With a mischievous smile, Hylany said, "Well, if I could. I would cut his balls off and shove them down his throat. I hope that clears up my feelings towards him." Looking at Becca in a lighthearted tone, she asked, "Becca, how about another glass of wine. Layla needs one to hear the other reason I am in town."

Looking intently at Marianne, Layla then called out to Becca. "I am ready to hear the truth but forget the wine. Hard truths go down much easier with a glass of bourbon on the rocks."

After the drinks were served, everyone took several sips and then exhaled, waiting for what was to be a dramatic telling of the truth. Marianne Hylany did what she did best. Inspire passion in impassioned women.

Layla Brazini was unsure how long she had been listening to Marianne Hylany as she was mesmerized by what Hylany had told her. Had it been minutes or hours? After looking at her watch, she realized she had been transfixed by what Marianne had told her for over an hour. She told Layla of the struggle she was fighting, not just for herself or women, but for humankind. Like many strong and successful women, Marianne found a receptive and willing audience in Layla Brazini. Lauren and Becca had assured Marianne that not only would Layla Brazini be receptive to her call to action, but she would also be invaluable because of her role as a doctor in the IVF field. They knew that Layla was a born leader. While it was a shame that her clinic had to be robbed and lives potentially taken for her to be more open to this message, Hylany understood that the loss Layla Brazini and her patients suffered would be building blocks to a movement more significant than they all could imagine.

Marianne laid out to Layla who she thought broke into her clinic and why they did it. "I, and many more like me, believe your clinic break-in was the beginning of an assault, started by some pro-life supporters and some Christian conservatives that would take place around the country. The break-in and others like it were a warning shot to people out there who foolishly believed they would be allowed a choice, especially as it applied to human life, whether the human life was an embryo conceived in a test tube or in a woman's womb. When it comes to embryos and the formation of human life, people who are pro-choice would be considered, not only on the wrong side of current and future laws, but also the laws of God. Additionally, the use of IVF to use science to circumvent God's will incense even a more conservative faction of the pro-life crowd. These are people who believe strictly in the teaching of the Bible, and to use science to conceive through a test tube, in their opinion, is an abomination. Another abomination is gays using IVF to create life."

Taking a breath and a sip of bourbon, Hylany continued, "Additionally, because IVF might create multiple embryos, those who use it seem, to some pro-lifers, to be more representative of how animals would breed versus humans. All of this conflict on the use of science, the turning against God's will, and the ability to create multiple embryos, including weeding out genetic abnormalities and picking a specific gender, drive people crazy. Now, the biggest issue, especially since pro-lifers temporarily had the wind in their sails after the Roe v. Wade decision, is the clinics and the woman's ability, if she chooses, to destroy those embryos and end life. While the most fanatical of the pro-lifers, especially the ultra-conservatives, believe that these women should be forced to personally use every embryo themselves and establish large, loving families; short of that, they believe the embryos should never be destroyed. If they are, those that destroy them, either the clinic or the patient, would be a murderer. In fact, they are mass murderers in the eyes of the religious right. They would not let an embryo be destroyed. If not used by the woman and man whose eggs and sperm created the embryo, then they should be required by law to give them away to couples, preferably to one comprised of a white Christian man and a woman, who want to start a family. Science may have created these test tube miracles. However, laws now and in the future, pushed more frequently by extreme right politicians in the state houses around the country, would give more rights to the embryo to become a human, a product of God, than the man and woman who created and technically own the embryo."

Becca chimed in, partly to give Marianne a breather but also to add, "Layla, part of my divorce fight is about my right to make decisions about my embryos, as you know, and Marianne has been giving me insight on why it is so important that I protect my right to do so. And if I need money for lawyers' fees, which I don't, I could count on Marianne and her allies to back me."

"Marianne," Layla asked, "I could possibly understand the reason for taking the embryos but transporting them and storing them to be viable for a long period is a very complicated and, may I say, costly endeavor. No crazy pro-lifer off the street, no matter how wealthy or how motivated, would have the scientific know-how to do that."

"Layla, that answer is simple. Not every owner of an IVF center believes in pro-choice or even morally believes they could destroy the embryos if the couple does not want them. I know the disposition of unused embryos is part of the contract the couple signs with the IVF clinics. Still, you and I know historically there have been a few cases of IVF doctors either impregnating eggs with their own sperm or sold eggs and probably embryos on the black market. Where there is money, there is motivation, and an IVF doctor or technician, I am sorry to say, is human, and as such, possesses the ability to commit a crime whether for money, political or religious beliefs."

Layla had not considered her stolen embryos might be in the hands of a pro-life IVF owner, or sympathizer. However, she knew what Marianne said to be true, as a few doctors did unscrupulous things to fatten their pocketbooks over the years. In conversations she had had with many doctors at IVF conventions, the topic of destroying the embryos had always been a sensitive one, and many doctors weighed their contractual obligation against perhaps their religious beliefs. She had learned over the last several years that regardless of the education level or societal level attained, people's views on things were multi-faceted and contradictory. Many brilliant scientists and doctors were against vaccines, not because they thought they were ineffective, but because they did not want them to be forced on people. Some doctors put science and patient care second to political beliefs and lining their pockets. She guessed that the same thing could be happening in her business. Many IVF centers were owned by doctors who were devout Catholics or very much pro-life, and she knew they really agonized over the destruction of the embryos or eggs. Layla and her other IVF clinic owners reviewed the embryo options with all their patients. Still, Layla wondered if a pro-life doctor tried to steer their patients to give the unused embryos up or, in fact, never destroyed them when contractually they were required to. Layla knew from her own feelings that she wished so many times the patients would give up the embryos for medical research. Many did, but at the end of the day, it was their choice, and that choice is what Layla firmly believed in.

"Marianne, let me play devil's advocate for a minute. You outlined why you think my break-in and possibly others are being conducted or influenced by pro-lifers and the religious right zealots. They might be, but as you and I know, others have their own agenda, maybe for profit or to ensure their rights are not taken away. You are very passionate about your beliefs and agenda, but have you ever thought that as passionate as those people are about protecting the rights of the unborn, there may be others who are passionate about protecting their choice before it is taken away from them?"

"Like whom?" Marianne asked.

"Like people who have multiple embryos in storage who have had a few successful IVF births and are slowly aging out of their interest and ability to conceive another child. Maybe those people are fearful of losing their rights to do what they want with their embryos and, more importantly, fearful of legal consequences if they exercise their right to destroy them. I think some of my patients worry about this, especially because Missouri is turning ultra-conservative. State reps like O'Dell and others in Jefferson City, our state capitol, are starting to talk about charging those who have an abortion with murder. I think my patients are wondering whether they will be charged with murder if they destroy their embryos. So maybe my patients who know they don't want any more kids and who don't want their viable embryos given to the highest bidder are deciding now to destroy them before they no longer have the choice," Layla answered.

"But if these people were behind your break-in, why go to all the trouble? Why not just make the call to destroy the embryos they own? Why would they go through an elaborate break-in and systematically remove all the vials containing embryos?"

Layla countered, "Well, for a couple of reasons. First, maybe to make a point, to create a false flag and point the finger at someone else, to rally and wake up the pro-choice troops who never thought they would lose their right to choose. Sort of like what countries do, when they create a fake incursion of a foreign enemy on their land to get their citizens believing they have been attacked and should declare war. Or maybe, these people want to protect their rights and make a buck out of it. Many couples spend upwards of $100,000 or more going through IVF, especially if they want multiple births or had trouble in the first few rounds of IVF. Maybe they figure they own their embryos to do what they wish, including selling them off for financial payback to them for their pain and misery. A good friend of mine once said, 'all crime is tied back to money,' and perhaps that is the motivating factor to whomever might have stolen them, pro-choice, pro-life, or just couples, medical providers, or other outsiders who just see a way to make some serious money. All these people, for all these reasons, are just like you, Marianne, social disrupters."

"We can always use more social disrupters" was Marianne's response.

It was getting late, but Layla asked Marianne to share what she knew about IVF break-ins in other parts of the country. This information would be of value to Rhonda and Richard. The answer that Hylany gave Layla was unsettling.

"Unfortunately, it is beginning to happen nationwide, which is why I am on the road so much. I used to go to cities to participate in pro-life vs. pro-choice protests, and I still do that. Often, either before or after a protest, I learn that an IVF break-in has occurred in the city where the protest also occurred. That is part of the reason I came to St. Louis," Marianne said.

"I thought you came to track down Billy O'Dell?" Layla asked.

Hylany just smiled at that last comment, and Layla was unsure why. Perhaps because what Layla said was true and possibly the real reason why Marianne Hylany was in St. Louis or perhaps because it gave Marianne Hylany another idea.

"I did. I try to see him in every city I visit because where there is a protest, there is Billy O'Dell."

"Are they all connected?" Layla asked. "Are the protests part of the IVF break-ins, and is Billy O'Dell part of both?"

"Perhaps it's only a coincidence that the IVF break-ins occur close in time to organized protests. Still, something tells me it is not a coincidence," Marianne answered.

Layla now had a feeling of dread in the pit of her stomach that, while she had bought into some of the things Hylany was saying and wanted to join up with her on the crusade she was on, at some time, she would have to fess up to Rhonda about what she now knew and who was giving her this information. But how could she do that and keep Hylany's name out of it? Layla did not want Rhonda to know she was meeting with Hylany, but she also wanted to be honest with Becca, Lauren, and now Marianne about how involved she was with Rhonda and others in this case. She had listened to Rhonda about her suspicions, and now, in a way, Marianne confirmed that Rhonda may be on the right track.

She thought the best course of action was to bring her relationship with Rhonda and the investigation out in the open and get input from the three women in this room to whom she was beginning to feel a unique closeness. Becca and Lauren Stevens were Layla's closest friends, and she was extremely loyal to them. Also, she did not want to endanger them as potential co-conspirators with Hylany. They were all smart, with deep convictions and passion but so was Rhonda. But only recently had Layla begun reconnecting with Rhonda. Layla was still scarred from their shared past and unsure if she would ever forgive or trust Rhonda again. Layla also believed that honesty always won out. Still, she wanted to let this play out before determining how to tell the truth about what she knew and where her loyalties lay. Layla did not know where all this would end, and when it did, who would remain close to her and stay in her life.

While Layla was lost in her thoughts, Becca broke them up by noting that it was nearly 10:30 and she was wiped out and ready for bed. Lauren indicated the same. Trying to determine how much time she had before she would have to be honest with Becca, Lauren, and Marianne, Layla wondered how much time Hylany would be spending in St. Louis; Layla figured the longer she stayed in town, the greater the possibility that Rhonda and Hylany would cross paths. Layla knew that Rhonda was too good of a detective not to discover Hylany was nearby. With Richard Leary doing his online snooping and tracking magic, it might be only hours before he tracked down where Hylany was located and digitally who she was talking to online. Knowing what she knew about Rhonda and Richard's tenacity, she decided to ask Marianne a few more questions and give her a subtle warning.

"So, Marianne, it was great talking to you, and we will have to continue this another time. Are you in town for a few more days?" Layla asked.

"No, I leave tomorrow to head up to Minneapolis and then out west for a few weeks. I know they are having a protest in Minneapolis the day after tomorrow, and I want to be up there ahead of time to see if my good friend Billy O'Dell will be there whipping up the crowd. I will stay a few days to monitor any IVF clinic activity."

Layla thought that would get Hylany out of the area and out of sight of Rhonda for a while, which was good.

"I am curious, Layla. Do you know any owners of IVF clinics up in Minneapolis?" Marianne asked.

Layla knew several peers who owned clinics up there but decided not to tell Marianne about them because she was unsure if she wanted to get her peers involved with Hylany. She would, however, give them a heads up on the break-in at her clinic without going into all the other points of information and theories she was now collecting and now seemed to be in the middle of. Instead, she told Marianne a little white lie.

"You know, at conferences, I have met some folks from up there, but I would not say I know them more than a five-minute cocktail party conversation. Can't really help you, unfortunately."

"I understand," was all that Hylany said, but how she said it indicated to Layla that she did not believe her. Hylany could read people, and she read instantly that Layla was holding something back.

Saying their good nights and promising to all meet again, Dr. Layla Brazini and professional shit disturber Marianne Hylany left Becca's condo and departed into the night to their homes and to ventures unknown.

Chapter 28
BILLY O'DELL

While Marianne Hylany knew how to inspire passion in people for a cause, Billy O'Dell also possessed above-average skills in the same area. He had to keep track of his Missouri constituent's acceptance and support of his ideas. He tested his hard-right ideas within Missouri, then, he would bring the ones that got the most positive reception to the national stage, which was always Billy's end goal. While Billy O'Dell started out as just a small-town insurance salesman, going nowhere, his ambitions took hold once he ran for and became a Missouri state representative, riding the deep red cultural wars favored by his southwest Missouri constituents. As his term began, he and his constituents initially focused their ire on overreach and mask mandates, then overall government interference in citizens' lives. Still, now that the pandemic was over, and while minor culture wars erupted over things like transgender rights, Billy knew the core of his power was ensuring Roe v. Wade ended. With it, abortion would forever disappear as an option for all women. But once the Supreme Court overturned Roe v. Wade as a national mandate and turned it over to individual states, Billy sensed the steam was dissipating from a cause that galvanized so many of his followers. He needed a new, but closely aligned, cause and enemy.

Billy knew the evangelical Christians, which were widely represented in his district, at the end of the day, were total hypocrites but not as hypocritical as Billy. They wanted the government to stay out of their lives and not force decisions like masks and vaccines on them but wholeheartedly agreed with the government stepping into other peoples' lives by deciding It should have a say over what a woman can do with her body. Anything in their mind to outlaw abortion was worth being hypocritical over. Hell, they held their noses and voted known liars and philanderers as leaders because they wanted conservative Christian domination of the U.S. Supreme Court. They ignored transgressions, saying all of us were sinners, and God was there to help sinners repent. Billy always feared they would walk away from him if they knew what he was like and what he had stood for and done in his past. But his past remained hidden, and in his first election, in part because of his radical ideas including charging women with murder if they have an abortion out of state, he got eighty-nine percent of their vote, so right now, Billy felt emboldened to do whatever he wanted, and what he wanted was taking shape, especially after the St. Louis protest and IVF clinic break-in.

Billy O'Dell loved chess, and in life, he was a master chess player, moving his pawns in places to do his bidding, mowing down the defenses so he and others like him could come in and crush the more serious opposition. But one of the opposition, a woman from his past, would be taken care of personally by Billy O'Dell like he had done so many years ago while a student at Mizzou.

While Billy and Marianne Hylany had left each other's orbit twenty years ago, Billy kept track of her from afar, and he imagined or hoped that she would keep track of him. Despite their differences, their passion for each other burned hot until it didn't. Frankly, he hoped they would reconnect under different circumstances, but they never stayed in touch, and both went on in their lives.

But Marianne Hylany was different than any other woman Billy had known. She was an intellectual equal to Billy, but with more pure fire, drive, and conviction deep in her soul. Billy was just an opportunist. After she left Billy and Mizzou behind, she went on to do great things or at least great things based on liberal beliefs. After she earned her law degree from Georgetown, she joined the attorney general's office in Maryland, then became legal counsel to several human rights groups, and finally to a grassroots-driven cause that gave her national prominence as a liberal political agitator. Billy had to hand it to Marianne; she had made a name for herself nationally before Billy had. In fact, Billy guessed Marianne had an FBI file on her before Billy had one on him, if such a thing existed. Marianne Hylany, while opposed to almost everything Billy stood for in college and even more so now, was, ultimately, a brilliant, passionate, fearless leader who could incite great emotion in people, just like she did in Billy when she first met him after a political debate and post-debate party at college. But now, Marianne Hylany was an adversary of Billy O'Dell. After college, they traveled widely different roads, yet their paths converged, and soon they would meet again. But now lives were at stake, many lives, and all hell was about to erupt to make amends for not only what happened twenty years ago but for what would be happening around the country today.

Chapter 29

NOAH SHARES WITH HARVEST

While the night for Layla was ending, it was just beginning for Noah Sharpe, who had driven back to St. Louis from his family compound. He was brimming with excitement as he would try and connect with Harvest this evening to tell her how much progress he had made. In the last four months, he had been back and forth from Ottery twenty times. He delivered almost everything Harvest expected from him. Noah was so excited to be able to talk with Harvest again as so much had happened both at Ottery and locally with the break-in at the IVF clinic and the protest shooting. Noah felt he had earned Harvest's trust, but more importantly, since it was personal, he had earned her admiration and perhaps love.

Harvest, like Noah, seemed to be a night owl because it was the only time of day Noah could reach her. Noah often tried to reach Harvest during all hours of the day by sending her personal messages. She only connected with him late in the evening and early morning hours. He assumed she was so busy spreading her message to her other followers that she saved the night to talk with him. And tonight would be a special night as Harvest promised Noah that they would video chat rather than just send instant messages to each other or talk on shared chat threads. Waiting for Harvest, Noah spent the evening catching up on his on-line *NoahItAll* social, cultural, and sports commentary postings. Soon he knew those postings would be a thing of the past. His online friends and followers would gain a new sense of awe when talking to Noah because he, and not anyone else, had been chosen by Harvest. His online commentators were now the losers in Noah's mind. Not Noah. Not anymore. He was so nervous waiting for her that while not a big drinker, he sipped on a few glasses of whisky, which softened his eyelids enough that he was sound asleep when his computer pinged, indicating Harvest was on a video chat and ready to connect with Noah.

Groggily, he clicked the link, and there she was, beautiful as always, and she was a woman who was all his for the first time in his life.

On-screen, Harvest looked like she was in a bedroom, perhaps in a hotel or in her home, sitting on the couch, comfortable and very sexy. However, as far as Noah was concerned, she could be in a parking lot dressed in sweatpants. He was so hot for her it did not matter where she was, how late it was, or how she was dressed. *"How late was it? Where was she making this call from?"* he wondered because every time he talked to her online, he tried to envision himself being where she was, sharing her life and her home. While the words tumbled randomly from Noah, Harvest was always so concise and crisp whenever talking to Noah.

"Noah. Are you ready for me? How are your plans going?"

Noah responded excitedly, "I have been doing what you have asked me to do at a perfect place where our plans will be secret until they are completed."

Harvest asked, "Is it secluded?"

"It's very private, and it's a place that meant so much to me when I was younger, but it will mean even more to me now, as an adult being there with you." Noah talked for a full ten minutes about his childhood escape, Ottery.

"Harvest, you will love it. We will love it. It was my family's second home, a retreat for my father and mother. It is ninety miles southwest of

St. Louis at the beginning of the Ozark Mountains, which are more hills now. Over three hundred acres are crisscrossed with clear, cool streams and hillsides where the orchards my family planted years ago continue to bear all the fruit we may need. Also, while much of the land is rocky, my mother and father, when they were alive, cleared acres and acres of rich soil to plant vegetables that we would store in our root cellar. My father built several houses designed to function off the grid, with all the power we needed coming from the sun and batteries and the water coming from the heavens. While it has fallen under some bad times since my parent's death, I have been making the property what it once was, and we can all live there in peace and harmony. Just like you want us to, Harvest."

"And we can live peacefully without government interference or even knowing we are there?" Harvest asked.

"Yes. There is only one way to get to the property: an unmarked road hidden from any paved highway. Besides, any neighbors or law enforcement that may be aware of the property will probably be patriots and support us for what we are trying to do. Not only will they leave us alone, but I think they will join us," Noah answered enthusiastically.

Noah was excited, talking about the plans Harvest and he had discussed. He was proud that he was accomplishing something that someone important in his life had asked him to do. However, he was troubled that Harvest still seemed to keep him on the periphery of her life, and she determined when they would talk and when they would meet. And while he was emotional and enthusiastic when talking to her, Harvest was more stoic. All business, Noah observed. Thinking about this, he started to go into the dark place he had gone to when he was most lonely. Were there other men in Harvest's life that she was involved with? Did she also count on others to help her with her plans? Were the others also involved with Harvest personally? Noah knew she had thousands of followers online, and he was sure there may be others that Harvest was also close to. Darkness and bad thoughts continued to envelop him as they did most nights.

Harvest was silent, her image flickering on screen. Noah wanted to make sure Harvest knew how he felt.

"When will we finally be together? You know I love you and need and want you so badly. I am out of my mind thinking about you every waking hour." Now Noah was almost pleading with Harvest to be his, now and forever."

Finally responding, Harvest said, "Noah, you and I will be together for eternity. We, our children, and our followers will live in utopia. Just trust me, Noah, and always do what I ask of you."

A smile crept across Noah's face. Harvest always knew the right things to say to him. "Noah, before I go, here are your next assignments. You need to take care of them as you have done all the others. Continue having faith and patience, Noah." And with that, the screen went dark, and Noah was content and happy again. He slept blissfully, although, he would get up in less than two hours, but he did not care. His life would change forever. Harvest was his, and only his, and the family he lost when his parents died would become born again, thanks to Harvest.

Chapter 30

RICHARD FINDS MORE CONNECTIONS

In her direct, almost militaristic manner, Rhonda had marshaled the troops, Richard, Officer Moloney, and Layla Brazini, and given them their assignments to continue working on the parallel cases of the protest shooting and the IVF clinic break-in. Richard could see the wheels turning inside Rhonda's head as she tried to piece together all that she knew and did not know, but the wheels were also turning inside Richard's head. His job was to monitor the online chatter and determine if the local cases were connected and with whom, but more importantly, to determine if this was a one-off local incident or the spread of a more significant nationwide conflict.

Richard knew from his work as an online snoop that there was no such thing as a "lone wolf," as the police and media pundits liked to label killers. There was too much influence with online chat rooms, the dark web, and fanatical organizations sowing seeds of hate for anyone who lived online not to be influenced by what they hear and read. Richard knew that any mass shooting or hate crime, whether it be against Jews, Blacks, LGBTQIA, liberals, or conservatives, began with the killer reading a manifesto or two written or espoused by people who shared the same view of hate and violence. While thousands may share the views, it only took one totally fucked-up, crazy person to act on those views. Richard's job was to find the totally fucked-up, crazy person or persons, but to do that, he had to find the one connection between one person and another or one conversation among thousands of conversations, which was as difficult as finding a unique snowflake in a snowstorm.

He would discover what Rhonda would need him to discover. But for his own curiosity, he planned to discover something that perhaps Rhonda did not want him to discover: the relationship between her and Layla Brazini. In a way, it was none of Richard's business because Rhonda certainly had a life before she knew Richard, but what exactly was Rhonda's relationship with Layla, and why had it remained dormant and hidden for so many years, only to reemerge now? As it reemerged, Richard could tell that Rhonda, while not hiding or denying its existence, was undoubtedly not forthcoming about its origins or why it remained somewhat hidden in Rhonda's current life. Was Layla a past friend, work associate, or something more. A dalliance with Rhonda, who perhaps tried a relationship with a woman?

Or was Rhonda related to Layla in some way? He could easily explore that as Rhonda was open about her life growing up in rural Missouri and her relationship with her parents and sisters. If Rhonda was to become important to Richard, and she certainly had, she would have to come clean with him at some point. Of course, Rhonda would expect the same from Richard, to become clean with her on his past, which he was not embarrassed about, but he was concerned his past deeds and sins would scare Rhonda off.

So, putting his personal investigation of Rhonda and Layla aside for the time being, Richard turned his attention to finding out more information about the main people of interest. He knew if he focused on the typical criminal motivators of passion, power, and money, he would connect the dots, and those dots would lead him to the culprit or culprits in these crimes.

Richard had focused his research on the three principal characters that seemed to be leaders connected and active online: Harvest, Billy O'Dell, and Marianne Hylany, but he also focused on Noah Sharpe, who would not be considered a leader, more of a follower, but perhaps this trait made him the "lone wolf" or the local dupe that one of these individuals used to achieve their objectives. Richard had learned that each of them had a shared commitment to a battle centered around pro-life vs pro-choice. However, they also discussed or shared information about IVF centers being a part of future battles. The most significant link connecting them was Harvest's most recent postings that Richard had flagged.

"Today, in addition to the battles fought between citizens in our town squares and city streets, a new battlefront has begun to protect the unborn, not only in utero, but where science and nature clash at IVF centers around this country."

In posting this, did Harvest connect in-person protests like the one in St. Louis to the IVF break-in? Was she explicitly talking about the St. Louis events, or was this much larger? Richard needed to answer that question for Rhonda, but Harvest could provide the response herself as she ended her most recent posting.

"Over the next days and weeks, I will share the blueprint of how to achieve this new society rapidly with the living and the unborn."

Richard thought, *"What was the blueprint, and who would she share it with?"*

While most of what Richard investigated was national online chatter and connections, he knew he had to make a local connection. So far, the only local he knew about was Noah Sharpe. Plus, according to Rhonda, he was the only person with a personal relationship with Harvest, perhaps going beyond online communication. Did Harvest convey her most important messages to and through Noah Sharpe? Did she do it only online or in person? Who was this guy? Why him? Was he a conduit for Harvest? Was he a local soldier, and were there others like him around the country?

Most importantly, would Noah physically lead Rhonda to Harvest? Just as it is difficult to convict a murderer without finding a body, it is difficult to charge someone with a crime without knowing the person existed beyond their online persona. If Harvest was a ringleader of a crime, she would be arrested when she surfaced. Noah could be the critical link to Harvest.

Richard, to organize his thoughts and see where connections and relationships intersected, turned to the tried-and-true Venn diagram but in a modern digital application. He created an algorithmic formula that would identify and populate the intersecting circles with the shared characteristics of data variables belonging to each person, themes or positions, political affiliations, personal history, etc. This would allow him to focus on his main characters. Still, as other suspects, crimes, or manifestos surfaced, he could expand the diagram, which now centered on the known people and the known events, the protest, and the IVF break-in. Where they and the actions intersected would give him and Rhonda an answer or a better direction on where this was all going. But Richard was concerned that the answer would not be simple. In fact, it would be complex, and the concentric circles containing events and people would grow and grow like a virus overtaking the country. He laughed when he thought about the analogy of a virus, as the country had just mercifully gotten out of the Covid hysteria. He wondered if now we had a cultural virus, that rather than being curtailed by vaccines and time, may be unstoppable as people infected with it don't build up immunity; they build up hate.

Richard built his profiles of the primary suspects by assigning a numerical value to each person and the traits they possessed, with the higher numbers indicating more commonality and overlap. He factored in what their motives might be: power, passion, or money, and whether they would sacrifice their principles of one of them over another.

Harvest: Online influencer talking about a new society that needs to be born. Seems to be apolitical; now brings IVF centers into her focus and perhaps battle plan? Power and passion are her primary motivators.

Billy O'Dell: State representative from Southwest Missouri. His main goal is political gain beyond Missouri and into the national political picture. Power and eventually money. The aphrodisiac and Achilles heel of all politicians. But politicians need money and backers with much to gain, with O'Dell as their puppet. Who were O'Dell's backers, and what do they want?

Marianne Hylany: The opposite of O'Dell in every way. Far left position. There is no seemingly upward professional tract but perhaps a political agenda. Happy being a general shit disturber and irritant to the far right. Passion, above all, motivates her. But she also needs money and a power base to do what she does. Who provides it? History with O'Dell?

Noah Sharpe: Does not fit in with the others as he seems just a local loser. Works at the St. Louis Zoo. Has a personal relationship with Harvest, but how? His personality would indicate he is not interested in any of the three motivators, power, passion, or money. What would a loser or loner like Noah Sharpe want? Vindication? Respect? Very dangerous, usually the trait of those who shoot up schools or commit other crimes where notoriety is the primary goal. Who is his puppet master? Delusional?

He stared at the list and his description of each person. He then instructed his computer program to create a diagram using Political Protests, Pro-life, Pro-choice, IVF embryos, New World, and End of World to see where each person landed within each circle or circle. He would follow this process to track people and themes and see where and when they intersect. If able, he would also see trends occurring with other people, perhaps in other cities. If Richard was lucky, perhaps he could head off another violent protest or IVF break-in by knowing when the activity would occur, where it would occur, and, based on the GPS tracking of each individual, who would likely be involved.

He knew that every one of these topics written in his circle could be read about every day in every mainstream media outlet. They were discussed in every legitimate and dark or conspiracy-laden online forum. He did GPS tracking based on IP addresses and cell phones, indicating with a high degree of certainty when these people were on the move. Interestingly, the only person who did not change locations was Harvest. She never seemed to go anywhere based on phone activity, and her IP address based on her postings was stagnant. She was in southeast Missouri, near Caledonia. In one way, it seemed odd that someone with such a large national following would remain stationary. Still, Ted Kaczynski, the Unabomber, followed that approach living undetected in Montana for years. Rural southeast Missouri made sense if Harvest wanted to be isolated to express her viewpoints and hide from the feds, perhaps with help by the locals who aligned with her. This location could be perfect. Was she a Ted Kaczynski copycat, believer, or follower? Whatever she was, whoever she was, she covered her tracks to make sure it would be difficult to find her. Noah Sharpe, a loner from St. Louis, who based his cell phone GPS, traveled to Caledonia many times. Is this where he found her and make a personal connection. *"How odd, of all people, he found her, or she found him,"* Richard thought.

Aside from the mysteries surrounding Harvest, which Richard knew he would eventually solve, Richard knew his other big problem was separating fact from fiction. Richard knew that most people understood that the internet was filled with disinformation. For most people, they assumed disinformation about political positions centered around elections, but it was much, much more than that. Richard knew where the real danger lay. Much of the disinformation was about conspiracies or hatred of anyone who did not think or perhaps look like you. To him, the online sites were like carnival barkers of his youth, yelling out to passersby to try their food or their games and take a chance to win a prize. Today, internet carnival barkers were called influencers. Many legitimate influencers made a good living promoting fashion or music. They got paid based on how many followers see their posts promoting a product. But other influencers with millions of followers were also getting rich, whether it be through payment to subscribe to their online hate messaging or, in some cases, by those advertising the tools to facilitate hate and violence, such as gun manufacturers or survival gear and clothing with political or social statements.

Additionally, to get around the regulators and attract unsuspecting viewers, many sites that on the surface seemed benign, like American Democracy Inc., BLM, or even TikTok, were really gateways to darker and more disturbing sites such as IChan, developed and followed by QAnon supporters, white supremacists, and antisemites. Some sites were even gateways to foreign governments who would use data to spread disinformation to unsuspecting Americans.

For every race, for every lifestyle, there was a site devoted to hatred of that race or lifestyle. For every culture war, such as BLM, pro-choice, or pro-life, there were many supportive sites. Still, there were just as many sites that advocated hate and violence against those who disagree with them on societal issues. These sites were like hidden doors in a carnival fun site. Open the wrong door or click on the wrong link, and you will find yourself in a world you did not expect. Even organizations that use the telephone, posing as fundraisers to support police or firemen, were automated bots that threw out catchphrases like "defund the police," which would capture people's attention and then their money when, in fact, the fundraisers were nothing more than a fraudulent scheme to pay themselves every dollar raised as the charities they supposedly supported did not exist. It was hard enough to know a fraud when it was standing in front of you, but the use of A.I. and ChatGPT made scamming almost undetectable, especially for poor souls who wanted to be led or needed something or someone to believe in or to blame for their woes. Unsuspecting people, intelligent or naive, could have an entire conversation with a bot and would not know it.

This is where people like Harvest lured people like Noah. Into the shadows of the internet, with backlinks, Deepfake videos or posts trapping an unsuspecting and susceptible person looking for a place to belong. When the internet first came into existence, parents only had to fear their children accidentally looking at pornography. Richard now scoffed at that antiqued idea as he knew there was much more dangerous material already influencing and permeating not only the minds of younger people but people of all ages and all walks of life. In doing so, they turned those usually ordinary and law-abiding citizens into zombies, reciting and believing what they read and seeking out only those who share their warped, demented, and in many cases, violent views.

In many cases, followers just had online connections or relationships. But in other cases, online relationships became real, in-person relationships, perhaps like Harvest and Noah Sharpe. It was not a crime in the

U.S. for people to be part of or even share bizarre or hateful views. The crime was taking these views and putting them into action against real people or property. That was what Rhonda needed Richard to do: connect online activity with actual events. In many cases, that connection only happened after the fact. After a fateful event when people were murdered, the investigators could trace the murderous intentions back to their online presence.

Richard knew that the internet contained those who influenced or gained something and those who acted upon a movement and lost something. People like O'Dell and Hylany used the internet, and their involvement with online groups aligned with their thinking to gain something, whether that be riches, political power, or followers. However, they would not jeopardize their bigger goals to do something as pedestrian as committing a crime. They had others, their followers, commit the crimes. While some influencers encouraged others to buy a legitimate product, dark web influencers, like Harvest and others, used their online influence to give mass murderers, school shooters, and other copycat criminals, not only a reason to act, but also a reason to live. While the internet was dangerous enough, the explosion of social media was more dangerous because it gave the most vulnerable people bragging rights to do the most heinous crimes. And because social media clearly identified the haves and have-nots, Richard knew the have-nots, the most vulnerable losers in society, were most influenced by hate and action. They knew they had to act to make a name for themselves when, in life, they had lived on earth invisible to most people. The key to solving these crimes, wherever they may lead, was to find those whose participation in the crime would elevate their status from loser to somebody. And the only loser on Richard's piece of paper so far was Noah Sharpe. Richard believed he was an unsuspecting foot soldier for Harvest, but who were the others he did not know about? Others who shared the strange, demented view of the world and would act upon their urges by communicating with those who have the same sickness?

Rhonda wanted him to try to connect the IVF break-in and the protests, both in St. Louis and other cities around the country. To do that, he had to have a direct connection between the most prominent influencer, Harvest, and her messengers, foot soldiers, losers, and malcontents like Noah Sharpe.

Chapter 31

Layla Talks with Her Peers

For her assignment of trying to find any other activity at IVF centers around the country, Layla mapped out how she would give Rhonda and her new friend Marianne Hylany helpful information while keeping them and their relationships with Layla hidden. While Layla, in her head, knew Rhonda would always have her back, she was not sure that would hold up if Marianne was on Rhonda's radar screen as being a crime suspect in her case. From Layla's perspective, while she did not know Marianne Hylany for very long, she felt a strong bond between her and her views, as they were also shared with her best friends, Becca, and her sister Lauren. But Layla also knew to be pragmatic about Hylany and learn more about her before she could trust her completely. Once Layla trusted her completely, she would tread very lightly with Rhonda to ensure that Rhonda saw Hylany as an ally, not the enemy. Layla hoped Hylany was not the enemy. While Layla had some digging to do on her end, both with her IVF contacts and Marianne Hylany, she knew Richard Leary was also trying to connect the dots. She was afraid that what he might find would implicate Marianne Hylany. Still, she wanted to know what he knew, so she called Rhonda and asked to meet with her and Richard later that evening when she got off work. Before that meeting, however, she needed to make some calls to her colleagues.

Last summer, Layla attended a conference focused on the issues surrounding the IVF industry, which was now nearly fifty years old and, as such, had seen changes in technology, science, success rates, and, unfortunately, politics, impacting the future of IVF. A hot button, long before the recent Dobbs v. Jackson Supreme Court decision, which effectively gave states the right to overturn the Roe v. Wade decision, was the discussion on how potential abortion trigger laws being contemplated by the states would impact IVF. When Roe v. Wade was the national law, states could not outlaw abortion. However, some states over the years passed abortion trigger laws which would criminalize abortion in the event that Roe v. Wade was ever overturned. When that happened, it triggered the enforcement of laws that would restrict or ban abortion in that state. At the conference, she attended a seminar, along with other peers nationwide, put on by the American Society of Reproductive Medicine in which they reviewed their white paper on how abortion triggers, enacted by fifteen states, would impact reproductive medicine. While the seminar itself was a bit dry as it went through each state's current position and the current legal interpretation of that position, conversation in the bar afterward was much more animated. This was in no small way attributable to the combination of unlimited alcohol consumed by overworked, very intelligent, and opinionated people, primarily doctors, blowing off an average level of steam but now supercharged based on the potential threat to them and their businesses.

At the bar that evening and at break-out groups or coffee breaks, certain attendees gravitated to each other based on various factors. There were some past professional or medical school overlap, perhaps some geographic-based alliances of IVF clinics located in the same city or town and some by peer groups, IVF Centers owned by young women doctors, such as Layla, who felt comfortable getting to know other doctors with shared experiences and genders. Each state had unique interpretations of how they viewed IVF embryos relative to abortion trigger laws. Comparatively, some states had no trigger laws at all and were fast growing as abortion sanctuary states. Layla made her connections with other female doctors. Specifically, she sought out doctors in states such as Minnesota, Illinois, Washington, and California as she thought these would be places where, if need be, she would relocate her clinic or engage in some sort of referral network. The doctors she got to know were also intelligent, dynamic women with whom Layla immediately bonded. They also had another trait that Layla admired. They were activists. They were not going to sit on their asses and let the state government, especially primarily male legislators dictate how they ran their businesses. Perhaps that is why she liked Marianne Hylany so much. She was just like the doctors she met at the seminars. Bad Ass Bitches.

Thinking about what Hylany had asked her about peers she may know in other states, a question which Layla dodged, she pulled up her contact list of the conference attendees. She scrolled to the four to five doctors she felt closest to. She would contact them and ask them what they had seen regarding violence or protests surrounding their clinics or communities. As she thought about it and the potential reasons for the IVF break-ins, she decided to also reach out to doctors in states that had abortion triggers, such as Missouri, whose IVF clinics were potentially under fire or threat of extinction. She would then contact doctors whose clinics were in safer states. She wondered if there was a pattern to the violence and perhaps to the objective of the IVF break-ins that were unique to IVF clinics that were under threat of extinction or ones that were in safe havens.

Since her clinic was still temporally closed due to her break-in, she could spend all day contacting her professional colleagues. Once she assembled her notes, she could share them with Richard and Rhonda to give them a trail. In turn, she hoped Richard would provide information that Layla could secretly share with Hylany if she wanted to. Layla rationalized in this way that she would not compromise her integrity with Rhonda or Hylany.

It took her all day to reach out to the doctors on her list. Many of them had heard about the break-in at Layla's clinic. After sharing sympathy, Layla got to the point with each of her peers, asking them if they had had similar problems, if they had seen an uptick in violence or protests in their community or around their clinics, and if their patients were asking about the protection or destruction of the embryos. Many had seen the uptick in violence and vitriol surrounding their clinics. Some had even reported their clinics, or others they had connections with, had been broken into but with limited damage to the embryos, just as Layla had encountered. She also asked them a very important question. Why was it happening? Who did they think could be behind an act like this? Were they hearing anything among their contacts and peer groups? Did they think it could be someone doing it for political or moral reasons or just the most common reason, money? Finally, she asked if they felt the crimes could be emanating from within other doctors or owners of IVF clinics? They had all heard the rare stories of unscrupulous doctors stealing a woman's eggs or impregnating them with their own sperm to sell them on the black market, or worse, implant them in an unsuspecting patient.

While those days seemed behind the IVF industry, nothing surprised Layla, and based on the responses she got, nothing surprised the other doctors as well. Finally, before ending each conversation and proceeding cautiously, Layla felt each doctor out about the information Hylany had shared regarding the group or ideology that might be behind these break-ins. While she kept the specifics vague because they were vague, Layla wanted to see if her fellow doctors would take this concern and interest to the next level and do whatever was necessary to protect their patients and their businesses. Layla also wanted to understand if she could trust each of the doctors. Layla was asking them to join her and Hylany in a crusade they perhaps did not believe in. But, while she could not see their faces, their conviction and passion, amplified by a resounding yes when Layla asked them to join her, gave Layla a sense of warmth that she had finally found the true family she had sought her entire life. She now had enough information to share with Rhonda and Richard.

Chapter 32

SUSPICIONS ARISE

After spending the day talking to her IVF peers around the country and putting her notes together, Layla was ready to drop some bread-crumbs and see if Richard and Rhonda would follow them.

Rhonda decided it would be best for Layla to meet with her and Richard at Richard's home. They might need to access Richard's digital spying technology to do his research in real-time. Layla arrived at 7:00 p.m., and after greeting Rhonda with a hug and Richard with a hand-shake, they made their way into the man cave to discuss whatever was on Layla's mind.

"Rhonda, when we last met, you mentioned that you wanted me to reach out to my peers in the industry and see if any of them have had any issues with protesters and break-ins."

"That's right. I assume you have found something because you asked to meet with us," Rhonda replied.

"I am not sure what I found, but I have talked to some peers about my situation, and they are seeing the same things at their clinics and in their cities. They have had break-ins at their clinics, and they are concerned about increased chatter relative to IVF being the next battleground in the pro-life vs. pro-choice cultural wars."

"Who did you talk to?" Rhonda pressed. "I would like to compare notes with their local police departments."

"I would rather not say as I want to respect their confidentiality, but I can tell you the cities or states where their clinics are located, so at least you and Richard can use that information to compare what their local police force is finding, as well as local online chatter."

Layla thought about Rhonda's business-like tone, and maybe it was nothing. Still, she wondered if Rhonda saw Layla as just a victim of a crime she was investigating versus someone more important in her life. As long as Layla had known Rhonda, she knew Rhonda was a cop first and a caring person second. Perhaps that was the problem that has always plagued their relationship.

In silence, Richard once again noted this odd, subtle friction between the two women. So, hoping to move the conversation along, as he was itching to share his digital spying results, he asked Layla, "What cities and states are your friends in? I can build some algorithms to start tracking off my keywords in those geographic areas."

"Ok. That sounds like a good place to start. First, I reached out to some peers I had met at a conference I attended last summer regarding the impact of abortion trigger laws on reproductive medicine," Layla said.

"Good. If you have any materials, speeches, or white papers from that seminar, give them to me, so I can add some of those agenda points and takeaways into my algorithm," Richard added.

"Yes, I can give you all of that. While the conference dealt with many reproductive medicine issues, most were about medical or operational changes. Success stories or, in some cases, failures. Some seminars were about business practices and the nuts and bolts of running a profitable business. I attended most of the seminars, but the buzz in the conference was about the impact of the Dobbs v. Jackson decision on IVF."

Rhonda asked, "How big of a buzz was it, Layla? Are your peers concerned?"

"Yes, they are to a degree, and that is a lot of what we discussed when I reached out to them today. On paper, of the fifteen states that have abortion triggers, none of them mention IVF directly, but a few use some terms that potentially could impact IVF depending upon how a court or state attorney general may interpret the wording in the trigger laws."

Richard asked, "Give me an example of terms by state, if possible, as they can help me in my search. These online influencers are smart and can use specific terms, almost like industry jargon, to drive true believers to their posts or weed out non-believers."

"I will give you the entire white paper, and you can see, state by state, some of the ambiguous language, but for example, in Missouri, while there is no mention of IVF, the state does define abortion as the act of prescribing or using any means with the intent destroying the life of an embryo or fetus in its mother's womb. The lawyer that gave the seminar said while they mention embryos, which could be IVF related, they refer most of their language strictly around an abortion once the embryos are in the womb, in essence, after our IVF work is completed."

Rhonda added, "The lawyer is right. Anytime there is ambiguity, it is open to interpretation, a legal or political stalemate then followed by a bundle of lawsuits."

Continuing, Layla said, "When the lawyer brought up state laws in places like Arkansas and Kentucky, he mentioned the word, "Unborn Child" as potentially being problematic. For example, in Arkansas, the statute does define "unborn child" to apply from fertilization to live birth, and in Kentucky, the definitions of "fertilization" and "unborn human being" could theoretically apply to the process of creating in-vitro embryos."

"This is good." said Richard, "All this information will aid me in developing my search parameters. I hope you reached out to those peers in the states that had trigger laws, as that would seem to be the most likely place for a protest or future attacks against IVF centers."

"I did if I knew someone in that state, but I also reached out to peers in other states that I would consider safe states. I think understanding the political dynamics in those states is just as important. Plus, I need to keep my contacts in those states as you never know what might happen to my clinic in Missouri. The state legislators seem to be becoming more and more emboldened. Even if a vote ever came up to protect the rights of women regarding abortion, like they did in Kansas and Ohio, I am not even sure our state legislature, filled with people like Billy O'Dell, would honor the vote. Missouri is fast becoming one of the most conservative, religious right states in the country, and I am beginning to doubt my long-term presence here," Layla said, somewhat melancholy.

Upon hearing that comment, Rhonda surprisingly switched from cop mode to human mode and squeezed Layla's hand, saying, "I certainly hope you don't leave the area. I would miss you." Both Richard and Layla seemed surprised by the sentiment Rhonda had just displayed.

"You would make a good investigator, Layla, as you can combine facts with instinct, and you are right about Missouri. Anytime some local politician has greater aspirations, they need to become more radical and controversial. Billy O'Dell is a good example of that," said Richard.

While Layla added Billy O'Dell's name as a sidebar to Missouri conservative politics, her real reason was to ensure Richard and Rhonda kept him high on their radar screens, as any information they found out about O'Dell would be fed back to Layla who would quietly feed it back to Marianne Hylany. Layla knew that while all politics were local, all vendettas were personal, and Marianne seemed to have a personal vendetta against O'Dell that stretched beyond political differences. *"Maybe Richard was right. Perhaps I would be a good investigator or a double agent,"* Layla mused to herself.

Layla then explained to Richard and Rhonda, in general, what she had learned but not from her peers as much as from Marianne Hylany. "While my peers seem to be somewhat worried that the debate about IVF will center on political or cultural reasons, they seem to be equally concerned that IVF debate could also focus on moral codes or for financial gains."

"How so?" asked Richard.

"Sometimes morality and greed overlap, as proven so often with some of these super evangelicals' churches and pastors. The same could happen with IVF. As you may or may not know, over the history of IVF, there have been insidious acts where a doctor personally fertilized a woman's eggs with his sperm instead of the woman's partner's sperm. Why they did it may have been due to a God complex. It gave IVF a bad name, but luckily, it also made us tighten our security protocol. But there were also doctors selling a patient's embryos without their permission on the black market. These doctors would tell a patient they had nine viable embryos when maybe they really had fifteen, and how was the patient to prove them wrong? There is an incredible trust between IVF patients and their doctor, as in many cases, the doctor is the last hope for a desperate couple, and the bond and trust between them is unbreakable. I know my patients are entrusting me with more than their lives. They are entrusting me with the lives of babies they so desperately want."

"So how do morality and greed come into play?" asked Richard.

"Let's first talk about morality. We all know from the era of political divisiveness that you can't always judge a book by its cover. This means that many of us go out with friends or family we have known for years, and we suddenly discover their views on politics or cultural issues, whether far right or left, are not what we thought them to be. We usually leave that conversation shaking our heads, saying, I never believed Brian or Leslie would think like that. We are always surprised when we really dig deep into someone's beliefs. The same is true of the IVF industry. Just because a doctor opens an IVF clinic does not mean he or she is comfortable destroying embryos if the patient no longer needs or wants them. So perhaps a doctor does not destroy them. Perhaps they decide to sell them for financial gain. This is where a doctor's morality might overlap with their greed. Now add to that the possibility that if IVF becomes a focus of abortion triggers, and doctors potentially could be accused of murder if they destroy an embryo, the motivation to do something else with that embryo becomes even more acute."

"Have your peers seen any evidence of that happening?" Richard asked.

"Not hard evidence, but my peers are involved in bizarre conversations along those lines with doctors they thought they knew very well.

Richard, you need to see if these conversations are going beyond casual living room chatter and are starting to have a large presence in the online community."

Richard nodded while banging out additional keywords in his digital algorithm.

Layla continued, "The flip side is that many of my peers see and hear the reverse conversations. That is, how do we keep the pro-life advocates from taking the decision away from our patients about what they can do with their embryos? Obviously, being forced to have more children than you want or being forced to give up your embryos and have your offspring being raised by other families unknown to you is not appealing to many IVF patients. But they and we, the IVF clinic owners, also want to ensure no one will be criminally charged if the embryos are destroyed."

"Interesting." Richard added, "So that tells me if IVF clinics and their embryos become the next battle of pro-life vs. pro-choice, the battle may protect the right to destroy the embryo by either the patient directly or the clinic upon request of the patient or the saving of embryo to protect future life although that life may not be raised by the actual owner of the embryo."

Now Rhonda jumped in, as she was getting antsy discussing all these "what ifs" because, at the end of the day, she had a local crime to solve and solve quickly. "Layla, based on what happened to you and your conversations with your peers, do you have any more conclusive ideas on who may be responsible for your break-in? Do you think it was the pro-lifers, pro-choice, or neither, just a common variety criminal?"

Layla hesitated a second before answering, taking a sip of her water as she needed to be very careful how to answer this question as her response was going to be based more on what Hylany had shared with her on the possible connection of the protest and the break-in than any feedback her peers had given her.

"There are several theories my peers and I are debating. Some believe there is a connection between the protests occurring around the same time a clinic is broken into. If you had to press me on it, I would say both are being orchestrated by pro-life groups. They have more to gain. Plus, they are talking about IVF embryos being the next battleground." While Layla may have harbored these feelings, they were reinforced by her conversation with Marianne Hylany.

Almost reading Layla's mind, and as if he was listening to the conversation she had with Marianne Hylany, Richard jumped in asking, "Ok, perhaps this break-in and others is the work of pro-life advocates, and while we know they are very organized and very determined, what they did and how they did it at your clinic takes more than organization; it takes money, medical technology expertise and an intimate knowledge of the daily working of your IVF process. They knew exactly when a large supply of embryos would be in your clinic based on the implantation cycle. Who would know that information, Layla?"

"Well, the only people who would know that would be my employees, my patients who were scheduled for implantation, and the large Cryobank warehouse where we now send embryos for storage because we don't have the space and can't cover the insurance costs." Layla then added, "And specifically for my business, private equity companies that have toured my facility with the possible intent of buying it. Many of my peers are selling to private equity companies and in their due diligence, they learn about every aspect of our operation.

Rhonda jumped in, "I know I cannot get the names of your patients due to HIPPA, and to me, that is the least likely groups to have pulled this off, but I need to get the names of all your employees, plus the names of the Cryobank and private equity companies you have been dealing with."

Layla nodded to Rhonda affirming she would provide her with the names she requested.

Richard then broke the silence by asking the obvious. "OK, we have a good list of who might have done it and may have the financial resources to do it, but I am still wondering about the 'why'. I get the pro-life vs. pro-choice battle ground over IVF, but this seems like a very expensive and complicated way to make a political point, and before we go down that path, let's take the easier route and follow the financial gain for stealing embryos."

"Layla, can you give me an example of the amount of money that is at risk or potentially to gain if existing embryos are taken from current patients and resold. Because, as time and crime have always told me, follow the money."

Thinking about what Richard asked, Layla waded in. "Okay. Putting aside the moral, political, and religious rationale for anyone deciding what to do with unused embryos, money could be the sole reason for the break-in at my clinic and others around the country. A woman can have perhaps fifteen viable eggs after extraction. Depending upon age and other factors, some may only get a few, and others may get more, but fifteen is a good average. We then fertilize the fifteen eggs, and after fertilization, we test for any abnormalities or potential birth defects. Let's say that cuts our viable embryos from those fertilized eggs to ten. After the implantation of a viable embryo into a woman's uterus, the woman may have nine other viable embryos for future use if the initial implantation is not successful or if the woman wants to use the remaining embryos for additional children. My initial fee until the first embryo is implanted in the patient is approximately $40,000. I am in the middle of the road fee-wise, but $40,000 is a good number. Let's say a woman wants to or needs to use the other embryos. Every time she uses one based on my fees and tests, it will cost her about twenty five percent of the original cost, so around $10,000."

Richard then interrupted. "So based on this scenario and my quick math, one woman with nine viable embryos could be worth about $130,000 to an IVF business if she ended up using all those embryos over time."

"Yeah, rough guess that seems right, but of course, the embryos are used over time, and fees go up, but for purposes of this example, let's use $130,000 per patient." But Layla explained that her figures are the cost or revenue of an existing patient using her own embryos. But the revenue is exponential if those nine embryos are somehow taken and sold to new women or parents, not the rightful owners of the embryos, and those parents go through a completely new IVF process. Then, nine new patients each use one of those embryos. Using my $40,000 per new patient, those nine additional embryos may be worth $360,000." And then with some anger in her voice, Layla added, "and that does not even include what a couple would pay for a stolen embryo that was not theirs. Anyone willing to cross that moral threshold probably would pay and outlandish amount of money for the embryo."

This time, Rhonda jumped in, "So there is tremendous value in using all the embryos. So much so that any person or entity would have reason to steal them."

Layla waded in, "Tremendous value is an understatement. These are rough numbers and only U.S. based. They vary widely based on the woman's age or ability to produce eggs. Still, there is an average of one hundred thousand IVF babies born yearly in the U.S., and it's probably ten times that worldwide. Now, using my earlier math, those one hundred thousand IVF babies are a tenth of the total viable embryos the couples created. Using ten embryos on average, that would be one million other embryos available for use. Now IVF success for women under thirty-five is about fifty percent, so cut the remaining available embryos down in half to five hundred thousand. At $40,000 per initial IVF procedure, you are looking at potentially a is $20 billion per year, and that is in the U.S. only."

"That is a huge number that would get anyone's attention," Layla continued. "But I think you are just seeing the tip of the iceberg. Think about supply and demand. If IVF centers are under siege, current embryos would be in high demand, thus perhaps doubling or tripling my estimates. Plus, suppose all these babies are being born all the way down the line. In that case, everyone cashes in from hospitals, doctors, maternity services, baby clothing suppliers, nannies, pre-school etc. The list goes on and on. It costs about $20,000 for a baby born in a hospital and let's say conservatively a couple spends another $100,000 over a child's lifetime. Every year, if five hundred thousand IVF babies are born by not destroying unused embryos, the windfall to all those companies in the baby and childcare business would be astronomical. Billions and billions of dollars and if these embryos and future children are somewhat controlled by one entity, and if that entity has its fingers in all aspects of the creation, birth, and caring for a baby, the financial gain to that entity would be unfathomable. Perhaps this whole pro-life religious fever is not just about protecting the unborn. Suppose it is about protecting the profits of those who want to profit on the future unborn."

Richard then asked a fundamental question, "Layla, correct me if I am wrong, but don't fertilized eggs or embryos lose their viability the older they get.

"Not necessarily. An appropriately stored fertilized egg or embryo can be used for up to ten years. For example, you must remember that the egg taken from a woman created in 2023 would not have aged at all if it was implanted in 2033. It is still a 2023 egg, "and Layla added, "The numbers I just gave you were based on one year's worth of egg extraction and embryo creation. So, the numbers I gave you over time can be multiplied exponentially. Basically, embryos could be a never-ending pipeline for childless couples."

"And," Richard added, "if someone is creating uncertainty now regarding the future of IVF, my guess is people who could not conceive, or who want to delay having a baby, would be flocking to your business before they have no other option, so by causing chaos, it may be increasing the urgency to use IVF, and with that urgency is an increase in eggs, embryo's etc., therefore creating, if you will, a huge inventory of laboratory created embryos."

"Well, my business and those of my peers are booming, more because of the increased difficulty for a variety of factors for women to have a baby naturally. This has been a phenomenon for years now. Environment, women's health, stress have all made a woman's ability to conceive naturally more difficult. Add to the fact women want to have a baby when they are ready, financially, career-wise, or even partner-wise, and this has made our field very lucrative. Nowadays, couples, especially those with money, can also choose the gender of their baby using IVF, making an IVF-produced embryo perhaps more valuable than one produced naturally. Wealthy people live in an 'I want what I want society and will do or pay anything to get what I want."

All three were quiet for a while, and then Richard, thinking about what Layla just said about the "I want what I want society" spoke up. "I hate to bring this up because it sounds so incredibly crazy, but as you know, I am in the 'find the crazy people business,' but what if, aside from a political or social agenda or a sizeable money-making scheme, the people or organizations behind this assault on the IVF industry had another motive and that is creating an on-going supply or pipeline of future humans started from test tube babies that followed a specific ideology to benefit the organizations for their present and future agendas. Let's label this thought as the 'Harvest conundrum' due to her rantings because we should not discount any possibility."

Both Rhonda and Layla laughed out loud, with Rhonda adding, "Richard, you have been in the deep, dark web too long, my friend. You need to get outside for fresh air."

Richard held up his hands as if to say, I know this sounds crazy, but then he continued after their laughing subsided. "Think of this in this way. Every day, as adults and even children, we are bombarded with messages from the media, entertainment, sports, our peers, families, and friends that, in some ways, are designed to shape our thinking about issues. This is what I am investigating now and that is how Influencers are trying to shape how we think about political or social causes and positions. We hear so much from the far right that uncontrolled immigration is being encouraged by Democrats because they see these immigrants as potential voting blocks. Whether that is true or not, it is a conservative position echoed constantly. It is the same with the liberal policies seen throughout Hollywood and even taught on college campuses. Do you agree that this is, in fact, a political reality and is, in fact, a perceived strategy that the right believes the left is doing?"

Both Layla and Rhonda nodded affirmatively, so Richard continued. "Now, what if the right believes, as warped as this may sound, that if they control the production of babies as procured and created through IVF, they can, in a way, control the beliefs of future generations, and they do so by requiring the future parents of a purchased IVF embryo as part of the purchase agreement would be that they must raise the child in a pro-conservative, religious right, environment. Does this sound more or less plausible than the Fox News drumbeat that hordes of illegal immigrants and their children are coming into the country to be future liberal voting blocs?"

Rhonda looked at Richard, then at Layla, and she said, "Plausible, I guess, but it sounds more like a science fiction movie plot than reality."

But before Richard could respond, Layla jumped in. "You know, Rhonda, one of the things I have learned through science is never to underestimate it, especially in the hands of brilliant and driven people. Perhaps you would call me crazy if I told you twenty years ago that a couple in the future would be able to determine what gender they wanted their baby to be, maybe even eye color, hair color, athletic prowess, and likelihood of intelligence. All these attributes can be calculated by the testing we do with eggs and sperm to give a couple the 'perfect child.' If we can create a chromosomally perfect child, we could also create a child who is programmed to think and act in a certain way. Especially if you control the environment the child is raised in."

"Layla is right, Rhonda," Richard said, "if you were a chemist, or an athlete, or a musician, and you had a child that you wanted to follow in your footsteps or had an interest in these fields, you would expose that child as best you could to help shape and influence their decision to follow those pursuits. It happens daily with normal American parents and their children in households and towns throughout the country. Why couldn't it happen with overzealous believers or influencers who are so wrapped up in this country's political and social direction that they would do anything to ensure their ideology remains protected and dominant in American society? They are already doing so in a way based on these insular communities popping up all over the place. Many people, regardless of the reason, want to live among their own kind, so this is just taking that idea and laying out the possibility of how these communities might be populated in the future."

Rhonda sighed, perhaps both to accept the argument Richard and now Layla were making, but also perhaps to reflect the weariness she felt on her shoulders that society as a whole was getting more sinister and as such, crimes, like an individual murder, were becoming more frequent without any rhyme or reason, but almost blasé, and new crimes and criminals were becoming more complex and intelligent.

Rhonda said, "So let's say that the reproductive industry is under siege, perhaps for political or religious reasons, perhaps for money, and now perhaps for control of the hearts and minds of mankind. My question to you is, who or what could be behind this? They have to have the financial means and perhaps political clout to change the arc of reproductive medicine to favor them for money or political power. Also, let's not forget we have real-life individuals breaking into IVF clinics, being killed at pro-life vs. pro-choice protests and, based on your research, posting manifestos, as Harvest did about future battle grounds and societies. Are these people the foot soldiers of something or someone bigger?"

"That is what I need to find out, Rhonda," Richard answered. "I may be totally off-base, and we may only have run-of-the-mill criminals acting of their own volition, but we may have something much bigger, where these people are pawns and are directed by those people or institutions where morality is overtaken by greed and power. My money is on a company or companies, or an extremely wealthy group of individuals is behind this, whatever this is. Companies are still run by people, and people reconcile their morality and beliefs versus the financial realities of making a dollar, or in this case, billions of dollars, every day. Can you imagine the internal dilemma and discussion among the board of directors at a business who could profit tremendously from IVF embryos and the use of science in reproductive advances?"

"On the one hand, they want to protect IVF procedures from possible future inclusion into abortion trigger laws because the reduction in people choosing IVF would impact their business. On the other hand, they also don't want women to be allowed the option of destroying unused embryos as those could be, in essence, their future pipeline of product and revenue in their business. Does morality or greed win out in that discussion?" Richard asked Rhonda.

Rhonda answered, "Based on my experience, people faced with moral dilemmas vs. financial windfalls usually try to get ahead of the issue and manage the desired expectations. I believe Alex Finnegan was doing that with his Arch City Transplant Center. He saw a way to make huge profits by owning the conversation on the ability to choose between life and death situations. I see the same parallels here, including using unsuspecting individuals as foot soldiers. Alex got very rich using others to act on his orders. Others who lost their lives for it. I hope there is not another Alex Finnigan-type person out masterminding this plan."

Richard was pounding away at his keyboard and stopped to say, "I call what Alex Finnigan did being a market maker. He created a market by creating a product because of legal ambiguity. In this scenario, I would say whoever is behind this, whether a person or a company, or maybe a government, foreign or domestic, is years ahead of pending legislation and plans to create a market that will impact future legislation. And just like Finnegan did, the market is made if there is enough money to pay off the politicians who make the laws. You are instantly the market leader."

Rhonda responded, "Ok, your view on possibly the sinister motives of a corporation or rich individuals gives us maybe the traditional white-collar criminals or a faceless corporation, using lawyers and political clout to create revenue for their business, but what about the other cast of characters you are investigating? How do Noah Sharpe and the mysterious Harvest fit in? How about Marianne Hylany and Billy O'Dell? How do they fit in, if at all? For every large-scale criminal plot, you need foot soldiers or dupes who do the dirty work, knowingly or not for others. Maybe that is who these people are. Maybe they are part of an organization or a political movement and have their own agenda. We need to find it out and do it quickly."

Richard talked while entering commands into his computer. "If there is a connection to corporations or wealthy individuals, I will find it. I will search for the ownership of any business that could gain profit from the increase or decrease of viable embryos and what political donations they may make to pro-life or pro-choice organizations or politicians. Knowing that and knowing who owns them may lead us back down the trail to who may be behind these IVF break-ins. And because they are politically active, I will see if O'Dell and Hylany are connected to each other and potentially a political organization or movement controlled by a company or an individual."

Rhonda added, "Try to track Hylany's and Harvest's whereabouts so I can interview them. I know where I can find Sharpe, and O'Dell as a public figure is easy to track, but Hylany and Harvest seem like ghosts. Knowing where they are and what they may be up to may generate some needed answers."

That last comment made Layla shutter, as in about ten days, Marianne Hylany would be at Layla's home as they had planned to meet up again when Hylany returned from her trip to Minneapolis and the West Coast.

Chapter 33

Rhonda Presses Noah

Since most of the people central to the case seemed to be unreachable or unfindable, the following day, Rhonda decided to pay a visit to the one person she could locate, Noah Sharpe. She paid him an early morning visit at the zoo, hoping to be able to talk to him as he did his work and before the visitors started to arrive. The St. Louis Zoo is over one hundred years old and located in the largest urban park in America, Forest Park. It is widely considered one of the best zoos by experts and the public alike. Marlin Perkins was a director for eight years while doing his TV show Mutual of Omaha Wild Kingdom. In fact, the zoo was the first job Marlin Perkins had when he was just twenty-one. Because of all its history and diversity of wildlife, as well as its setting and its free price, it is one of the top attractions in St. Louis and a place Rhonda always loved visiting.

Arriving before it was open to the public, Rhonda flashed her badge to an attendant at the front gate. With admittance free, the attendant didn't pay much attention to her. On a personal visit, Rhonda would look at other exhibits as she wound her way to the primate habitat. Today, she made a direct and swift route there to find Noah. She did not know if

Noah worked with the big apes in The Wild area or in the Historic Hill area where the smaller primates like monkeys and chimpanzees lived. Since Noah specifically said he worked with the monkeys when she last interviewed him and knowing that people in his field would be very specific about what type of animals they worked with, she headed to the monkey enclosures.

While enjoying the early morning antics of the monkeys and keeping an eye out for Noah, she strolled around the enclosures. She approached a woman dressed in a zoo uniform and asked if she knew where to find Noah Sharpe. The woman obviously knew Noah well and replied, "It's too early for him to be goofing off, so I guess he is cleaning out the inside enclosures around the corner. If you see one with no monkeys, look for Noah, as we usually move the animals around when cleaning an enclosure."

Rhonda did as directed and soon came upon one of the last inside enclosures still used to house the monkeys, as a sizeable outside canopy had opened up last year to allow primates and humans to interact more naturally. Perhaps Noah literally got the shit duty and only worked inside because he was too much of a goof-off to handle a more complicated assignment. But soon she saw the man she was looking for. She knocked on the glass window, an act typically frowned upon when monkeys were in the enclosure, but she got Noah's attention. He looked up at her, then back down to what he was doing, seemingly ignoring her. She knocked again, flashing her badge, and signaling him to come out. He indicated he had a few more piles of monkey shit to clean up, then pointed to his right, indicating an exit door where he would meet her.

After about five minutes, Noah appeared at the door and did not offer to shake hands, thankfully, as Rhonda did not know what those hands had touched. Noah said, "The zoo is not open yet, lady. Is there something I can help you with?"

"I am Detective Simon, Mr. Sharpe. Do you not remember me?"

"No. Not really. Have we met before?"

Getting slightly irritated, though it would not be surprising that Noah did not remember their conversation several weeks ago, Rhonda decided to retain her composure as she needed Noah to talk and remember some details. She also did not know if Noah was just being shifty or if he was dumb. After her first meeting with him, she did not think he was dumb. She thought he might be off the charts for intelligence despite his menial job.

"We talked after the shooting at the protest at Tower Grove Park and the New Beginnings Fertility Clinic. Does that ring a bell?"

"Hesitating like he had to think hard to remember Rhonda, he said, "Oh yeah, now I remember. The shooting, I told you, Detective, I did not see the shooter."

"Yep, you told me that, but you also told me that your girlfriend--what was her name—Harvest-- might have known the shooting was going to occur. That is why I am here, Noah, to discuss and hopefully find your girlfriend, Harvest."

"You must not be a very good detective if you are still looking for her. She is not that hard to find."

Ignoring that comment, Rhonda pressed on, "Well, I have found her rantings online but have been unable to track down where she is physically located. Can you help me on that, Mr. Sharpe?"

"Can I and will I are two different requests, and the answer to both is no."

"And why is that, Mr. Sharpe? Why would you not help me with a straightforward request to keep you out of hot water and off my radar screen, where I can tell you is a place you don't want to be?"

"Because I keep my relationship with my beloved Harvest private, though I did talk to her the other day."

"Really, you talked to her the other day. And did you talk about anything related to the protest, or perhaps her views on the ending of the world and the need to form a new society? Anything along those lines, Mr. Sharpe?"

Upon hearing this, and perhaps forgetting he had told Rhonda about Harvest's vision, Noah shifted his feet and looked down before he answered. Rhonda knew she had hit a nerve with Noah, so she pressed him harder.

"You know, Mr. Sharpe, since I initially talked to you about the specific shooting in the park, my interest in you and Ms. Harvest has grown in scope immensely. She has captured the attention of not only me but some of my law enforcement associates, both local and federal."

Typically, threats by an authority figure would unnerve Noah. However, since he had met Harvest, Noah had transformed from a meek observer of life to a bold participant. He felt more confident and aggressive in dealing with Rhonda. "What associates?" he huffed. "The feds? FBI? Homeland Security?" Noah rapidly threw out federal agency names with a hint of disgust in his voice. "Harvest and I are not worried about any government agency looking into our dealings. Those people will be rendered castrated soon enough."

"Well, Noah, who is looking into you is information I cannot tell you. Unless, of course, you start talking about Harvest. Where is she? What is she planning?" Rhonda asked with anger but tempered anger as she knew the only associate she was referring to was Richard. She was bluffing and needed to be careful that Sharpe did not pick up on her bluff. She also noticed Noah's demeanor had changed from being philosophical a few weeks ago to being angry and confident.

She matched his intensity with hers to put him off stride and give her the upper hand in this conversation. What she also knew from being a cop is that the bad guys almost always want to talk and brag about their crimes. And while she was still not sure Noah was a bad guy, perhaps just mentally unstable, she pressed on. "You know, Noah, when my associates and I start hearing words like 'the end of days' and 'forming a new society,' our alarm bells go off. You and Harvest would not be part of any radicalized group planning some civil unrest, would you? Maybe an armed militia uprising or an anti-government cult? Are you Mr. Sharpe?" she asked, inching closer to his face.

"The only cult is the deep state and our government. They currently are an armed force designed to protect our freedoms, but rather than protect them, they trample on them. But that will soon change as our force grows and thousands of others who believe what Harvest and I believe will join us. But one thing to remember, Detective, is that today, we are not a violent group, but that could change if we are challenged. Today, our group is all about love, family, and a future shared by those with common goals and beliefs," Noah said.

"Tell me about this future with you, Harvest, and maybe some of your pals. What does it look like?"

Laughing, Noah looked at Rhonda and said with some degree of incredulity. "Come on, Detective. I am not stupid, and I know you aren't either. If you have done any online research about Harvest, I assume you or some of your 'associates,' using air quotes to emphasize the word, "already have some understanding of Harvest's beliefs and her call to action. If you didn't, you would not be here hassling me and trying to find her."

"Yeah, you're right, Mr. Sharpe. I do know a little bit about Harvest and her beliefs through online research, but I am a local cop investigating two local crimes: a shooting at the park and a break-in at an IVF clinic. I fear online conspiracies and manifestos are beyond my pay grade." Rhonda was bluffing because she wanted Noah to believe she was just some local cop doing her nine to five and focusing on her daily caseload. In fact, thanks to Richard, Rhonda was deeply interested in conspiracies and manifestos. While she couldn't prove yet that the Tower Grove Park protest and the IVF clinic break-in were connected or done by the same people, she felt they were because the world was fucking crazy. People, especially a person like the loser Noah Sharpe, were easy prey to be radicalized and drawn into a national movement. She was also losing her patience with Noah Sharpe's evasiveness, so she thought she would try a new tack.

"Now, Mr. Sharpe. I have let you rant and rave about Harvest, her new world order, and your mutual distaste for the government, but before the world comes to an end or you and Harvest save it, start answering my fucking questions on the whereabouts and activities of you and especially Harvest. Were you involved in the shooting, and did she instruct you to undertake that?"

"No. Fuck you," said Noah.

Now more angry and closer to Noah's face. "Don't push me, you asshole. Were you involved in the break-in at the New Beginnings IVF Clinic, and if so, did Harvest instruct you to do that?"

"Same answer. No." and being a bit of a smart ass, added with a smile, "No, Ma'am."

The direct approach seemed to hit a stone wall, so Rhonda wanted to get deeper into Noah's psyche, which she assumed was fragile.

"Well, Mr. Sharpe, I hope you are telling the truth because if you aren't, and if you are involved in any of this, the only new world order you will see will be in the prison yard where a loser like you is sure to be someone's play toy. It will be hard for you to change the world and see your love Harvest if you are doing life. From what I know of Harvest and her beliefs, she would not be paying you any visits, and in fact, you would be easily replaced, and she would go on with her big plans with someone else. I think I read one of her manifestos that said there will be casualties in the battle. Maybe, Noah, you are already a casualty. Maybe Harvest had you do what she needed, and she has moved on. My associates who are tracking her postings tell me there are several people like you all over the country that she has connected with to help make her dream a reality. You are replaceable, Noah. In fact, you already may have been replaced."

Rhonda's comments seemed to shake the bravado off Noah, and self-doubt crept into his face, much like it did the last time he talked to Harvest online several nights ago. He had been concerned and even jealous that Harvest had others in her life, but she assured him she did not.

"You are wrong about Harvest. She and I have a special relationship, although she reaches out to thousands of followers. Harvest and I believe in a new world and are trying to build a life together."

Sensing Noah had a blind spot about Harvest and, in fact, was not as self-assured as he initially came across, she decided to soften her tone a bit to make Noah feel maybe she was on his side, at least from understanding how women think. "So, tell me about your life together, Mr. Sharpe."

"Harvest and I are planning our life together and building a home on some property my family owns in southeast Missouri, near Caledonia."

Now Rhonda pulled out an ace that Richard had found out about Noah. "You mean the property where your parents died in a flood, perhaps from your stupidness, Noah?"

That comment caused Noah to change his demeanor entirely. He was no longer an angry, psychopathic man. He reverted to an abandoned child, bottling up years of guilt and sorrow.

"I did not cause them to die. That was not my fault. It was God's fault. He made it rain and flood and told them to go look for me."

Pressing hard since she felt Noah would reveal a critical piece of information, she asked, "Noah, I know your parents died over twenty-five years ago. According to my cousin, the sheriff in Reynolds County, your property is now an abandoned wasteland. People have tried to buy it over the years, but you refuse to sell. Why does this property haunt you, Noah? Why have you not been back, Noah? Guilt? Shame for what you did?"

Now yelling loudly enough to attract stares from some early morning zoo visitors, Noah responded, "Leave me alone, Detective. I am finally in a good place in my life. I am finally doing something my parents would be proud of and doing it on the land we all loved. I am bringing the land back to life, so you or your cousin, the sheriff, do not know what you are talking about."

"What are you doing down there, Noah? What would make your parents proud of you or at least cause them to forgive you for their deaths? " She added the last comment to break Noah, who was already emotionally destroyed from this conversation. If ever a confession would be had from him, it would be now, but no confession was forthcoming as Noah turned and ran away from Detective Simon.

The reaction from the card Rhonda played shocked her a bit and frankly sickened her that she would use the tragic accident and deaths of a person's parents to help her solve a crime, but she had to do it as she was getting nowhere with this case. But her jurisdiction was St. Louis city, so she would have to enlist the help of her cousin, a call she would make immediately.

Chapter 34
SHERIFF TOMMY WILCOX

After confronting Noah Sharpe, Rhonda returned to her car and called her cousin, the sheriff of Reynolds County, Tommy Wilcox. After a few rings, she heard the familiar voice from her past, heavy with a southern rural Missouri twang that seemed more exaggerated every time she talked to him. However, their conversations were increasingly infrequent.

"Sheriff Tommy Wilcox here. What can I do you for?" the voice boomed through the phone at Rhonda.

"Tommy, Rhonda. How have you been?"

"Well, hell has frozen over, cuz. I have not heard from you in years. I've read about you and all your big-city detective crime-solving exploits, and I expected a call to your favorite country cousin just to rub it in my face. I am hurt, Rhonda," Tommy said, laughing.

Laughing as well, Rhonda said, "Tommy, it takes me months to solve a case. If I had your bloodhound of a nose with me, all the crime in St. Louis would be solved in days."

"Rhonda, if I was in the big city, there would be no crime. No street punks want to mess with Tommy Wilcox. Down here, we don't try them;

we tie them up, lock the door, and throw away the key. Maybe even fry em if we get the chance but those bleeding-heart liberals up by you don't like that so much. Justice takes too long, if at all, up in St. Louis."

Rhonda knew that while Tommy was kidding and using a euphemism from years ago, there still was too much revenge justice or courthouse step lawyering for her liking in rural Missouri. While she hated that in St. Louis, so many criminals seemed to walk and weeks later were involved in another crime, she also knew her peers in the rural parts of the state, while mostly law-abiding, were also not opposed to busting some heads in the name of suspect cooperation and retribution. Her cousin Tommy Wilcox was a good and popular cop, elected sheriff several times in Reynolds County, and she knew he would help her, if he could, in this case. Rhonda got to the point of the call after a few more good-natured ribbings and catching up on mutual relatives.

"Tommy, I could use your help on a case I am working on here. This may be a long shot, but instead of begging my supervisor to let me drive two hours to maybe chase a ghost, can you do some checking for me on a landowner down your way?"

"Cuz, you know I will if I can. I know darn every landowner down here and which ones to tread carefully with and which will cooperate more with the law. Who or what are you looking to find?"

"I want you to visit the Sharpe property on 32 off of A. They have a few hundred acres that wrap around Ottery Creek. Do you know the place?"

"Sure do, but not much going on there, Rhonda. After the Sharpes died in the freak flash flood drowning years ago, I think the place has been abandoned. Maybe the occasional lost hiker stumbles upon it or local meth cookers, but as far as I know, it is deserted. What's your interest in it?"

"A case I am working on has a suspect named Noah Sharpe. I think he was the only child of the Sharpes. Well, he's done all grown up and living in St. Louis. Perhaps he is involved with some odd behavior occurring on that property."

"Noah Sharpe? Wow, that is a name I have not heard in years. He was an odd kid back then, and he slipped deeper from reality after his parents died. What's he like now?"

"Odd is being kind. Sharpe is also a loner. Maybe he has even worse psychological problems. I think he could have become radicalized and even maybe a part of end-of-world conspiracies. He may be involved with some crimes up here, perhaps with a girlfriend of his, and just now, he flipped out when I brought up his family property and his parents' deaths. He indicated perhaps he has been doing something on that property that will make his parents proud. It made me shiver a bit about what this psycho could be doing down there. Before I make a trip down there, I am trying to find out if anything is going on with his property and maybe try and find the whereabouts of his girlfriend, who could possibly be hiding out there."

Laughing, Tommy said, "Well, Rhonda, from what I remember about Noah Sharpe, he did not live up to his name's sake. His nickname among the townspeople was Noah Dull. But when it comes to end-of-the-world conspiracies spun by religious or radicalized groups, he would fit in perfectly down here. After every "hi, how you doing" greeting, the conversation always goes into an end-of-the-world conspiracies, revolutions, and revolts. Shit, most people spouting off this stuff could not get to the end of their driveway unless they had a map. I would put Noah Sharpe in that category."

Now laughing herself, Rhonda responded, "I hear you, Tommy. Sounds whacked out, but I tell you, the stuff we see online that starts as ranting and raving, we, unfortunately, see turned into action with some nutcase thinking they have been summoned to act on another crazy manifesto. That is what I am worried about. Noah Sharpe may be one of those guys influenced by others and could do something crazy. I would appreciate it if you would just do your cousin a solid. After all, I know what you and Mary Jean Renner did underneath those bleachers back in high school."

"You got it, Rhonda, and you don't have to remind me what Mary Jean and I did under those bleachers. I remember every day when I talk to my beautiful daughter, who is now twenty-eight with a baby of her own."

"That's great, Tommy. And say hi to Mary Jean for me. If you find something happening at the Sharpe property, it will give me a good excuse to pay a visit."

"Well, whether we find something or not, our door is always open. It's been a long time since a family reunion, and I know your life and family have also changed, so we need to all connect. Not getting any younger, and in the line of work we are in, every day upright is a blessing. I will be in touch."

Rhonda hung up the phone and realized Tommy was right. It had been a long time since there had been a whole family reunion, and she did have a dangerous profession, which made every day something to savor. She wanted her cousins to meet Richard and her whole family.

Chapter 35
OTTERY SEARCHED

Sheriff Tommy Wilcox decided to drive down to the old Sharpe property himself rather than pawn it off to one of his underlings. He was pretty sure that whatever Noah Sharpe may have told Rhonda was probably delusional because he was sure that after the accidental deaths of Noah's parents, the boy lost what little sanity he may have been holding on to. Driving down Missouri 32 to Highway A, Tommy Wilcox knew the entrance to the Sharpe property was hidden, about one hundred yards off the road, and access to it went through a shared easement with a neighbor's piece of land. Turning right off of A, he drove down a rutted trail to a locked gate. The gate was locked and seemingly covered with an overgrowth of low-hanging tree branches and encroaching bushes and weeds. Tommy did notice some of the branches looked freshly broken and perhaps detached from the original tree or bush they sprouted from. They seemed to be loosely placed on the gate, indicating that someone wanted to make the gate seem unused when, in fact, it may have been used recently.

Additionally, Tommy looked down both in front of and behind the gate. He noticed while the gate seemed overgrown, there were obvious tire tracks, somewhat fresh as if they had been made recently, and just like with the gate, there was a feeble attempt by someone to try and obscure the tire tracks for thirty or forty yards or as much as Tommy could visualize from his position. Enough seemed out of place that Tommy decided to call several deputies to join him before he entered the Sharpe property. As much as he believed at most some squatters or maybe some meth cookers were temporarily occupying the Sharpe property, back here in the woods, everyone was armed, many times with more firepower than he possessed. While residents respected the law, generally, if you were entering someone's property where a criminal act may be taking place, the law was the enemy. It would be about fifteen minutes before backup arrived as they had limited sheriff's deputies covering a huge county. He waited and listened, perhaps for voices or something else. As an avid outdoorsman, Tommy knew that to hear the noise in the forest, you had to first hear and separate what you expect to hear and then, and only then, could you hear the unexpected. He began to let the silence of the woods envelop him, isolating and locating the noises from distant cars on the road to tree birds, ground critters, and running water. He enjoyed this momentary peace and quiet because he knew that it could be shattered as soon as he stepped foot on someone's property, especially in rural Missouri, where shoot first and ask questions later was the law of the land.

After about fifteen minutes, two additional deputies arrived. Tommy quickly covered why he was investigating the Sharpe property, showed them the tire tracks on the rutted path, and discussed handling the situation. Technically, they would need a warrant to enter private property, but they could do it without a warrant if they had reason to believe an uninhabited property may have been broken into. This was frequent in Reynolds County and many rural counties, as many properties were second homes or hunting properties that were usually unoccupied. In fact, many remote owners never even locked their properties, knowing that in the woods, a break-in would occur unheard. It was better to let the trespassers enter the home, providing it was devoid of any valuables, rather than having a door or window busted to attain entrance. While the Sharpe property, to the best of their knowledge, had been vacant for years, the signs of recent vehicle and foot traffic observed by the entrance told them, at a minimum, it had been visited recently.

While normally they would have tried to contact the homeowner before entering since they had seen the tire tracks on the property, they could use the excuse of "suspicious behavior or activity" based on what Detective Simon had told her cousin as a reason for entering. It also helped that the presiding county judge was Tommy and Rhonda's cousin. They decided to enter on foot instead of trying to drive their cars to ensure the secrecy of their presence along the paths. They did not know what shape the gravel roads were after years and years of weather, disuse, and neglect.

The property was over three hundred acres, but it also adjoined thousands of acres of uninhabited state land. It was very isolated. Based on their local knowledge, the sheriff and deputies knew the housing complex when the Sharpes last lived there was in the southeast portion of the property. The Sharpes had built several homes, a barn, a root cellar, and several other outbuildings on the flattest part of the property overlooking Ottery Creek and its crystal-clear swimming holes and slow-moving current. They expected all the buildings to be in disrepair, if not completely uninhabitable. Still, as they got closer, approximately two hundred yards away, they could see the main buildings. The houses where the Sharpe's friends and families had gathered were in good shape. This surprising discovery raised the hairs on the back of Tommy's neck. It was not what he had expected. It was the exact opposite. Instead of finding abandonment, he saw rejuvenation in the buildings and surrounding grounds. The property was in the same pristine state it was twenty-five years ago when the Sharpes lived there. *"Had someone bought the property and was living there?* Tommy wondered. He would have to check the county's tax records to see if that was the case.

Regardless, something was off. Tommy was sure. He motioned his two deputies to fan out in a safe but hidden distance on three triangle points surrounding the Sharpe family compound. He wanted him and his men positioned on three sides of the property, figuring the side perched high above Ottery Creek would form a natural barrier to anyone trying to run or hide.

Tommy was still determining if the houses were occupied. However, he saw no vehicles, but there was access to the property by back trails that locals were sure to be familiar with. If there were people in the houses, he needed to ascertain how many people he might be dealing with and if they were armed. He and all his men had hunted together and knew how to move quietly in the woods and communicate using hand signals and natural bird calls. He gave them instructions to indicate how many people each of them might see with a common bird call. They chose to use the calls of a Winter Wren and a Wood Warbler, common birds in Missouri in the winter whose sounds would not surprise or be noticed. The call of the Wren would be issued to count the number of people they saw, and the Warbler called once would indicate if they saw weapons. One call for standard shotguns, and two calls for more deadly firepower such as AR-15s.

After waiting five minutes, each of them, starting with Tommy, gave a sound indicating the number of people and the presence of weapons. What Tommy heard back from his two deputies relieved him as none of the men could identify any sign of people in the houses or on the property. He then gave the call to the deputies to meet in the original spot so they could re-group and discuss what they thought might be going on and their next step.

Taking time to compose themselves, Tommy asked each deputy their assessment. Jason had positioned himself at the back of the house and had the most unnerving findings.

"Boss, something creepy is happening in that house and on this property. I didn't sense anyone was in the house, so I moved closer to peer into the back windows, and you have got to see it to believe it," he said to Tommy.

Knowing Jason was rock solid but also knowing he would have to see for himself what Jason saw through the back windows, the three men moved closer to the house, pistols drawn. Quietly, Tommy walked up the first steps onto the back porch, which he noticed was not weather worn but looked almost new. Peering inside and glancing into what he assumed used to be the Sharpe's living room, Tommy was surprised by what he saw because it was the last thing he was expecting. Turning to his men and slowly signaling to ease back off the porch, they eventually went outside the gate, returned to their cars, and drove them back out of the Sharpe property and onto Highway A. They would head to the sheriff's station to debrief each other in detail and determine the next steps. On the way back to the station, Tommy called Rhonda, gave her an update, and told her to get her St. Louis ass down here. Quickly. The second thing he did was to call the Reynolds County judge, his cousin Bobby, and have him execute a search warrant immediately, so when Rhonda arrived, they could go back to the property to enter the buildings because what he had seen may have confirmed Rhonda's worst fears.

Chapter 36
RHONDA CONFRONTS NOAH

After hearing from Sheriff Tommy Wilcox, Rhonda immediately met with Lieutenant Tarallo to tell her what they found and to recommend she try to convince Noah Sharpe to go with her to his family property. Rhonda and Tarallo agreed they needed to see firsthand what Noah was doing on his property, but also use Noah to access Harvest. What Tommy Wilcox had told Rhonda about what he saw convinced Rhonda that perhaps Harvest was down at Ottery and was the ringleader of whatever operation was being conducted down there.

Based on what Tommy Wilcox told Rhonda, she knew she had to play to Noah's delusional ego versus arresting him because, at this time, she was not even sure what she would be arresting him for, plus she did not want Noah to lawyer up before she could figure out if he was working alone or was being helped by others. She also asked to take Officer Moloney with her since she was on the case, and Rhonda needed another set of eyes on Sharpe. Tommy told her he had the men to handle the ground operation as there were three hundred acres they would need to search. Tommy reminded Rhonda that it was his jurisdiction because not only was there a potential crime in his county, but he also wanted some recognition for uncovering it. He and Rhonda had been competitive ever since they were kids, and he certainly did not want her to have all the limelight in this case. Tarallo agreed to all Rhonda's requests. Rhonda did not tell Tarallo that she was also taking Richard Leary with her because, on the way down, she needed Richard's mind to play chess with Noah's mind.

Leaving Tarallo's office, Rhonda headed to the zoo to talk with Sharpe. She told Officer Moloney to meet her there for backup. Entering the zoo, they walked to the primate area where she had last met Noah. She walked among the enclosures, looking at ones that seemed empty, indicating that the enclosure might be being cleaned. This is where she assumed she would find Noah at work. Sure enough, she spotted Noah down in the man-made ravine that created a water source for the apes and served as another barrier between them and their human visitors. Yelling down at him, she got his attention and asked him to meet her around the corner of the enclosure's staff entrance. While he seemed nonchalant to her request, he gave a sense that he acknowledged her and, in a few minutes, came out the staff door and locked it behind him. He was dusty and dirty from a long day of work and, frankly, smelled like the ape shit he was cleaning.

"Ah, Detective. Another visit. Have you considered buying a yearly membership to the zoo if you plan on visiting so often," he sneered, adding, "With all the crime in St. Louis, don't you have any other cases to work on?" However, his glance also saw Officer Moloney with Detective Simon, and his bravado quickly changed.

"You know what, Noah. I have a ton of cases to work on, but they are so black and white. Boring really. They are pretty basic murders based on rage or money. But sometimes, I run into a case involving someone who is a criminal genius. Usually, a brilliant person is always underestimated. Sort of like you, Noah, which keeps me returning to this case. It is interesting because I know so little about it and you, even after weeks of investigating it. I must say, I have solved hundreds of cases, but this one perplexes me. So, congratulations, Noah. You have stumped me so far." She could see a subtle smile across Noah's face. The face of a true delusional narcissist.

"I should take that as a compliment, Detective. You know, I have always found that everyone has underestimated me until they find out who they are dealing with. I know I have what might seem like a low-intellect, crappy job, but I think you are starting to realize I am more intelligent than most people walking the planet."

"I noticed that, Noah. I have been following your social connections and commentaries online, which is where you command a great deal of respect. Your online followers listen to what you say on various topics. You are usually listed as one of the top commentators on most forums you participate in. As a matter of fact, I have heard that the Cardinal's management specifically reads your comments about improving the team. Congrats man. You have a skill and seem to be a natural-born leader."

Now Noah was practically beaming, and he completely seemed uninterested that Rhonda had mentioned she had been probing his online activity since most people would have heard that and considered it a huge red flag. Rhonda could tell Noah interpreted her comment as a badge of honor. She decided to push the conversation to gain more of his trust.

"One thing I wonder about is that online influencers make so much money. Have you monetized what you do like these other influencers? I know some of them, even those not super famous, make hundreds of thousands of dollars. I know you are a bright guy, and you could if you wanted to do it. It sure would be better than cleaning monkey shit out of cages."

Noah looked at Rhonda with a mixture of caution and maybe doubt but perhaps also intrigued. Rhonda sensed Noah's apprehension, so she pushed on.

"You know, Noah, I have a friend I work with who is considered one of the most advanced digital and social media investigative experts, and he consults with influencers on how to monetize their influence. He told me that, based on his experience, you have tremendous potential to grow your online following beyond your predominately sports commenting, which while prolific, is such a crowded field with many professional influencers."

"Yeah, I have thought about that, but many ex-athletes or news sports outlets seem to have the market cornered on paid influencers. I am not sure I could make any real money in that field. Does your friend have any other ideas on what other subjects I should be talking about?" Noah was still contemplating whether to trust Rhonda and this conversation's direction. After all, she was a cop, but since in his mind, he had not done anything wrong, she seemed to have information that could be useful to him. Noah always thought his intuition and intelligence would make him a good detective.

"My friend follows a lot of hate or anger influencers fueled predominately by disinformation and conspiracy theorists. My friend told me that guy Alex Jones made billions of dollars primarily promoting the conspiracy and disinformation about the Sandy Hook shooting. It was unbelievable to me he made so much money."

Noah shook his head in the affirmative. "I follow him, but I did not realize he made that much money."

"My friend also told me there are dozens in the field, all with niches that are raking in the dough and, more importantly, gaining the adulation of millions of followers. Like your friend Harvest, they are rock stars in the online influence world. I bet she is making millions of dollars based on the size of her following," Rhonda added.

Mentioning Harvest changed Noah's disposition slightly, and Rhonda knew she had to tread carefully here. Noah had proclaimed his love for Harvest, and Rhonda assumed his unwavering loyalty to her. Rhonda had one angle she thought she could play, but this would be her only and best chance to get Noah to bite.

"What does your friend know about Harvest?" Noah asked, not defiantly but with more curiosity, as he wondered what more there was to know about Harvest. He thought he knew everything about her, but even to him, she remained mysterious.

"Noah, I don't want to get in the middle between you and Harvest, and as you have been tight-lipped about her to me, but my friend perhaps knows a lot more about her than you may even know. You have only shared her philosophy and, I guess, her manifesto about forming a new world order."

Rhonda continued, "Harvest is one of many trying to gain supporters and generate money for an idea shared by many. In a way, she is running a business, and other end-of-world conspiracists are her competition. Her niche seems to be targeting the upheaval caused by pro-life versus pro-choice supporters which probably has some big financial backers, as it is all business like everything is these days. My friend knows she is targeting IVF centers and perhaps the abduction of embryos to potentially start this new society, as you call it. You and I both know it takes lots and lots of money to create a following and do what Harvest is asking you and, I assume, others to do. Do you have the kind of money that Harvest needs?"

Noah shook his head no.

"In many ways, Noah, while you may be her lover, you may also be just an employee. An employee that may be disposable when she is done getting what she needs out of you. That is why I think you need to start monetizing what you do, so she looks at you as a true equal, and my friend can help you do that."

"That's not true. Harvest loves me and needs me. She and I will build this new future together. She told me so," Noah said but not with much conviction as perhaps Rhonda was beginning to sow some doubt in his brain.

Rhonda needed to interlace the pure fiction she was spinning about Harvest with the reality of what Tommy found in Ottery. "So, Noah, is Harvest the one who told you to build that operation on your family property down in Reynolds County?"

"How did you know about that? Only Harvest and I know about that."

"I told you, Noah, everyone is looking into you and Harvest. My cousin, the sheriff in Reynolds County told me that the townspeople are all talking about it and are so proud of what you are doing down there. They call you their prodigal son and want to welcome you back. In fact, because my cousin was concerned that your notoriety might lead some trespassers to your property, he visited it to make sure everything was ok and saw the operation with his own eyes."

Now Noah was truly pissed and raging.

"What I do on my own property is my own business, Detective. And you and your cousin have no right to snoop around down there. I have my rights!"

"You are right, Noah. You do have your rights, and what you are doing down there may be completely innocent, or it may implicate you in the crime of the protest shooting or breaking into the IVF clinic, crimes that right now you are a primary suspect. But if it is something you are doing on the wishes of Harvest, we should know that because you are a small fish in this, and perhaps Harvest is the big fish."

Taking a moment to assess how Noah was reacting to all of this, Rhonda continued, "While what you are doing down there may be something you and Harvest are doing for your future, if anything is illegal, you, as the property owner, will be charged, especially since Harvest seems so elusive. She may vanish like the wind if she feels she is at risk legally. Let me assure you, Noah, people like Harvest, the ring leaders and the visionaries, seldom spend time in jail. It is those that they instruct to carry out their work that end up serving time. In my line of work, that is a certainty."

"I can't believe she would do that to me. We love each other," Noah said with a weakened sense of certainty. Rhonda could sense more doubt, now with some rage creeping into his mind.

"Perhaps, Noah, but as they say, love is blind, but you are smart enough to know you should protect yourself, and who knows, maybe even make some money and achieve national and maybe worldwide notoriety for yourself. You have wanted that for so long. You have wanted not to live in the shadows. Not to be underestimated. To be someone. To make your parents proud. Right, Noah? Whatever you are doing is perhaps righting the wrongs in your life. Filling the holes your parents' deaths have caused you."

On the mention of his parents, Noah began shaking, then sobbing uncontrollably.

"My parents died because of my stupidity, and my stupidity has left me so alone. They were all I had, and my life was empty until Harvest came along. She has given me purpose."

"That is great, Noah, that she gave you purpose, but let's make sure for your sake and their memory that you don't fall into a deep, dark place again. Maybe what you are doing is completely legitimate, and it is something that will make your parents proud, but I can't know that unless you take me down there with you and show me around. If you do, I can take my friend with us, and he can also tell you how you can make millions of dollars on your own as an online influencer. How about we drive down there right now? Would you like that, Noah?"

Noah nodded, with an eerie calmness about him. Almost has if his personality had flipped yet again. No longer weeping and no longer defensive. He was back to defiant and cocky. Turning to Simon, he said, "Let's go, Detective. I will tell you about my great awakening on the way down and how I hope to impress Harvest."

Chapter 37

NOAH'S SECRET DISCOVERED

They left the zoo, jumped in Richard's truck, and headed down to Noah Sharpe's property in Reynolds County. They took Richard's truck as Rhonda wanted Noah to feel this was an off-the-book trip, and being in a cop's car might spook him. She also gave her cousin Tommy Wilcox a heads-up that she was headed down. She asked him to be on standby a few miles away to avoid Noah being spooked that more law enforcement was involved in this. She wanted to continue to gain Noah's trust and hoped he would implicate himself and possibly Harvest.

On the way down, it also gave Richard some time to talk to Noah about both Richard's skills as an online investigator and continue to inflate Noah's ego about his skills as an online influencer. Richard also hoped to understand more about Harvest and his influence on Noah. Richard knew of Noah's family tragedy that happened at Ottery, so while he wanted to dig deep into his mind, he did not want him to retreat to some dark hole that was caused by his parent's deaths. He needed Noah talking and, more importantly, trusting Richard. This was a skill Richard had learned in the military, interrogating enemy combatants before, of course, he tortured them.

"Noah, this is beautiful country down here. Are you much of a hunter?" Richard asked casually.

"No. I had a BB gun as a kid and would sometimes try to take out a squirrel, but usually I felt bad about it, so I just target shot. My mom and dad were the same way. We all liked the land to foster nature, not destroy it."

It was good that Noah could talk about his parents without retreating to a dark place.

"Are your views on nature and animals what got you into your job at the zoo?" Were you always interested in zoology?"

Noah in a monotone voice commented, "I am not sure if you call feeding and cleaning up after monkeys 'zoology,' but I have always liked working with animals. I wanted to be a vet because I liked or was liked by animals more than humans. When my parents died, vet school was done for. I was also good in science and biology, so I wondered if I could combine those interests with my interest in animals."

"In what way?" asked Richard.

"I studied the work of a doctor in St. Louis, a leader in human reproductive methods, but then he started using his knowledge in that field to find breakthroughs to help endangered animals reproduce. He was the genius I never became, until now."

Richard asked, "You mean Dr. Durell and his work in the field?"

"Yeah. He is considered a pioneer and visionary in reproductive medicine. Now I want people to think of me as a visionary, and maybe they will because of what I am doing down here."

"Now Richard perked up on Noah's comments about reproductive medicine as this could be the connection they needed to tie Noah into the New Beginnings break-in. Noah, as Richard hoped was close to confessing his crimes by first bragging about them as all narcissists do. He also thought that the conversation was going exactly as planned, as Noah had been talking more freely than Richard had thought he would. Rhonda told Richard that she felt Noah had delusions of grandeur and believed he was an important person and that people wanted to hear what he had to say. Richard, who was not a trained psychiatrist, concurred based on Noah's online comments. Like many delusional commentators, Noah believed he had more knowledge than the professionals whose decisions he was mocking. In the old days, they used to call people like Noah 'armchair quarterbacks.' Now, they were online commentators or influencers with followers, who were sometimes paid to give opinions. *"What a narcissistic world we live in,"* *Richard* thought. *"Everyone thinks they have something important to say."*

They drove silently for a few minutes as Richard focused on navigating the winding roads, traveling through rolling hills, and passing clear-running streams on the way to Noah's property. It really was a remote and beautiful part of the state. However, he wanted to get back to Noah's comment and how this might all tie into the purpose of their visit to Ottery.

"Noah, you mentioned you were interested in how human infertility breakthroughs have helped endangered species. Can this type of science have a significant impact on saving endangered species?"

"Sure, it can. All species can be saved by human infertility breakthroughs. Animals, insects, humans."

Richard continued, "Is this what Harvest believes in, Noah? Is that why she has told you to build this operation on your property? I am open-minded about this, and I think what you are doing could have a major impact on your life, but I have to be honest, some of Harvest's beliefs sound a little far-fetched."

Noah and Rhonda were silent for a while, with Rhonda wondering where Richard was going with this conversation as he was almost ridiculing Noah, a guy Rhonda was trying to nurse along. They had fifteen miles to go before they got to Noah's property, and she was concerned Richard's comment would piss off Noah and cause him to stop cooperating. She waited for Noah to speak, and after a minute of deep thought, he spoke very quietly but not angrily. "You know, Mr. Leary, when we get to my property, we will walk past these little creeks crisscrossing the area. You will look at the creeks, and if I told you that they could swell to a raging river in a matter of seconds, you might think that concept is also far-fetched. Sort of like the bible when the original Noah built an ark to save mankind from the great flood. That was far-fetched, but it happened, Mr. Leary."

"Well, perhaps it happened, Noah. But I believe the story about Noah's Ark is just that, a story," Richard commented in a non-confrontational way, but it obviously set Noah off.

"It did happen!" he screamed. "God asked Noah to save mankind and he did. You are all non-believers. You will all suffer the same fate as the non-believers when Noah built his ark." Then, continuing with a little less anger, "My parents are dead because of a concept that could be described as far-fetched. So perhaps, describing our project to create a new society as far-fetched is a bit short-sighted."

Now, an uncomfortable silence settled over them in the car. Still, it was a critical silence, perhaps as Rhonda and Richard thought about what motivated Noah to embark on such an audacious plan. Maybe it was under the direction of Harvest. Maybe it was part of some large national end-of-the-world cult or conspiracists. Or maybe it was just about Noah trying to make amends for the deaths of his parents he felt he caused.

The silence was interrupted by Noah quietly but with still anger, saying, "The turn-off is two hundred yards on your right, just past the three pine trees."

Richard turned where Noah instructed and, after another one hundred yards, came up the rutted path to a metal gate in the same shape as it was when Sheriff Tommy Wilcox and his deputies visited. Noah hopped out of the car and used a code to open the gate.

Unlike Tommy Wilcox, who wanted an element of surprise on his visit, Noah instructed Richard to drive his truck down the path and through the clear running creek. Although he had a truck that should easily traverse the creek, Richard instinctively asked Noah how deep it was, so he could gauge if he needed to find a more shallow area for the crossing.

"It's only about a foot deep, about ten feet to your right, but when the rains come, it is not far-fetched that the creek becomes four to five feet deep very quickly." Richard steered the truck towards the crossing Noah suggested and made it across without any problem. However, on the far side of the creek, sand deposits had built up, and Richard put it in low gear to move through the sandy soil. Once they were on a firm, though now a very rock-strewn path, Noah instructed Richard to follow the path another seventy-five yards. Once Richard rounded the last bend in the path, Noah's family compound appeared. They came to a stop, and Richard turned off the truck engine.

To Noah, so many of his happiest memories were when his family would pull up to this point to enjoy the property's tranquility. Those memories were darkened by one of Noah's last memories, the coroner pulling away from the property with the bodies of Noah's mom and dad. It was only since he decided how to make amends for his parents' deaths and when he met Harvest that he started coming back to this place. She convinced him that from death comes life and that he was destined to create a new life for himself and others.

He exited the truck and proudly waved his arms to show Rhonda and Richard all he had developed. The land and property that had been discarded and left in decay for nearly twenty-five years was brought back to life by Noah. Noah pointed out the main house to Richard and Rhonda. What Tommy Wilcox and his men saw in there is the reason Rhonda rushed down here, so silently Rhonda undid the safety on her gun. Then, they turned to the guest cabins Noah's parents had built for their friends who would visit. When Noah was a kid, his parents had always hoped he would invite some friends to the property, but no friends came because he had none. While his parents were concerned Noah's lack of friends was painful for him, Noah was happy being here and being with nature. He could feel his happiness as a kid returning to him as he rebuilt the compound to complete his and Harvest's vision. Noah pointed out a new tire swing he put up to replace the old one whose tire and rope had rotted and the horseshoe pits that he spent many days playing on. He had rebuilt those as well.

He told Richard and Rhonda, "This is where all the kids will play, just like I did as a kid."

As they walked to the main house, Noah pointed out where the orchard and vegetable gardens would be, just as when his mother tended to them daily in the summer months. Noah rambled on, discussing the property and what else he wanted to show them. As he rooted for the key to the main house in his pants pocket, he turned back to Rhonda and Richard, saying as he opened the door, "Of course, our dream starts here with all the babies."

Every time Rhonda had met with Noah Sharpe, she came away bewildered about the oddity of the man. But what Rhonda saw when she opened the door to his family home changed her feelings about Noah Sharpe. While he was odd and a loner, now Rhonda saw him for what he really was: a monster. Looking at Richard, who had seen every horror in his life and who also had unholstered his gun, she could tell he had never seen what was behind the door in Noah Sharpe's family cabin. And the smell when they entered the room was nauseating.

Throughout the home were fifteen makeshift cribs, bassinets, and cages, the types used for animals. Hanging over each of the units was a small music box and the lullaby "Rock-a-Bye Baby" was playing over and over. In each enclosure was a pink or blue blanket covering what was causing the smell, and around each blanket, flies swarmed.

"But we must be quiet as the babies are sleeping," Noah said, shushing Rhonda, Richard, and Officer Moloney. While they could not take their eyes off the cribs and what might be under the blankets, they scanned the room. On the walls were hundreds of photos of babies, but next to each were also photos of aborted fetuses. It was gruesome and Noah noticed everyone looking at the photos and said, "the photos remind me what our mission is, to save the unborn who have been so brutally murdered for the last fifty years."

With fear in her voice, an emotion Rhonda had never had in investigating any crime scene, she asked quietly, "Noah, do you mind if we look at some of the babies? I promise we won't wake them." When Noah nodded yes, Rhonda walked up to one of the cribs, as did Richard and Moloney, each pulling back a blanket. Their reaction was physically sickening, with all of them holding back from vomiting at what they were now looking at. In each crib was not a living baby, but one that was dead, and based on the decay, dead for a while. Some were missing their limbs, some were opened up where an empty chest cavity revealed no heart, and some were decapitated and looking over to the shelf on a wall, the severed heads lay, rotting, infected with maggots. Rhonda and Moloney had never seen something so gruesome and looked away. Richard, however, hardened because he spent so much time in war zones and had seen mutilation and death, especially of children, beyond what Moloney and Rhonda had in their lives, steadied himself and stared more intently at the corpses in the cribs. He hovered over, then looked into the cribs Moloney and Rhonda were looking at, then started turning over the blankets in the other cribs. Rhonda and Moloney stared at him, wondering how he could hold in the contents of his stomach. They were then startled, as was Richard, as he laughed, turning to Noah saying, "You are one sick fuck, Sharpe. Does the zoo know you are killing baby monkeys?"

"What did you say, Richard?" asked Rhonda as she edged closer to and carefully peaked into one of the cribs, whose blanket Richard had removed. "I said, these, I believe, are monkeys, chimps, apes, all primates, but not human, I think, and I hope. Am I right, Sharpe, these are all animals?"

Noah responded without emotion but more puzzlement at the question, "Of course they are not human, but their sacrifice will help mankind become one, with a common sense of purpose and beliefs."

"What do you mean Noah? What did you do to these animals and why did you do it?" asked an angry Richard.

"I experimented with them to see if I could shape their behavior by whatever means possible. Some I implanted transmitters receivers in their brains and used electric surges to control actions, some I starved or withheld medicine until they behaved as I wanted them to and some I just dismembered to study their organs and skeletal systems. I studied many of the greatest experiments ever done on animals, and came up with some of my own."

Now, with a surprising degree of compassion Rhonda asked, "But why Noah, you love monkeys. Why would you torture them like this?"

"For Harvest, Detective, and our goal of creating a new world order. I had to understand how animals would respond before we began breeding, raising and socializing the humans to thinks as we want them to. I did not want to do it at first, but I know that if I was to earn Harvests' trust, I had to do it. I have never had a real person who loved me since my parents died, so I needed to make some sacrifices, and the animals needed to be sacrificed before we get to work on the humans I have on the property."

Then, shocking everyone Noah said, "Humans are kept in the other houses on the property. You want to see them?"

As shocked as everyone but Noah was, Rhonda whispered in Moloney's ear to get on the radio and call Tommy Wilcox and his team to get down to the property immediately. She was unsure what they would see but knew it would be bad.

"Sure, Noah, let's go to the other houses," Rhonda said. Noah gently put all the blankets back on the decaying primate corpses. Then, tiptoeing out of the home and signaling everyone else to be quiet, they all left and, and once in the fresh air, stopped to catch their breath and process what they had just seen. They were not sure what they would see in the other houses: humans, who were really animals, or real humans who had also suffered from cruel experiments? Whatever it was, they were prepared to be shocked and possibly sickened.

As they walked to the other houses on the compound, Noah cheerfully told them what they might be seeing as if he was a tour guide.

"I have them all organized based on their race, gender, religion, political beliefs, or purification status, determining if they are close to being true believers or not. Some men and women who came without children I have put in the same cell to force them to breed. This is another thing that will make Harvest so proud of me."

Opening up the door to the first home, Rhonda noticed it did not smell like death as the home with the decayed primate corpses did. But it smelled nonetheless of feces, urine, and discarded food. In addition, Rhonda could clearly see signs of rodent droppings through the home. When they entered the main room, there was no sign of humans. Still, the house did look lived in, as books and magazines, covering everything from the bible to medical journals to survivalist tips and child caring manuals, were strewn all over the house, along with half-eaten food and spilled soda bottles. Noah took them through the living room, then the kitchen, and then unlocked a door leading down to what they assumed was a cellar or basement.

As he did, he told them that his parents had originally built all these underground caverns to store roots and vegetables as well as keep them all safe if the country was bombed in a nuclear attack. As they walked through the cavern Noah pointed out the endless rows of canned goods, powdered food, munitions, water, medical supplies, all the items needed in a nuclear attack, or the end of the world by self-implosion. As they reached the end of a tunnel, he turned on a light, and what they saw, while not as sickening as the decayed primate corpses, was every bit as shocking. In now a well-lit basement were ten what could be described as cells, and each cell contained a bed, a chair, two people and a child or baby, and in some cells, there were just two people. All of them were naked and so emaciated and shriveled they did not look up, perhaps out of weakness or hopelessness, at the three new people with Noah, including one with a cop's uniform on. Rhonda and Richard were not sure the babies and small children in the cells were alive.

Noah turned to Rhonda, Richard, and Officer Moloney, saying," I would like to introduce you to the first inhabitants, future breeders and parents who will populate Noah's Ark and become the new society that Harvest, and I are planning."

Rhonda had one question before she cuffed and placed Noah Sharpe under arrest. "Noah, could you tell me where these people came from and what are you planning to do with them."

Noah responding as if he was doing a school tour at the zoo, pointed to each cell, highlighted the inhabitants. "Well, these people here, I found at the St. Louis Zoo, the ones next to them were visiting the animals at zoos in Omaha, Columbus, Wichita, and Milwaukee. I visited zoos around the Midwest to see how different people from different places would treat animals, especially monkeys, so I could decide if they would be good parents and breeders for our new society. And the ones who are in the cells without a child or baby, they need to show me they can breed so we can begin populating the Ark."

As Richard and Moloney started to assure and calm the cells inhabitants and look for ways to unlock the doors, Rhonda kept interrogating Noah, "Noah, is there anybody else helping you do this work?

"No Detective. Just me. I told you I am a genius, and everyone underestimates me. They won't anymore as soon as they will find out what I am capable of doing, and how I and Harvest will be the overseers of this great new society."

"But Noah, so far your great society consist of dead monkeys, emaciated and scared humans, and a fantasy woman you have never seen in person. You can't believe you have been called upon to create a new society Noah?"

"It's my destiny Detective. Once I lost my parents, I asked God for all these years to show me the way to start a new family. Once Harvest and I get my hands on the IVF embryos stolen from Dr. Brazini's clinic and begin to birth them and raise them this will the foundation of our new society."

The mention of Layla stopped Rhonda cold. "You know Dr. Brazini, Noah?"

"Of course I do. I have been following and tracking her for months. I was hoping to take her from the IVF clinic and that is why I was outside her clinic the day you and I met. We need her medical expertise, but she is also so pretty and smart. I think she would make a good breeder not just to carry existing embryos, but maybe to breed with me. Don't you think we will have beautiful children Detective?"

While Rhonda heard sirens from Tommy Wilcox and his officers' cars, who were now descending on the property, she reacted from Noah's comments in the only way she knew how. Taking her gun and bashing it into the head of Noah Sharpe, who crumpled on the ground, she stood over him saying, "Noah Sharpe, you bastard, you are hereby under arrest for the kidnapping of these people. Do you understand your rights? I will read them if you do not understand them."

Chapter 38

THE TRUTH COMES OUT

After Tommy showed up, Rhonda and her cousin got into a piss-ing contest about who would process Noah Sharpe. Rhonda used a call into Tarallo, who convinced Sheriff Tommy Wilcox that since it was possible these kidnappings took place in many locales, multiple agencies would be involved, and he would be inundated with paperwork. She told him he would get more publicity arraigning Noah in St. Louis because it is a larger media market, and she promised him some exposure on local and national news outlets. That was enough for Tommy to let Rhonda take Sharpe with her, and he could get back to hunting, fishing, chasing moonshiners, and meth heads.

Rhonda knew solving the kidnappings, multiple unsolved cases that had not been on the STLPD radar screen because they took place in various cities around the Midwest and the connections between them all had not been made. And like many cases in overworked and understaffed police departments in the Midwest, they got pushed to the back burner and never solved. This would be a feather in both Rhonda and Tarallo's caps, especially Tarallo's as Rhonda would let her take the credit for the overall strategy of the investigation. Plus Rhonda had bigger fish to fry.

Rhonda still had doubts about Noah's involvement at the IVF break-in and theft of the embryos as he really did not confess to doing the break-in but knew about it and more importantly knew and was obsessed with Layla. Perhaps his obsession with Layla led him to believe he was also involved with the theft of the embryos in some way. He was definitely delusional, and Rhonda believed he could be suffering from a degree of transference regarding his desire to kidnap Layla and his involvement with the IVF theft. But he was about to be locked up, probably in a mental institution for a long time, and she needed some answers from him now on the ride back to St. Louis. She and Richard still had to figure out if anybody helped Noah in the IVF break in and if Noah was involved in the protest shooting. There was still the matter of Harvest, who she was and where she was and perhaps the loose ends understanding if Marianne Hylany and Billy O'Dell fit into this in any way. To answer these questions, she and Richard would have to huddle up again in his man cave to dig deeper into the online community, but right now they had about ninety minutes to interview Noah Sharpe, uninterrupted and without lawyers present or the media feeding frenzy which would undoubtedly take place.

Noah was not very talkative on the ride home.

"Noah, who told you what to do on your family property?

"Harvest and God," he said.

"How can we find her, Noah? We might be able to help you get a reduced sentence as we think she is the ringleader of all of this."

"She is not hiding."

"Noah, did you also break into the IVF clinic?"

"No."

"Did you take the embryos from the fertility clinic, Noah?"

"No, others did. I was going to break into the clinic in the very early morning, when the pretty doctor came into exercise but when I got there the clinic had already been broken into, so I left. I really wanted to take that cute little doctor and make her a breeder, then adding, and sending shivers up Rhonda's spine, "You know she sort of looks like you Detective Simon. Too bad I did not get her."

Rhonda said nothing but Richard stole a glance at Rhonda, wondering if the two women did look alike.

"Noah, did you know who broke into the clinic?"

"No, but I am sure they were instructed by Harvest to do so as Harvest has the plan."

"What is the plan? How did Harvest or her followers do this?"

"Figure it out yourself. Like everyone always says, follow the money."

Changing tack, they then asked about the shooting.

"Noah, did you do the shooting at the protest?"

"I was there to do it for Harvest but someone else did it before me and I was worried Harvest would be disappointed in me, but she wasn't. Everything I do is for Harvest, Detective. Don't you understand yet, the power she has over me? The power she has over everyone," Noah responded, then was quiet.

Everyone now in the Richard's truck fell silent, trying to comprehend what had happened in the last three hours. It had been a long day, and they were anxious to dump Noah off at the city jail and let him be the St. Louis City Prosecuting Attorney and the city-appointed psychiatrist's problem. Once they did that, they returned to Richard's place for some well-needed whisky and sleep.

Chapter 39

MISSING SECRETS

It had been over a month since Layla had first called Rhonda about the clinic break-in, but it seemed much longer with all the cases Rhonda and Richard were trying to solve. They both needed a break from their work for a couple of days. Richard had been bothered by all the unanswered questions regarding the Noah Sharpe confession on the way back from Ottery. Richard knew that whatever said in the car would not hold up as Noah did not have his lawyer present and as soon as the news about what he did hit the media, some of the highest paid criminal lawyers in St. Louis would line up to represent him. But Noah lawyering up or his case being discussed ad nauseum in the media was not Richard's concern and while Rhonda slept, he stewed and paced his man tech cave. They were also no closer to solving who really was involved in the IVF break-in unless they could find Harvest or evidence that anyone else had helped Noah. The public though was fascinated with the case, as ever special interest group, from animal welfare groups, end of times doomsdayers, pro-choice and pro-life groups marched in support of or against Noah every day and night in front of City Hall, New Beginnings IVF Clinic,

STLPD police headquarters and even the zoo. In some circles Noah was described as pure evil, in others he was a messenger of God. Noah certainly was getting the attention he craved all his life. But Harvest, whoever she was, and wherever she was, truly captured the hearts and minds of the lunatic fringe and was the focus of constant speculation in the right and left-wing media. In a city like St. Louis where crimes and public unrest flowed constantly like the mighty Mississippi did as it past the city, this crime opened the floodgates of chaos and once again put St. Louis in the national spotlight for all the wrong reasons.

The headlines and stories appearing online bordered on ridiculous, with no factual basis to any of them.

"Messenger from God, starts a new civilization"

"Christian conservatives find their Messiah"

"Noah Sharpe, the product of a failed mental health policy"

"IVF business booms…babies for sale?"

"Ark building kits for sale"

What they saw at his property told them that Noah was insane. Still, although Noah said someone else beat him to the shooting, Richard was not convinced, He was convinced however, Noah was not sophisticated enough to steal the embryos but his story about someone breaking into the IVF Clinic before him seemed to convenient. However, from all accounts, after looking into Noah's finances, he did not have the money or technical expertise to steal the embryos and store them safely. No evidence of embryos was found at Noah's Ottery property or his house in St. Louis, and they could not find a weapon that might have been involved at the shooting at either of Noah's properties.

But what about the mysterious Harvest? If she existed, she seemed to be calling the shots for a lot of sheep that blindly wanted to follow her and do her bidding. She stumped Richard like no other person he had tracked digitally. Where was she, who was she, and why could they not find her? She was not hiding as she continued to post online messages, including commenting, and spreading more end-of-times prophecies whenever stories about Noah Sharpe's gruesome discovery were discussed in online forums. She also touted Noah as a hero in the cause and, at least for the time being, gave Noah the spotlight he craved. Also, her IP address would indicate she was still in southeast Missouri. Sheriff Tommy Wilcox was assigned to track her down as it was in his jurisdiction, and someone as mysterious as Harvest would stick out like a sore thumb in rural Missouri.

"Hmm, Richard thought. *"What if Harvest was not as exotic as Noah painted her to be?"* Noah had described her to Rhonda as a beautiful blonde with long flowing hair, stylish clothes, and an athletic figure. Richard laughed to himself. *"What if she was like one of those 1-900 sex line workers who had a very sexy voice, which could turn a man's credit card into an ATM machine, who you thought looked like a model but was really a three-hundred-pound crack whore with brown teeth and bad skin? What if, what if, what, if… shit, what if Harvest is not even real? What if she was just a figment of Noah's imagination, a delusion? What if she was Artificial Intelligence, a Deepfake virtual influencer? What if she was not real, but she or it was built based on the commands of someone or some organization or even some foreign government, to create upheaval in our society for what reason…financial gain, challenging social and cultural norms, creating chaos and anarchy, making money, gaining political power and influence?"*

After thinking about Harvest and what she could be, he returned and looked at all the notes he had gathered over the last month. There had to be a connection to someone or something he missed, and the connection had to be tied to money. Someone in line to make a lot of it, based on the future viability of IVF and controlling one way or another the embryos it produced. The first place he prioritized was the source or center of the opportunity: IVF clinics and their ownership. Many crimes were often described as an inside job. In this case, inside could be one of Layla's competitors or someone with a personal axe to grind, breaking into her lab with the simple objective of driving her out of business, or it could be a social and cultural statement by either pro-life or pro-choice groups shining a light on the embryos and the ownership and disposition of the unused ones. Or it could be some crackpot, like Noah Sharpe, who still was the main suspect until Richard found a better one.

While Layla was in the IVF industry and knew firsthand about the industry, she knew who owned IVF clinics but only those in her network. It was big business, and Layla did not know all the players. Richard had to build a more extensive database of information through online sources beyond what Layla had provided to him. When he finished his research, he felt he would know as much or more than Layla regarding the good and evil side of the IVF business and those who drove the industry. Richard first followed the money: where it was flowing, who it was flowing from, and who was on the receiving end, both directly and indirectly. Following the money always leads to the motive and usually the perpetrator. To do that, he built a computer program to look at three groups of organizations who all could profit from upheaval in the IVF business and reproductive medicine. Based on the discussion he, Layla and Rhonda had regarding who could have broken into her clinic specifically he first targeted her IVF clinic employees, the owners of other IVF clinics, then the Private Equity groups who were buying up IVF clinics as fast as possible, and finally the large medical affiliated corporations, perhaps comprised of birth beneficiaries: hospitals, biolabs, adoption agencies, and social service agencies. With all these groups he would of course look at any political positions, pro-life or pro-choice that may be a motive, beyond financial, for the thefts of the embryos. He would look locally and nationally for affiliations and financial contributions company owners, board members, politicians, and business groups may have made to any other organization, whether private or public. Affiliations could be as formal as being a member of a company's board of directors, an adjunct faculty member at a university, or something as common as being a church, golf club, or school board member. He would hack into financial databases and accounts including offshore and Bitcoin to track money flow. To understand what types of communication his targets were having and with whom, he would hack into social media accounts, email servers, and text streams. The algorithm would then compile a database of thousands of prime suspects, most completely innocent and uninvolved with any crime, except the crime he was committing, and what he did was criminal. Still, he needed only one needle in the haystack to unravel the mystery, but he also needed time, a luxury he did not have as every federal and state investigative organizations plus hundreds of on-line spies were all trying to solve the case, but they did not know all that Richard did so far, nor understood what was in his gut about where the tentacles of this crime led to and from. Richard was glad the media ran with the story nightly because in his mind the media took the direction to a different place than Richard currently was searching.

Once he had all the data compiled, he would pan for gold to determine if anybody among the groups he was monitoring was colluding with one another for something nefarious. He expected ninety nine percent of the conversations and data to be completely innocuous. Still, his experience had told him that human nature would assume that one percent of those he followed had something to hide. In contrast, what they were hiding might not have anything to do with what he was investigating. Sometimes, these random unassociated hits led to other opportunities with clients looking for dirt on someone or something and Richard was not above selling his information to the highest bidder or black mailer.

He also knew he would most likely find connections in the smallest subset of a group, such as an individual owner of an IVF clinic versus a CEO of a large company or a local or state politician versus a national one. The higher up a person in the food chain, the more they took caution or had more sophisticated software and firewalls to keep others out of their business. It was the individual, perhaps naïve about digital spying and hacking, who would not take any caution with whom they were talking or contributing money. If people thought their every move was not being tracked, then they were stupid.

These individuals were the ones who would use the same passwords on all accounts because they were lazy or used well-known search engines and social media sites, unaware of the sophisticated digital spying that was taking place by everyone from foreign governments, the U.S. government, or just very smart schemers and scammers working around the world individually and for their own financial gain. Richard was like all of them, but in his mind, he was better than them, so Richard knew that the digital spy they should be most afraid of was him. He was at the top of his game in sophistication but more so than that, in secrecy. Nobody knew who he was or what he knew. Still, Richard had been infiltrating some of the world's most sinister people and corrupt governments and companies for years. He looked forward to solving this puzzle.

Before executing his final commands to his algorithm, he wanted to test it on a small level to ensure he had no hidden doors or windows where others could find him. And the best way to test it was to run the code against one person in his target set and see what he would find. In this case, a benefit of a test run would allow him to kill two birds with one stone. Still, it could also have a negative side effect as it was a personal connection. He felt like a creep spying on someone he knew, especially if it revealed secrets that were private but not criminal. But he had a job to do, so he plugged in Layla Brazini's information to see where it would lead him. On the one hand, he was hoping nowhere. However, he knew peeking behind the curtain of a person's private life had always surprised, intrigued, and excited him.

Typing in the final commands in his program, Dr. Layla Brazini's life, based on her digital footprint, began to take shape. The basic information was plentiful and easy to access. All her immediate family was identified, and it was surprising. Although it was not uncommon nor a red flag, the data indicated that Layla had been adopted by Tony and Carla Brazini. No information, as he anticipated, was found on Layla's birth parents. The adoption occurred in Reynolds County, Missouri. Was it a coincidence that Rhonda grew up in that part of the state, and Noah Sharpe's family property was also in Reynolds County? In his mind, he wondered if they all knew each other from their down-state upbringings. But Rhonda never mentioned she knew the Sharpes, and since it was close to a sixteen-year age difference between Rhonda and Layla, he put it out of his mind for the moment. He made a note, however, to try and hack into some of the adoption and hospital databases to find out more about Layla's birth parents. Richard also considered building a profile on Rhonda to see if she and Layla's paths had crossed in rural Missouri. Richard knew if he did that, he was crossing a threshold of trust with

Rhonda he did not want to cross. If Richard needed to, he would ask Rhonda directly when the time was right.

Pulling away from his thoughts on Rhonda and Layla's possible history, he focused on her educational background, from her high school records to her progression through college and medical school. Everything about her early life, including photos, grades, and past jobs, was quickly found. All this data told him was that Layla Brazini, while perhaps starting out as an abandoned child, had adoptive parents who loved and supported her and perhaps built a fire within her that allowed her to excel academically and professionally.

Layla completed her medical residency specializing in reproductive health and then worked for several hospitals in the St. Louis area. This work history took Richard up to when she started the New Beginnings IVF Clinic. Richard could see the history behind financing the clinic as Layla had taken out a $500,000 bank loan to get started. Since she had taken a bank loan versus private investments, Richard did not think he needed to follow this aspect of her business as he did when he investigated Dr. Alex Finnegan. That proved fruitful in investigating Finnegan and connecting him to some unsavory characters. For now, nefarious financing was not part of Dr. Brazini's backstory. Richard knew he was already getting too deep into the personal background of someone on their side, especially Rhonda's side. He felt guilty about digging into Layla, but he had to know more about her personally. Digging deeper into her business and finances would come later if a trail of Layla's life were compromised by finances or financial backers of Layla's clinic. Richard hoped that was not the case.

What he wanted to discover was what causes Layla believed in and, more importantly, did she support financially? Once he found her favorite causes, he would create a program hacking into her financial accounts to determine if she was transferring money to any of these organizations. He then began searching her social media accounts, Facebook, Instagram, Twitter, and LinkedIn, but also several medical-oriented social sites, including Sermo and Doximity, which he could see Layla utilized for professional networking, information, and best practices. He could see who in the medical community she was connected to at the organizational and personal levels. To no surprise to him, he noted increased activity and participation in online chat forums discussing IVF and its potential impact on abortion trigger laws. These were intense debates. Scanning the conversations, Richard sensed that most doctors fell into two camps. The "not concerned at all camp" or the "we need to do something about this now camp." It was the second camp and those group of doctors that Richard would come back later to investigate more thoroughly.

He would see a more personal side to Layla in her Facebook, Instagram and even dating sites if she used those types of sites. This was bothersome to Richard. Her history would indicate that she was a young, educated, and wealthy professional in St. Louis interested in social and cultural connections. She was on the board of Forest Park Forever, a non-profit that cared for the well-being of the crown jewel of St. Louis, Forest Park. She was also a benefactor to the St. Louis Zoo and the Botanical Garden and Art Museum. She contributed to charities dealing with child welfare, the placement of foster children, and newborn medical support for underprivileged women. He also noticed Layla was on the Arch City Transplant Center board, the business now run by Dr. Ellen James-Calabrese, after the scandal caused by the former owner, Dr. Alex Finnegan. Usually, this would not raise any red flags because St. Louis was a tight-knit community, especially in the medical field, or was this strictly a medical connection with Calabrese serving as a mentor to young female doctors? Richard wondered if Rhonda had been instrumental in introducing Layla to Ellen, which seemed odd because Rhonda still harbored doubts about Calabrese's involvement in the Arch City case. Was this the secret Rhonda was possibly hiding from Richard, and if so, why? Nonetheless, he would mention that to Rhonda and see her reaction.

After assembling and reading about her professional and personal background, Richard realized Layla was an incredibly decent human being, and he hoped nothing he would find out about her would change that perspective. Finally, while Layla did not seem outwardly active in political organizations, he did notice she contributed to some local and statewide candidates, primarily Democrats, but some Republicans and Independents, and almost all the politicians were females. Understanding the politicians' positions on IVF and abortion would be the next step in piecing together any connections. Was their position on these issues or their influence over them why Layla supported them? Lastly, he decided to query her friends, and of course, Layla had hundreds of them, so Richard knew he would have to build some sort of hierarchy to see which friends perhaps shared political or social associations with Layla. Richard assumed many of her friends might have also been patients, so he did a crossmatch on them with a list of women who may have gone through IVF based on their Instagram, Twitter, and Facebook posts. He ascertained that at least twenty online friends were also her patients over the last four years. This information did not violate HIPPA as Layla's patients and friends volunteered the information, discussing their IVF success and promotion of Layla and her clinic. Richard was always amazed at how much people were concerned about their private lives but would make any aspect of their life so visible on the most easily accessible social media sites in the world. If people knew what he and others could find out about them, they would never post on a social media site again. Taking a breath for a minute and thinking about what society has become, he continued his research. He decided to dig much deeper into the friends that Layla seemed to have most activity with, especially since the clinic was broken into. Because of the break-in, many of her friends reached out to her out of curiosity and empathy, but there was one friend, Becca Stevens, with whom Layla seemed to be in almost daily contact, sometimes up to ten times a day. Most of the contact was straightforward. Richard ascertained that Becca was first a close friend and entrepreneurial peer of Layla and, most recently, had become one of her patients.

There was enough said between the two women, but more importantly, unsaid within the conversations. When they were broaching certain subjects, they almost began talking in code, almost as if they knew someone was monitoring them or that they had something to hide. While Richard's initial focus was to find connections between owners of medical services such as Cryobanks and IVF clinics, or politicians bought or sold, or supporters of political movements, Richard knew that while he would always catch a big fish, it was the little ones like Dr. Brazini and Becca Stevens that led him there. Richard was beginning to think that he could get lucky and find out both Layla's secret connection to Rhonda and Layla's deeper connection to those who may be behind the clinic break-in. In the worst case, he would learn a lot about Layla, and Rhonda would not be angry at him if his learning was part of the larger goal.

To expand his research further into Layla, he decided to drill deeper into her conversations and connections with Becca Stevens to see where that might lead. After a few minutes of research, it was obvious that Becca Stevens was not only a patient of Layla but was a very good friend, perhaps her best friend, as they both were up-and-coming women professionals in St. Louis with a lot in common, both in viewpoints, causes, and personal connections. Richard started branching out to their shared contracts or friends, and he could see they had a similar circle of mutual friends, including Dr. Ellen Calabrese. He understood the medical connection between the two doctors, but what was Becca Stevens's connection with Calabrese? Becca Stevens was not in the medical business but owned a successful online swimsuit company. That was yet another interesting path to follow, but, for now, Richard wanted to stay focused on the two younger women to see where that led him. Both Layla and Becca Stevens crossed paths with each other regarding St. Louis civic activities and causes. Both seemed to be politically active in the pro-choice movement. Still, Becca was much more active and vocal than Layla. Richard assumed that being a doctor in reproductive medicine, Layla took a lower profile position regarding her stances. But not Becca. She seemed to be part of every rally and every lecture and made numerous donations. In fact, she had posted photos of herself at the protest in St. Louis where the shooting had occurred. That, in Richard's mind, erased some guilt over his spying. Perhaps he could justify that since she was at the protest and was an IVF patient, she was fair game to investigate. But digging deeper, a connection of Becca's stopped him in his tracks. Becca was also connected online to Marianne Hylany, who was on Richard and Rhonda's radar screen regarding the protests and the IVF break-ins. Based on his past research,

Hylany was a nationally known political agitator and radical. She was on the radar of the feds and local police, and here she was, a friend of Becca Stevens, who was a good friend of Layla's. In his gut, he knew Layla also knew Marianne Hylany or would know her through Becca Stevens. Their causes were too aligned not to be introduced at some point. Richard dug further into the conversations between Becca and Layla. Eventually, he found what he thought he was looking for. A connection between all three women.

At some point in time, perhaps two weeks after Layla's clinic was robbed, the conversation between Becca and Layla became more philosophical, less about who may have broken into her clinic, but why. As he dug deeper into social and political upheaval, rocking their generation, gender, and the country in general, Becca, the more active politically of the two, began almost recruiting Layla to join her cause. Becca even suggested to Layla that she had a friend who had information that would clearly open Layla's eyes as to what was happening in the world and how it was up to their generation to stop it. Continuing his reading of their shared messages, he ascertained that at some point, Becca, Layla, and Becca's sister Lauren, the woman Rhonda thought was hiding something, all got together one evening. That evening proved to be a turning point in Layla's thinking. Reading their conversation after their night together, Layla thanked Becca for introducing her to the little redheaded Chicago shit disturber and helping her see more clearly than ever before. This got his attention. Two women, very good friends, having an important night together, would mention the person who impacted them so meaningfully, and they would not use her name. Unless, of course, they were hiding her name for a reason. Thinking, Richard pulled up another screen and brought up all his information on Marianne Hylany. What he was looking for was easy to find. She was from Chicago, petite in size, and a redhead. In fact, on Hylany's personal profile, she proudly described herself as a "social agitator and shit disturber for social and women's causes." It had to be Hylany the two women were talking about.

So now Richard had almost certain confirmation that a woman, Marianne Hylany, that he and Rhonda were investigating possibly for both the shooting at the protest and the IVF clinic break-in, had met in person with Dr. Layla Brazini, who was in turn working with Rhonda and Richard on a criminal investigation that Hylany was part of. Richard thought about how he would tell Rhonda what he had found out about Layla and Marianne Hylany. He had to be very careful not to implicate Layla unless he had direct evidence that Hylany had committed a crime and Layla had known about it. He continued scrolling down and skimming additional conversations Becca Stevens and Layla had.

The last one, held only two days ago, stopped Richard in his tracks upon reading it. Marianne Hylany was in St. Louis, and she was staying at Layla's home. She was also here for a meeting with a potential large donor that Marianne had hoped to enlist in her pro-choice cause. Based on reading the communication between Layla and Becca, the meeting was set up between Dr. Layla Brazini, Becca Stevens, Marianne Hylany, and a person who knew and respected Layla and Becca enough to agree to this meeting. A woman only described by Layla and Becca in their communication as Dr. Ellen.

Richard thought that while there could be many people named Doctor Ellen, there was only one Doctor Ellen who knew both women because they sat on her board and who was rich enough and socially conscious enough to support women's causes such as pro-choice. Dr. Ellen James-Calabrese, the former partner of Dr. Alex Finnegan, he the former white whale who got away from Rhonda and escaped to the U.A.E. Richard now knew what he had to do with this information and do it in a way that would not endanger whatever relationship Rhonda, his lover, had with Layla Brazini, his lover's mystery woman.

Chapter 40

DR. CALABRESE RETURNS

The following day, Richard made a surprise visit to Dr. Ellen James-Calabrese's office and, flashing an old F.B.I. badge, was granted immediate entry to see the Doctor.

While professional, strong, and always in control, Dr. Calabrese was still on edge, as most people are, when the F.B.I. visits. Although Richard was not really F.B.I., his physical presence and manner were convincing enough for Dr. Calabrese to take note. She was sure this man was here to talk about Alex Finnegan, as most federal officers seemed to be when they paid her a visit.

"Good morning, Doctor. Thank you for seeing me on such short notice."

"Well, I really did not have an option, now did I? Agent Leary, is it?"

"Yes, but let me clear one thing up. I am Agent Leary, but I am not with the F.B.I. currently. I was with them for quite a while, as well as other federal and some foreign agencies, whose initials, missions, and kill tallies shall remain secret, as my visit here shall remain. Are we good on this, Doctor?"

If the presence of who she thought was a real F.B.I. agent unnerved Dr. Calabrese, whoever this man was had downright terrified her.

Richard continued, not waiting for an answer from Dr. Calabrese. He had made his point, and his presence was felt.

"Doctor, I assure you everything discussed is confidential, and even under torture, I don't reveal my sources."

Dr. Calabrese did not think he was exaggerating about being tortured, and she sensed it was he, rather than the torturer, who left the torture sessions voluntarily.

"You had a meeting with three women of interest to me. Dr. Layla Brazini, Becca Stevens, and Marianne Hylany. Please tell me the nature of those conversations assuming they were not protected due to some HIPPA law. I would not want to violate any patient confidentiality, after all."

Knowing the violation of patient confidentiality was the least of her concerns and holding down her still shaking legs, Calabrese answered with a little more bravado than she felt, "Mr. Leary, much like your proclamation of protecting sources, even if tortured, I will protect my patient confidentiality." She was bold enough to say this because what she told the three women had nothing to do with patient confidentiality.

Richard Leary just smiled, but the smile was not comforting. Dr. Calabrese continued because she wanted Richard Leary out of her office and, she hoped, out of her life soon.

"I talked to the three women regarding my favorite subject and the subject of every actual F.B.I. visit, my former partner, Dr. Alex Finnegan."

"And what did you discuss?" asked Richard.

"They were investigating some rumors that they had heard, specifically that one of the women, Marianne Hylany had heard, that Alex Finnegan, still in the U.A.E., was taking up a new cause: the upheaval of the IVF industry, under the guise of the pro-life vs. pro-choice debate, to create legislation that unused embryos, or eggs for that matter, could not be discarded and by law required to be turned over to government approved medical providers and facilities, to help ensure the continued population growth of pre-selected, pre-ordained, primarily white, U.S. born citizens in the United States," Calabrese concluded.

Richard looking shocked, asked, "He wants to control our population growth and the racial mixture by taking ownership of every birth done through some artificial means? Is that what you are telling me, Dr. Calabrese? Why? Why would he want to do that? How would he do that?"

"The why, Mr. Leary, is because he is fucking insane, pardon my French. He is an insane megalomaniac with a God complex. He wants power, money, and wealth like an Arab sheik, and he has become a white nationalist. Since he has been exiled, he is, Mr. Leary, the composite of all that is evil in the world. He is bitter and wants revenge because of his failed vision for right to die and organ transplant upheaval. He caused chaos to create change in that field and now he is doing it to upend reproductive medicine for his own purposes." Taking a breath, Dr. Calabrese continued, "He is doing this because he believes that with lower birth rates of white couples in the U.S., the influx of non-white immigrants, and the loss of abortion rights in the U.S., more non-white and lower-income children will be born or raised in the U.S., shifting the balance of power and votes in the next one hundred years. The statistics bear this out. Abortions are overwhelmingly had by lower-income women of color and if they quit having them, more babies of color will be born. Secondly, IVF treatments are primarily done by wealthier, more educated, white and Asian women. In his warped mind, Alex wants to even the playing field racially and then politically and culturally by controlling who gets these embryos, based on their political beliefs and commitment to white nationalism."

"Well, now please excuse my French, Dr. Calabrese, but that is fucking nuts. He would not live long enough to see the changes he is trying to make if he could even make them."

"Oh Mr. Leary you truly underestimate what drives Alex Finnegan. It's immortality. He wants to be remembered in history as the man who righted the wrongs of the decline of a white, Christian civilization, not only in the United States but around the world. With population declines predicted across Europe, China, and Russia plus with population gains predicted in Africa and in Southeast Asia, he believes it is his manifest destiny to ensure America remains dominant, by ensuring its population of white Christians remains the dominant race for the next 100 years. But he does not just want the population to look the same, to believe in the same god, he wants it to be aligned socially, morally, politically, financially with the same goals and visions. His warped fucking vision. He wants to written about in history books as the man that saved not just America but the world.

"Tell me how he plans to do this," Richard said, shocked at what Calabrese had told him.

"By using A.I. driven disinformation, deepfakes, virtual influencers to sow chaos and division in American society, and from that chaos, an opportunity arises for him. It's already happening as the sheep are looking for a new messiah to follow, but I don't know the actual specifications of his operation."

"And how do you know all of this? Are you still in contact with him?" Richard pressed.

"No, I am not. But my financial backers, who are legitimate business-men or as legitimate as you can be, amassing billions of dollars, have been contacted by Alex. In turn, they told me because they felt I should know."

"Was this the information the three women, especially Hylany, want-ed?" Leary asked.

"Yes, but I sensed it was mainly for Hylany to do something about. The meeting was set up by Becca and Layla specifically for Hylany to find out information. I do not believe either of the other women are actively looking for vendettas for the cause, so to speak, as much as Hylany. She is a woman on a mission."

"Ok, what else was Hylany looking for that you may have provided?"

"She wanted to know Alex's political base. Who was he hoping to get in his pocket to change legislation so that he could pave the way to make his warped ideas law? You may not know this, Mr. Leary, but I suspect you do. Alex Finnegan had politicians in his pocket to do his dirty work on the transplant revolution he was pursuing."

"Were you of help to Hylany regarding this information, Doctor?"

"My financial backers are not exactly tight-lipped when they have a few drinks in them or if they think they have a chance in hell of bedding me one night. They mentioned a dozen people, including one Missouri guy who is becoming a significant national player in the pro-life debate."

Richard Leary did not wait to let Dr. Calabrese answer. "Missouri State Rep. Billy O'Dell, correct?"

"Yes, he was one of several I mentioned, but he was definitely the one Hylany was most interested in. If I was that guy, based on the hour I spent with Marianne Hylany, I would watch my back because he is definitely on her radar."

Getting up to indicate this meeting was over, Calabrese added, "Oh, and one last thing that may help you, Mr. Leary. Since Alex has moved, or escaped I should say, to the Middle East, he has become extremely wealthy and somewhat of a religious scholar. The shell company in which money is being invested and funneled to politicians like Billy O'Dell and others is called Noah's Ark, a testament to Alex's delusion and megalomaniac complex. I hope that helps."

After Richard Leary left, Dr. Calabrese thought about Finnegan and the rumors she had heard, which were too audacious to believe unless you consider a man like Dr. Alex Finnegan was involved. As much as she hated him, she knew him to be brilliant, resourceful, conniving, and vengeful. She hoped Richard Leary and Alex Finnegan would meet one day and not in a courtroom.

Chapter 41
HYLANY AND O'DELL

O'Dell had always been on Hylany's radar, regardless of the new information Dr. Calabrese told her about Billy O'Dell in his current role in creating havoc within the IVF and thus pro-choice business, thanks in part to the funding by Alex Finnegan. Marianne Hylany knew that the moment she had been waiting for after twenty years would be more momentous because of the paths she and Billy O'Dell had taken since they had last seen each other. Had their respective paths not been taken with so much passion, they probably would have just been content to live their lives separately in anonymity, and if they ever did meet, it would be an awkward but brief encounter between people who had spent some formative years together in college.

But Marianne Hylany was always a fierce liberal, counter to Billy's stringent conservatism, and while their causes were many and ever-changing, Marianne was now a strict pro-choice warrior, fighting for years the battle to protect a woman's freedom to choose. However, it became much more personal and vital after the Dobbs v. Jackson decision, which effectively overturned Roe v. Wade in some states and, in the future, the entire country if the balance of power shifted. That decision made women's rights the focal point of the 2022 election cycle, as it would in 2024, and as such, elevated previously unknown, predominantly male, conservative politicians into cultural warriors whose bombast extended well beyond the district or state they represented. That is who Billy O'Dell had become. His standard brand of conservatism was now more toxic and, like Hylany, focused primarily on the most prominent cultural hot button, pro-life vs. pro-choice. Many conservative voices were competing daily to see who said the most outrageous statements, who could rally their base to a fever pitch, and most importantly, who could get on conservative news and social media outlets where their one and only goal was to raise money in their pursuit of national exposure and possible national political office. And Billy O'Dell was soon becoming the best at it.

While Hylany followed and harassed all the pro-life politicians she could, she was shocked when a formerly mild-mannered, in her mind, somewhat reasonable politician from southwest Missouri began appearing in social media forums and local and national news as an extreme voice in pro-life and thus in Hylany's mind, anti-woman. For Hylany, it was personal; while all these politicians were bad, Billy O'Dell was the worst, and not necessarily because he was the best at generating red meat talking points but more so that he was a complete and utter hypocrite and fucking liar, a fact that Marianne Hylany knew better than anyone. Billy O'Dell, the man she knew so long ago, or perhaps he was just a boy she once loved or thought she did, traveled through life first as a failed insurance salesman and father, then a local politician, then as a fire breathing, hate-mongering anti-abortion warrior. What made Billy O'Dell a hypocrite and a liar was one small part of his history that never made it on his official bio. That small piece of history fueled Marianne Hylany's hatred of him and the personal vendetta she pursued vigorously.

Billy O'Dell was once Marianne Hylany's lover. He was also once, for a moment, the father of Marianne Hylany's child. Until, of course, he forced, almost threatened her to have an abortion when she was just twenty. Thinking about it as she did daily in her life, perhaps Marianne rationalized an abortion at twenty, unmarried and still in college, was the right decision, but she would never forgive Billy O'Dell for forcing that decision on her by deceiving her, telling her that while he was not ready to have kids yet, he did know that Marianne would be the woman he would marry eventually. They could have children when they were more established in their careers and married life. She believed him, and in her heart, she guessed she still loved him, and they planned a life together. But then, she hated him, and the hate continued to burn over all these years.

After she had the abortion, Billy broke off his relationship with Marianne to head back home to marry, unbeknownst to Marianne, his long-time, ongoing girlfriend and high school sweetheart, a woman Marianne did not even know existed in Billy's life. However, her current hatred towards him, still heated with her college-age trauma, was now a raging inferno caused by his current actions. Whenever he was able, he preached to all those who would listen, at rallies, at churches, at fairgrounds, on social media sites, or on national T.V. that abortion was evil, women who had abortions were murderers and morally corrupt, and only Billy and people like him could correct the great mistake the country had allowed to happen. Billy did not realize that the great mistake he had made twenty years ago was about to be corrected, and the one doing the correcting was Marianne Hylany, who waited years to exact revenge.

Marianne Hylany followed the violence, or maybe she caused it. She also did not mind it, as in her mind, only violence creates actions. And she was all about actions. After spending the night with Becca, Layla, and Lauren in St. Louis, women who now she felt were, not only her allies, but her friends, Marianne, as planned, headed on a road trip to Minneapolis then out west to visit San Francisco, Portland, and Seattle, centers of intense battles between the right and the left over many culture wars, but now specifically women's rights to choose verses pro-life stances and the outlawing of abortion. Her destinations were also places she knew Billy O'Dell would be visiting. While these cities and the states they resided in were traditionally liberal strongholds, they increasingly were flashpoints of confrontation. The best place to incite intense anger was to take your message to a crowd that was overwhelmingly against you and your message. You may be overrun, overruled, or worse, be a victim of violence, but you would be a newsmaker, which was Billy's goal.

While Hylany followed the violence, she also followed the newsmakers, and Billy O'Dell was one of them. O'Dell was perfectly cast as a southwest Missouri aw-shucks rube. He enthusiastically supported and generated money from those who shared his far-right viewpoints. Hylany had been tracking O'Dell since he went from a small southwest Missouri town jerk wad to an overhyped right-wing blowhard. And while he might have been charismatic based on intelligence and, yes, looks, in college, he was now a pencil-necked twerp, but a twerp that was becoming more dangerous with his rhetoric and growing national profile. It was incredible to Hylany that someone like Billy O'Dell would be taken seriously and, more so, start to receive some recognition about potential national aspirations, but first, perhaps even a future United States senator from Missouri.

She knew he would be organizing or attending, if not the primary speaker, all the protests in the cities she was visiting. Hylany also knew that the best place to come face to face with O'Dell was at the planned protest in Seattle, as she had missed him by days in Minneapolis and by hours in both Portland and San Francisco. She also knew that within a day or two of each protest, there would be yet another break-in and theft of embryos at an IVF clinic. This seemed to be a pattern that Hylany and perhaps others had figured out. Some break-ins weren't as clean as the one at Layla's clinic, where embryos were removed with precision. Some of the break-ins were less about removing the embryos for their protection. Some were about destroying the embryos and all other aspects of the IVF clinic. No one really knew if the violent break-ins or the sterile break-ins were done by people with the same shared ideology. And she liked the fact that no one knew who was conducting the break-ins. Billy O'Dell seemed to be front and center during the protest but always seemed absent when a break-in occurred. The break-ins, while possibly affiliated with a protest being executed locally, might be directed from a remote and national voice, not by Billy O'Dell, who, while being a jerk wad and a blowhard, was still very smart and ambitious. He knew that being a voice of a movement versus being involved in a felony or worse had vastly different repercussions on a politician's success.

The protest in Seattle, an event that seemed to be almost a daily occurrence, was planned to be held on Saturday at Pioneer Square, one of Seattle's oldest traditional urban parks and gathering places. Hylany loved that Seattle had websites highlighting the day's protests to reinforce the residents' activism and because it gave her information about O'Dell's whereabouts. She knew who the speakers would be through his social media sites and her local contacts. Billy O'Dell was a speaker, scheduled between 2:00 p.m. and 3:00 p.m., assuming a riot did not break out ahead of time between protesters or between protestors and police.

She arrived early, as protests nor the speakers could ever be dependable, which was why she had never been able to confront O'Dell yet in person. She staked out a spot one hundred yards from where the speakers would be as she did not want to spook O'Dell if he saw her, but she wondered if he would even recognize her. Had she changed physically, besides getting older, from when they last were together in college? She, of course, had recent photos and videos confirming what he looked like due to the many sound bites he put out there and his constant video blogs. While he and Hylany were both activists and disrupters, O'Dell was a social and political climber and thus was more about publicity than Hylany, who preferred to make her point silently and in the shadows.

The protest, organized by a pro-life group, started on time, maybe, she laughed to herself because right-wingers were much more organized than the radical left, who, in many cases, were as organized as a litter of kittens. Although the protest was promoted and organized by the right, they were outnumbered and out vocalized by nearly ten to one. Hylany thought the pro-choice speakers, rather than being cowered by the large group yelling obscenities at them, were getting energized. This was certainly the case when Billy O'Dell took the stage. While she had followed him online, this was the first time in over twenty years that she had seen him in person. Hyland was not interested in being nostalgic or reminiscing. She knew his words, so she was not interested in his speech but only in one thing. Vengeance for his actions today, and in reality, her anger for his actions twenty years ago. She was still determining which version of Billy O'Dell she would eventually see, but it did not matter because she knew what the end game for Billy O'Dell would be.

Marianne was unsure how many in the group would have even heard of Billy O'Dell as there were so many local and regional Billy O'Dell wannabes out there, but based on the boos he received from the larger group of pro-choice attendees when he introduced himself, Hylany thought Billy O'Dell had finally made it to the big time. Not just hated by her, and probably his ex-wife, she thought sarcastically, *"Well, good for him. The little jerk wad has made something of himself."*

Grabbing a microphone and bounding on stage, Billy said, "I am Billy O'Dell, and while I represent the great state of Missouri in upholding our conservative values, I jumped at the invitation to come out two thousand miles to Seattle, the bastion of woke radical liberalism. I bring a message from Missouri and the country I want to represent. Liberals, your time is over. Your values, or what passes as values, are over when we are done with our movement: the right movement, God, the American flag, the sanctity of marriage between a man and a woman only, and protection and conception of the unborn naturally as God intended, plus the protection of embryos conceived in a lab. These are our values, and they will completely and unequivocally guide our America, the right America, in the future."

His words were met with a smattering of applause from his supporters but overtaken by a large round of boos and many "Fuck you O'Dell! Go back to Miserable Mizzerah, redneck!" Hylany enjoyed the moment but hoped the crowd did not rip apart O'Dell before she got her shot at him. O'Dell spoke for a few more minutes, more of the scripted talking points he had used so many times, so Hylany tuned out, knowing his five minutes were up. She worked her way to the stairs left of the stage, where she knew O'Dell would be exiting. This time, he would not escape her.

She was in place, in a mob jostling among themselves and alternatively yelling platitudes or condemnations to O'Dell as he left the stage and walked down the stairs. He came face to face with Hylany, but if he recognized her, he did not indicate so.

"Nice speech," she said.

Sizing her up quickly to determine if she was friend or foe, all he said was, "Thank you. Glad you enjoyed it." But, as he began to walk away, Hylany asked him, "So how does what you believe in today reconcile with what you did when you were younger?" Stopping again, he realized Hylany was a foe. However, still not acknowledging any awareness of who she was, O'Dell said, "When we are young, we all make mistakes in what we believe in or how we think, but through time, those mistakes evolve into our beliefs that make us who we are today. I know you probably made mistakes when you were younger, but my guess is you never evolved, as you seem to be one of the woke, entitled leftists that I hope to snuff out over time. You're probably the same woman you were when you were in college, being indoctrinated by leftist viewpoints. It is sad, really, that you have not achieved any personal growth."

"Well, Mr. O'Dell, I am not the same woman as I was in college. If I was, I would have a twenty-year-old child, but I don't because I was forced to abort that child because of several mistakes I made."

Looking at her, slowly and now fearfully with perhaps a sense of recognition, he just said, "Well, there is still time to repent for your sins and the murder of your unborn child."

"Have you repented, Billy? Have you repented for forcing me to have an abortion of our unborn child?" Now, with her voice rising and seeing both recognition and fear in Billy's eyes, she continued, "Or has your blind ambition allowed you to push aside what you did, you fucking hypocrite?"

Although Hylany could clearly see the recognition that now came over Billy, he tried to swat it and her away like any skillful politician. However, Marianne Hylany did not travel across the country waiting for this moment, only to be swatted away.

"You must be off your meds, lady. I don't know you, and certainly never would anyone I was involved with have an abortion."

"Keep believing that Billy. But I have some documentation that would prove otherwise, and while destroying your career would be delightful, destroying everything and everyone you love would be better. I know you remember me, and I know you will never forget me after I am done with you." And using Billy's own words from his recently concluded speech, she said, "That's the future of America I am hoping for."

Knowing that Billy probably had some sort of security detail close by, she started to walk away. Before she did, Billy O'Dell grabbed her by the arm and said, this time with complete knowledge of her, "Marianne, we were kids, and kids make mistakes. Don't make one now that will ruin your life or mine. Let's peacefully co-exist. It's a big world out there, plenty big for us to lead our separate lives."

"It's too late for that O'Dell. If you led a quiet life, it would be different, but you have chosen fame and power and are doing so by trying to eliminate what I have been fighting my whole life to protect: my rights. I know you would like it to be nice and tidy, and perhaps we will see each other passing on the protest circuit, but you won't see me, Billy, until it's too late. You did not give me a choice twenty years ago, and you will not have a choice of how this will end. I will!"

With that, Hylany walked into the crowd, now not a safe place for Billy to follow as he had seen an angry mob of pro-choice protesters listening in on the argument he and Hylany were having, so he ran towards the exit. He wondered if harm to himself or his family or worse was the price he would eventually pay for believing and fighting for something. He told himself it was and would not let Marianne Hylany, or anyone, stop what he and others had started. She might have surprised him today, but he handled her twenty years ago and planned to do so again if need be.

Chapter 42

SETTLING THE SCORE

After her encounter with Billy O'Dell in Seattle, Marianne Hylany stayed in the area to talk to other advocates of her pro-choice, woman's rights causes. She found a large and welcoming group of people in Seattle, and for a moment, she found some peace that many were aligned with her. She found peace, ironically, because she also found many who would, if necessary, use violence for political purposes, just as she would. During the heat of a protest, Marianne Hylany often glared at the opposition. She felt the venom and hatred rise in her. She really believed she hated those who opposed her. In her dreams, she saw herself harming or even possibly killing others. But she was always awakened from her dreams or those thoughts by the words of her parents and grandparents, who were role models to her and had been political protesters their entire lives. They always told her that violence is like giving dangerous fuel to the other side. They believed in using logic and reasoning as weapons of compromise or convincing because when you break down political disagreements, you realize that in many cases, not all, there is more in common with your enemy than there are differences. The debates centered around ideology, but finding a solution agreeable to all should always be the end goal. They would remind her of some of the greatest strife in the country, such as civil rights, which started out violently but ended up resolved in peace because, generally, people were good. While painful, in the end, those who understood the big picture realized that for American society to move forward in a positive direction for the greatest number of people, compromises must be made with your enemy.

Hylany knew in her heart that her parents and grandparents were right. The extremes on every side of the argument made compromise so tricky. The extremes wanted all or nothing, and those in the middle seemed weak or silent in the national debate. However, Hylany always reminded her parents that social media was not around in their heyday. Now, the extremes use social media, sound bites, and clickbait as the fuel that creates notoriety, then fundraising, then violence. She thought about her parents and her grandparents and the advice they would give her now, specifically with the hatred she felt towards Billy O'Dell, whose voice and political position would be enough to be targeted by her. But she had a personal connection to him, and while she liked to think that she had stuffed all the personal baggage away years ago, it actually never left her mind. She had never moved on from her relationship with him and the abortion of their shared child. And while she had never married or had any meaningful relationships with anyone, she rationalized that it was more about her work and causes than Billy O'Dell or any lost baby. In fact, Billy O'Dell was a nobody until his political ambitions and position on pro-life and pro-choice made him somebody. While Billy O'Dell was basking in his rising notoriety, he probably would have regretted it if he had known what was in Marianne's heart and head. Marianne Hylany was in dogged pursuit of righting wrongs on national societal issues. But righting a personal wrong would be resolved on their next encounter.

Marianne Hylany, because of her work, was really a nomad. She traveled across the country, aligning herself and sometimes staying with others who shared her cause. She did not need to financially as she was backed by powerful voices and their large pocketbooks. They preferred to be hidden while she did the hammering. She stayed with people because as much as Marianne had a national following, she was, at the end of the day, lonely for friendships. This is why she began to make more frequent trips to St. Louis as she got closer to Becca, her sister Lauren, and especially Layla. They not only had shared social causes, but they were also close in age and intellectually in the same place. In fact, most of their conversations always started with heavy subjects, primarily what Marianne was up to, but their days and nights together were usually fun filled with laughter intermixed with intensely personal conversations about love and losses. On their group text streams, which were now daily occurrences, they called themselves the Fab Four. And while they all loved Beatles music, influenced by their parent's taste in music, their favorite song was "Revolution," a song by John Lennon. While Lennon penned the song about the end of war, they used his lyrics to remind themselves that their job was *to change the constitution, the institution and the minds of people that hate.*

When she returned from a road trip, she would stop in St. Louis and stay at either Becca's house or Layla's, depending on each woman's work schedule. While she had an affinity for both women, she was becoming much closer to Layla as it was her IVF business that was violated. In a way, Marianne felt that her cause was now Layla's cause. Becca was a much wealthier entrepreneur who, while aligned with the cause, tended to throw money at the problem versus rolling up her sleeves and doing the grunt work necessary to keep a movement alive. Layla also seemed more sympathetic to Marianne's history with Billy O'Dell and the psychological impact an abortion had on her. Layla also had upheaval in her life regarding her birth, so their conversations seemed to be much more intense and meaningful. So now, several weeks after her confrontation with Billy O'Dell in Seattle, Marianne sat on Layla's couch, making phone calls to supporters, and managing her next trip and protest. She was exhausted, and her downtime with Layla was a welcome break. Layla was also exhausted as she needed to put in long days to clean up the physical, legal, and psychological mess the break-in at her clinic had caused.

After each of them relaxed a bit and realizing they had nothing to eat at Layla's house, they made plans to have dinner out, venturing down the street to The Crossing, a restaurant in downtown Clayton, the government center of St. Louis County and now the default location for many businesses and restaurants moving out of St. Louis city. The Crossing was one of Layla's favorites as it was small and quiet, and the food was phenomenal. They settled in, ordering a bottle of wine, and then each of them tried the tasting menu, which was too much food, but they were both famished, having missed lunch. After spending nearly two hours there, they decided to walk down the street to grab a nightcap that neither of them needed in the lobby bar of the Ritz-Carlton. While the bar was quiet on a Tuesday night, a group was attending a meeting in one of the large ballrooms down the hall. From the noise they could hear from the group, evening-end applause to a speaker's comments, the quiet sanctuary of the bar was soon broken up by the meeting attendees who also had the same idea about having a nightcap. The women decided to finish up and depart as this group soon became loud and obnoxious after an ample supply of drinks was consumed. As Layla and Marianne started leaving, a comment stopped Marianne in her tracks. "Hey, O'Dell, what do you want to drink? I am buying," boomed a male voice twenty feet from Marianne, who turned around, focused on a group of ten or so men seemingly encircled around one person. As a few members of the group drifted to other corners of the lounge, Marianne could see who the comment was directed at. Billy O'Dell was the man at the center of the group's attention.

Whether from stress or liquid courage, Marianne wasted no time marching up to O'Dell and getting in his face. "What the hell are you doing here, O'Dell?"

Because he had some liquid courage as well and knew he was surrounded by those who adored him, O'Dell was more aggressive than he had been at their last meeting. Rather than answer Marianne directly, he yelled to the group surrounding him, "Hey guys, you want to meet our enemy? A real life, left-wing, radical, in person? Well, here is one in the flesh. Marianne Hylany."

Sensing a potential confrontation was about to occur, and because many surrounding Billy were well dressed, professional people, probably well known in St. Louis, a few tried to neutralize the situation, assuming Marianne and Billy had some personal history and some alcohol in their veins. A few, though, made unflattering comments toward Hylany, who in turn was met back with her intense stares from now, not only Hylany but from Layla as well.

That was enough to have some men slink away from the brewing conflict. Sensing he had lost a few of his loudmouth backers, Billy said, "Come on guys, this is only little Marianne Hylany, a little girl I dated in college. I guess now," looking leeringly over at Layla, "she has decided women may be more her style."

Marianne and even Layla, women in a male-dominated culture, were used to these taunts, usually from men whose advances they ignored who then relied on their standard fallback. *"If I am not a good enough man for you, I guess you must be a lesbian."* Layla looked around at others in the room and recognized a few men and women, she knew from her civic work. They recognized her as well and knowing there had always been mutual respect and friendships among many of these people and Layla, they gave a nod of both acknowledgment and then embarrassment for the scene Billy O'Dell was initiating.

Several walked up to Layla to say hello, which reduced the tension a bit. O'Dell realized while he might have a following of people with shared interests, he was in St. Louis to raise needed money and support from this crowd. Many of the people were civic leaders and had reputations to uphold and some knew Layla. Sensing he had put his foot in his mouth regarding the lesbian comment and his overall boorish behavior, he tried to defuse the situation, especially since many of these folks contributed quite a bit of money to Billy, and he knew that faucet could be turned off immediately if they thought they were backing someone unstable.

Billy said sheepishly, "Hey, folks. Just kidding around here. Just some old college friends reliving the past and maybe too many Old Fashioneds loosening my tongue."

Layla also thought it best to diffuse the situation, and she grabbed Marianne's elbow, saying to all still witnessing the scene. "Folks, enjoy your time tonight. Marianne and I are going to take off."

For her part, Marianne was itching to get into a fight here and now. Still, she also read the room and sensed Layla's discomfort. She also heard Layla whisper into her ear...."Another time, another place." They then left the Ritz-Carlton lounge and headed home, but Marianne knew she would not be home for long.

It was only a short Uber from the Ritz-Carlton lounge to Layla's home in the DeMun area north of Clayton Road. The two women did not speak on the ride home, but the wheels were turning inside Hylany's head. Layla was glad they were in a public place, and the civilized outnumbered the uncivilized. The incident was only uncomfortable at worst. But something was spinning inside Marianne's brain, and Layla could tell that her mind was elsewhere while she was physically present in the Uber.

Once they got home, Layla commented that she was tired and was going to bed. Marianne mentioned she was too wound up to sleep, so she was going to take a walk. Neither woman was lying, but one was not telling the entire truth. Layla, in bed, heard the door open and shut as Marianne walked into the night and into a scenario she had imagined for over twenty years. While Marianne was somewhat unfamiliar with the area surrounding Layla's place and the Clayton entertainment district less than a mile away, she had a plan in mind before her feet hit the pavement. As Hylany walked, she dialed Billy O'Dell's phone number, a number she had in her contact list ever since she started stalking Billy. Hylany knew she would use it someday, and this was the day. Answering his phone after a few rings, Billy's voice sounded more slurred than clear. It was quiet in the background, indicating to Marianne that perhaps Billy had left the bar and was back in his room. She was not sure it mattered as Billy was an egotistical man, and Marianne knew his curiosity and libido would get the best of him regardless of whether he was in bed.

Unsure if Billy would recognize her voice, whether he was sober or drunk, she said, "Billy, this is Marianne. I hope I am not disturbing you."

"You didn't, but you probably don't give a shit one way or another," he answered.

"Or better put, I hope I did not interrupt you if you have company."

Billy was silent for a minute. Perhaps thinking. Then he said, "So what do you want, Marianne? Our last two meetings were ugly, so I'm sure you are not calling to ask about my well-being. What do you want calling me this late, or are you as fucking crazy as I think you are?"

"Not crazy, Billy. I was never crazy. But always curious, as you know."

"So, what are you curious about Marianne to call me?" Billy said.

"Well, you said I went to the dark side, though you knew I was always aligned with liberal causes in college. I have the same question for you. Why did you go to the dark side? Why are you such a champion of the right and against a woman's right to choose? You seemed to be so even keeled in college. Is it just political ambition, Billy? Is that it?"

"Jesus, Marianne. After twenty years, you want to engage in political discourse at 11:00 at night?"

"Billy, my parents and grandparents always told me to understand what those I disagree with think. I want to understand, and this may be the only chance I get to talk to you away from the crowds and cameras. Just you and me, Billy. Two people who knew each other, maybe even loved each other twenty years ago."

Billy was silent again, so Marianne pressed on. "Billy, we are both busy people and might not be in the same town at the same place again, so let's spend an hour having a drink and trying to understand each other. Maybe we can co-exist if we do. Perhaps even find some common ground."

After thinking for a second, Billy said, "What are you suggesting? I am game for it, but it isn't wise to meet at the Ritz after our little spat was witnessed in front of my supporters, many of whom may still be in the bar."

Knowing Billy was now intrigued, she picked a place she knew he could not resist. Hylany knew Billy loved music, especially the blues and Chuck Berry, so she picked Blueberry Hill, a legendary bar and musical shrine to Chuck Berry. "If you are up for it, how about we meet at Blueberry Hill on Delmar. Might be able to catch the last set of some blues. I can catch an Uber and meet you there in ten minutes."

Silence again. Decision time for Billy. He was never a huge risk-taker, but he was curious about where this meeting with Marianne Hylany might take him. Plus, he loved the blues. "Be there in fifteen, Hylany, and laughing to perhaps lighten the future encounter, he said, "Why don't you leave your weapons at home."

The following day, Layla woke up early and checked on Marianne, who was sound asleep in the guest room. Not wanting to wake her, she set the Keurig to start in thirty minutes, knowing the smell of the coffee would be enough to rouse Marianne from her sleep. She began to know her patterns after spending so much time with her. Layla had an early morning, so she wrote a note wishing Marianne a great day and then headed off to work. In her car, she turned on the local news, KMOX, because she liked to get local news directly rather than having it filtered through national online news sources. But what she heard was not what she expected, or maybe, after last night, it should have been. The lead story that morning was another murder in St. Louis. This one, though, was of a prominent state politician and one rising in national prominence. The news anchor stated in a voice made for the radio, *"Billy O'Dell, Missouri state representative and growing national voice in the outlaw of abortion, was found murdered last night around midnight in an alley behind the popular music venue, Blueberry Hill. Police have no suspects at this time."*

Layla slammed on her brakes and thought about Marianne. *Could she have been involved in this?* If she was, Layla needed to find out quickly to protect Marianne and herself. Layla knew the murder of a prominent politician would be investigated by STLPD's best homicide detective, and that person was Rhonda Simon. Marianne being investigated for murder by Rhonda was bad enough, but Rhonda finding Marianne at Layla's house would be catastrophic. Layla turned her car around and headed back home, hoping beyond hope that Billy O'Dell's murder was just the regular nightly violent crime St. Louis residents were used to waking up to but her gut, told her it wasn't.

Chapter 43

THE PAST HAUNTS US ALL FOREVER

Detective Simon got a call from Lieutenant Tarallo that last evening in the back alleys of The Delmar Loop, in mid-town St. Louis, prominent Missouri politician Billy O'Dell, a pro-life activist and organizer of the recent St. Louis protest, was found murdered. Tarallo knew that O'Dell was already on Rhonda's radar screen, so she sensed his killing was connected to the protest murder, perhaps revenge, or something more significant. Tarallo instructed Rhonda to get to the scene immediately and keep a lid on her findings and instincts until they talked again. Rhonda would head down to the murder scene, but she was anxious to tell Richard about the news to see what conclusions he would draw from it. However, Richard had some news for Rhonda that could also alter the ongoing investigation of the IVF break-in but would possibly tear Rhonda apart, professionally, and personally.

Since Richard had gotten back from Dr. Calabrese's office, he continued doing additional research based on what Calabrese had told him and organized all he had found to present to Rhonda. Before Richard could set the stage, Rhonda busted in and said, "Richard, I know you wanted to go over your information on the cases again, but I have almost no time. I just heard they found Billy O'Dell's body in the alley behind Blueberry Hill."

Oddly, Richard did not seem shocked by that news, and Rhonda noticed.

"Richard, what's wrong? Did you know this already?"

"I did not know it, but it did not surprise me. But what I am about to tell you will surprise you, and I hope not to shock you."

While in a hurry, Rhonda sat down. "Go on, Richard, tell me what you know."

So, Richard did, eliminating how he found the information and not trying to connect any dots because Rhonda would ask him how they were connected. He also knew Rhonda was pressed for time, and he needed more time to sort all this out and try to make sense of it.

"First, Rhonda, based on all my research, we, you, and I guess Tommy Wilcox, can stop looking for Harvest. She does not exist, never did. In fact, she is an A.I. algorithm. A Deepfake, A digital mirage. She is programming code to create chaos and social upheaval, controlled by someone or some organization to spread their message and protect their real identity and intentions."

"But how is that possible? Rhonda asked, "Noah Sharpe seems to have an intimate relationship with her."

"Well, I think we might find out after Mr. Sharpe's psych evaluations that while he may have felt she was reaching out to him personally, he was delusional. Her messages to him may or may not have been real, but what she asked him to do was probably activated what already may have been in Noah's mind. She was like a fake bot or virtual influencer telling you to buy shampoo or drink a certain soda. Or, in this case, convince you of some grand conspiracy or societal change that needs to happen in the world. For most sane people, it is harmless disinformation, but for Noah, it was deadly. And while Noah might convince himself Harvest told him to break into the IVF Center or kill the protester, I don't think he did either of those crimes, though his delusion supported that claiming responsibility would impress Harvest."

"If he didn't, who did?" Rhonda asked.

"I don't have exact proof yet of who committed those crimes, but I think I have a thread of who was giving the marching orders to do them and probably others around the U.S."

"Ok, who or what is the puppet master?" Rhonda asked impatiently.

"Remember I told you that in my research, I track an individual's location based on their IP address, and this allows me to track who links on specific sites or influencers like Harvest, for example, whether she is real or not. In fact, finding an authentic influencer, a fake A.I. bot, or a Deepfake can be done this way. These IP addresses are worldwide, so I need to continue building more information and finding more links to put this digital jigsaw puzzle together."

Now showing a lack of patience, Rhonda bluntly stopped Richard and said in an unusual tone. "Get to the point, Richard, please! I have got to get to O'Dell's murder scene."

But Richard wanted to proceed slowly as some of what he told Rhonda would be of value to her, and some would be hidden for now as much to protect him and his sources and not destroy her.

He decided to get to the point, "One of the most frequently trafficked IP locations between Harvest postings, article clicks, and links was one address found of all places in the U.A.E."

When Rhonda heard the word the United Arab Emirates, Richard did not have to say anything more.

"Dr. Alex Finnegan. Fucking Alex Finnegan is connected to all this shit? Is that what you are telling me?" Now yelling, "IS THAT WHAT YOU ARE FUCKING TELLING ME!" Rhonda now drained of life, just plopped down in a chair trying to comprehend the news.

Rhonda could not believe what Richard was now telling her. Dr. Alex Finnegan, the cunning scumbag who escaped to the U.A.E. after possible murders of innocent people, and bilking millions of dollars from his investors in the Arch City Transplant Center, was once again playing God with people's lives, and this time creating chaos and social warfare by stealing the embryos of the unborn. Finnegan had tried to change the rules of transplants and end-of-life decisions as he felt profit overrode laws and ignoring morals overrode everything. Now, based on Richard Leary's research, Finnegan, seemingly untouchable from the U.S. and living in the U.A.E. where the feds were trying in vain to extradite him, was at it again as the owner of a secretive company called Noah's Ark. The company per the information Richard could find vaguely described their mission as "a global technology influencer over the future of human life, human racial make-up and personal choices."

The mission statement was purposely vague and grandiose, allowing Finnegan to weave his magic among politicians and naïve investors in a world that has too many, uber-wealthy individuals that have so much money they will chase anything, moral or immoral, because of FOMO, their fear of missing out. Just like he wanted to control the time when you die to harvest organs for Arch City Transplant Center, now it seemed he wanted to control life and the makeup of our society by somehow inserting himself legally or illegally in the reproductive medicine business, including IVF centers and Cryobanks. To those who did not know him as well as Rhonda, his reasons, while probably financially based, were no different than the goal at Arch City. His motive, however, was beyond riches; it was power and disruption of social norms. It seems that his company, Noah's Ark was more interested in life or owning life by owning possibly millions of embryos around the U.S. and the world and to create a singular, pre-ordained society, programmed by Alex Finnegan's A.I. technology, to carry out his political vision.

It was not lost on Rhonda that Finnegan set up Noah's Ark in the Cradle of Civilization in the Middle East on the shores of the Persian Gulf, where the original Noah's Ark was possibly built. Being agnostic to a degree, Rhonda thought much in the bible sounded like a fairy tale, but the story of Noah's Ark more so than most. However, she knew that Dr. Alex Finnegan was real, his company Noah's Ark, and his thirst for money and God-like power was absolute. Ever since Finnegan had escaped Rhonda's clutches, she had nightmares about him. Today, however, the nightmares became her new reality, and rather than scaring her, they energized her. She thought of another fantasy tale, Moby Dick. Well, perhaps Finnegan was Rhonda's white whale, and she was committed to capturing him this time.

Rhonda, now seeing a text from Tarallo asking, "Where the hell are you?" started to get up. "Richard, all of this is too big for me to wrap my head around now. I will have to deal with it when I get back from the O'Dell murder investigation."

Richard swallowed, then blurted out what he had to say, Rhonda, I think I know who the prime suspect in O'Dell's killing may be."

Sarcastically, Rhonda said, "Oh, don't tell me, Alex Finnegan killed O'Dell."

"No, not directly," That comment stopped Rhonda.

"I believe he was killed because of his association with Finnegan. He was one of Finnegan's political operatives in the U.S., but I believe he might have been killed by someone whom we have both been tracking. Marianne Hylany."

"Ok, Richard, since you have already been looking into her, continue, but she is like a ghost, like Harvest. Any great ideas about where we can find her, or is she A.I. also?"

"If you want to find her, I would start at your daughter, Layla's home. She is likely there ," said Richard soberly and most importantly, knowingly.

Rhonda turned white. Looking for a minute like she would vomit. She sat deeper in the chair unable or unwilling to move, collecting her thoughts and not sure what shocked her more, that Marianne Hylany a possible killer was at Layla's house, or that Richard somehow discovered Layla was Rhonda's daughter, who she gave up for adoption so many years ago. Ashen, she got up weakly from her chair. "Please, Richard, find the killer of Billy O'Dell, and please let him or her not be involved with Layla. I lost her once, and I cannot lose her again."

And with that, Detective Rhonda Simon, weary from thirty years of police work, a past life, and past mistakes, got up from her chair to solve Billy O'Dell's murder, thinking numbly that it was just murder number fifty-three of the year, but this murder, like every murder in St. Louis, the most dangerous city in America, would change the lives of the living, the survivors, forever and permanently. This time, unlike murders Rhonda coldly and emotionally would solve, this one would change Rhonda's life forever.

THE END

About the Author

Steve Pizzolato is originally from Chicago but has lived in St. Louis for most of his life. Steve comes from a large Italian American family complete with seven brothers and sisters and over thirty nieces and nephews. He met and married his wife, Nancy, of forty years in St. Louis. Together, they have three daughters and four grandchildren. Steve acquired his love of reading and writing from his mother who was a librarian. *The Perfect Match* was Steve's first full novel, and he has followed it up with *Noah's Ark,* which is the second in a series of three books featuring some of the same interesting characters, solving crimes in St. Louis and in life. Steve owned a successful digital marketing agency for 21 years. He is an avid and talented fisherman, an enthusiastic but mediocre golfer and a passionate foodie, especially when it comes to the delicious food at the many Italian restaurants St. Louis has to offer.

If you liked reading Noah's Ark and are interested to learn more about how Detective Rhonda Simon and Dr. Alex Finnegan first crossed paths, please read the first in the series, The Perfect Match. A synopsis of that story is below. Happy reading.

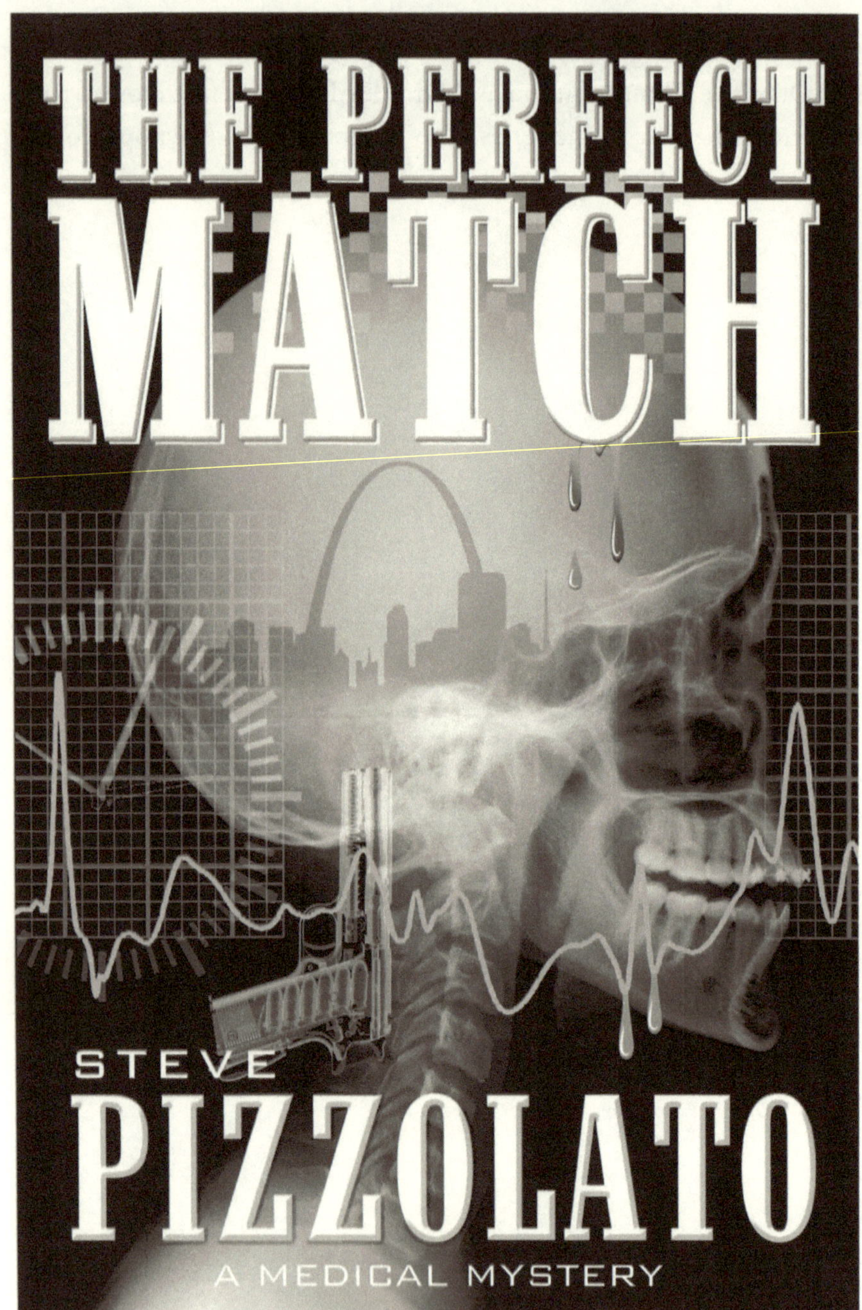
THE PERFECT
MATCH
STEVE
PIZZOLATO
A MEDICAL MYSTERY

THE PERFECT MATCH

Frank Esposito has an incurable lung disease and needs a double lung transplant in a matter of months to survive.

Arch City Transplant Center just opened in St. Louis, MO, and is challenging cultural and ethical paradigms in end-of-life decisions and in the organ transplant business. ACTC is run by brilliant doctors: Dr. Alex Finnegan and Dr. Ellen James-Calabrese who will push each other and society to create a business that will be worth billions of dollars but unbeknownst to Dr. Calabrese, Finnegan is using his colleagues, investors, and the poor as pawns to get what he truly wants.

While Finnegan seems to be unstoppable and untouchable, a series of carjackings and murders being investigated by St. Louis homicide Detective Rhonda Simon threatens Finnegan's plans. With the help of a compassionate organ transplant nurse and one of Finnegan's business partners, Detective Simon realizes her current cases are connected to a crime bigger than she originally thought.

Meanwhile, Dr. James-Calabrese's ex-husband, Vinnie Calabrese will stop at nothing, including jeopardizing his ex-wife's career to get his brother-in-law, Frank, the lifesaving double lung transplant he needs.

Inspired by first-time author Steve Pizzolato's brother-in-law's battle for a double lung transplant, The Perfect Match is a crime-filled adventure of murder, everyday people, ethics, the U.S. healthcare system, the

'My Body, My Choice' movement, and how it is all connected to impact our future in more ways than we can imagine. The novel set in St. Louis will introduce readers to a city known nationally for its crime statistics but also a city with world-class health institutions, old-world neighborhoods, and parks that make St. Louis, despite its national reputation, a very livable community.